Meet Me in Marco

Published by Sunset Publishing LLC, Akron, Ohio
www.sunsetpublishing.com

Library of Congress Control Number: 2025925491

First US Paperback Edition 2025
ISBN 979-8-218-87678-4 (paperback)

Printed in the USA
Illustrations, cover design, and interior design by Jen Elmore
www.jenelmore.com

Maggie and Kevin's Playlist

- ♡ **Love Is You** — Santana
- ♡ **I Will Wait (Candlelight version)** — Matt Johnson & Amber Leigh Irish
- ♡ **You and I** — John Legend
- ♡ **Where Have You Been** — Kelly Clarkson
- ♡ **Break My Heart Again** — Finneas
- ♡ **I'm Gonna Love You** — Cody Johnson and Carrie Underwood
- ♡ **Love You Out of Your Mind** — Byrne & Barnes
- ♡ **Until I Found You** — Stephen Sanchez
- ♡ **Wildflower** — Billie Eilish
- ♡ **There You'll Be** — Faith Hill
- ♡ **The Other Side** — Brendan Walter
- ♡ **She's Everything** — Brad Paisley
- ♡ **You Save Me** — Kenny Chesney
- ♡ **A Song to Sing** — Miranda Lambert and Chris Stapleton
- ♡ **Die With a Smile** — Lady Gaga & Bruno Mars
- ♡ **Is This Love** — Whitesnake
- ♡ **I Don't Want to Miss a Thing** — (feat. Felix Irwan) Music Travel Love
- ♡ **The Prayer** — Pentatonix
- ♡ **If the World Falls to Pieces** — Young Summer
- ♡ **So Easy (To Fall in Love)** — Olivia Dean
- ♡ **Growing Old with You** — Restless Road
- ♡ **Love Like This** — Lauren Daigle

Meet Me in Marco

ANITA CALLERI

 Sunset Publishing LLC / Akron, Ohio

*To every hockey mom
who's come into my life.
Our friendships are eternal.*

1

Maggie

"Pay attention, girls!" my best friend Annie yelled at the top of her lungs, trying to sound like she had complete control of the situation, which I suspected she did not. "We have five interested men who've answered Maggie's Want Ad."

"It's a dating profile, not a Want Ad," I said.

"Pfft." She waved her hand. "Same thing."

"Not the same thing," I muttered.

I was a fifty-year-old widow who'd done her fair share of grieving. I'd been on more than a few dates over the last year, but my friends had a zero-percent success rate with their matchmaking skills. I was ready to move forward, but if I were being honest, the idea of falling in love again felt like a fairy tale, rather than real life.

My friends thought online dating would be "fun." I thought it had disaster written all over it. But they loved me enough to want to help, and I loved them enough to let them try.

"My point is…we're experiencing success, ladies!" Annie said.

"Operation 'Get Maggie Some Tail' has begun," my friend Jules said as she thrust her hips in the air, making the letters on her shirt dance.

"Jules, you cannot do that thing with your hips or say things like that while wearing an '*I love Jesus*' T-shirt," I said.

"Maggie's right, you know," Annie said to Jules. "You can't wear that to Girls' Night. Seeing it makes me feel like I should go to confession." She dropped her voice low. "And believe me, no priest wants to be on the other end of that."

"This is the best idea EVER! It's like we're one big, lovable dating team," Joy cheered. "Team Maggie!" She sprang into action, launching herself into some kind of herkie jump, then took off toward the living room and attempted a cartwheel.

Katie, who had zero rhythm and plenty of self-confidence, jumped on my coffee table and started singing "Let's Get It On" completely off-key. One hand clutched her wine glass, the other thrust to the ceiling like she was a back-up dancer for JLo.

"Get down!" Annie scolded her, which was ironic, coming from the most misbehaved one of us all. But she was right, Katie should keep her feet on the ground. Last year, she climbed on top of the table in the rink's parking lot while tailgating and broke her arm celebrating our hockey team's tenth consecutive state championship.

She gestured dramatically to herself, followed by a curtsy. "I'm a great dancer."

I didn't know *what* she was doing, but it wasn't dancing.

Can't sing. Can't dance. Loyal friend.

The five of us met through our town's hockey team. In

Hattrick Harbor, babies didn't leave the hospital with a crocheted beanie and blanket—they left with their first pair of skates. Hockey wasn't just a sport our kids played—it was the beating heart of our small town.

Between road trips, parking lot tailgates, a book club that was never about the books, and the occasional summer vacation, we'd logged more hours together than with our husbands. Girls' Night Out was the backbone of our twenty-year friendship and had kept us sane when our kids were young. Now that we were all empty nesters, we'd had a lot of time on our hands. Oftentimes, that got us in trouble.

Girls' Night rules were simple: everyone brought their pajamas and a bottle of wine to share.

No one shared.

Another cork was popped, and obnoxious cheering from all of us ensued.

"Whoop! Whoop!" Glasses were being refilled, and we totally overserved ourselves as we celebrated success on the first response to my team-initiated dating profile.

"Listen up, everyone." Annie clicked on the Second Chances icon. She'd fired questions at me all evening between sips and heavy pours, and while I answered, the other three had chimed in with their two cents.

We gathered around the kitchen island, elbows on granite and wine in hand, as Annie skimmed the comments from the men who'd answered my profile.

"Let's see who's taken the bait," she said, clapping her hands together, eyes lit up like she was heading for the clearance rack at Saks. "Maggie!" She pointed the computer screen in my direction.

"Phillip would like to assure you that he takes Viagra and, I quote, 'will not disappoint.'" Annie's eyebrows waggled.

My tipsy friends doubled down on the evening's theme—inappropriate hip thrusting, dangerous gymnastics, and terrible dancing. Katie started singing "I Want Your Sex," sounding *nothing* like George Michael.

Complete circus.

Totally on brand.

I studied Phillip's picture. "Ummm. No, thank you," I said, as politely as possible, staring at a man who looked to be approximately half my age, half my height, and half my weight.

"Next." Annie swiped her finger across the screen. "Let's meet Trent."

She went quiet for a few seconds.

"Oh, wow." She stopped reading.

"What?" we all shouted, riveted, and waiting for her to continue.

"Trent is looking for a woman who has a 780 credit score, weighs under 120 pounds, and wears at least a double-D, naturally. She should wear makeup 24/7, look incredible in lace, leather, or a combination of both. She should plan surprise vacations and be willing to try 'anything' in the bedroom. Bonus points if she laughs at all his jokes and doesn't talk during football. Do I seriously need to keep reading?"

"Hard pass," I said.

"Total douchebag," Jules added.

Annie kept skimming the matches with several continuous swipes. "Wait a minute," she said, her voice turning hopeful. She spun the MacBook around and raised it over her head like the Stanley Cup. "Meet Walt."

"Oo-la-la," Joy cooed.

Annie placed the laptop back on the counter and scrolled through the six pictures Walt had posted with his profile. Handsome. Chiseled. A rugged beard that screamed *I chop wood for fun* and one hell of a cool tattoo across his chest—probably with a backstory involving fire and motorcycles.

"Holy hotness!" Jules leaned in closer.

"What's wrong with him?" I asked, skeptical that this couldn't be real after the last several profiles we'd swiped through—all red flags, shirtless bathroom selfies, or men posing with a monstrous catch or dead deer.

"Nothing!" Annie said, delighted. "He says he's just a guy who loves good food and great company. He's looking for adventure, meaningful conversation over a bottle of red wine, and apparently has an uncanny ability to parallel park anywhere. He could stay in and watch a movie one night or hike and paddleboard the next."

Annie sighed and read the last part with admiration. "I've been told I'm charming, loyal, and an excellent hugger. I love holding hands and promise to let you pick the movies we watch. I may not be the best at writing bios, but I'm excellent at dating."

"SWIPE RIGHT!" my friends shouted.

Their laughter rang out, while mine felt a little forced. What if by "excellent hugger" he meant something creepy? What if he showed up wearing orthopedic sneakers? What if he hated hockey? My heart did a little jitterbug in my chest, with the tiniest flicker of hope—God help me. I rolled my eyes at myself because this was supposed to be a pajama party, not my audition for *The Bachelorette.*

Within ten minutes—and after a few cartwheels and a broken lamp—Walt and I had planned to meet for a drink.

Three days later, I was sitting at the Riverview Lodge staring at the clock behind the bar. The place had rustic charm—white lights strung between wooden beams, a solo guitarist playing softly in the corner, and the warm scent of woodsmoke made it all feel like a Hallmark movie with a liquor license.

Low-key. Perfect for a first date. Although I regretted that third cup of coffee because my foot tapped like it had a mind of its own. A mix of hopeful butterflies and *please-don't-be-a-serial-killer* battled for my attention.

5 p.m. Showtime.

I swiveled on the barstool as the door swung open—in walked a full-blown thirst trap right off Instagram. Thirst trap meets GQ. I did a cartoon double-take—eyes bugging, pulse racing, and head whipping like *People's* Sexist Man Alive just walked in. Except hotter.

That must be my tattooed lumberjack.

He paused to smile and held the door for an elderly man with a walker.

Thank you, Jesus. Handsome *and* a gentleman.

I love my friends. I owed them the first round of drinks at Margarita Night, heck, maybe three rounds, and a kidney! This guy was my age, didn't look like he'd stuff me in his freezer, and I checked his shoes…hallelujah, no thick soles.

From across the room, he didn't look *exactly* like his pictures, but close enough.

Mr. Lumberjack strode toward the bar, heading straight for me—until he veered off at the last second and joined a group of professionally dressed men.

Before I processed my disappointment, I felt a soft tap on my shoulder. The elderly man, hunched over his walker with green tennis balls on its feet, peered at me through thick glasses. "Excuse me." His voice was raspy, crackling with excitement. "Are you Maggie?"

I hesitated, debating whether to stick out my hand or lie.

Catfished by Grandpa.

"Here you go, Maggie." Bartender Brett set my drink in front of me.

Busted.

I turned to the toupee-wearing gentleman, wondering if he had his own teeth—and panicked. I didn't lie or stick out my hand. No, I did something much, much worse. Awful, in fact. I started to use sign language.

The only problem? I had no idea *how* to sign. It was a total free-for-all.

I started making wild gestures—arm circles, fingers flying, and jazz hands. To anyone watching, this was a total disaster.

Bartender Brett raised his eyebrows, so I started signing to him. He made a rolling gesture with his fists and pointed down the bar—pretty sure he just called an offensive penalty for a "false start"—then walked away with a smirk, shaking his head.

I turned back to my "date," making peace with the fact that I was going straight to hell. An apology letter to the entire deaf community was already drafted in my head.

Walt pulled out the barstool next to me, looking like he'd just won the lottery. I'd let Annie talk me into a more formfitting dress than I was comfortable with—although, thankfully, I'd ignored her advice about not wearing a bra.

"You're as pretty as my late wife, Mabel," Walt said with tears in his eyes. "She had the prettiest eyes I'd ever seen…just like yours."

If there was a place worse than hell, then that's the place I was heading. He must be a computer genius because I completely fell for the stock photos he posted. And now, apparently, he was playing the *lost-my-wife* card. Slap the word "sucker" on my forehead and call it a day.

I should've gotten up and left, but I was already in too far. And, truthfully, pity got the best of me. Walt wasn't just old, he was lonely. And that was something I understood all too well. Walking out and leaving him by himself felt cruel, even if he lied to lure me here.

Maybe I was trying to justify my terrible misstep. Maybe my brain preferred catastrophic choices over rational ones. But maybe Walt just wanted some company. And that, I could give him.

I had to give him credit, though, when—with great confidence—he draped his arm around my chair and signaled for Bartender Brett to bring him "whatever she's having." Silently, I prayed that the alcohol wouldn't mess with the medications he was surely taking.

After looking around to make sure the bar had a defibrillator handy, I turned around just in time to see Walt leaning in. I moved my head in the nick of time—barely dodging a very sloppy, whiskery kiss on my cheek.

Pointing to his lips, Walt locked eyes with me and started talking loudly.

"Do!" he shouted.

"You!" Louder this time.

"Read!" Practically yelling now.

"Lips?" So loud that the entire bar turned around.

Please don't let his teeth fall out.

Immediately, I sent the poop emoji to Annie and shared my location—the SOS we'd come up with in case I'd needed a quick extraction.

She replied within seconds.

> **Annie:** I'm on it. ETA 10 minutes.
>
> **Me:** When you get here, pretend I'm deaf.
> Just go with it.

Grinning from ear to ear, Bartender Brett approached us, shot me a sly grin, and started making his own hand gestures. This time, he let me know that there was an "illegal man downfield."

No kidding.

I sneered and held my glass up. Walt said to make his a double, then started yelling at me again.

When Bartender Brett delivered our drinks, he added a shot of tequila for me. I said, *"Thank you"* in my imaginary language, then typed a question to Walt on my phone.

"What do you do for a living, Walt?" I handed him my phone.

Instead of typing back, he just yelled again with over-exaggerated lip movements. "I'M A RETIRED TEACHER!"

I reached for a cocktail napkin, dabbed my face, then typed

another question. "What did you teach?"

More shouting. "PHYS ED!" Then, wriggling his caterpillar eyebrows, he added, "AND SEX EDUCATION!"

Shoot me now.

It was time to put an end to this charade. Just as I was about to confess my horrible decision to Walt and end this tragedy for both of us, my night took another unfortunate turn.

"Excuse me." The husky words came from behind me. "I couldn't help but notice the trouble you're having. My grandparents were deaf. Can I help translate?"

Slowly, I turned to face the velvet voice that sent a shiver down my spine, and my blood pressure spiked. Yep, the walking Instagram model.

I couldn't get out of my own way if I tried.

I searched for hidden cameras to make sure I wasn't being Punk'd, but I wasn't that lucky. The man I'd initially prayed would be my date was now offering his services as my criminally good looking translator.

My eyes went straight to his muscled arms. The seams of his shirt were hanging on for dear life, and I felt like my brain was short-circuiting. Who needs power tools with forearms like that?

Should I double down or wave the white flag since I was already knee-deep in bad decisions?

If I confessed now, it wouldn't just be to Walt. It would be to this man, too—the one with the unfair jawline. I'd had a plan. A good one. I was going to quietly apologize to Walt and hope nobody else in the bar would notice my miraculous recovery. But my brain had different ideas. Somehow, humiliating myself in front of a hot stranger felt safer than humiliating poor Walt.

The lie had momentum now. So, I panicked—again.

It was true what they said. One bad choice always led to another.

2

Kevin

I didn't pick up women in bars—they picked me up. Ever since my divorce ten years ago, they'd been nothing more than company, a way to fill empty hours. Work had all my focus these days. I'd learned after heartbreak that serious relationships had already cost me enough. And at fifty, I sure as hell wasn't giving my whole heart away again.

But then I saw *her*. A stunning brunette at the other end of the bar doing her best to keep the elderly man's wandering hands—and lips—from landing anywhere near her. The flailing arms were a dead giveaway, like a distress signal.

Message received.

Who was I to turn down a beautiful woman in need of a rescue? By the time I was halfway across the room, I'd convinced myself that she was flagging me down—that she needed *my* help. And maybe I wanted to get a closer look.

Truth was, I was drawn to her. And the chaos looked fun, too.

"It's been a while. Both my grandparents have passed away, but I'm sure I can still help translate," I said, grinning widely at the woman who momentarily took my breath away.

"Well, thank you, young man," the old man said, sticking out his wrinkled, unsteady hand. "My name is Walt, and this is my girlfriend, Maggie."

So, that's her name.

Maggie closed her eyes, took a long swig of her drink, then looked straight at me. That's when I noticed her eyes. Green— not just green, but the kind that made you look twice. Clear and striking, impossible to ignore. For a moment, I lost my train of thought.

Maggie tilted her head, eyes wide, daring me to say something. I was all in. I faced the old guy, who was grinning like a lucky son of a bitch. "Is there something you'd like to ask Maggie?"

I fought off a smirk. No idea what I'd just stepped into, but damn if this wasn't going to make my day. After a week in the office with my father and brother, this should be a welcome distraction.

Walt's eyes lit up. "Can you ask her if she wants to go back to my place?"

Maggie coughed and spat up the drink she held to her lips. Her body froze, shoulders tense, one hand gripping the cocktail napkin. Then, she whipped her head toward me with a silent, *Did-he-just-say-that?*

I nearly lost it. Walt had guts—I'll give him that. Not sure I'd have taken that approach, but points for effort. And Maggie? Those eyes weren't letting me off the hook, and I wasn't about to disappoint.

"Did you drive here, Walt?" I asked, barely managing to keep a straight face.

"The bus is waiting for me outside."

Sure enough, a big white van from St. Francis Assisted Living sat at the curb—doors open and the wheelchair lift deployed.

Trying like hell not to laugh, I faced Maggie and started signing Walt's very forward, and painfully hopeful, request. "Walt would like to take you to a place a little less crowded."

Maggie's jaw tightened just enough to betray her frustration with me. She shifted her gaze from me to the bartender, who had his elbow resting on the bar, watching.

Apparently, we had an audience.

The three of us waited. Two wanted to see how Maggie got out of this, and the third one seemed to be praying she'd take him up on his offer.

This trainwreck had my full attention—you couldn't have paid me to walk away.

Maggie didn't skip a beat. Her hands and arms got back to work. This woman had spunk—the kind that didn't back down, even under pressure. And I liked it.

Then, I decided to kick things up a notch. If Maggie wanted to continue to play this game, then I'd go along—anything to keep those incredible eyes on mine. There was fire there, and I couldn't remember the last time a woman had met me head-on, instead of trying to charm me.

I figured if we were going to put on a show, I might as well go full tilt. I began translating with just enough improv to keep Maggie guessing. "Maggie thinks it's best to take things slow," I said with a serious face. And just when she thought I was done,

I added, "But she's intrigued. A second date might be on the table—something romantic, like dinner and soft music. Maybe dancing, if you're up for it."

Maggie's eyes flared—missiles locked and loaded and aimed squarely at me. A stunned half-laugh caught in her throat, then her hands launched into motion, and determination set in her jaw, like surrender wasn't in her vocabulary and tonight wasn't the night to test her.

Sparring with her was addictive—the more she fought back, the deeper I wanted in.

The rapid fly-swatting started up again—arms, fingers, and elbows, whipping through the air like she was trying to kill a wasp and throttle me at the same time. She was definitely trying to say something...and it sure wasn't *thank you*.

She looked at me—full-on death stare. And damn if my heart didn't pick up. Gorgeous, pissed off, and holding her ground. I liked her immediately. Maybe I'd pushed it a little too far, but I couldn't help it—she was even prettier when she was mad. And something about the spark in her eyes made me want to stay in the game a little longer.

From the corner of my eye, something—or someone—was heading our way fast. Maggie's face broke out in relief as a frantic woman came bursting up beside us, waving like a maniac, trying to catch her breath. She skidded to a stop, bent over, hands on her knees, and sucked in air like she had just outrun security.

Maggie's smile twitched, a laugh slipping out before she could stop it. She pressed her lips together, trying to stay composed, but her eyes gave her away. When I looked at the ground, a pair of pink, floppy-eared bunny slippers came into view. I blinked. Sure enough. Bunny slippers.

Man, this night was getting better by the minute. I haven't had this much fun in…hell, I didn't know how long.

Bunny Slippers popped upright, came face-to-face with Walt, then recoiled a step. "Whoa," she muttered. Her eyes bounced from me to Maggie. "Please tell me *he's* Walt," she said, her head pointed in my direction.

Maggie gave Bunny Slippers *the look*.

"Oh, right," she corrected herself, snapping into character. Then, as if Maggie's fake sign language wasn't already a shitshow, this woman jumped in—arms slicing through the air that looked like…*letters?* Even throwing in a random leg kick.

I leaned over, close enough to catch the scent of Maggie's shampoo. Lemon and citrus, and something…hypnotizing. "Did she just spell out Y-M-C-A?" I whispered.

Maggie huffed and pointed to her ears, reminding me we were still playing this ridiculous game.

"Oh, we're still doing this?" I questioned, leaning back with a raised brow. All I wanted was to hear her voice. Say something. Just one word. Because if it was half as gorgeous as the woman herself, I wasn't leaving without her number. And that was saying something.

The bartender snorted. "This night is epic!" He shook his head and walked down to my friends at the other end of the bar, all of whom were watching this debacle unfold. Leave it to them to treat this dumpster fire like prime-time entertainment.

Bunny Slippers bounced back into character, cranking the crazy up a notch. "Maggie, we have to go," she gasped, arms circling, knees knocking, and voice pitched high with panic.

"While I was babysitting your emotional support gooooooat—" she dragged out the word like a bleat—"it ate a box of condoms and started blowing purple bubbles."

She spread her hands wide, as if waiting for gasps of horror. Maggie and I were speechless. Then, she placed her hands on her hips, lifted her eyebrows in a *Nailed It* kind of way, waiting for applause.

Maggie shot her a look that screamed *Seriously, that's the best you've got?*

Bunny Slippers arched her eyebrows right back, *You're welcome.*

Not a word was spoken, but somehow, with nothing but eyebrows, they were having a full-blown conversation.

I had no idea who this Bunny Slippers woman was, but I sensed the two of them could find trouble in a locked room. And the way Maggie's friend came barreling in like she was on a pure adrenaline, zero-logic rescue mission? I should've been backing away slowly. Instead, I couldn't get enough and caught myself grinning. Loud, messy, totally unfiltered—and hilarious. And kind of awesome.

Maggie jumped off her stool and slapped a hundred-dollar bill on the bar. She leaned in close enough for only me to hear. "I'm really not a terrible person. And by the way," she whispered, lips curving like she almost enjoyed saying it, "you're a terrible translator."

Bunny Slippers apologized to Walt, and the two women sprinted out of the bar.

Finally. Her voice. It just didn't hit me—it pierced through me. It was wispy, and breathy, and sultry all at once, and it sent my pulse into overdrive. For years, I'd trained myself not to react, not to let anyone get close enough to matter. But this woman—with the hundred-dollar exit strategy—left me rattled, hooked, and deep inside my own head.

I wanted to yell after her, but I didn't. Instead, I watched her drag Bunny Slippers out the door. I'd met plenty of women in bars. Very few had left me wanting anything more than a good time. But Maggie had gotten under my skin and flipped the script. She didn't bat her eyes at me; she challenged me. She didn't play coy; she met me head-on. Instead of bruising my ego, she left me wanting more.

I excused myself from Walt, shoved my way through the crowd, and rushed out the door. My eyes swept left, then right, searching for her. Nothing. She was gone.

On the sidewalk in front of the Riverview Lodge, I started cataloging details about the woman who momentarily upended every rule I thought I lived by. My chest tightened. And my heart did something it hadn't done in a long time—I almost didn't recognize it.

I didn't even see it coming. But damn, I felt it.

3

Maggie

Mother Puckers 4-Life

Maggie: Margarita Night. My house 6 p.m. You're all in trouble.

Annie: Spanking doesn't scare me.

Maggie: Do you always need to go there?

Annie: You left the door wide open!

Joy: Can't wait to hear about Walt!!!!!!!

Annie: I told you not to bring that up.

Joy: You said there was a hot guy there.

Annie: That's not exactly what I said.

Katie: Define HOT. Because if you say George Clooney-hot, I call BS.

Jules: Jason Momoa hot?

Maggie: Not even close.

Annie: Time to regroup, girls.

"You guys are fired. No more set-ups, no more blind dates, and certainly, stay away from the dating apps," I said, plunking the margarita pitcher down in the middle of the coffee table.

"Fired?" Joy gasped, dramatically clutching her heart and nearly spilling her drink.

"You guys are *terrible* at this. Walt was at least a hundred years old, and to make matters worse, I faked a disability." I buried my face in my hands. I'd had enough of embarrassment, reliving the steadfast determination on Walt's face, who refused to let my "disability" deter him.

"Maggie, you probably made his day," Annie said, tilting her glass toward me. "And he got some fresh air, some exercise, and had the attention of a beautiful woman."

"Well, that's not the worst of it," I said, sinking deeper into the couch cushion. "I made a fool of myself in front of half the bar at Riverview and a random stranger."

"A random stranger who looked at Maggie like she was prime rib," Annie deadpanned, smirking over the rim of her glass.

"He did not," I shot back. I grabbed the bowl of chips and set them in my lap. If anything was going to make me feel better, it was chips and guacamole. What woman didn't rely on emotional eating to help solve emotional problems? It was practically in our DNA.

But even as the words left my mouth, heat crept up my neck. That smile—just a slight tug at his lips, like he knew how ridiculous I was, and liked it. Random Hot Stranger didn't try to save me—he played along, and he hadn't looked at me with pity or sympathy. He was amused by the mess I'd made and poured fuel on the fire, daring me to keep up. He was fun, and our banter was exhilarating and sharp. And infuriating.

That voice—low and gravelly, the kind that could melt butter. And that body? It could probably melt a lot more than that.

"Look at the bright side," Annie mused. "The greater Charlotte area has a population of 2.8 million. Chances of ever seeing him again are slim."

Well, that was sobering. Because for the first time in a long time, I felt…something. And that was the problem. This pull toward a stranger was just a cruel reminder of what I didn't have anymore. Odds of ever having it again weren't just slim—they were impossible. An idea I'd been getting used to.

I'll just figure out how to do life on my own—even if part of me ached for more. So, I plastered on a brave face and said, "I'm hoping to wake up and realize it was all a bad dream, but since that won't happen, I'm going to relieve you of your matchmaking duties and do this on my own. Plus, you guys aren't very good at it."

"I take great offense to that statement," Katie declared, her back stiff and proud. "I matched my cousin up last year."

"Didn't your cousin have to get a restraining order against that guy?" I asked.

"Minor details. Chemistry was off."

Jules cut in. "And what was wrong with Rodney?"

Rodney was the man that she'd insisted was a "cross between a Viking and Brad Pitt." He ended up being ninety-nine percent Viking. He arrived for our date dressed in head-to-toe leather, smelled like beef jerky, and had the bushiest face I'd ever seen. Every time he talked, I wondered where the sound was coming from. I couldn't stop staring at his face like a *Where's Waldo* puzzle, trying to locate his mouth through all that fur.

"He sobbed like a baby when he told me his goldfish died," I explained. "I think he was a little *too* sensitive for me."

And too leathery, too bushy, and not enough Brad Pitt-y.

"Take note, girls." Jules lifted her glass in mock salute. "Cross sensitive animal lover off the list of characteristics for Maggie's possible suitors."

"You guys are batting zero. I'm pretty sure I can do that on my own." I scooped up the pitcher and refilled everyone's glasses, reasoning with my friends, who were helpful in theory, but hazardous in practice.

Annie came to my side, eyes hopeful. "Before we give up on the Second Chances app, let's just look one more time. They can't *all* be Walts. He had to be an anomaly, right? Although, give the old bugger credit for his stealthy computer skills."

With renewed determination, Annie sat on the floor in front of the coffee table and flipped open the laptop like it was a treasure chest.

I sighed and shook my head. This is like fighting with a teenager—hopeless and exhausting. Even the name *Second Chances* sounded desperate, like it was for someone who'd gotten it wrong the first time. But I was neither of those things. I wasn't desperate, and I'd gotten it *completely* right the first time. So right, that nothing else will come close.

"Maggie!" Annie gasped, eyes glued to the screen. "You have one hundred and twenty-two matches!

Annie's fingers flew across the keyboard. She clicked on the first match. The longer she stayed silent, the wider her eyes grew.

Now, what?

I moved to the edge of the cushion, instantly suspicious. "What? Why are you making that face? Don't make that face. You're scaring me."

"I can't read these out loud." Annie's face was frozen in disbelief.

That stopped me. Nothing made her blush—not public nudity, not even her clients' bedroom sagas. The word "vagina" floated in and out of everyday conversation like most people say *thank you*.

"Let me see." I got up and sat beside her, afraid to know, but more curious not to.

My hockey moms huddled around the computer, and for the first time, I actually checked out the profile—*my* profile.

And there it was. The first page. Front and center.

My pictures.

My jaw dropped. "Annie, you did not—"

I slapped my hand over my mouth.

Oh, yes. Yes, she did.

The reason behind all the explicit messages and mismatched men was staring me straight in the face. Annie uploaded the maximum number of photos—eight in total. And every single one of them? Bad. Horrible, even. Internally, I was scolding myself for ever letting a vino-inspired Annie be in charge.

This was all my fault. I'd basically gift-wrapped my dignity and handed it to her with a note that said *Have at it*. She'd been half a bottle of Pinot deep when she told me she had the "perfect" pictures.

My main profile picture was a joke photo we'd taken years ago—back when we thought stuffing fruit down our shirts was hilarious. My fruit of choice? Cantaloupes. Clearly, the picture was taken in jest. Clearly, one hundred and twenty-two men didn't care.

I opened my mouth to say more, but nothing came out.

"To be fair, we did finish all the wine," Annie said, like that was a legal defense.

Annie grabbed the corner of the computer and tried to pry it out of my hands. "Let's just delete it right now to avoid any more surprises."

"Wait a minute." I started reading the small bio underneath the pictures. The text was so small I hadn't noticed it before, or the pictures were so bad, I skipped right past it.

I began reading my bio aloud. "My name is Maggie. I'm a fifty-year-old widow. I've been back in the dating game for a year now. Sex is important. It's excellent exercise."

Silence.

I looked up at my friends. Katie stuffed her mouth with chips, Joy tilted her head back and started whistling at the ceiling, and Jules announced she "had to pee."

My eyes about popped out of my head as I whipped toward Annie, giving her the universal *what the fuck* look.

I kept reading. "I'm not opposed to having sex on the first date, and I'm looking for a man with equal stamina…"

"Maybe we should stop there." Annie reached for the laptop, but I stood up and walked away.

"I'm flexible, and my best friend is South Carolina's most sought-after sexologist. She's taught me how…" I stopped reading and gasped.

Joy's eyes shot to me. "Taught you what?"

"Maggie, I'm so sorry. I truly am. I knew we never should've opened that bottle of Fireball." She took the laptop from my hands, and her fingers moved quickly and dramatically.

"There." Annie shut the lid. "Profile deleted."

My throat burned. I was horrified, pissed, and sad, all rolled into one giant mess. This wasn't just about bad pictures or a bio written in the middle of Girls' Night. The words on the screen were a version of things I never really said out loud. Yes, I was lonely. Yes, I hated how quiet my house was at night. But reading it in black and white for the whole world to see, I felt exposed.

If I didn't love these women so much, I'd be plotting their slow, painful deaths. But these were the same friends who had held me together when Joe died—the ones who wouldn't let me crawl back into bed when all I'd wanted to do was fall apart.

I wanted to yell at them, tell them that none of this was funny. But the anger got lodged in my chest, caught up in everything they'd done for me. These were the women who had brought laughter back into my life.

So, they got a free pass tonight.

I knew they wanted what was best for me and always had my back. Their hearts were as big as their wine pours. This batshittery, however, was not their finest moment. But I had plenty of good examples filed away. I gave them a lot of grace tonight. They deserved it.

When I had decided to give dating a try, they were supportive. They had taken it upon themselves to even "help." Blind dates, casual introductions, and…this.

I loved them, but didn't have the heart to tell them that they'd taken on the impossible. Life with Joe had been once-in-a-lifetime.

And lightning?

It didn't strike twice in the same place.

4

Kevin

"This has the potential to be the biggest—and most profitable—project our company has ever seen," my father, Conrad Mitchell, declared in front of the board of The Mitchell Development Company.

My brother Ben and I, both co-CEOs, flanked our father, who sat at the head of the table as Chairman of the Board. A position he'd been holding for years.

This was all I'd ever known. The Mitchell Development Company had been part of my life since the day I was born. While other kids were drawing superheroes, I was sketching skylines. Job sites were my playground, and I'd had a hard hat instead of a baseball glove.

No one ever asked if I wanted this life, and honestly, I didn't need them to. I never dreamed of doing anything else. Running the company was ingrained in me, as much a part of me as my damn fingerprint.

I loved the Mitchell family legacy. The history. My great-grandfather built the company from nothing, and my father had turned it into something massive. One day soon, it will be mine—the fourth generation of Mitchells to run the family business.

What I loved most was the challenge. Given a desolate piece of land, I recognized its purpose. I saw an opportunity. Where everyone else saw something broken, I pictured what *could* be. And this was exactly what I'd found in our next project.

"Kevin, if you pull this off, it will be the one that puts us on the map," my dad said, slapping me on the back while my brother rolled his eyes.

My brother…younger by two years, and nothing like me. When I worked, he coasted. When I planned, he flew by the seat of his pants. He was the definition of nepo-baby and resented almost everything about me. Other than our last name, we didn't have much in common.

But he was my brother, and my only sibling. Even when he tested every ounce of my patience, and his jealousy seeped into the boardroom, I still had his back. I'd like to think he had mine.

"Hey, Golden Boy, remember we have that thing tonight," Ben said, popping his head into my office right before the end of the day.

Exhausted, I sighed. "You don't have anyone else you can ask?" It'd been a long week. Going out with my brother only made it longer. And besides, it messed with my usual Friday night routine.

"No. Besides, you already answered all the questions and committed. You can't back out now."

"Ben, you don't need me. You know I hate these kinds of things," I pleaded, hoping he'd let me off the hook to attend this event he'd roped me into

Ben sounded annoyed. "Of course, I don't *need* you, but it looks better for both of us if we show up together."

"What about Gary in accounting? He's always up for something like this."

"No offense, but Gary is not good-looking."

"You didn't ask him because he's *not attractive?*" Disbelief must have washed over my face, because my brother just laughed and shrugged.

"Pretty much."

How are *we* related? I've always known that my brother and I were just wired differently. I heard about it all the time—how two people with the same parents turn out nothing alike. Even though his confident arrogance was what attracted most women, it was what pushed them away, too—the good ones anyway.

"Fine," I conceded. "I'll go."

Ben clapped his hands as if he knew all along I'd end up going. He turned toward his office and tossed over his shoulder, "It starts at six."

This was not how I wanted to spend my Friday night.

Fridays were reserved for happy hour at Clancy's in Uptown Charlotte, where the city's post-work crowd filed in like clockwork after a long week of depositions, brokered deals, and business meetings that ran too long. By six o'clock, the place was shoulder to shoulder with professionals in tailored suits, who were ready for the weekend. Half of them were divorced or single, and the other half pretended not to be looking.

Some were regulars. Some new in town. Charlotte was like that—constantly changing. People moved here for a new opportunity and left just as fast for the next big thing. I'd lived here all my life, and I still saw new faces every week. That's what I loved about the area. I could drive an hour in either direction and go from uptown city bustle to a quiet lakeside town that felt stuck in time. The diversity made this area appealing not only to people, but also to businesses and developers like me.

I'd met my fair share of women at Clancy's on Friday nights. We had a mutual no-strings arrangement. I wasn't the kind of guy to do strings-attached, and I never pretended to be. Every time it ended the same way—consensually, honestly, and always at her place. Never at mine. I liked my space and my freedom. I protected it. That's why no woman had ever set foot into my house. Not one.

After the divorce, everything changed. I built a house on Lake Wylie across the South Carolina border. Bought the lots on either side of me as well. The home I'd shared with my wife was full of memories of everything I'd lost—I couldn't live there. I hadn't just lost my marriage—I'd lost a dream. A life. The possibility of a family. When my wife walked out, she took the last bit of hope I had for something lasting. And in the fallout, I'd rebuilt my private world in a way *I* could control.

But my new house wasn't just about privacy—although that was a big part of it—it was about peace. My home, tucked away from noise and chaos, was the only place that felt entirely mine. No pressure from my father to find or close our next blockbuster. No performance to be the next Mitchell heir. Just quiet. A boundary never crossed. A line no one ever got to step over. Maybe that made me guarded, perhaps even lonely at times—but it was safer that way. Easier. I needed that house as much as I needed air.

I didn't host dinner parties or invite friends over for Monday night football. My family? They'd never seen the place—not that they'd ever asked to. And that was fine with me.

My house was mine. And mine alone.

Ben's idea of fun was already a total failure. Two hundred singles packed in a hotel ballroom speed-dating their way through small talk. Charlotte's Speed Dating Extravaganza was held a couple times a year for anyone looking to find an alternative to dating apps or blind dates. I'd never had an interest in either, nor did I need the help. But Ben had asked me to be his wingman, and I'd agreed. Wing-manning, against all better judgment.

Last week, Ben had asked me to fill out an online questionnaire. I'd done it—reluctantly—but now, I was seriously regretting it. Ten dates. Ten minutes each. Plus a cocktail hour after. Several hours of speed-date torture.

If there was a way to make dating feel like jury duty—this was it.

First came Sarah, who wanted to gain TikTok stardom by doing makeup tutorials. She was hoping to boost her followers to fifty thousand with her dollar store finds—whatever that meant. I hated social media. Not a good match for more than one good reason.

Then, Amanda only asked transactional questions—*How much money do you make? What kind of car do you drive? Do you own a vacation home?* It was like a job interview for a Sugar Daddy. Another swing and a miss.

The dates were supposed to get better as the night went on, ending with my most compatible match—according to the one hundred questions I'd answered. Unfortunately, they were only getting worse. Hostage-situation bad.

I was debating blowing off my tenth and my most compatible date—thank you, algorithm—but figured I could suffer through ten more minutes before heading to Clancy's and catching the tail end of happy hour, like I'd originally planned. On the other hand, Ben was probably loving every second of tonight, charming his way through each date like it was an audition for *Love Island.*

I wound my way through the crowd with five minutes to spare before date number ten arrived. I looked at my watch, already hoping she didn't show.

And that's when I felt it. A shift. Like the whole room exhaled all at once, leaving me on edge. The air charged—alive and humming beneath my skin. There wasn't enough oxygen in the room. I couldn't explain it, but I knew something was about to happen.

I felt her presence before I even turned around—like gravity had tilted and every part of me leaned in her direction. And then I saw her. Walking toward me.

The green eyes hit me first. They went straight to my chest, just like they had that night at the bar with Walt. I searched for words, but nothing came out. Just her standing there, lit up by the overhead lights like she was on stage. I was starstruck. The curve of her mouth, the steady confidence in her eyes, and those legs that could make a grown man forget his own name.

Every thought, every plan, every reason to leave went right out the window.

Hell, my night hadn't ended—it had just found its reason to start.

5

Maggie

"Hi, I'm Mag…" My outstretched hand froze, and my smile faltered mid-introduction.

I was momentarily stunned. If a giraffe had walked through the lobby of the hotel, I wouldn't be more surprised. In fact, I was praying that would happen. I looked around. Planned my getaway. There were really tall trees, with great big, beautiful leaves. They looked delicious…for a giraffe.

It wasn't out of the question, I hoped.

"Hi, Maggie. I'm Kevin," he said, taking my hand and shaking it.

My pulse tripped. My first reaction—fury. But underneath it, the unexpected tingle of his touch shot all the way through my body and caught me completely off guard. The man single-handedly managed to stir me in ways that no one else had since Joe died. Even if it came wrapped in irritation, it was something. Heat. Pull. Dare I say…attraction.

"Does Walt know you're here?" he quipped.

There was no escaping my shame, and I didn't see any safari animals saving the day. My cheeks burned, and my stomach did an unhelpful little flip. I'd been caught, cornered, and there was no graceful exit strategy.

I jumped in with both feet. "I have a confession to make."

The corners of his mouth ticked upward. "Oh, yeah. What's that?"

Our hands were still connected—well past the window of a normal handshake—but neither of us pulled away. There was something electric threading through our fingers, keeping us locked in place. I swallowed hard, wondering who'd let go first.

"Walt and I broke up," I confessed.

"Did the age difference finally catch up with you two lovebirds?" His thumb brushed once against my hand before I pulled mine back, and we slid into the brown leather booth.

My heart did something funny, but I recovered quickly. "Age is irrelevant when it comes to true love," I deadpanned, then added, "Walt and I had irreconcilable differences."

Kevin leaned back, his grin slow and a little wicked. Then, he shifted forward again, planting his forearms on the table. "Shouldn't your first clue have been the name? No offense to all the Walts in the world, but it's like the female equivalent of Ruth. Those names are just screaming nursing home."

I mirrored him, folding my hands on the table and matching his stare. "Bold words from a man named Kevin."

His smirk deepened like he was enjoying every second of this verbal ping-pong. And I hated to admit it, but so was I.

We both sat there, locked in, fighting the smiles threatening to break loose. Stalemate. I bit my lip, and his eyes tracked the motion. A low laugh slipped out of him, and he shook his head.

"So, Maggie, what made you show up here today?"

After declaring my four best friends fired from all matchmaking duties, I surprised even myself by signing up for this event. The thought of spending another Friday night alone with a pint of cookie dough and binge-watching the new season of *Virgin River* made this seem less pathetic.

"Well, you had a front row seat to my attempt at online dating."

"And how is tonight working out for you?' he asked.

"Well…Ryan told me he's living with his mom temporarily because he had a 'disagreement with his boss.'" I made air quotes around Ryan's explanation of why a fifty-three-year-old still lived with his mother. "Plus, she does his laundry and cooks for him—so there's that. John wanted to know if I'd be into a joint OnlyFans account. And the last guy asked what kind of condoms I prefer." I crossed my arms, daring him to top that lineup.

Kevin threw his head back and burst into unrestrained laughter. It was so genuine that it triggered mine, and just like that, the tension disappeared.

"And how about you?" I tilted my head, trying to get a better angle of that smile I felt somewhere deep in my gut. "What brings you to Charlotte's Speed Dating Extravaganza?"

"My brother asked me to join him, although I don't know why. He's never needed my help finding a date. But I thought I would agree since we don't get to spend a lot of time together outside of the office."

"Have you had better luck than me?"

"Five minutes ago, I would have said no." His voice trailed

off, and his body leaned in.

"And now?" I asked, feeling bold. I hadn't even realized I was doing it—flirting. I was so wildly out of practice, yet sitting across from Kevin, I didn't feel rusty or ridiculous. Instead, it felt natural. Playful. And I was totally into it.

"Now…" Kevin began, but before he could finish, the emergency ringtone on my phone went off. I dug to the bottom of my purse, heart racing, until I found it. The loud, shrill buzz cut through the moment like a bolt of lightning in still air.

Kevin flinched at the noise.

The moment between us—whatever it was—was cracked in half.

My heart dropped into my stomach, and a cold rush zipped down my spine. "Excuse me, but I need to take this."

I didn't even wait for a response—I just slid out of the booth, my skitterish heart pounding, and stepped far enough away to be out of earshot.

I tapped the green accept button. "Hello?"

"Maggie, it's Liam." His voice was weak and very unlike him. "I'm really sorry to bother you. Is this a bad time?"

Maybe it was, but not anymore. "No. Not at all," I answered, already bracing for whatever came next.

"I shouldn't have called," he said, and my stomach tightened. "But it's been a bad day… Are you free?"

He wouldn't ask if it weren't important. I knew that about Liam. The timing was awful—but then again, when had it worked in my favor?

I exhaled and swallowed down the disappointment already creeping in.

"I'm on my way. Send me your Pin." I hung up and walked back to the booth, my head swimming with all kinds of thoughts. The warmth from before—the lightness I'd felt sitting across from Kevin—had been replaced with a knot in my chest.

Liam needed me. I had to go.

Kevin stood outside the booth, waiting. The laughter that had swum behind those chocolate eyes just moments ago had vanished—replaced by something quieter, more serious.

"Everything okay?" he asked with concern, leaning slightly forward like he already knew the answer was no.

I nodded, though it wasn't entirely convincing. I couldn't even answer the question because I didn't know. I reached for my purse. "I'm sorry, I have to go."

The words scraped out, heavier than I wanted them to. I hated how much I didn't want to say them.

He didn't pry or ask for an explanation. Just held my gaze for a beat longer than expected. Part of me wanted to slide back into the booth. But Liam's voice echoed inside my head.

I was leaving—and the night was ending. Abrupt and final.

Kevin studied me for a moment—quiet, thoughtful. Then with a small nod, he said, "Of course."

I started to turn, but his voice stopped me.

"Hey, Maggie?"

I looked over my shoulder.

"For the record—this was the best ten minutes I've had in a long time."

His smile was soft, sincere. Leaving shouldn't have felt this hard—but it did.

6

Kevin

For the second time, I watched Maggie walk away from me. And for the second time, I felt like she'd taken the air from my lungs right along with her.

I stood by our booth, eyes locked on her, unable—no, unwilling—to look away. This wasn't me. I didn't get disappointed over women. I didn't get caught up in maybes and what-ifs. But there was real, unmistakable regret pressing right behind my ribs.

I'd spent years building up walls around myself. Around my life. Then she showed up with her green eyes and sharp wit and blew a hole right through them. I told myself to shake it off. To let it go. That ten minutes couldn't mean anything.

But my gut said otherwise. She felt different. Real.

And I'd just let her walk away from me. Again.

She weaved in and out of the tables quickly, somewhere between a walk and a jog. I stood staring as she headed toward the exit. Her black dress wasn't tight enough to spell out every curve, but it skimmed her body perfectly, leaving enough room for my imagination to wonder what it looked like underneath. Thin straps, bare shoulders, and tan skin that shimmered like silk. One thing was for damn sure—that dress was made for her.

Part of me wanted to follow her—race after her, even—but the other part, the prideful side, couldn't believe she'd left.

The adrenaline spiked and crashed in a matter of five minutes. I didn't know how long I stood there, watching the door, but eventually, the bell rang. The final date was over.

Cocktail hour began, but the only reason I had for staying was gone.

I found Ben at the bar, standing with a voluptuous blonde who was very much his type—low cut, tight sweater, equally tight skirt, high heels, and red, plump lips. Injected, I was sure of it.

"Could I get a vodka soda?" I asked the bartender.

While I stood and waited for my drink, I scanned the room— my eyes drifting to the door Maggie had walked through, hoping she'd come back at any minute. Without her, the room felt duller. Less alive.

Meanwhile, my brother was busy trying to pick up the young blonde beside him. "You must be the most beautiful woman here tonight."

She giggled, batted her too-long eyelashes, and thanked him, slapping his wrist. This conversation had been overplayed one too many times. I knew exactly what was coming next.

He leaned in and whispered, "Are you going home with anyone tonight?"

Yeah, there it was.

So much for brotherly bonding.

"Let me just freshen up, and then we can get out of here," the blonde whispered back.

Hook. Line. Sinker.

She brushed past him, hips swaying like a metronome, leaving a trail of men gawking in her wake. Overdone. Overdramatic. Exactly his type.

"How'd it go?" Ben chewed on a piece of ice, surveying the room over the rim of his glass. He continued to peruse the crowd, looking for the next prospect in case the one in the restroom didn't work out. He liked options.

"This really isn't my scene." I took a slow pull of my drink, ready to throw in the towel and head to Clancy's.

"I'm pretty sure I'll have all ten women I met tonight begging me to take them out," Ben bragged. This guy was unreal. There was more than one good reason he'd never been married.

"How about you? Anyone with enough potential for your high set of standards?"

"Maybe one…" I trailed off, not wanting to give away too much on the off-chance Maggie came back before I left.

"I'll be right back," Ben said. "I'll get our results."

The lobby was still packed—hundreds of hopeful singles, all laughing, flirting, clinking glasses, and making plans to meet later—but it didn't feel the same. Just minutes ago, the room had been electric. Now? It was just noise.

Maggie left the room, but somehow, she was still the only thing in it.

And that bothered me. I'd told myself that I didn't believe in fate—but what were the odds? Twice in a month, this woman had crossed my path. Women came and went in my life. It was the way it worked. They never stuck. They never made me feel like this. Curious and wanting more.

Was that what I wanted? More? The thought alone threw me. I didn't do more. I didn't even think about it. But standing here, all I could think about was her. I wanted to brush it off, chalk it up to timing, coincidence, anything that made sense. Anything that could explain why she'd crossed my mind more than a few times over the past month.

Maybe I was losing it. Lack of sleep, stress at the office, or the fact that I'd been running on fumes for months. But deep down, I knew better. None of these things could account for the way my pulse picked up when I saw her tonight or what her eyes did to me when I stared too long. This wasn't chance. And whatever it was, I couldn't shake it. Couldn't shake her.

"Here you go." Ben handed me the computer printout of the dates from the evening. If anyone were interested, they would've included their numbers in the results.

I looked at my list. The only number I'd hoped to get was missing. A hollow thud landed in my gut. I folded the paper in half and looked around for the trash can.

"What the fuck?" Ben studied his results, then crumpled them up and angrily stuffed them in his pocket.

"Only nine out of ten wanted my number. There was one

holdout. Someone's playing hard to get." He slammed his glass on the bar and motioned to the bartender for another.

"Ben, come on. Watch your tone."

"Don't you worry. I know how to treat the ladies," he huffed and took a long swig of his second drink.

Again. Still single. Not surprising.

By the time I scanned the room one last time, Ben was already talking to another blonde who wandered up to the bar, programming her number into his phone.

I checked my watch. "Okay, little brother. You're on your own."

I slapped his back and moved in for a bro-hug. The first blonde was back, freshened up, and ready for part two of her evening to begin. Ben draped his arm around her.

"Thanks, Kevin. Catch you later, man." Ben threw a wave over his shoulder and ushered the blonde out the door.

I nodded. He never introduced me to her, but it didn't matter. I'd never see her again. And after tonight, Ben probably wouldn't either.

Clancy's was packed just like every other Friday night, but the buzz didn't hit the same. I found a barstool next to a familiar brunette I'd met a couple of months ago. She was pretty—nice smile, long legs, and a tight red dress that didn't leave much to the imagination—but if I was being honest, she wasn't Maggie beautiful. This woman's eyes didn't sparkle or pin me in place like Maggie's did. They weren't playful or daring, and didn't shoot straight through me. This woman was a poor substitute, but she was familiar. And right now, familiar felt easier. Familiar didn't stir anything up. Familiar didn't leave me standing speechless in a booth with my chest tight.

She smiled like we had unfinished business.

"Angela, right?" I asked, not knowing if I had the right name or not. Not really caring either.

"Amy," she corrected me.

Close enough.

She crossed her legs, and the slit of her dress opened. I offered her a drink—more out of habit than interest—hoping the routine would dull the disappointment gnawing at me.

"I'll take an espresso martini," she said, her voice smooth and confident as she shifted on the stool. Then she turned, just enough that her knees moved between mine—close, intentional. She knew exactly what she was doing. After all, we'd been here before.

But even as she moved closer, laughing at something I didn't really hear, I was barely aware. My body was here, but my mind wasn't. All I could see were green eyes and a black silk dress weaving through rows of speed daters.

Maggie had left early. And I couldn't stop thinking about it. About her. Maybe there was some way I could track her down. Contact the hotel that put on the event. Surely, I could find her number.

Amy said something about work, maybe her boss—I couldn't really tell—and I nodded along, offering the occasional "yeah" and "no kidding," like I was paying attention. But I wasn't. Her eyes were a light hazel, maybe greenish in the right light, but they didn't hold the same zing. They didn't challenge me like Maggie's did. These eyes batted at me, waiting for a response, and I realized I hadn't heard a damn word Amy said.

My mind was replaying an entirely different conversation.

And that's when I looked at the end of the bar.

And froze.

There she was. Black dress. Dark hair. Elbows on the bar, shoulders relaxed, head tilted toward the guy next to her.

Maggie.

In deep conversation. Drinks in front of both her and the man she was talking to.

Not just any guy—a total disaster. He wasn't even good-looking. Not that looks were everything, but the dude looked homeless. His hair was a mess, and his clothes looked even more of a mess, wrinkled and disheveled. And yet, there she was locked in some kind of private conversation with him. No smile. No laugh. Just her eyes—those damn green eyes—focused completely on him. The fire alarm could've gone off, and they wouldn't have heard it. I doubt they would've moved.

My gut twisted.

What the hell?

I thought something terrible had happened, but in reality, she had a better offer. So much for her "emergency."

Their conversation looked intense. He leaned in and whispered something in her ear, and Maggie placed her hand on his forearm. It was sensual. Intimate. And *not* me. I was jealous, no question, but mostly I felt duped.

I tried to concentrate on Amy or Angela—whatever her name was—and put my attention toward something else, but I couldn't do it. I was getting more furious—maybe more jealous—by the minute, and I couldn't stay put. Once Maggie's "date" got up to use the restroom, I excused myself.

I hadn't been dumped since my divorce. I didn't like it. In fact, I was a little pissed about it. Before my bruised ego could think it through, I was heading toward Maggie, sitting alone fifty feet away.

She saw me approach, and her eyes looked surprised, then softened a bit when I finally made my way beside her.

"Maggie," I said, my voice curt, unrecognizable even to me.

"Hey, Kevin. How did the rest of your night go?" she asked, her voice sweet and breathy.

"Not as planned." My voice was flat. No apology in it.

"I probably owe you an explanation as to why…"

I cut her off. "You don't owe me anything, Maggie. I think I get it. You don't need to spell it out for me." The words came out bitter and sharp.

Her head tilted, her eyes narrowing, lips parting like she was about to fire back. But then *he* returned—the Bob Dylan look-alike. He placed both of his hands on Maggie's shoulders, casual but possessive. A line I hadn't even realized existed until he crossed it.

I glared at his hands, then at Maggie. Her eyes narrowed further.

Before sitting down, he stuck out his hand. "Hi, I'm Liam." He tried to smile, but it looked forced.

Up close, this guy looked more of a mess than he did fifty feet away. Hollow-eyed, unshaven, wearing worn-out jeans, and a faded Harvard sweatshirt. No way he'd gone there. And if he had—good for Maggie. Ivy League *and* younger.

My sarcastic side surfaced.

I left his outstretched hand hanging longer than any decent man should. God, I was being such a dick. Maggie knew it, too—her glare confirmed it.

Finally, I shook his hand. "Kevin," I said, squeezing harder than necessary.

He took his seat next to the woman who'd momentarily jump-started my heart an hour ago. His eyes flicked between us before landing back on me. A stare-off. No way I was losing this one.

"How do you know Maggie?" he asked.

"We just met briefly." I tore my eyes away from him, then looked at Maggie. "I don't *really* know her at all."

At that, Maggie's eyes caught fire. I'd just stepped on a landmine, and we both knew it. But I didn't care. Seeing her catch fire reminded me of when we first met, and immediately, I wanted to turn back the clock.

Liam started to say something, but Maggie shut him down. Her eyes zeroed in on me when she spoke. "It was nice seeing you again, Kevin."

Then she turned her back—clean, unapologetic—and leaned toward Liam as if I was no longer a part of the conversation.

Dismissed. And it landed harder than I ever could've expected.

For a man who had sworn he didn't get attached, I sure as hell felt it now.

I returned to my seat and ordered another drink. This time, when Amy moved in, I let her. I turned in my seat and let her press up against me, hoping the whole time Maggie was watching.

Even though I wanted to forget I'd ever met her and continue with my night, I couldn't help but glance Maggie's way every so often. What did Maggie see in that guy? Opposites attract, I guess, and I was watching it live and in person.

After thirty minutes of trying to keep Amy from climbing onto my lap, Maggie and Liam stood up to leave. She grabbed her purse, and Liam helped with her jacket. As they made their way through the bar, they walked past me. Liam nodded his head, while Maggie pretended I didn't exist.

Paying attention way more than I should, my eyes followed them out the door. Liam stepped ahead of Maggie and pushed on the metal bar, letting her walk out first. Again, Amy was laughing, and instead of playing along this time, I couldn't stop staring out the window. Blatantly not listening, watching the woman who had me acting like a fool.

And now she was disappearing with someone else, while I sat here, pretending I didn't care.

Outside, Maggie and Liam embraced for a long time. When they pulled apart, he leaned down to kiss her cheek. For some reason, that small gesture was like a match to a fuse, and jealousy ripped through me from head to toe.

A moment later, he got in an Uber and left.

He left Maggie sitting on the iron bench outside the window, by herself.

I interrupted Amy in the middle of her saying something about her dog. "Can you excuse me for a second." I wasn't asking.

I pushed through the Friday night crowd, exiting the same door that Maggie and Liam had. I was fired up, ready to confront her, demand answers, call her out—something. But when I got close enough, I saw it. A tear trailed down her cheek, and I lost all steam.

Something inside me softened. For as much as I was disappointed that Maggie chose to spend time with some other guy, seeing her cry, alone on this bench, made me forget about every petty reason I had for being angry. All I wanted in that moment was to *not* see her cry.

"You know, if you're going to run out on our date, at least pick a guy who's going to make sure you get home."

There was no bite in my words when I walked up beside her. I was going for humor, but I was pretty sure I missed the mark. God, I was a dick tonight. She didn't deserve that.

"Let me get you a car," I said softly, pulling out my phone.

Maggie sucked in a breath and let it out slowly. "That's not necessary."

When a black sedan pulled to the curb, Maggie stood up and approached the car. Before opening the door, she turned back to face me. "You know, Kevin. Things aren't always what they appear."

With those last words, she lowered herself into the back seat and shut the door. I stood on the sidewalk, watching the taillights disappear, feeling worse than I had any right to. Like I'd missed something important. Like I'd let Maggie down.

And now her words clung to me, circling in my head like there was no way out.

Things aren't always what they appear.

What did that mean?

Maybe the bigger question was—why did it matter so much to me?

7

Kevin

The next evening, I was back at Clancy's. Same barstool. Same drink in front of me. Same sour attitude.

I hadn't slept well last night. Something was off, a weight I couldn't shake. I didn't like the way things had ended with me and Maggie, and how upset she'd been. I might not have liked the idea that she left in the middle of our date—especially to meet with another man—but watching her cry on that bench did something to me. Jealousy was one thing. Watching her hurt was something else entirely. And no matter how hard I tried to brush it off, it was all I could think about.

Work wasn't helping either. The new project would be presented to the city council next week, and although I was confident they would approve it, my dad had a way of turning up the pressure. *"If anyone can pull this off, it's you. Failure's not really in our family gene pool, is it?"*

He knew what the project meant for the company—and for me. Words like legacy, reputation, and "not dropping the ball" were practically his anthem. I'd always handled the pressure, but carrying the weight of Conrad Mitchell's expectations wasn't for the faint of heart. I should know—I'd been doing it my whole life.

If it were just about contracts and city councils, it'd be easy. But with my dad…it was never just business. I was always trying to prove myself worthy of the empire he'd built, constantly on the hamster wheel while he kept raising the bar. Nothing was ever good enough. He never had enough land, enough money, enough of anything. He wanted more. And being Conrad Mitchell's son meant I was expected to want it too.

And if my mood could get any worse, it just did. Because sitting at a table in the middle of the bar was Liam, the wanna be Harvard grad, eye-fucking some redhead seated across from him. Last night, he was breaking Maggie's heart, and tonight, she'd been replaced.

The dude worked fast.

I knew I shouldn't care, but tonight was not the night to test me. The volcano inside me was about to blow. All I kept seeing was an abandoned Maggie, her sad eyes, and the tears she conspicuously tried to wipe away. Strong and fierce, even when she wasn't.

Pushing myself away from the bar, I did what I knew I shouldn't. I made my way to the center of the room.

Five. Six. Seven. I counted my steps in my head to keep my pissed-off attitude in check.

Ten seconds and twenty-five large strides later, I was standing beside Liam, who was pretending to be charming and lovable, laying it on thick.

Looks like he found a hairbrush since last night…and a shower.

My hand clamped down on his shoulder. Definitely harder than I'd intended, but it felt good. Liam flinched, turned, and for a second, he looked startled—until he recognized me, and his face lit up like we were old fraternity brothers.

"Kevin, right? Maggie's friend?" he asked, trying to remember our introduction not even twenty-four hours ago.

The guy was caught. I was about to call him out, and he was pretending we were *actually* friends. He couldn't be more wrong. He stood and offered me his hand again. Had he not learned anything the last time he tried to do this?

I pulled him into me as we shook. He was my height, but I had a good twenty pounds on him. I gripped his shoulder with my other hand and leaned in to spare his date the embarrassment.

I spoke slowly and quietly so only he could hear. "Do me a favor. Make sure this date actually gets home, and you don't leave her crying on the bench out front." When I'd said my piece, Liam's eyes shot up, caught somewhere between guilt and disbelief.

Fucking asshole.

I stalked back toward my spot at the bar, furious that the guy had the nerve to look upset. I wasn't five steps in when a hand grabbed my forearm. I spun around fast, fists forming at my side, nearly ready to fly—

"Maggie was crying after I left?"

The nerve of this guy. He actually looked *confused*. Irritated at the fact that this piece of shit believed that leaving a woman—after he'd clearly dumped her—to find her own ride home was *acceptable*. I wanted to punch him in the face.

"Yes, she was upset," I said through gritted teeth, my finger poking his chest. "What do you think happens when you break a woman's heart and leave her alone, not even concerned about how she gets home? And from the looks of it, you've moved on quickly." Nodding my head back toward his "date." My fist tightened with every second I stood there.

"Wait," Liam said. "What exactly do you know about me and Maggie?"

I huffed, shaking my head. "It's not my business, but I know your type." I glanced toward the redhead still waiting at the table. "Consider this your warning. Just make sure you treat her better than you did Maggie."

She wasn't mine. But the thought of anyone hurting her bothered me.

Liam ran his hand through his hair and expelled a harsh breath, like the weight of my words had just landed straight on his jaw.

Better my words than my fist.

Liam rubbed the back of his neck and looked genuinely thrown. "I called Maggie last night because I was having a rough day. I didn't stop to think how dumping all that on her might make her feel."

"You're unbelievable. She left me mid-sentence to come to your side. And then what—she ends up outside by herself, crying on a bench, and now you're here with someone else like nothing happened?" My voice was low and tight. "I don't know what kind of game you're playing, but from where I'm standing, it looks like you're a pathetic excuse for a man. Maybe I'm old-fashioned, but when you're dating someone, you don't leave her in tears and move on before the night's over."

Did I really just give him relationship advice?

Liam's eyebrows jumped. "Wait—what?" His voice rose an octave. "Maggie and I weren't on a date. We're just friends. And yeah, maybe that's no excuse if she was upset after I left, but we both called Ubers—mine just came first. She was fine when I got in the car. I had no idea she was crying."

All I heard was *not on a date.*

"Wait—what did you say?" I asked, blinking like I must have heard him wrong.

"After my wife died, I met Maggie at a widow's support group. She always seems to be so strong." He paused. "Guess I forgot that no one who's been through what we've been through has it together all the time."

My brain tripped over itself trying to make sense of it all.

"Maggie's a widow?" I repeated to myself, piecing it together.

"How well do you know Maggie?"

"Apparently, not that well," I muttered, the shame settling in like I'd missed something important because I was too caught up in my own assumptions.

"My wife died giving birth to my son two years ago. I lost the love of my life and became a father on the same day. Maggie's been my rock. She helps with Parker—she's actually babysitting him tonight. Yesterday was Courtney's birthday, and I was struggling. I just needed to talk to someone who understood. Maggie lost her husband three years ago."

I'd just won the Biggest Asshole Award. Instead of giving her the benefit of the doubt, I'd been tearing her down in my head. Jesus. What kind of man does *that?*

I'd jumped to every wrong conclusion, led by nothing but my

damn pride. "So, you called Maggie, and she met you," I said more to myself than to him, finally putting all the pieces together.

Liam nodded. "Yeah, she dropped everything—like she always does." He dropped his head, the guilt of it hitting him all at once. "I was so caught up in my own grief. I need to apologize."

"Liam, wait." I stopped him. "I think I have way more apologizing to do than you do."

After giving Liam the full rundown of my major fuckup, I begged for Maggie's phone number. He'd given it to me only after taking a picture of my driver's license. I tracked down her address in no time because this apology couldn't wait.

Forty-two minutes later, my deflated ego and I, along with the biggest bouquet of flowers I'd bought at the corner farmstand, were pulling onto Carlton Drive.

The driveway to Maggie's house was long and winding, lined with old trees that hung over the top like a drooping canopy. At the end of it sat a big blue cottage with a killer view of Lake Hattrick, window boxes full of bright flowers, and a porch swing where I could picture Maggie having morning coffee and reading a book.

I killed the engine and sat in my car for a second, knowing damn well I needed to make this right. Finally, I shoved open the door, flowers in hand, and made my way to her porch. Apologizing wasn't something I was used to doing, but I needed to fix this.

I lifted my hand and knocked.

Laughter and the patter of little feet echoed inside. When Maggie opened the door, everything in me paused. She wore white joggers and a soft green sweater that lifted just enough to show a sliver of her toned stomach. Her hair was piled on top of her head, she had no makeup on, and a barefoot toddler was resting on her hip. She was gorgeous last night, but standing here like this—I think I liked this look more. Effortlessly beautiful. Naturally magnetic.

Her bright smile faded the second she saw me. "You're obviously lost."

This was going to be harder than I thought. Every word I'd rehearsed disappeared. Every bit of confidence I had vanished as this woman left me fumbling for words.

"I owe you an apology," I said quietly, ready to eat crow.

Maggie lifted her eyes.

My throat went dry. For maybe the first time in my life, I felt nervous standing in front of a woman. Maggie had me flustered, and all she had to do was stand there and look at me with those green eyes of hers.

The child in her arms wriggled free and bolted down the hallway, his little arms pumped wildly. "I wun fast!"

"Parker! I'm gonna get you!" She laughed, chasing after him. Just like that, she disappeared, leaving me standing alone on her front porch.

She didn't slam the door in my face, so I took that as an invitation to follow. Rounding the corner, I found her in the kitchen, strapping Parker into his highchair, like she'd done it all the time.

Her place was wide open and full of light. I could see the sun setting over the lake through the wall of windows on the back of the house. Everything was soft—the walls, the furniture, the blankets thrown over the large sectional. Built-ins were filled with books, a couple half-opened on the ottoman, like she'd been reading earlier today. Her kitchen looked like it belonged in a magazine, but somehow felt like home. It wasn't showy, but it was beautiful. Like her—simple, elegant, and way more impressive the longer I looked.

She emptied a small container of cereal in front of Parker, and his fingers got busy. When she turned around, her eyes softened just enough to open the door for me to talk.

But I stood in her kitchen, just staring, watching her babysit Liam's little boy. My heart stuttered. None of what was happening to me made sense. My heart didn't flutter. My gut didn't clench, and I sure as hell never reacted the way I did when I saw Maggie sitting at the bar last night. I barely knew her, yet she'd gotten in my head in a way no one else ever had.

I took a deep breath. "I was an asshole."

Parker pointed his pudgy little finger at me and babbled, "Ath-hole."

Maggie choked on a laugh and covered her mouth. "I can't wait to hear you explain that to Liam."

On cue, the front door opened, and a voice came booming through. "Where's my little monster?"

Legs started kicking, and squeals erupted from the little guy in the highchair. Maggie's smile leapt to her face. "Parker, who's here?"

Liam bolted around the corner and made a beeline straight for the curly-haired blond, who was stuffing a Cheerio into his mouth. Parker's eyes lit up, and his arms reached for his dad like he hadn't seen him in days. Liam scooped him up with a grin, then leaned in and kissed Maggie on the cheek.

"Thanks again, Maggie," he said, before turning to me, a smile tugged at his mouth, "I had a feeling you'd beat me here."

"Some things can't wait," I said.

Maggie tried to scowl, but her eyes betrayed her. She let out a sigh, then gave her head a slow shake.

Liam bounced Parker in front of him and pointed to me. "Did you meet Maggie and Daddy's new friend?"

Parker pointed to me again. "Ath-hole." More giggles and more clapping. Maggie stifled a laugh.

Liam baby-talked to his son, laughing at his new vocabulary. "Which one of Aunt Maggie's boys was here? Or did Auntie Annie stop over for a visit?"

"Kevin taught him that word all by himself." Maggie smirked, throwing me directly under the bus. "And since when did you start giving my address out to strange men?"

"It was just your phone number, not your address." Liam laughed. "He tracked you down like a bloodhound."

"Impressive, by the way," Liam muttered, shooting me a look before turning to Maggie. "And he's not strange—he just had a moment."

"Don't mind me, I'm right here," I said, dryly. "I'm not deaf." I glanced at Maggie, who narrowed her eyes at me.

"Fair," she whispered.

"He seems harmless," Liam went on, taking a minute to gather Parker's stuff, slinging the diaper bag over his shoulder, and walking toward the door.

Maggie said, "If by harmless you mean rude, assuming, and full of himself."

"Again, I'm right here," I said. "Always great to be slandered in surround-sound." This was fun. Dangerously fun. The kind that made my pulse tick. But even with every jab she threw, I couldn't help but smile. She was sharp, quick, and completely in the right. I deserved every bit of shit she tossed my way. Funny thing was, it hit harder than I expected.

Outside, Liam buckled Parker into the back seat of his SUV while Maggie stood in front of me, waving to Parker as he pressed his hand against the glass. Once Liam shut the door, he climbed back onto the porch and pulled her into a hug.

"Give him a chance to apologize, Mags."

"I'm not sure his ego will allow him to do that," she fired back, smirking at me over her shoulder.

Liam released her, leaned toward me, and whispered just loud enough for Maggie to hear. "She's going to make you earn it, man."

He offered his hand, and this time, I didn't crush it like a vice. Liam grinned, hopped off the porch, and climbed into his car.

"Nice seeing you again, Kevin."

"Hey! Don't just leave me here with him," Maggie called after Liam.

He rolled down the window. "I told you—he's harmless."

"You'd better call and make sure I answer my phone later," she deadpanned.

I could've reminded them both that I was still standing there, but honestly? Watching her like this was the best part of my night. My confidence grew by the minute, and I was ready to shoot my shot. She hadn't asked me to leave, and I took that as a win.

Liam gave a quick wave and drove off. As soon as his car

disappeared down the driveway, Maggie abruptly spun on her heels and walked past me through the front door.

"You have five minutes."

Five minutes was more than I had last night.

I'd take it.

8

Maggie

Why was I even considering letting Kevin apologize? As much as I wanted to stay angry at him, I couldn't shake the way I'd felt when I opened the door and saw him, holding the biggest bouquet of flowers I'd ever seen. The sight of him—stubbled jaw, shoulders that filled my doorway, and an unsure smile that had bordered on vulnerable. Everything contradicted the man I thought I'd pegged.

Even under my fury ran a current of electricity I hadn't felt in a long time. Still, every man should learn to grovel at one point in his life. Something told me he hadn't had a lot of practice, and I figured I was doing him a favor.

"Alright, this better be the granddaddy of all apologies." I crossed my arms and leaned against the island in my kitchen.

Kevin exhaled and rubbed the back of his neck. His eyes flicked down at the floor before meeting mine. "I'm sorry," he said quietly.

I let the words hang there, waiting for more. "That's all you got?"

"You leave me at a loss for words." His mouth curved like he wanted to smile but thought better of it.

I tilted my head, unconvinced. "I can tell this is hard for you," I said. "Let me help."

He looked at me, one eyebrow arched.

"Repeat after me." I gave a dramatic wave of my hand. "Dear Maggie."

He suppressed a smile, eyes locked on mine. "Dear Maggie."

"Please forgive me for being a complete and monstrous ass."

"Please forgive me for being a complete and monstrous ass," he repeated, barely able to contain a grin.

"It was inconsiderate and rude."

I was enjoying this way too much, leaning back just enough to watch him squirm.

"It was inconsiderate and rude," he said.

"I also made a gigantic, colossal fool of myself in front of Liam and the entire bar."

He smirked, dragging his hand down his face. "I also made a gigantic, colossal fool of myself in front of Liam and the entire bar."

I needed to think of more adjectives. *Where was the thesaurus when I needed it?*

"Okay, now put it all together. Feel free to adlib, freestyle, or grovel a bit more. The stage is yours," I rambled, making a sweeping gesture with my arm.

Kevin cleared his throat and looked right at me. Steady. Intent. Tender. The heat in his eyes made the temperature notch up a few degrees, taking my pulse along with it. I crossed my arms tighter, more to ground myself than anything.

"Dear Maggie," he began, his voice carried a weight I hadn't heard before. "Please forgive me. I was an ass. I made a complete fool of myself and handled the situation poorly. And the worst part is, I knew it the minute you walked away from me."

He paused, searching for the right words. "What you saw last night—that wasn't me. I jumped to conclusions without giving you a chance to explain, even when you offered. I reacted when I should've listened."

His eyes softened, the sarcasm was gone now, replaced by something earnest. I kept my arms crossed, digging my fingers into my biceps, afraid to let them fall to my sides. "From the minute I saw you on your date with Walt, I was intrigued. I was smiling before I knew your name. And then you walked up as my tenth and final match? I thought there was a reason you and I were thrown together again."

Kevin took a breath, slower this time. And as I stood there, rooted to the floor, my breathing started to pick up. "I should've asked if you needed my help when you said you had to leave. I shouldn't have jumped to conclusions when I saw you with Liam, and I shouldn't have reacted like a jealous idiot." He paused. "And when I saw you crying outside…"

He took a step closer. "It broke me."

The heat rolled off him, his gaze holding mine. "I'd like to take you out. On a real date. And if you say yes, I promise I'll show you that I'm not that guy at the bar."

I'd spent the better part of the last year trying to date again. Trying to move forward. Was I ready? Yes. Had I been through every stage of grief? Also, yes. And I survived. So I said yes to setups and casual coffee meetups, with nice men who had held doors for me and dished out all kinds of compliments.

I'd smiled through small talk, had polite conversation, and even kissed a few goodnight. Some of the dates were uncomfortable—yes—but not all. Some were fine. Actually…vanilla. Not Chocolate-Almond Raspberry, and surely not Everything But the Kitchen Sink. Just plain, safe, uninspired vanilla. Nothing that made me think of extraordinary ice cream flavors.

But with Kevin? It was different. Every time I'd been near him, there was a pull I couldn't quite explain. I just knew it wasn't vanilla. The air felt heavier. It sizzled a bit. It wasn't just his smile or those stupidly good looks. Something simmered. Like a match had been struck and I was holding my breath, waiting to see if it stayed lit or got blown out.

He took another step closer, his voice dipped lower. "Please?"

I forgot the question.

"You're a quick learner," I whispered, swallowing the lump in my throat and letting out a deep breath—one I didn't even know I was holding.

Something in his eyes and the way his words tumbled out of his mouth made my entire body hum. The air between us was charged, the kind of energy felt before a storm broke. Our eyes locked. I felt it. And I knew he did too—because that was when he closed the last bit of distance between us.

He placed his hand on top of mine. The unexpected contact lit up my nerves, a slow burn working its way up my arm, making me catch my breath. "Our compatibility score was off the charts."

My pulse skyrocketed, and the energy between us cranked up a thousand watts. He towered over me, body just inches away, his gaze never breaking as he reached over and tucked a loose strand of hair behind my ear. My skin buzzed where his fingers brushed.

Nope. Definitely *not* vanilla.

"Ninety-eight percent," he said, voice low and maddeningly confident. "That was our score. Pretty sure no one even came close."

I blinked. Swallowed. My throat was drier than dirt. "I'm sure those scores are inflated." I managed to push the words out.

He grinned, and it was a problem. "How about we test the theory? Let me take you out."

I stepped back and drew in a breath—because if I didn't, I was going to either spontaneously combust or kiss him. Maybe both. And I wasn't ready for either. Not tonight. I couldn't stand this guy an hour ago.

"I'll think about it."

"Give me a second chance to redeem myself."

A date. With Kevin. The thought alone made me want to practice my deep breathing or reach for my weighted blanket. He'd probably freak out and change his mind if I sank into child's pose right in front of him. My pulse was all over the place, nerves and want battling for front row parking in my brain. Maybe this was what moving forward felt like.

"Friday. Take it or leave it," I said.

A wide grin broke out across his face. "Pick you up at six?"

Fear was easier than hope. I'd learned that over the last three years. I'd hidden behind it one too many times. It kept me safe—but lonely. Hope asked too much from me. But I didn't want to say no, not after that apology.

"Yes," I said softly. "Six o'clock Friday." I nodded, already knowing I was in trouble because Kevin didn't seem like an ordinary man, and this didn't feel like an ordinary yes.

9

Maggie

Mother Puckers 4-Life

Annie: We will be there tonight.

Maggie: Tell me you don't plan on making a grand entrance or anything.

Katie: Would we do that kind of thing?

Joy: I thought we were wearing our matching cheer uniforms.

Jules: JOY!!

Annie: That was supposed to be a surprise.

Joy: Oops. Cat's outta the bag.

Maggie: Oh, my gosh. What do you guys have planned?

Jules: Nothing illegal.

Katie: Debatable.

Maggie: With you guys, I always wonder.

Joy: That's so sweet, Maggie.

Katie: That wasn't a compliment.

Annie: Maggie, relax. We got you! You focus on your speech. We'll focus on making it unforgettable.
Maggie: That's what I'm afraid of.

Hattrick Harbor's city council meeting was on the first Monday of every month. In our little hockey-lovin'-town, it was quite the social event. For days leading up to the meeting, everyone talked about the agenda, and for the week after, everyone gossiped about who was there, who missed it, and who fell asleep during the budget report.

Even our town's nursing home, Sticks & Slippers, provided a shuttle to the event. Businesses closed early, or at least dimmed the lights and pretended to, so that they could be there. Tonight, Peggy from Top Shelf Pastries was bringing her "pucking delicious" apple twist cookies. That alone guaranteed standing-room-only, and maybe even a minor stampede to the refreshment table.

After the monthly financial report was delivered and the new history teacher at the high school was introduced, it was finally time to discuss the sale of the Daniel Taylor Farm. The property I'd been waiting five years for to hit the market. It was perfect. It wasn't just a piece of property—it was a dream Joe and I had together and never got to finish.

I knew our entire city council. Because I was a guidance counselor at Hattrick Harbor High School, I knew all their children, too.

Our city council was made up of three men, three women, and

Fred Cummings, who somehow wrangled the title of President.

Fred Cummings thought he was very important and had made it known to almost anyone who'd listen. He'd even created his own parking place at the hockey rink:

This parking spot belongs to
City Council Member
President Fred Cummings
Violators will be towed

Nothing says "power move" like reserving a front row space next to the Zamboni.

I'd been preparing for this meeting for months. Truthfully, it should've been Joe standing here. He had loved this kind of thing. Standing up in front of a crowd, charming everyone with his ridiculously easy smile, and then, undoubtedly, winning everyone over. I should've been cheering him on with my friends on the sidelines. But that wasn't how life played out. Over the last three years, I'd been left trying to make our dream a reality, and the one figuring out how to do all the hard things on my own.

For most of my marriage, I lived in a world full of pillows. I never fell too hard or too far without Joe there to catch me, steadying the world around me. He took on all the heavy stuff, trying to make my life easier. Not because he thought I couldn't handle it, but because he'd loved me that much and wanted to carry the weight for both of us. That was Joe.

But he wasn't here now. These days, it was just me. Learning how to live as a half, not a whole. Some days, I got it right. Others, I was still working on it.

"If all the old business is taken care of, we are moving on to new business. Next up…the sale of Daniel Taylor's Farm on Old Forge Road." Fred shuffled a few papers, adjusted his tie, then looked up. "Ms. Bentley, the council will hear from you now."

My stomach flipped as every head in the room turned toward me. I gathered my notes, stood up, straightened my skirt, and walked to the podium. Gripping its sides, I took a calming breath to settle my nerves and opened my mouth to speak.

But before I could say a single word, the back door burst open. My four best friends came prancing down the aisle, wearing cheerleading skirts, waving the most enormous red pom-poms I'd ever seen, and dragging a speaker, blaring the *Rocky* theme song like they were leading a pep rally rather than crashing a city council meeting.

And this was considered not making a scene. I couldn't help it—a wide grin broke free, and a wave of relief followed right behind it.

The crowd erupted in cheers. A few people even stood up and started shadow boxing; the rest clapped along like it was Friday night at the hockey rink. The council members did their best to hold it together, but a couple of them were clearly losing the battle.

This behavior was nothing new to Hattrick Harbor. Ninety-nine percent of the people loved their energy. Unfortunately, Fred, who'd been born with a stick up his ass, represented the other one percent.

He did *not* look amused. His jaw was tight, his face a shade redder than usual, and he pounded his beloved gavel, like it would actually make the madness stop.

Whack! Whack! Whack!

I wouldn't be surprised if he slept with the thing.

"Ms. Bentley, can you control your groupies?" he snapped.

"Have you just met them?" I said, half-smiling, relieved that these women were here to support me. They always made me feel braver. With them around, courage always came with a side of chaos.

I glanced over at my blue-glitter-eyeshadow-wearing friends. They winked and waved, giving me a double thumbs-up and a loud, "You got this, Maggie!"

I rolled my lips together, trying my hardest not to laugh, but I could already see trouble brewing. And then I looked at Katie, tilted my head toward the table where the council members sat, and gave her a warning shake as if to say telepathically—*Don't even think about it.*

She saluted me.

Fred pounded his gavel again.

"Quiet." Whack! Whack! Whack! "Settle down."

A hush settled over the crowd, and a few chuckles still bubbled as everyone turned their attention back to the front, back to me.

"Ms. Bentley, please continue."

I cleared my throat. "Thank you, Fred."

He leaned into his microphone. "Umm…you mean *President* Cummings."

Was this guy *serious*? I mean, *come on*. His oldest son had played hockey with the twins for ten years. We'd been to more tailgating and weekend tournaments together than I could count.

I started again. "Thank you, *President* Cummings."

He looked smug.

"My name is Maggie Bentley."

My friends waved their pompoms like it was play-off hockey, hooted and hollered, and threw in a few leg kicks that should've never been attempted without stretching first. Joy did another cartwheel.

Whack! Whack! Whack! "Ladies!"

Fred's gavel was seeing more action tonight than it had all year.

The hockey moms settled down.

"Most of you know who I am. You knew my late husband, and you know my children. We moved to Hattrick Harbor right after we were married, built our life, and raised our family here. We love this town. We love its people. It's more than just a place on the map—it's always been home. It's Friday night tailgates, it's potluck dinners, it's neighbors borrowing lawnmowers and eggs, and babysitting each other's children."

Then, I set my notes aside because when it came to talking about how much I loved this town, I didn't need a script. The words just spilled out.

"As you know, ten years ago, Joe and I started a foundation called *New Hope*. This foundation helps support foster children after they turn eighteen. Over the last ten years, we've been able to support and mentor these young adults in many ways. We help find them a place to live, a job, and a path toward more education." I stopped, letting the weight of my words settle. "But this isn't enough. Some kids have nowhere to go and no one to turn to because, quite frankly, our social workers have too many cases, and sadly, some kids slip through the cracks."

My eyes scanned the city council members, hoping they all understood how deeply this mattered to me.

"My vision for the Taylor Farm property would be life-changing. I want to turn it into a safe home for young adults who've aged out of foster care and have nowhere else to go. These kids would live on the farm, fully supervised, while they attend school, learn life skills, and build a future. I wouldn't destroy any of the land. Minor repairs would be needed, but I would preserve it—the barn, the land, the house. The property offers space for so many possibilities—stabling horses, maintaining a large garden, and operating a farm store where the kids could sell what they grow. They'd learn how to work, manage a home, and run a business, all while they continue their education. It's not just about putting a roof over their heads—although it's a serious necessity for many—it's about giving them a foundation. A chance to stand on their own feet and build something lasting. Something stable. Something that, until now, most of them have never had. It's about hope."

When I finished, I let out a slow breath. In that exact moment, I felt relief. I knew that Joe would've been proud of me. This wasn't just a speech—it was a dream I first brought to him years ago. And like he'd always done, he'd believed in it—and in me. Before he died, we had developed a business plan and started fundraising together. We'd mapped out a five-year plan. Tonight, I finally brought it to the town's attention because the perfect property presented itself.

The council thanked me, and I nodded, ready to head back to my seat. But before I could take a step, Annie jumped to her feet. "New Hope Farm!" she shouted.

Then came the other three—pom-poms in the air, cheering loud and proud. "New Hope Farm! New Hope Farm!" The chant caught on like wildfire. People stood. Clapped. Some danced. Heat rose to my cheeks, but it wasn't from embarrassment. Who knew that pom-poms, gaudy blue eye shadow, and oversized hair bows could make a girl feel so loved?

Katie climbed onto her chair with her fist pumping along to every word like we'd won the Stanley Cup. Even a few council members cracked smiles.

Everyone except Fred. Red-faced and flustered, the stick was still firmly embedded.

The whole room was chanting when Fred finally lost his patience. He banged his gavel like he was playing Whack-A-Mole. "Order!" he barked. "Enough! We're moving on!"

The room quieted just as the next interested buyer stepped to the podium.

I looked up—and froze.

Kevin.

The last person I expected to see.

His wide eyes found mine, and my stomach lurched. For a moment, everything else fell away. The cheers. The chants. Even the sound of Fred's stupid gavel.

Our eyes locked. Six feet of space didn't matter. The heat felt the same as when we stood inches apart in my kitchen. Shock and disbelief rolled through me as we both stood motionless in an invisible standoff, neither willing to look away.

I thought I was fighting for a piece of land.

Turns out, it was a whole lot more than that.

10

Kevin

When Maggie looked up and our eyes met, the air left my lungs. She had this crazy effect on me—every damn time.

She stood there—surprised, but steady—flushed with emotion, carrying that same quiet fire I'd seen in her kitchen. The kind of calm strength you don't expect until it knocks you flat. She spoke with passion. Every word of her proposal came from her heart, raw and honest, and now I was the guy standing on the other side of something obviously important to her.

How the hell could I have known?

"Mr. Mitchell, are you ready?" Fred Cummings' voice cut through the room and echoed in my head.

I couldn't answer right away. I was still watching her. She blinked once, slowly, then turned away and headed back to her seat. My eyes followed, but she didn't look at me again.

My chest tightened. I turned to the podium, heart pounding like a drum in my ears. I glanced at my father. His expression was a mix of annoyance and simmering impatience—like he couldn't tell if I was sick or wasting his time.

This never happened to me. I loved getting up in front of people. The larger the crowd, the better. I loved selling our proposal. *My* proposal. I thrived on it—the strategy, the pitch, the negotiation. I knew how to own a room. But right now, I was choking.

For the first time in my professional career, I was off my game.

This deal—this farm—was the project I'd been hammering out for months. Losing sleep over. Living and breathing it every damn day. It was *the* deal. The one my father was counting on. The very one that—until just now—had me fired up and ready to lock down. Conrad Mitchell went for blood in every negotiation—he'd taught me to do the same. This was mine to win. My project. My validation. And now? Maggie was standing in the way of it.

I hadn't expected to see her. Not meeting her with Walt. Not on that ridiculous fluke of a speed date. Not in her kitchen when I placed my hand on top of hers and felt the immediate rush of heat to my core that I still couldn't get out of my head. And definitely not here, standing in front of the same crowd, pouring her heart out for the same piece of land I came to take.

I opened my mouth, but nothing came out.

This woman—beautiful, witty, quietly fierce—had taken up space in my head like no one else had in years, and I hadn't even taken her on a real date yet. In fact, I hardly knew her that well, but I felt her. And now she was the one thing standing between me and everything I was supposed to deliver.

Opponents? Maybe. Enemies? My father would think so.

And that would be dangerous.

Ben cleared his throat in warning. I looked to where I'd been sitting minutes ago, and my father shot daggers straight through me. His jaw tense, his brow drawn low, silently telling me to *get on with it* and *pull it together*. I could practically hear the words he wasn't saying—*Don't. Blow. This.*

I tried again.

"Good evening…"

My voice cracked. I grabbed each side of the podium and looked down at my notes, hoping they'd tell me what the hell to do next.

They didn't.

This wasn't just about a piece of land anymore. It was about her. And me. And suddenly, the weight of it all felt a whole lot heavier than I ever expected.

"Good evening, President Cummings." I nodded to the guy who was rude to Maggie. "Thank you for hearing us out tonight." I exhaled.

"Mitchell Developers would like to acquire the property known as the Taylor Farm on Old Forge Road," I said, steadying my voice, "to build the Hattrick Harbor Resort and Casino."

For half a second, there was silence. And then—

A collective gasp rippled through the room, followed by murmurs, sharp whispers, and the unmistakable sound of someone saying, "You've got to be kidding me." A few people audibly groaned. One woman, the one who supplied the cookies, stood up and shook her finger at me before sitting down again.

I made the mistake of looking at Maggie.

She didn't flinch. Didn't gasp. Didn't move a muscle. But her eyes—God, her eyes—were fixed on me like I'd just knocked the life out of them. The warmth I'd seen in her eyes earlier was gone, replaced by something quieter.

Her hands were folded in her lap. She blinked once, then a second time, like she couldn't believe what she was hearing. Then, she looked down like she couldn't bear to watch the rest unfold.

It felt like a punch to the ribs.

And I still had more to say.

Fred Cummings had that gavel out again. Pounding it furiously to restore order. I could think of a few things to do with that gavel after the way he talked to Maggie. But he never rattled her. She was impressive.

I didn't know how long I stood there watching Maggie study the floor, but my mind went blank. The crowd had gone quiet—quiet enough to hear my father hiss, "Get it together, Kevin… Now!"

Fred Cummings spoke into his microphone. "Mr. Mitchell, are you alright?"

Without answering his question, I continued. "Mitchell Developers has done extensive research on Hattrick Harbor." I steadied my voice to the quiet tension in the room. "We believe this project offers more than just construction and development. It offers opportunity. *Real* opportunity."

A few murmurs swept through the crowd—skepticism, maybe confusion—but I pushed forward, white-knuckling the podium. "This project would bring hundreds of jobs to the area—during construction and beyond. We're talking about sustainable employment. These are jobs for *your* citizens. *Your* kids. *Your* future."

More murmuring now. A few head nods. A few council members were frothing at the mouth.

"We'd bring year-round tourism to Hattrick Harbor, not just

a few weekenders during hockey season or the summer months. That means steady business for local shops, restaurants, coffee shops, bookstores—places that currently struggle to stay afloat during the off-season."

I paused for a beat. I could feel her there—somewhere off to my right. But I didn't look. I was too afraid of what I might see. Disappointment, maybe. Or worse, disgust.

My throat tightened, but I kept going, careful to keep my focus on the front of the room.

"Increased revenue from the resort will go straight back to the community—into schools, county roads, public services, things that matter. It's money the town can use *right* now."

A few people shifted in their chairs. Someone up front leaned over and whispered to their neighbor. Fred sat up straighter.

"We know this is a town full of pride. We're not here to change that. We're here to help it grow. Property values will rise. Homeowners will benefit. Small business owners will thrive. This isn't about replacing what Hattrick has. It's about making sure it has a future."

I finally let myself glance across the room—just *not* in her direction. I didn't trust myself to look at her. Not after the way her words about Hope Farm had hit me. She wasn't like anyone else in this room, and I couldn't figure out why that mattered so much. Only that it did.

I'd planned to say more, but I stopped. I'd said enough. The room was quiet when I finished. Not warm. Not hostile. Just… uncertain. Which, honestly, was exactly how I felt, too.

I told myself the uncertainty would pass. It should've been simple—land, numbers, strategy. But it wasn't. Not anymore.

Not with her fighting for the same piece of land, and not with the way her words still lingered—*foster care*, *slip through the cracks*, *Hope Farm*. Maggie offered something completely different than Mitchell Developers. The two business plans couldn't be more opposite.

I returned to my chair, taking a seat between Ben and my dad. Ben looked at me with confusion, while my dad slapped me on the back.

"I don't know what happened to you up there, but good recovery," he said, his voice low and clipped. His hand remained clamped on my shoulder.

Whack! Whack! Whack!

The council meeting ended the same way it started—with Fred banging that damn gavel. "The council will review both business proposals over the next few weeks," he announced. "We'll hear from both parties again at next month's meeting, where a vote will be held." He slammed the gavel one last time, louder, sharper than the fifty times that came before it—full of self-imposed authority.

The room stirred. Chairs scraped. People stood, and conversations resumed. But I barely heard any of it. I straightened slowly, scanning the crowd. Looking for her. Maggie's seat was empty. Like she'd vanished. Like she was never there.

I lingered, pretending I wasn't affected, pretending it was just another meeting. But I knew differently.

This was supposed to be just business. Just another deal.

But somehow it felt like I lost something I never really had.

11
Maggie

Kevin: Maggie, can we talk?
Kevin: Maggie, please pick up.

Not here to change your town…

> *It offers real opportunity…*

> *We want to secure its future…*

My ass! They want to secure *their* future. It was money *they* could use right now.

I was talking to myself, alone on an elevator, heading straight into the lion's den. My palms were damp, and my heart was beating faster than I'd liked, but I needed to do this. I don't know what possessed me to wake up and want to confront Conrad Mitchell and his son, but that's exactly what I was about to do.

Conrad Mitchell didn't scare me.

Kevin Mitchell…different story.

The elevator dinged, and I stepped out, immediately greeted by sleek floors, oversized portraits of million-dollar Mitchell projects, and a receptionist who looked like she'd stepped out of a beauty campaign—flawless makeup, glossy hair, and full-blown lips.

I couldn't tell if I wanted to pass out, throw up, or pee my pants. All three felt like reasonable options.

I was going to march into the office of Conrad Mitchell—the man standing in the way of everything I'd just poured my heart out for—and his ridiculously handsome son, whom I may or may not have a date with Friday night.

I couldn't concentrate. Kevin's face kept flashing through my mind—those eyes, that stunned expression when he saw me last night. His words still rattled around in my head—job security, revenue, increased tourism—all of which irritated me.

He hadn't been expecting me—just like I hadn't been expecting him. The surprise in his eyes matched my own. And for a flicker of a second, I saw something in his face—regret, maybe. Conflict. Something honest.

But then reality set in again. His family business wanted the land. And no matter what he felt—or what I thought I saw—we were standing on opposite sides.

Every assistant I passed was a young woman with perfect hair, perfectly polished nails, tight skirts, and tailored blouses. I felt like I'd stepped twenty years back in time. I had a feeling the #MeToo movement would have a field day with this place, and I had half a mind to call Gloria Steinem and start handing out protest signs.

I asked the young woman at the reception desk to direct me to Conrad Mitchell's office.

Her nameplate read: Stacey.

"I'm sorry," she said, all pleasant professionalism, "but Mr. Mitchell is in a board meeting right now, and his schedule is full for the day. Would you like to make an appointment?"

I wasn't leaving here without talking to that man.

That's when I saw it—the glassed-in corner office at the end of the hall. A handful of men in suits were gathered around a table, deep in conversation. Whatever was happening in there, it looked serious. And I had an overwhelming feeling I needed to be in that room.

"Is that the board meeting?" I asked.

Stacey nodded politely. "Yes. They will be there most of the morning."

Without another word, I turned and walked straight past her—no hesitation, no stopping to think.

"Ma'am—wait!" she called, heels clicking behind me.

She gave chase, but she wasn't fast enough, and her skirt made her waddle.

I reached the glass doors, pushed them open, and stepped inside like I belonged there. The room fell silent. All eyes swiveled in my direction, brows raised, and the conversation froze mid-sentence.

Perfect. Now what the hell should I do?

I swallowed. "Good. You're all here."

There were eight men seated around the large, polished, cherry table that looked rather elegant and expensive. The room smelled of old money and cologne—leather chairs, crisp suits, and aged cigars. Power radiated off the walls. No smiles. No softness. Just a boardroom full of men who were not used to being interrupted. Especially by a woman.

If I had a penis, this might be easier. Instead, I squared my shoulders, planted my feet firmly in the middle of the room, and let my voice cut through the air. They weren't going to roll into Hattrick Harbor and destroy our town by building a casino. Not without a fight.

Conrad Mitchell sat at the head of the table, hands folded in front of him like he expected me to bust through the door. Kevin whipped around in his chair—and the look on his face stopped me cold. Surprised? Definitely. But then I saw something else flash through. I thought I might've imagined it, but then he hid a smile and dropped his head.

Focus, Maggie.

Stacey came toddling in, winded and flustered. "I'm sorry, Mr. Mitchell," she puffed. "I told her you were in a meeting. She just ignored me."

Tattletale.

Conrad Mitchell stood. He was a man who exuded power— older, yes, but clearly still used to getting what he wanted.

"That's alright, Miss Ross. I'll take it from here," he said coolly.

Stacey nodded quickly and backed out of the room with her tail between her legs. Dismissed, rudely, with a wave of a hand.

I should drag her to the picket lines when I leave here.

Conrad Mitchell turned his full attention back toward me— eyes sharp, posture straight, confidence so thick it bordered on condescension. He didn't just look at me—he assessed me like I was a problem to be solved, not a person to be heard.

Kevin sat to the left, looking nothing like him. His expression was softer, conflicted even, like he didn't quite belong at the table. I wasn't sure what to make of him. But the man on the other side of Conrad? Him, I knew right away—*Mr. What-Condom-Do-You-Prefer?*

Ben leaned back in his chair, slowly dragging his tongue across his lips, and stared at me in a way that made my skin crawl.

Pig!

I was the only female in a room of eight men. And every inch of me knew it.

"Ms. Bentley, is it?" Conrad said, smiling—but it was the kind of smile that liked the game more than the outcome.

"Correct."

He motioned to the chair across from him. "Please. Join us."

"I'll stand, thank you." My voice was calm, even if my insides weren't.

"What can we do for you today, Ms. Bentley?" He talked like we were friendly.

We were not.

"There are plenty of other properties in the Charlotte area that are better suited for your resort and casino. Why Hattrick Harbor?"

"I believe my son made all of our motives clear last night. This plan is mutually beneficial for us *and* your town."

"But that was before you knew there was someone else who wanted the property."

"Correct. We were under the impression we would go unopposed."

"And now that you know you're not, and that I would like to retain the integrity of the property for a good cause, I'm hoping you'll reconsider."

Ben choked out a laugh. And several board members shook their heads.

Asshats.

"Now, why would I do that, sweetheart, when my son has thoroughly researched your town as the perfect spot for our project?"

Sweetheart. Are you kidding me? Conrad Mitchell was the kind of man who still thought women should smile pretty, keep quiet, fetch coffee, and let the men talk business. Guaranteed he was the type of man who called the waitress "darlin'," still used the word "secretary," and called her "honey."

"First of all, I'd prefer Ms. Bentley to sweetheart. And second…" I said, "because it's the right thing to do."

He laughed. He planned to intimidate me, but he had no clue who he was up against. I'd faced bigger bullies than a man in a power suit. And here I was, still standing. Still fighting.

I stood, waiting for an answer. He sat, waiting for me to leave.

Kevin spoke up. "Dad, can we have a private conversation?"

He looked at his son. Maybe the only other man in the room he had an inkling of respect for was Kevin. But Conrad Mitchell wasn't going to back down. He didn't have it in him.

"I was hoping to come here today and respectfully—and professionally—ask you to reconsider. To leave Hattrick Harbor out of your casino plans." I dropped a folder on the table. "I'm going to ask you to take a look at these alternate locations for your project."

I would beg him to reconsider, but I wouldn't bring myself to look weak or desperate. So, if it were a fight he wanted, he'd get one.

"Thank you for taking the time to listen to me. But I want you to know, I'm not going away."

I walked out of the boardroom with my shoulders back and my head held high. I had no idea if I'd just poked a sleeping bear—or flat-out invited him to come for me.

Hey Siri: Add bear spray to shopping list.

Maybe I'd made things worse. I probably did. But I didn't care. They needed to know I wasn't going to roll over. Not for Conrad Mitchell. Not for anyone.

I didn't like the man. I didn't trust the way he smiled like he'd already won, and he looked at me like I was a minor inconvenience. Something about him felt cold. Unmoved and strategic. He never raised his voice. He never got rattled. In fact, that politician's grin never left his face—he was calm and calculated, and that was worse. The man had an attitude that came from decades of success. And I got the distinct impression that stepping on anyone who got in the way was something he liked doing—probably thrived on.

He didn't care about Hattrick Harbor—he cared about his bank account. And when a rich man smelled money, he didn't walk—he circled, like a vulture.

And Kevin Mitchell. He had started the ball rolling because he had chosen *my* town for his dumb casino. The man who stood in my kitchen apologizing, asking me out, begging for a redo.

My heels hit the marble floor as I stormed down the hallway, each step mixed with fury and something I hated to admit—a hollow weight low in my chest. I swallowed hard, refusing to let it rise. Anger—I could handle. Disappointment—I'd had enough of.

Hope Farm wasn't just a cause. It was personal for me. Joe and I dreamed about this for years, long before we had a plan.

It was an idea we'd talk about on Sunday mornings or on long drives. But when our twins, Jack and Andrew, turned twelve, we took in our first emancipated foster child, Ethan, who was eighteen at the time. Over the years, we would take in three more young men who had nowhere to go. No family to call their own.

This was personal.

Joe understood how deeply Hope Farm mattered—he'd wanted it just as much as I did.

And now he wasn't here to fight for it. That battle was all mine now.

It wasn't just about the farm, the kids—not entirely. It was about finishing something we had started together. About turning our dream into something lasting. About fulfilling a last promise.

Hope Farm needed to happen—for the kids, for me, for Joe.

12

Kevin

I've never been more impressed by anyone in my life. And I meant *no one*.

No one had ever barged into a Mitchell board meeting. Not without an invitation. Definitely not without a suit and tie. And not without knowing exactly what they were stepping into. But Maggie Bentley did.

Not only did she hold her ground—she fucking owned it.

She looked incredible, too. Not stiff and sharp like half the women who breezed through our office, but real—confident and disarming in the same breath. Hair straight down her back, a navy pantsuit tailored to walk in and kick ass. Stilettos that sent my mind to a different place.

Honestly, a silk dress or cotton joggers—it wouldn't have mattered. I had a feeling she could wear a trash bag, and I'd still think she was the most captivating woman I'd ever laid eyes on.

But it wasn't just how she looked or what she wore—it was her presence. She carried herself with purpose, her posture confident, her chin lifted, her eyes dialed in. And when she spoke, the room full of stuffy suits didn't know what to make of this stunning woman standing toe to toe with my father.

And somehow, in under five minutes, she managed to do the one thing I'd never seen anyone pull off—she caught Conrad Mitchell by surprise. Just for a millisecond. But I saw him crack. And in this building? That's rare enough to be a seismic event.

And me? I wasn't thinking like a Mitchell at all. I was thinking like a man who wanted to know more about the woman who'd just shaken the ground under his feet.

I should've been focused on the deal—but I wasn't. All I thought about was her fire. Her passion. It was a combination I'd never seen. Not in this room.

No one opposed my dad.

Until today.

The boardroom emptied out, leaving just me, Ben, and our father.

Ben stood staring after Maggie, practically foaming at the mouth. "If you two will excuse me, I have a meeting," he said, grabbing his folder like he suddenly remembered he had somewhere to be.

I watched him head for the doors, moving fast, like a wolf chasing something he had no business catching.

My jaw tightened, grinding my molars. My blood simmered.

"Is this going to be a problem, Kevin?"

I froze. Did he see the way I looked at her? The way my whole body responded to her. To him, distractions were a weakness, and my father never tolerated weakness in anyone, especially me.

"What do you mean?"

"Maggie Bentley and this…this idea of a kid farm." He waved his hand dismissively in a way that made Maggie and her idea inconsequential. It bothered me. A lot.

"Well, Dad," I paused, "I think we're in for a fight. This town clearly loves her. She's got people behind her—loud ones. And if we bulldoze our way through, we're not just risking the deal—we're risking our name. Forcing something a town doesn't want? That kind of backlash sticks."

"Who cares about that? It's a farm for a handful of throwaway kids. This town needs to decide—sentiment or millions in revenue. I know which one I'm betting on."

His words hit like a slap.

Throwaway kids? Shock ripped through me. When had he started thinking like that? Or had he always thought that way and I'd been too eager—too blinded by loyalty—to see it?

I studied him, trying to read something behind that harsh, polished exterior. There was nothing. Just calculation. Cold ambition in a Tom Ford suit.

I used to think he was ruthless for the sake of business. Now I wasn't so sure. Maybe ruthlessness was just who he was. I'd spent my whole life trying to live up to him, prove I was cut from the same cloth. But in that moment, I wasn't proud of the resemblance—I hated it.

A bitter taste coated my tongue, the same one I'd swallowed down for most of the meeting. For a second, I was so stunned I didn't know what to say. I just knew I had to keep my voice level because he wouldn't respond to anything else.

"Well," I said, swallowing hard, "maybe this town won't see it like that."

My phone buzzed, and I looked down to see who it was. Annoyed, I silenced it and sent it to voicemail.

I tried the tactic of redirection. "I know this deal is important," I said, keeping my tone even, "but maybe it doesn't have to be this property. As smart businessmen, we should at least consider the alternatives Ms. Bentley presented. There are other options to build something great without steamrolling the town."

Conrad let out a short, humorless laugh. "Not a chance. A week ago, you were the one selling me on Hattrick Harbor. *You* said it was perfect. *You* said it was *the* location. That wasn't a suggestion—it was a pitch. *Your* pitch."

His words landed hard.

My pitch. My plan.

My mess to defend.

I shifted in my chair, ignoring the buzz on my phone again.

"I'm not saying we walk away," I said carefully. "I'm just saying we should look at the options. We owe it to ourselves to see what else is out there before we dig in on a property that's already got this much heat. That's smart business."

Dad leaned back in his chair, eyeing me like I was speaking a language he didn't understand.

"We stick with the original plan," he said flatly. "Don't go getting soft on me now."

I didn't say a word. Just turned and looked down the hallway. Maggie stood by the elevator, arms crossed, while Ben, all swagger, leaned against the wall with smug ease and an arrogance convinced that every woman enjoyed his company. Clearly, one did not.

Meeting my ass. He wasn't even trying to hide it.

I inhaled. Some fight I was in—with the town, with my dad, and now apparently with my own damn brother.

My father lit a cigar and took one large puff. "You have one month to win over the city council. You'd better be prepared to crush Ms. Bentley's little farm idea."

I'd seen that look before. To him, every deal was war, and every opponent was disposable. Maggie wanted a fight—Conrad Mitchell was more than willing to give her one. Backing away wasn't even a consideration.

"Understood," I said. But my thoughts were already somewhere else—on a woman in a navy suit, and the quiet fire in her voice when she'd said *some kids have nowhere else to go.*

My chest tightened, and my fists curled and uncurled against my thigh. I was wired, like every word she'd spoken was burning in my lungs.

"Dad, I need a minute."

I didn't wait for a response. I walked out of the boardroom, every step fueled with intention.

"Where are you going? We aren't finished here," my father called after me.

Maybe not—but I was finished with him—for now.

When I reached the hallway, Maggie was still by the elevators. And Ben was hovering beside her like a dog ready to lift its leg and pee.

Not today. She wasn't his. He could take his swagger somewhere else, because Maggie Bentley wasn't up for grabs—not while I was standing there.

"Ms. Bentley?"

Maggie turned toward me, her eyes blazing, daring anyone dumb enough to come closer.

"I was just telling Maggie that I think we met a couple of weeks ago at that speed-dating thing." Ben's grin was a little too slick.

"And I was just telling your brother he doesn't look familiar at all," she said dryly.

I bit back a laugh. Maggie was all spunk. Ben, on the other hand, didn't appreciate her humor like I did.

"Sure, we did," Ben said, undeterred. "You were my little Miss-Hold-Out. The only one who didn't leave her number. I bet you're ready to change your mind now."

He leaned in, smug as hell. "How about I take you out and you can tell me all about this little farm of yours—and those kids you want to save."

Maggie didn't even blink. "I think I'd rather gut a pig and eat its intestines for dinner...raw."

God, I loved watching her stand up to the Mitchell men. She didn't waver, didn't back down, just knocked us on our asses with nothing but her words. Two for two today—and I was here for every second of it.

Ben chuckled, clearly amused. But like my father, he liked a challenge. Unfortunately, the only thing thicker than his unrelenting charm was his ego.

"May I validate your parking?" I asked, stepping in. "Let me walk you downstairs."

Ben's jaw flexed. "I was just about to take care of that for Ms. Bentley," he hissed, drawing out her name like it tasted good on his mouth.

I adjusted my cuff slowly, a quiet warning. "You're wanted in the boardroom."

Ben didn't budge at first. Then he smirked and stepped aside like he was doing us both a favor. "I'll be seeing you around, *Maggie*."

She didn't skip a beat. "I hope not."

The elevator finally dinged, and we stepped inside. I hit the button for the parking garage, and the doors slid closed, sealing us into a pocket of silence.

Maggie crossed her arms and leaned back against the wall. "Is your brother in some national database for perverts?"

I huffed out a laugh. "Some days I don't know how we're even related."

"He's an asshole," she said, almost to herself.

"He can be," I admitted. "I'm sorry about that."

She glanced over at me. "I shouldn't have said that. I know he's your brother."

Then, under her breath, dry as ever, "But he *is* an asshole."

I smiled, grateful she hadn't lost her spark. Grateful, she was still talking to me.

When the doors opened, we stepped out and walked side by side toward her car. The air between us lightened a little with each step, the tension from upstairs trailing behind.

"Your dad is intense," Maggie said as we walked toward her car.

"Yes," I replied, too quickly.

She glanced over at me. "Has he always been like that?"

I hesitated. "No. Maybe. I don't know." The words stumbled out before I could clean them up.

Lately, I started to doubt that the man I grew up with and the man running Mitchell Development were even the same person. Somewhere along the way, the bottom line became the only thing that mattered. If he wanted something, he just didn't go after it—he *took* it.

As Maggie and I walked, the silence stretched just enough to feel like something unspoken was hanging in the air.

Then she stopped and turned toward me. "Your dad isn't going to back down, is he?"

I rubbed the back of my neck, sighing. "I'm afraid not. He's like a dog with a bone when he sees an opportunity like this. He's convinced himself that what he's doing will not only benefit the firm's success, but also benefit the town."

She held my gaze for a moment, her keys dangling from her fingers. "If I remember, those were *your* words last night."

She wasn't wrong. I switched gears. "I tried calling you last night."

"I know," she said quietly, walking toward the end of the row where her car was parked. She pressed the button on her fob.

"In all honesty, Maggie, I'm not convinced it's not the better option for Hattrick," I said. "I do believe it will help the town. Create jobs. Bring more revenue to businesses. I wasn't lying about that."

She stopped by the driver's side and looked at me, her hand resting on the handle. "You haven't spent much time in Hattrick Harbor, have you?"

I shoved my hands in my pockets, trying to suppress a grin. "Not much. No."

"Then I'll have to show you."

The corners of my mouth inched up. "How do you plan on doing that?"

"I'm going to show you what my town is all about," she said. "Then you decide whether to destroy it or not."

I laughed under my breath. "Well, the vote is scheduled for next month."

"Perfect. That means I have thirty days to convince you to change your mind about the casino."

I wasn't entirely convinced Maggie was wrong—or right. The casino could bring growth to Hattrick Harbor in more ways than I could count—those facts I couldn't ignore. But facts have never left me restless at midnight, thinking about a woman with the most mesmerizing eyes. Maybe thirty days in her town would change my mind. Maybe it wouldn't. Either way, I was going to call this a win.

Her words lit me up as an undercurrent of electricity crackled to life, and I took a step closer. "Does that mean we're still on for Friday night?"

She smirked. "That means I'm showing *you* my town. So *I* make the plans."

"By plans, do you mean dates?" My eyebrows lifted in mock innocence.

"No. By plans, I mean…a month-long education of Hattrick Harbor," she said, like it was a challenge. "I'm going to show you all that Hattrick Harbor has to offer—how a casino will strip the soul right out of it—and that Hope Farm is the better option."

Maggie opened the door to her SUV, stepped on the running board, and climbed into the gray leather seat.

I leaned an arm on the open doorframe, grinning up at her.

"And what if, after thirty days, I still believe that your town will benefit from our company's plan?"

She leveled me with a look that made my chest tighten. "You won't." Then she shut the door.

The window rolled down with a smooth hum. "I'll text you Thursday night with the plan," she added, then drove away

Silently, I counted the days, already restless at the thought of waiting that long before I saw her again. I did the math—Friday. Which meant every hour until then was going to drag like hell.

I watched her car turn out of the parking garage and disappear. A month of Maggie Bentley—her town, her rules, her fire. That smile, those eyes, the way she challenged me with every damn thing I said…hell, yes.

I hadn't felt this alive in a long time. And something about it breathed life into me, an energy I could barely keep contained. Every nerve, every muscle, every fiber in my body told me to chase whatever this was.

The clock had already started ticking, and I knew exactly what was at stake.

13

Maggie

Mother Puckers 4-Life

Maggie: I'm bringing Kevin to the game on Friday.

Annie: We'll be on our best behavior.

Katie: That's a lie, and you know it.

Joy: Should I bake cookies? Wait—is this a date? Should I bring glitter?

Jules: Tell him if he doesn't change his mind about the casino, I'll key his truck. Also, I'm wearing my leather vest. It's intimidating.

Maggie: It's not a date. It's part of my plan. "Operation No Craps Allowed."

Annie: AKA "Thirty Days to Seduce the Developer."

Katie: Oh, good, I'll bring my label maker.
I'll tag everything as you show him around.
Joy: I'll make a playlist. Mostly Taylor Swift.
And one angry Carrie song—the one
about keying a car for Jules.
Jules: Thanks, Joy. I'm bringing moonshine.
For "Exhibit A."
Maggie: Just act normal.
Annie: You keep using that word...

Thirty days.

That's how long I had to convince Kevin Mitchell that his plan to build a casino in Hattrick Harbor was a terrible idea. To do that, I needed to show him the best of what I called home.

Growing up, home was just another word to me—four letters that didn't really have a meaning at all. My friends in school used the word so freely: *I need to go home for dinner. I'm just chilling at home tonight. I can't wait to get home.* They used it in everyday conversation as if it were a place everyone had—like it came with a key and a porch light left on just for them. It always sounded like a comfortable blanket, snugly draped over their shoulders, safe and secure. Two things I never really felt back then.

Home was something I'd never understood—not until Joe brought me to Hattrick Harbor, not until we'd planted roots here. For the first time in my life, I knew what I'd been missing all those years. Hattrick Harbor gave meaning to something I never thought I'd have.

Finally, the word had been defined for me.

The doorbell rang at precisely 3 p.m.

I answered it in my regular game day attire—temporary tomahawk face tattoos, our team jersey, and a hockey puck swinging from an oversized gold chain that even Mr. T would've been proud of. How I managed to open the door with two foam fingers on was impressive, even to me.

Kevin's dark eyes trailed down my body in the most unnerving and appreciative way.

"Why are you dressed like a '90s rapper?"

"This?" I grinned. "This will be considered underdressed. We're stopping by the team store on the way to the rink, so you don't stick out like a sore thumb."

He hesitated. "Where exactly are we going?"

"Our high school's hockey game, of course."

"What time does the game start?"

"Seven. But the pregame started at noon. And we're late."

"And we're going to the hockey game because…"

"This is all a part of my tour—The Best of Hattrick in Thirty Days," I said, jabbing a foam finger against his chest with a wicked smile. "You're going to fall in love with my small town so hard that putting a casino here will sound completely absurd."

He chuckled and shook his head. "Great. So, I'm being emotionally manipulated with nachos and high school hockey?"

"Exactly. And this is just the beginning."

By the time we left the team store, Kevin was wearing a maroon hoodie with the team logo on the front, a matching knit beanie, and—because I wouldn't let him out of the store without one—a foam tomahawk tucked under his arm. He looked ridiculously good. No wonder he was the face of the Mitchell Development Company. Put him in front of a crowd, and he'd win over the room. And if the crowd happened to be mostly women, he wouldn't even have to say a word. Game over.

Eye on the prize, Maggie. I had to remind myself I was on a mission—make Kevin see that Hattrick Harbor was worth saving. Do not get distracted by a charming—sometimes smug—smile, broad shoulders, and well-worn denim.

As we drove through downtown, Kevin leaned forward, squinting at all the CLOSED signs hanging in storefronts.

"Is...*everything* closed?"

"Yep."

"At three o'clock on a Friday afternoon?"

"It's a Friday night home game," I said as if it explained everything. "People have priorities, Kevin."

He glanced over at me, somewhere between amused and mildly alarmed. "And the *entire* town will be there?"

Hattrick Harbor had one main street. Eight stop signs and half the number of stoplights. On a normal day, people were out milling around, swapping stories in front of the hardware store, balancing iced teas in one hand and a dog leash in the other, and dodging kids on bikes on their way to Sweet Sally's ice cream shop.

But today wasn't a normal day. Not a soul in sight.

I gestured at all the signs as we passed.

> CLOSED for Pucking Business.
> We Break for ZAMBONIS.
> HALF-OFF MULLETS During Hockey Season.

That last one was at Harbor Barber.

"Welcome to Hattrick Harbor, Kevin. Hockey isn't just a sport, it's a full-blown religion."

He shook his head. "Remind me to make the sign of the cross before we go into the rink."

"That would actually earn you some serious respect."

As we entered the parking lot of the rink, Kevin blinked hard and sat back in his seat. "You've got to be kidding me."

The parking lot looked like someone dropped the state fair in the middle of our small town. To anyone seeing it for the first time, it probably looked excessive—some might've even called it obsessive. But once you'd lived here long enough, it didn't seem so out of the ordinary—it just felt normal.

Kevin's head was on a swivel as he took it all in.

A two-story inflatable goalie stood at the entrance, hard to miss. F150s were parked in every space with their tailgates open, loaded with coolers, crockpots, and enough food to feed a small army. Fold-up lawn chairs scattered everywhere. Blackstones smoking like factory stacks. The smell of sausage, barbecue, and woodsmoke drifted through the air as kids with maroon face paint and bare chests zipped between trucks. Cornhole games were already in full swing—everyone clutching a koozie. There was even a flat-screen TV strapped to the side of someone's camper, playing last year's championship game on a loop.

"Are you going to make me paint my chest?" he asked.

"Only if we go into overtime."

"At least I've been warned."

We hadn't made it ten feet past the inflatable goalie when I heard it—four unmistakable voices. "Maggie!" I spotted them instantly—Annie, Jules, Joy, and Katie—all wearing our matching jerseys and holding red Solo cups. We were set up in our usual spot—a maroon awning with string lights tied between two trucks, a folding table piled high with snacks, and a portable speaker blaring our favorite throwbacks. Their husbands lounged in camp chairs behind them, arguing about player stats from last season, and Annie's husband, Mike, manned the grill.

All four of my friends waved wildly. "Ladies," I said, gesturing to the man beside me. "This is Kevin Mitchell. We're on my Best of Hattrick Tour. Be nice."

They smiled sweetly, almost too sweetly, offering polite hellos that felt...practiced. This could go one of two ways: really bad or really, really bad.

Annie stuck her hand out. "Nice to see you again, Kevin."

"No bunny slippers today?" he asked, glancing down at her shoes.

"Only bring those out for special occasions," she shot back. "Bingo Night and fake emergencies."

"Kevin," I continued, "this is Mike." I nudged him toward Annie's husband, who extended a hand and offered him a beer. "Stick with him—it's safer."

The moment Kevin turned his back, Jules grabbed my arm

and dragged me to the circle of the other three. "Holy hell, Maggie. That man is a hot, walking felony."

"You can borrow my furry handcuffs," Annie offered.

Joy practically vibrated with excitement. "He has kind eyes. Don't you think?"

Katie leaned in. "I already made a drinking game for every time he asks a question."

Annie popped a jalapeno in her mouth and smirked. "If this is your plan to save Hattrick, consider me supportive. Does he come with a leather tool belt and shirtless calendar, because I want one?"

I gave them my most stern look. "Girls. Can we focus? This is about saving the town."

"Saving the town and appreciating the scenery," Jules said, licking the frosting off her fingers. "This is called multitasking, Maggie."

"You promised me your best behavior."

"And we delivered," Jules said, biting into a cookie. "We didn't even ask if he was single."

Joy gasped. "Wait—is he single?"

Annie winked. "Not for long if he keeps wearing those jeans. They should be banned."

I glanced over to check on him. That was all it was supposed to be—a quick glance to check and make sure Mike wasn't overwhelming him with refereeing conspiracy theories or his other favorite topic, the probability of Hattrick winning another state title.

But my eyes lingered.

Kevin was laughing at something Mike had said, head thrown

back and completely unguarded. His hoodie stretched across his back, clinging in all the right places, proving that this man wasn't afraid of a little CrossFit. I should've looked away, but I didn't. I stared a beat too long—and that's when he felt it. He turned, eyes scanning until they found mine.

His smile softened around the edges, and his eyes locked on mine like he was daring me to look away first. I didn't. Couldn't. My pulse picked up. It was only a few seconds, but it felt like a whole conversation. I finally gave the smallest nod, breaking the moment, and turned back to Annie, who was mid-story about her new idea for the hockey rink fundraiser.

I nodded and laughed along at the right parts, but my thoughts drifted. It'd been a long time since I'd stood there, surrounded by my closest friends, not feeling like the odd one out. Not because of anything they did. Of course, they'd never make me feel like that. But after years of being part of a twosome in a group full of couples, shifting to a onesome took some getting used to.

Some days, I'd adjusted just fine. Other days, it still caught me off guard—how quiet it could feel when the laughter faded, the night wound down, and I went home by myself.

But tonight…I wasn't alone. Kevin might be here under some kind of small-town saving mission of mine, but still…it made a difference.

He was here. With me. And somehow, that mattered.

Kevin wasn't just good-looking—which was the understatement of the year—he was comfortable with my friends. Awkward wasn't even in his vocabulary. He laughed at their jokes, they laughed at his, and he didn't even flinch at their teasing. And somehow made the whole thing look effortless. That in itself was pretty damn attractive.

I didn't know what was going to happen in thirty days, but for now, it felt good not to be standing here alone.

14

Kevin

Maggie: Pick me up at 6 p.m.

Kevin: What's tonight's small-town adventure?

Maggie: How to keep high school kids from making out in dark corners. Hattrick Harbor's senior citizens, too.

Kevin: You're scaring me.

Maggie: A word of advice: Don't wear those jeans again, and don't bend over anywhere near Handsy Helen.

Kevin: School Principal?

Maggie: Hattrick Harbor's Most Eligible Bachelorette. Ninety-three. Loves wine, bingo, and younger men.

Kevin: Is this your way of easing me into Hattrick Harbor?

Last night, I went to my first high school hockey game. And not just any game—this was a blow-the-roof-off, scream-till-you're-hoarse, half-the-town-called-in-sick-today kind of game. I knew hockey had its fans, sure. I'd seen enough highlight reels on ESPN to respect it—guys getting checked into the glass, gloves flying, the occasional tooth on the ice. But I'd always thought hockey was a northern sport, places with snowplows, blizzards, and frozen ponds.

I wasn't expecting this kind of devotion in a lakeside town in North Carolina where winter barely made an appearance.

In Hattrick Harbor? These people lived and breathed hockey.

There were foam fingers on every hand. A sea of maroon and gold. And a student section where every male had his chest painted. Texas football had nothing on Hattrick Harbor hockey.

And it all started with a tailgate party that was more fun than I'd had in years.

Maggie's four best friends were a trip—each one louder, bolder, and more unfiltered than the next. Their husbands? A protective force field. I was asked—half-joking, half-not—about my intentions with "their girl." Maggie had a crew looking out for her, that was for sure.

There was laughter, beers handed to me before I asked, and a few too many ribs shoved onto my plate, but under all that teasing, I got the message loud and clear: If I so much as made Maggie frown, I'd be walking home with a limp.

But damn it was easy to have fun with them. And Maggie— she was at the center of it all. The way her eyes crinkled when she leaned into her friends, completely at ease. That oversized high school jersey wasn't supposed to be sexy, but on her, it sure as hell was. It was impossible not to watch her.

Everyone around her lit up. Everything about her drew people in. And everybody wanted to be near her.

I was no exception.

This was supposed to be part of her grand plan, her Thirty-Day Tour of Hattrick Harbor, to convince me that Mitchell Developers should find an alternative location. But at some point during the night, it started feeling like more than that, and the mission became non-existent.

Maybe I was just caught up in the fun. Maybe it was the fact that I'd met a group of people who genuinely liked being around each other, and being folded into it was new for me. Or maybe it was Maggie—how my focus kept drifting from the conversation back to her, like my body was trying to tell my brain something.

Or maybe—if I were being honest—it wasn't any of that. Maybe it was something else entirely.

But Maggie was hell-bent on her mission. And I was hell-bent on letting her try. She made this little weird town feel like a place I wanted to learn more about.

The school gym smelled like popcorn, fruit punch, and whatever body spray teenage boys were overusing. Streamers hung from basketball hoops, the disco ball spun, and a playlist of pop songs blasted over a questionable sound system manned by a DJ with a handlebar mustache and sequined vest. Mix Master Merle was not only Hattrick Harbor's part-time postmaster and assistant to the assistant of the mayor, but also the reigning champ of the Tri-County Air Guitar Finals—three years running.

I didn't know whether to laugh or salute him.

Maggie leaned in close enough that I could smell her shampoo, something like coconut—soft, clean, and totally distracting. Whatever it was, it messed with my brain chemistry.

"Be honest," she teased. "You're rethinking your career choice right about now, aren't you?"

I smirked. "Only if the air guitar gig comes with dental and vision."

She laughed, and I swear I felt the sound somewhere in my chest.

Her long brown hair was straight and tucked behind her ears, simple and perfect. And her eyes—so green that they were impossible not to stare at. If I'd had a guidance counselor who looked like Maggie, I'd have faked a crippling existential crisis every damn day.

"Hey, Miss B." A tall kid with a wide grin sidled up to Maggie and pulled her into a quick hug.

"Cody!" Her face lit up. "This is my friend, Mr. Mitchell. Kevin, this is Cody. He's the captain of the hockey team and scored the hat trick last night."

Cody, polite and respectful, turned to me with a firm handshake. "Nice to meet you, sir."

"Great game last night," I said. "You had us all on our feet."

He smiled a little bashfully. "Thank you."

He then turned back to Maggie. "I'll have my college essay done by Monday. I'll drop it off."

"Perfect!" she said. "We'll start sending applications next week."

He hugged her again before he jogged back to a pack of his teammates. I watched him go, thinking how natural it all looked.

I didn't need a long case study to know Maggie was good at her job. She wasn't just kind to her students—they genuinely liked her. I could see it in the way they smiled at her—trusted her. Cody was only one example.

The phone vibrated in my pocket. I checked the screen, saw the name, and without a second thought, declined the call, powered it off, and slid it back into my pocket.

Annie was here, waving at us from the snack table with her husband Mike, who I discovered was head of the math department and the linebacker coach for the football team.

She twirled a piece of licorice. "Welcome to the sugar vortex."

Mike gave a nod, holding a tray of cookies, looking bored out of his mind. "Snack table duty."

"Mike's been eating more than he's handing out," Annie stage-whispered.

I laughed. "So, this is where the real power lies."

Annie lifted her brow. "Obviously. But you two have the real responsibility tonight."

I looked at Maggie. "What are we in charge of?"

She sighed. "PDA Patrol. Keeping kids from grinding to Ed Sheeran or sneaking off into dark hallways."

Annie laughed. "Basically, you're the fun police."

"Do we get a whistle?" I asked.

Mike tossed me a kazoo from the table. "That's all we got left. Budget cuts."

We took a lap around the gym, doing our best to look like responsible adults. There was something about seeing Maggie like this—in her world, with her friends, and completely in her element. It all tugged at me. I wasn't used to being a part of something that felt this…easy.

Nothing in my life ever looked like this. Never felt this natural. My world was all concrete and glass towers, deals measured in millions. Hers was this—school dances, real friends, and laughter. I couldn't remember how long it had been since I laughed so much or had this much fun in a weekend.

"You know if we built the casino, the school would benefit," I said, giving the kazoo a half-hearted toot. "Better facilities, no more budget cuts, maybe a new football field."

Maggie raised an eyebrow. "Ah, yes. The old strip club for scholarships argument."

I smirked. "I didn't say strip clubs."

She straightened, tucking her hair behind her ears as her chin lifted. Determined. Ready to make me understand. "Have you wondered why I brought you here? Why a school dance is part of my No Craps Allowed campaign?"

"The thought did cross my mind," I said.

"Look around, Kevin." Maggie pointed to the tables, the snack stand, and the bleachers.

We paused by the entrance to the gymnasium. Near the prize table a silver-haired woman in a sequined jacket was teaching two giggling girls how to do the Charleston. At center court, Mike was attempting a TikTok dance with some of his players while Annie filmed, doubled over with laughter.

Every round table was a picture of Hattrick's charm—

teenagers and residents from Sticks & Slippers Assisted Living Home, laughing, swapping stories, and sharing pizza and popcorn like old friends.

Then, DJ Merle queued up a Chuck Berry classic, and the gym floor flooded. High school kids twirled grinning seniors across the court, trying to master some form of the Twist with zero shame.

"Don't you see it?"

She gave me a minute to soak in the scene.

"This is what I wanted you to see—why I wanted to bring you here," she said. "It's real. It's a community. These kids aren't forced to include the residents from Sticks & Slippers—they *invite* them every year. The students look forward to it."

She paused, eyes scanning the gym like she was appreciating every part of it.

"It's not shiny or fancy," she said quietly. "But this is who we are."

I watched her as she spoke—not just her words, but the way she said them. The way her voice softened, like she'd rather be nowhere else. It made me wonder. Was there anything in my life I cared about that deeply, or was I only concerned about chasing the adrenaline of every new project? Had I missed out on something entirely?

"These kids will remember nights like this way more than any turf field," she added, staring at me with those eyes that should be illegal in small towns, or any town, really.

I stopped and actually thought about what she said. The simplicity of it all. The community. The connection. It wasn't what I was used to—I'd never experienced anything like it. But standing here, looking at Maggie, watching all this, I was starting to see the charm.

Then came a tap on my elbow.

I turned and immediately came face-to-hip with a tiny woman in a bedazzled cardigan and orthopedic shoes. "You must be Maggie's friend," she said, her eyes doing a full body scan. "I saw you from across the gym and thought to myself, 'Hello there, you tall drink of water.'"

"You must be Helen," I grinned. "Maggie warned me about you."

She smiled like a cat with a cornered mouse. "Smart boy. Save me a dance, Tall, Dark, and Delicious."

She winked and shuffled off toward the photo booth, humming along to the music with a little swing to her step.

I turned to Maggie. "Is she for real?"

"She's a legend," Maggie replied, straight-faced. "Last year, she ran for mayor. Annie was her campaign manager. She almost won."

I laughed. This town had some real characters. And that was the thing. Hattrick Harbor was the opposite of every place I'd ever called home, and against all odds, it was starting to grow on me.

We stood on the edge of the dance floor for another minute, watching what could only be described as coordinated chaos. It started as the Electric Slide and took a hard left into uncharted territory. I was still trying to process it all when Maggie suddenly gasped.

"Oh, no!"

She took off across the gym floor like a shot out of a cannon, and my eyes followed.

That was when I saw her—Handsy Helen herself—being

crowd-surfed across a sea of teenage hockey players, her sequined jacket flashing under the disco ball like a glitter bomb.

Maggie was half-laughing, half-scolding as she rushed to help Helen back to her feet.

Meanwhile, I stood watching, trying to process the mayhem. Handsy Helen thought she was at a Metallica concert. The hockey team was teaching Helen to crowd surf—or maybe it was the other way around. This town was insane. And completely one-of-a-kind.

Before I knew it, the lights were starting to come back on in the gym, and Mix Master Merle was packing up his speakers. We'd busted four teenagers and twice as many of Hattrick's seniors for inappropriate dancing and kept Helen grounded, which wasn't easy. The night ended before I was ready.

As we headed toward the doors, Annie stood proudly with a wicker basket, handing out items to the students as they left.

"What's Annie doing?"

"Oh, she's probably handing out condoms," Maggie said casually.

"Protection, people!" Annie called out, dropping foil packets into open palms like Halloween candy. "Make good choices! Or at least make safe ones!"

"I'd like a half dozen, Annie," Helen's raspy voice chimed in, holding out an open purse. "Kevin, wait up—I've got plans for you!"

Maggie grabbed my arm and dragged me toward the parking lot. "Let's go, Romeo, before Helen asks if you have a latex allergy."

I held up a packet and laughed. "Would now be a bad time to ask what our next adventure will be?"

And just like that, the chaos didn't feel quite so chaotic

anymore—it felt almost expected. Almost normal. And apparently, I liked it.

But therein lied the problem.

This weekend was full of Maggie—her green eyes, easy laugh, gentle curves, and this quirky little town that was starting to feel less like a business prospect and more like a place that mattered. The longer I spent around her and Hattrick, the clearer it became—this wasn't just about the bottom line anymore.

I had a feeling the next three weeks might mess with more than my schedule—they just might make what I had to do—what I was expected to do—a hell of a lot harder. And maybe that's what scared me most. I wasn't just drawn to Maggie—I was starting to want what she wanted. And I didn't know what the hell that said about me.

15

Maggie

Maggie: Ready to be wooed by small-town charm? Next stop on my Fall in Love with Hattrick Tour, the annual hockey rink fundraiser—For Puck's Sake.

Kevin: Small-town hazing?

Maggie: Jules and Joy are in charge this year. There's a surprise involved. Even I don't know what it is.

Kevin: That's not reassuring.

Maggie: Trust me, you're gonna love this. Bring your wallet!

It'd only been a week since my campaign kicked off, yet in that short time, life had already taken on a new rhythm.

In the days leading up to For Puck's Sake, I took Kevin on a bike tour, we kayaked on the lake, and I gave him the full rundown on Hattrick Harbor's history—the same one every sixth grader got in middle school. He teased me for sounding like a tour guide, but I was doing my best to make him fall for Hattrick the way the rest of us had—one bike path, one history lesson, and one sunset at a time. If he could see what made this town special, maybe the idea of building a casino would start to sound as outrageous to him as it did to me.

He never complained, showed up on time, and seemed interested everywhere I dragged him. And…I started to look forward to it. To him.

I kept reminding myself that this was part of the plan—to win him over with my town so he and his father would back away from their casino dream. But somewhere between the bike rides, the fresh mountain air, and the pumpkin fritters from Rinkside Donuts, it stopped feeling like a mission and started to feel like more.

Kevin was fun. Easy to talk to. Far too easy to look at. And when he smiled at me with those chocolate brown eyes, I forgot—just for a second—that I needed to keep my guard up. This mission wasn't about dark eyes, a smile that could reroute brain activity, or a body that most men his age had no business having without some kind of divine intervention. This was about my town and New Hope Farm—an idea that needed to come to fruition.

That was the logic. But my heart wasn't logical. The plan began to fray around the edges, the stakes blurred—and suddenly, I wasn't just fighting for Hattrick. I was fighting feelings I hadn't let myself touch in a long time.

"I thought kissing booths went out of style back in the fifties," Kevin said, as we looked over the town map, picking out all the places we wanted to hit before the fundraiser ended.

"They did," I said. "But try telling Helen that."

He followed my gaze across the lawn, where a red-and-white striped booth sat proudly under a blinking light that flashed "Pucker Up." The booth was a spectacle. A line of silver-haired men and women stood in shifts—some with canes, others with walkers and wheelchairs.

"Do you think it's a good idea that someone with the nickname Handsy Helen is in charge of a kissing booth?"

"I'm sure it's an HR disaster, but she insisted," I said. "Plus, that booth alone raised more money than the funnel cakes and snow cones combined."

Helen stood front and center, wearing fire-engine red lipstick, a pink feather boa, and a grin that could only mean trouble. She was flanked by two other residents from Sticks and Slippers— Geraldine was in charge of the cash box, and Miriam had the bullhorn. The three together were enough to strike fear in every man in Hattrick Harbor, married or not.

Helen spotted us and practically cackled. "Kevin, I've been waiting for you."

Kevin took a cautious step back. "She's looking at me like I'm the early bird special."

"Go on," I said, nudging him forward. "One kiss. It's for the kids."

He gave me the wary side-eye. "I'm going to regret this."

We walked toward Helen, and I quietly started humming the *Death March*.

"Not funny, Maggie."

Before Kevin could even hand over his five-dollar bill, Helen pounced like a jungle cat, grabbed both his cheeks, and planted her lips on his. Her grip was unshakable.

She went full throttle. Her lips were ironclad.

Kevin flailed—his arms half-raised, hovering uselessly in the air. A few onlookers stopped. One clapped. Someone wolf-whistled. And Geraldine gave a thumbs-up from her chair. I bit the inside of my cheek to keep from laughing out loud, even if some part of me felt a twinge of jealousy toward a ninety-three-year-old with a feathered boa.

When Helen finally released him, Kevin staggered back. She just grinned, lipstick smeared. "I still got it."

He stumbled toward me. "She's stronger than she looks."

Helen began fanning herself with the pink boa, feathers flying like confetti. "I'm here all day, Kevin," she purred.

"Get me out of here," he whispered, tugging on my elbow. I'd never seen a man make a faster getaway as we bolted to the next spot on our map. It had felt like we were partners in crime, in on the same joke, trying to escape Helen's lipstick posse. It had been a long time since I'd felt this light.

We finally slowed, laughter still bubbling between us, the smell of popcorn drifted through the air, and the noise of the hockey team heckling each other at the dunking booth faded the further we walked. On our way to the bakery tent, a blur of motion zipped past us—maybe seven years old, grinning ear to ear with a balloon animal perched proudly on his head.

Kevin squinted. "Is that kid wearing a hat made of condoms?"

I glanced in the direction he was looking. "Yes, it's a rooster. Made from a combination of balloons *and* condoms. Extra-large ones, probably."

Kevin choked out a laugh. "That doesn't make it better."

We turned the corner to find Annie's booth. A banner stretched above it that read: *Let's Talk About Sex, Baby*. Mike was behind the table, working double time, twisting inflated condoms into balloon animals. Looked like he was working on a porcupine. Annie was handing out her business cards to every adult walking by.

"Normal day at the office?" Kevin quirked a brow.

"Pretty much," I said, watching as Annie handed her card to a tired-looking dad pushing a stroller. "Welcome to Hattrick Harbor's version of health class."

Kevin's phone had been vibrating all morning. At one point, he looked so upset that he turned it off. I could imagine that with a job like his and a father like Conrad Mitchell, he was on the clock more than he would've liked.

We spent the next several hours walking from booth to booth, sampling every cookie, funnel cake, and slushie. Per Kevin's request, we stayed far away from the kissing booth.

"Hi, Maggie. Hi, Kevin," Casey from Slap Shot's Diner said

as she walked by, juggling her Bernedoodle, an apple pie, and a gallon of her famous sweet tea.

"This day must take a lot of planning," Kevin said as we made our way through the crowded sidewalks, our slushies dripping down the sides.

"It does," I replied. "As soon as it's over, we start planning next year's event."

"How much do you need to raise every year?"

"We have to raise a hundred thousand dollars just to keep the rink running," I answered.

Kevin was quiet for a second, his brow furrowing. I could tell he was debating whether to say what he was thinking. Then he glanced over and exhaled.

"You know the casino could make that kind of money in a weekend."

I stopped. He turned to me, his slushie halfway to his lips.

"It's not about the money, Kevin," I said, sweeping my hand over the booths, the kids running wild, the neighbors I passed, every one of them waving. "And it's not about the work either."

He waited, giving me his full attention.

"It's about this," I said, swinging with my arms out wide. "It's about knowing everyone you pass on the sidewalk by name. It's about showing up at the Harbor Pub and having your order at the table before you sit down because your waitress knows it by heart. It's about trusting your neighbors to pick up your kid from practice because you're running late. It's about knowing exactly who made the quilt for the raffle and how much time it took her to make it."

I took a deep breath and met his eyes. "Writing a check is

easy, but it's not what this town is about. This isn't work."

We stood in the middle of the sidewalk. He didn't say anything right away—he just looked at me. Really looked at me. And I could tell he wasn't just brushing me off. He was listening to what I had to say. Taking it all in.

"You know," he said. "I'm starting to see why you like this quirky little town so much."

Something about the way he studied me settled in my chest in a way I hadn't expected. It made me feel seen, not just for what I said, but for what I believed in. This was what I was fighting for. This town…my dream of Hope Farm.

"Sorry. I can get a little preachy when I start talking about Hattrick."

But he shook his head and took a step closer. "Don't apologize."

And just like that, I felt my heart lean a little closer to this man and the sincerity in his eyes. I was supposed to be convincing Kevin to build his casino somewhere else, that Mitchell Developers didn't belong in Hattrick Harbor. Instead, the ground beneath my feet didn't quite feel as solid as it had when the day began. Being attracted to the enemy wasn't exactly in my game plan.

"Kevin Mitchell." Joy's voice crackled over the loudspeaker, cutting through the moment. "You're wanted on the main stage."

Kevin froze. "This can't be good."

I smiled, already gearing up for what came next. "I think this is the surprise I was promised."

Kevin shot me a look. "Why do I feel like I'm being summoned to the principal's office?"

I wished I could tell him what Joy was up to, but I was in the dark as much as he was, which wasn't exactly comforting.

We made our way to the main stage, where Joy was bouncing on her toes in place.

"Kevin! Perfect timing. We need your help."

He slowed his step and pushed me in front of him. "This feels like an ambush."

"That's because it is," Jules deadpanned. "I said we needed to ask you first about this, but Joy said surprises were romantic."

Joy clapped her hands and hopped up and down. "Kevin Mitchell, you are officially this year's headliner for the Hattrick Harbor Bachelor Auction."

My eyes looked like saucers, and he blinked. "I'm what?"

"The Bachelor Auction!" Joy beamed. "It's the highlight of the night. We auction off a few brave souls. The highest bidder gets a date—dinner, drinks, nothing illegal. None of Maggie's boys were able to make it this year."

His gaze bounced from Joy to Jules, then over to me like I might swoop in and save him.

Jules just shrugged. "Last year's headliner raised eight hundred dollars. And that was for Deputy Dave. He's bald, a little portly, and he picked his nose on stage. You'll easily raise twice as much just standing there with your hands in your pockets."

Kevin blinked slowly. "Yeah…I really don't think this is a good idea."

Joy folded her hands under her chin like she was praying. "Please? We need a headliner, and you're tall, mysterious, and moderately charming when you're not trying to talk someone into building a casino."

He narrowed his eyes at me. "You're enjoying this, aren't you?"

"A little," I admitted, unable to hide my grin.

Kevin's eyes turned playful, and he decided to switch things up. "What's the most money a bachelor has ever brought in?"

"Maggie's twins, Andrew and Jack, did it a few years ago as a BOGO package. It caused a frenzy for all age groups. They pulled in a whopping five grand," Joy said.

He let out a low whistle. "Five grand for college kids?" He shook his head, then clapped his hands together and handed me his melted slushie. "Andrew and Jack are going down. Let's break a record, shall we?"

Then he leaned down, his voice low and warm in my ear. "You'd better be bidding, Maggie."

He winked, then followed Joy toward the main stage. The last thing I heard was her suggesting he lose the shirt.

Kevin Mitchell was about to help fundraise for our town's hockey rink. If this wasn't an oxymoron, I didn't know what was. And yet, some ridiculous part of me liked watching him fold himself into our town. For someone with the last name of Mitchell, there was something disarming in the way he genuinely charmed his way around Hattrick and its people.

You'd better be bidding, Maggie.

I stood anchored in place, goosebumps rising, eyes glued to the jeans he'd been warned not to wear. My pulse sped up, drowning out any trace of common sense. However, common sense was the only thing standing between me and the man whose family was threatening to bulldoze everything I loved. This town. This life. The only home I'd ever known.

I caught my breath, trying to steady the wild thrum of my heart. And just like that, my train of thought derailed.

By the time the Bachelor Auction kicked into high gear, the town square was jam-packed. The entire town was perched on hay bales, folding chairs, picnic blankets—any flat surface they could find. Even Mayor Billings was there, fanning himself with the church bulletin and sipping on a tall glass of sweet tea.

Mix Master Merle had gone up first, promising a front row seat to the air guitar finals and a personalized playlist for the occasion. He raised nine hundred dollars—mostly from a group of women from Bunco Night who wore matching blue wigs.

George, our seventy-something-year-old librarian, promised a romantic evening of poetry reading and meatloaf. He raised a solid five hundred and left the stage blushing so hard his glasses fogged up.

Then came Tyler, the gym teacher at the high school—young, cocky, and apparently very proud of his abs. He ripped his shirt off to a roar of screams and strutted across the stage like he'd just won a gold medal in Ego. He brought in fifteen hundred dollars and was the man for Kevin to beat.

By the time Joy called Kevin's name, my stomach was in knots. *You'd better be bidding, Maggie.*

He jogged up the steps like a man who didn't understand stage fright, waving to the crowd with a smile I could see from where I was sitting. The cheers were deafening. Long lines, sharp jaw, and that boy-band grin, wrapped in an easy confidence that drew every eye to him. Kevin Mitchell might as well have been standing under a spotlight, because no matter how hard I tried, he was the only one I could see.

So many thoughts collided in my head. None of them helpful. None of them useful.

Should I bid?

It would be weird if I didn't.

It would be weird if I did.

This wasn't supposed to be about dating Kevin Mitchell. This was business. A campaign. A tour to fall in love with Hattrick. And yet, watching him up there—charming, confident, way too handsome for his own good—something inside me twisted. This was supposed to be a fundraiser. Not a full-blown emotional crisis.

Joy picked up the microphone. "Ladies and gentlemen, we saved the best for last."

I swallowed hard. I had a plan. Right when all the bidding stopped, I would raise my hand.

The bidding started at a hundred dollars and climbed fast.

A thousand.

Fifteen hundred.

Then Helen, fanning herself with the pink boa like she was at the Kentucky Derby, shouted out, "Two thousand!"

The room roared with laughter, then hushed.

Kevin searched the crowd. When his wide eyes found mine, they held a silent, almost desperate, plea. *Save Me.*

My heart thudded. My stomach knotted in a way that had nothing to do with nerves and everything to do with *him.*

"Do I hear twenty-five hundred?" Joy called from the stage, her voice teasing. "Going once. . ."

I drew a breath, a slow grin started to spread as my hand rose.

"Going twice. . ."

Kevin gave me a lopsided grin, and my pulse jumped.

This was it.

But just as my arm lifted above my shoulder, a voice rang out from the back like a firecracker.

"Twenty-five thousand dollars!"

The air shifted. Gasps rippled throughout the crowd.

My hand froze in the air.

Joy blinked. "I—uh—did I just hear twenty-five *thousand* dollars?"

All eyes turned.

My hand retreated slowly, and my heart got jammed in my throat, wondering who the hell this gorgeous woman was who swooped in and bought the man I was supposed to be saving.

16

Kevin

Twenty-five thousand dollars.

I heard the number before I processed it. I was watching Maggie—her hand in the air. She'd raised it. Just like I'd asked her to. Just like I'd wanted her to.

The entire place fell silent—no cheering, no laughing. Just stunned silence, and every head turned toward the back.

And then I saw her.

My stomach plummeted. My jaw clenched so tightly my molars might've cracked. I'd been halfway through smiling at Maggie, hoping—really hoping—that she'd outbid everyone.

But then *she* showed up.

Standing there like she was better than everyone, in four-inch heels and a blazer that screamed *not from around here*. Not a wrinkle on her. Not a hair out of place. Eyes cold. And that same superior expression she always wore when she got exactly what she wanted.

Turning everything sweet to sour.

Joy practically squealed into the mic. "Holy Shit! Twenty-five thousand dollars for Mr. Kevin Mitchell."

The crowd erupted in applause, and I couldn't move. Couldn't smile. There was no faking it.

I took the steps off the stage two at a time, not stopping to shake hands or pose for any pictures. The crowd parted like it was the damn Red Sea.

I reached her, grabbed her by the elbow—firmly—not gently— and hauled her around the corner, out of sight from the crowd.

She enjoyed the attention—was fueled by it. This was all part of her plan, no doubt.

"What the hell are you doing here, Kristen?" I demanded, sharp enough to cut through glass.

She didn't flinch. Didn't blink. Just looked me up and down, assessing me like I was a pawn in some kind of game she'd already won.

"Well, if you'd answer your phone once in a while, I wouldn't have to go to such great lengths to see you," she said, dripping with arrogance, conceit, and any other word I could think of that would describe the most spiteful woman I'd ever known.

"You don't belong here," I said, practically spitting out each word.

"Is that any way to speak to your wife?"

"*Ex*-wife," I corrected her.

"An ex-wife you don't mind fucking now and then."

My jaw tightened as I stepped back, raking my hands through my hair, trying to control my temper, but failing miserably. I didn't have time for her shit.

"That's been over for a long time, and we both know it."

She laughed, all glossy control and confident, like she'd played this scene out a dozen times, each time getting what she wanted.

"What do you want, Kristen?"

"Your attention."

"You got it. Now what?"

She took a slow, sure step toward me, close enough for me to smell whatever expensive perfume she bathed in. "Conrad called me."

My back went rigid. "What for?"

She smiled, victory already looming in her eyes. "To close the casino deal."

If my dad was the most ruthless businessman I'd ever known, Kristen was a close second. Her showing up here meant one thing—my dad wasn't taking any chances of this deal slipping through his fingers, and he was willing to go to any length to make that happen.

None of it was good news for this town.

It sure as hell wasn't good news for Maggie and Hope Farm.

And that frightened me. Not only was I beginning to like this town, but I was starting to feel something for my tour guide.

I stared at Kristen, crossing my arms and keeping my voice controlled. "Why would my father call you?"

A slow, scheming smile curled at the corners of her mouth. "Because he knows that with you and me, we close deals. Always have. Plus…" Her smile turned downright menacing. "Our chemistry always transitioned to the boardroom."

She moved in with well-rehearsed presumption—a panther in heels—and placed her hands on my chest like she had every right to touch me like this whenever she damn well pleased.

At one point, she did. But she'd lost that right the day she walked out on me.

I grabbed her wrists and stepped back, putting real distance between us, praying Maggie wasn't seeing any of this.

"This isn't happening, Kristen."

She ignored me completely, like my words were just background noise and this was all part of her plan. Her voice dipped to that same sultry tone I'd heard so many times before when she wanted something. The same voice she used that once made me believe everything she told me.

"Are you dating anyone?"

I let out a sharp breath. "That wouldn't matter. You and I aren't happening. Not now. Not ever."

"So...you're single."

"Kristen." My voice was clipped, warning clear.

She just smiled. "Well…you owe me a date. I just donated twenty-five thousand dollars to this rinky-dink little town. They don't get their check until I get my date."

I dragged my hands down my face, glancing around. A few heads were already turning, several people narrowing their eyes in curiosity. Goddammit. The town needed that money. The rink needed it, too.

But more than anything, the kids needed that money, and that meant something to Maggie. And now this—Kristen's stunt—put her right in the line of fire.

"Dinner. That's all you get. And we're not calling it a date."

Kristen smirked. "Call it whatever you want, but it's a start."

I exhaled. "Let's get it over with," I muttered, already regretting every second of it.

Since my divorce, I'd been better on my own. My rules. My way. And since then, I hadn't wanted to spend significant time with any one person. No one was worth the effort. No one was worth the time. And no one interested me long enough to break down any of the walls I'd built around me.

But with Maggie? The moment we said goodbye, I was already counting the days until I'd see her again, wondering what adventure she had planned next.

At first, the thoughts were innocent. I'd picture her smile, the way she tilted her head when she laughed. Then they started to go beyond that. Who was she with? Did anyone else see the way she laughed like that? Did she ever think about me, even half as much as I thought about her? Before I knew it, she was the first thing I thought about when I woke up, and the last thing on my mind before I fell asleep.

This was uncharted territory for me. I usually saw a woman once, maybe twice, and that was plenty. I didn't do awkward mornings, never stayed the night, and always went home. I didn't want small talk or someone wondering if I'd call again. I wasn't going to take the chance of someone getting the wrong idea—or worse, someone getting too attached.

I had none of those concerns around Maggie.

The wall had started to crumble, and I hadn't even noticed how much until now. Somehow, she had effortlessly slipped through ten years of well-placed defense.

The night wasn't going according to plan. I thought I'd be

spending all day with Maggie, and then after her winning bid, I'd be planning a date with her. Instead, I was here—scowling and resentful—wasting my time with my ex-wife—the one woman who hardened my heart single-handedly.

Some things never change. Kristen was dressed to seduce, and full of entitlement.

Acting like she had some kind of hold on me.

She didn't.

Not anymore.

All I could think about was Maggie. Her soft laugh, the way she tucked her hair behind her ears, the way her eyes gave away everything she wanted to say, everything she felt. Nothing like the person sitting across from me now.

Kristen and Maggie, side by side, couldn't have been more different. The contrast was laughable. Where one was harsh and commanding, the other was soft and full of quiet strength. One demanded the room, while the other just naturally had it. Kristen thrived on power, while Maggie thrived on people. Night and day. There wasn't a person alive who could mistake one for the other.

They didn't even belong in the same orbit.

But here I was, sitting in a booth with the same woman who'd handed me divorce papers like they were nothing more than delivering a closing argument. The same woman who'd woken up one morning and ended our marriage—calmly, coolly— explaining to me *we'd grown apart, that the foundation of our marriage had changed, that we'd wanted different things*. I wasn't bitter about the fact anymore—my life was better without her—but the damage she'd left in her wake had stuck with me.

Kristen kept talking—something about the view, how good

I looked, about how she always did like me in black—but her voice faded under the strain of everything I wasn't saying. I didn't want to be here. I wasn't even sure anymore that I believed the casino would be a good fit in Hattrick, and I wasn't sure how to convince my father of that. And now with Kristen at my father's side, my fight just got twice as hard.

I'd had enough. The only woman I wanted sitting across from me was the one who had left the auction alone.

I needed to go and see Maggie—explain why I'd just disappeared.

Dinner with Kristen felt like a punishment. I pushed my plate aside and signaled for the waiter. Before I stood, I made damn sure to ask for Kristen's "donation." The astronomical number she'd written made my stomach churn.

"You can't come in here flashing that kind of money around," I said.

Her fingers tore across the paper. "Worth every penny getting your attention." Kristen coughed out a laugh. "This podunk town will be talking about me for years."

"Careful," I warned, already sick of her elitist attitude. A year ago, I might've agreed with her. Hell, a month ago I would've. But the change in me was like the tides turning—a slow pivot. Lately, nothing in my life felt the same. And having Kristen here only meant trouble. It always did.

After she handed me the check, she sipped the last of her wine, completely unbothered. "Just so you know," she paused, waiting to make sure I was listening. "I plan on sticking around for a while."

She didn't say it like a warning. She said it like a promise.

Then, without blinking, she slid her room key across the table. For a second, I just stared at it, the plastic rectangle sitting there like a live grenade. Typical Kristen—thinking sex would sway me—same game she'd always played. Years ago, it had always worked.

I picked up the key, leaned in, and made sure she could hear me.

"Never. Happening."

I dropped it, let it clatter on the table, and kept my mouth shut, walking away before I could say anything else.

We were at Matteo's—our place. The kind of place where the owner knew us by name.

"Mr. and Mrs. Mitchell, we have your table ready," the maître d' said, with a smile.

Our table—the one by the window with the best view of the city. The one with the bottle of Opus One already breathing, waiting for us, and a beautifully wrapped box with a white satin bow, resting on Kristen's plate.

Kristen barely glanced at it before sitting. "Kevin, what did you do?" Her tone wasn't playful or surprised. More like she was confirming something she already knew would be there.

She untied the ribbon and opened the box without ceremony to find the Cartier watch I had bought for just this occasion. No gasp. No smile. Just a tilt of her head.

She closed the box without trying it on.

"It's lovely," she said, as if commenting on the wine. Then picked up her menu without ever looking me in the eye. "You remembered I hate yellow

gold. Good."

She sat across from me in a red silk dress, her lipstick a perfect match. One hand curled around the stem of a crystal glass, and the other hand rested on the white linen. Everything about the night was perfect—just like us.

We were celebrating Kristen's latest milestone—she'd just been named partner in her law firm and listed as one of Charlotte's Forty Under Forty to Watch. We had everything we ever wanted. Two homes, vacations wherever we felt like going, careers we were killing, and more money than either of us had imagined at this age.

We were the couple everyone in our circle envied.

But lately I couldn't shake the feeling that something was missing. There was one piece left to the perfect puzzle.

I watched her for a moment—poised and in control as her eyes scanned the menu. Kristen had always been so sure of herself. It's what initially drew me to her. She was brilliant, unapologetically ambitious, and polished to perfection.

I took a sip of wine, confident and sure that our next step was a family. We were still young enough, and it felt like the right time. We were established, successful, and had checked every box on our Life Goals list. Children were never in our plan. But why not? We'd had it all.

"You ever think maybe...we were wrong?"

She didn't look up. "About what?"

"About having a family."

That got her attention. She blinked and, slowly, placed the menu on the table next to her.

"Excuse me?"

I leaned in slightly, trying to sound composed while containing my excitement. "I know we said we didn't want kids, but things change. People change. We've built an incredible life, Kristen. We've checked every box. The only thing left—the only thing we haven't done—is start a family."

Kristen stared at me like I'd just confessed to a crime. Her entire posture stiffened.

"You're serious," she said, her voice flat.

"I am," I said, probably too eager. But the more I thought about it—the more I said it out loud—the more I wanted it.

She didn't say a word. Just folded her napkin with slow, surgical precision and placed it neatly beside her plate.

I kept going, trying to lighten the mood. I started rambling about how we'd have one boy and one girl. I painted the picture—ballgames, soccer fields, campfires, scraped knees, and Saturday pancakes. I talked through most of dinner about Disneyland trips and baby swim lessons because we had a pool in the backyard.

Kristen sat and listened, never interrupting. The more I talked, the quieter she became, but I took her silence for intrigue. Maybe even thoughtful consideration.

By dessert, I had their futures mapped out. One would attend NYU and follow in Kristen's legal footsteps, while the other would be the fifth generation of Mitchell men to take over the company.

When we got home, Kristen said she had a headache and kissed me good night. She said she'd give it serious consideration. I poured a drink and sat on the patio, cigar in hand, watching the glow of the city, feeling like I had the world by the balls.

I actually felt good. Relieved. I'd done it. I'd approached the subject with Kristen, and it'd gone better than I expected. She was mulling it over.

She was gone before I woke up the next morning.

That day in the office, I was served with divorce papers.

17

Maggie

Mother Puckers 4-Life

Katie: Who was Cruella?

Annie: I was waiting for 101 puppies to trot in behind her.

Jules: She was definitely in the wrong zip code. Did you see those shoes?

Joy: Twenty-five thousand dollars. Are you kidding me?

Katie: His ass in those jeans—makes sense.

Annie: He looked pissed.

Jules: He went full statue mode. Didn't even blink. Not sure he was breathing, either.

Joy: She was stunning. And terrifying.

Annie: Maggie?

My non-judgmental side, the totally rational one, took one look at her and thought—she was the most beautiful woman I'd ever seen. She commanded the entire place. Confident. Controlled. And obviously, very rich. But my judgy, irrational side—which I was only just now realizing I *definitely* had—didn't like her. She and her Louis Vuitton bag had crashed our party and sent me home early—by myself.

I'd had my hand in the air.

One second, I'd been caught up in the moment—caught up in saving Kevin from Helen, and maybe, if I were being honest, caught up in *him—You'd better be bidding, Maggie*—and the next, that woman had appeared out of nowhere, looking like she'd walked out of the Sak's window in New York City. Just strolled up like a shiny penny—or more like an Amex Black Card—and dropped an enormous amount of money to get Kevin's attention.

Mission accomplished.

She'd gotten it—along with the whole town's attention.

Meanwhile, I'd stood there with my hand in the air like a total idiot.

What was I thinking? Letting my emotions get the best of me over a man I barely knew. Sure, he was attractive. Yes, he made me laugh. And yes, when I was with him, I didn't feel so...alone.

But tonight was another obvious reminder. I'd already had my one great love. Some people never even got that, and I was grateful. Another happy ending just wasn't in my cards. And certainly not with a man who was trying to build a casino in the middle of the town I loved most. A man who had no idea how much Hope Farm *had* to happen for me.

Why couldn't Kevin understand that changing this town—selling it out—wasn't progress? It was a mistake. Too much was at risk, and I needed to stay focused. My family and friends, the town, and Hope Farm…these were the things that mattered most. I needed to remember that.

Putting all that mental anguish aside, I was physically exhausted. I'd spent the entire week on the decorating committee, helping Jules and Joy get ready for today. It had taken the whole town to pull off the event every year, and it always came together at the last minute—late nights with Joy's glue gun, Jules threatening to run people over with her Harley if they didn't hustle, and me making late-night caffeine runs to Mel's Open Net Coffee Shoppe. Total town effort.

I'd been home in under an hour after Kevin disappeared with the runway model and her fat bank account. My weekend had hit a roadblock quickly, and my pride had taken enough of a beating. Some women drowned their emotions in wine—I chose stretch fabric and cotton. With my hair twisted on top of my head, and my favorite comfy sweatshirt on, I was torn between ice cream and popcorn—a classic Saturday night indecision.

"Calm down, Maggie. Save some fun for tomorrow night," I muttered to no one in particular.

There was a knock at the door just after ten. I didn't need to check the camera—I already knew who it was. Annie had texted me several times and called twice. I'd just sent her the thumbs-up emoji when she asked *Are you okay?* And I'd let her calls go to voicemail. I was too tired—and quite frankly too disappointed—to have to try and explain myself to my best friend.

I knew it was her. This was what she did. If Annie didn't hear from me, or only got one-word responses, she just showed up. Usually with a bottle of wine. Sometimes with a thousand-piece puzzle. Occasionally, both.

I pulled open the door with a sigh—ready to tease her for overreacting.

But it wasn't Annie.

It was Kevin.

My breath caught, and the lump in my throat doubled in size. Something in my stomach dropped—sharp and sudden—like I'd missed the last step of a staircase and caught myself just in time before face-planting.

He stood on the other side of the door in the same clothes he'd had on earlier, hands in his pockets, and those damn jeans that did nothing to discourage my inner teenager from taking notice. Hair slightly messy like he'd been running his hands through it—or making out with that woman who may or may not own a black and white spotted fur coat.

Ugh! Jealousy was alive and well tonight.

"Hey," he said, in a low husky voice that put every nerve ending on high alert. So much for playing it cool, pretending that just seeing him didn't affect me. His eyes searched mine, looking for any sign that stopping over unannounced on my wildly busy Saturday night wasn't a total intrusion.

"Hi," I managed. My hand stayed on the doorknob. I didn't move, unable to get any more words out of my mouth. My tongue felt heavy and swollen—maybe I'd been stung by a bee.

Then, finally, he asked, "Can I come in?"

I stepped back. "Sure."

My tongue started working again, thank God.

Crisis averted.

He walked in slowly, like he wasn't sure if he should be here or not, and followed me into the kitchen. I headed straight to the freezer and opened it.

"Mint chip or raspberry truffle?"

"Excuse me?"

"You're about to witness how I usually spend my Saturday nights. Ice cream and Netflix." I was praying I'd remembered to put on a bra. Saturday nights and Netflix didn't usually require one.

He wandered through the living room while I scooped each flavor into my favorite Saturday night ice cream bowls. I couldn't believe I had bowls just for Saturday night ice cream.

Maybe I needed a hobby.

I definitely needed a hobby.

I grabbed both bowls and carried them into the living room, slowing when I saw Kevin standing at the bookshelf. He picked up one of the framed photos.

"Is this your family?" he asked, still holding onto the frame.

"Yes. It's one of my favorite pictures." It was the last picture taken of all of us—Joe's forty-seventh birthday. He died one month later.

Kevin studied it for a moment longer, then looked over at me with something gentle in his eyes—almost reverent. He gave a soft nod before carefully setting the frame back in its spot.

"Six boys?" He raised an eyebrow.

"Yes. Andrew and Jack are our biological children. And the other four we adopted—sort of."

Kevin didn't react like most people did when they saw our family together. Andrew and Jack looked just like Joe and me, but the other four did not. Ethan looked much older, Kal and Evan were African American, and Mark had the most beautiful olive-colored skin. Most people who didn't know us tilted their heads or stumbled through an awkward pause before asking questions. Joe and I never cared. We loved introducing all six as ours. It always made us smile watching people figure out how our family fit.

I cleared my throat. "There are a lot of definitions of family. This was ours."

Kevin gave me a long look, something serious behind his eyes. Sadness, maybe. Loss. He didn't explain it, just said, "Sometimes family isn't what you thought it was."

The words hung there between us, and for a moment, I wasn't sure whose family he meant. Then, almost like he'd deflected, before things cut too close, he turned his gaze back to me. "Why is someone like you spending her Saturday nights alone?"

Professional side-stepping. I recognized it well.

How could I explain that I'd been both the luckiest and unluckiest woman in the same lifetime? That people only got one happily ever after—and I'd already had mine. That even though I didn't think love would happen for me again, I still missed it. The stubborn part of me believed it wasn't impossible—just unlikely.

Dating again hadn't changed that. The only available men either owned a walker, wore leather chaps, or had a running tab at the taxidermist. I tried, sure, but it always felt forced—like I was trying to make something fit that never really had the chance. And the thought of trusting my heart again with someone else—well, that was another story.

So, I offered him the version I could say out loud.

"I guess I'd rather be alone than pretend to enjoy being with someone who doesn't fit," I said with a shrug. "Spending time with the wrong person can feel lonelier than just being alone."

Kevin didn't say anything right away. He lingered near the bookshelf, still staring at the photo he'd had in his hands minutes ago.

"You really don't believe that there's someone else out there who can make you happy again?" he asked, concern etched all over his face.

"I've made peace with it. And right now, I have a farm to save and an entire company to convince to relocate their casino." I gave him a small smile, trying to refocus. "This is far more important to me. Operation No Dice is keeping me busy for the time being."

Kevin didn't say anything right away. He looked like he wanted to say more, but I handed him the bowl, and we settled on the sectional. For a moment, neither of us spoke. I let my brain silently debate about ice cream flavors—anything that kept it from drifting to the man sitting beside me and his reason for being here.

"I want to explain what happened tonight," he started.

"Kevin, you don't owe me an explanation," I replied quickly, taking a spoonful of mint chip.

"I know." His voice was soft and steady. "But I want to give you one anyway."

He set the bowl down on the end table and turned toward me. And that's when I saw it—not defensiveness, not anger. Something closer to regret.

"That was my ex-wife, Kristen."

I knew there had been a history between them. Anyone

watching figured that out. But there was no denying the slight sting of jealousy I felt when he disappeared with her.

"Well," I said, "she sure knows how to make an entrance."

He let out a dry laugh, then rested his head against the couch. "She'd always been good at that."

There was a pause before he added, "But she and I have been over for a long time." Frustration and exhaustion were threaded through every word. "I didn't even know she was in town."

"Well, lucky for us, she single-handedly helped raise more money than ever for the ice rink," I said, trying to sound unbothered. I wanted to focus on the win, but everything about her appearance felt like a loss.

So much for all my inner monologuing about keeping my heart in check and my head in charge. But something was becoming painfully clear to me—no matter how much I tried to convince myself that Kevin Mitchell was just a roadblock to Hope Farm, he was someone who woke up a part of me that had been lost. And right now, sitting on this couch, my hormones were getting a stern talking to from my head. They just weren't listening to reason.

Kevin was quiet for a second. He shifted on the couch and placed his arm behind me. "I saw you raise your hand, Maggie."

So much for flying under the radar.

Of course, he saw me raise my hand. He was looking right at me. The whole town witnessed it. Now, with him angled toward me, I tried to shake it off. "Helen was already planning your honeymoon. I figured someone should intervene."

I stirred my melting ice cream, having lost my appetite. "But honestly? I probably would make a terrible date. I'm too focused on the farm right now. The foundation is incredibly important to me for so many reasons. And no matter how much I wanted to—" I paused, the words catching in my throat. "Never mind."

Kevin gently took the bowl out of my hands and set it on the table beside his. Then, without saying a word, he reached out and brushed a loose strand of hair out of my face, his fingers grazing my cheek.

"Finish your sentence, Maggie," he said, his voice low and gravelly, laced with something raw and unspoken, eyes pinned on mine.

Kevin waited for me to answer. He didn't rush me, but it was clear he wanted to hear what I was about to say.

The air between us felt heavier now—thick with the kind of tension that made it hard to breathe, let alone think. I wanted to say something casual and clever, but nothing came. So, I dropped my gaze.

Maybe if I didn't stare into his eyes and ignored the warmth still lingering where his fingers had brushed my cheek, my heart would remember its place—tucked away safely in its box where it belonged.

But Kevin wasn't having anything to do with that either. He lifted his hand, fingers brushing along my jaw again before gently tilting my chin, coaxing my eyes back to his.

"Please, finish your sentence, Maggie," he said again, softer this time—a low, steady murmur that curled through me like a heatwave. "Even though you wanted to…what?" It wasn't a challenge. It was an invitation—intimate, patient—and he was making it impossible to think straight.

My heart wasn't going back in its box. Not tonight.

When he leaned in, I let him. The pull between us felt

inevitable, and every part of me screamed to close the gap. I wasn't thinking about land deals, Dalmatians, or anything beyond the space that separated us. None of that mattered. Not with him this close.

It wasn't distance anymore—it was time. How long before one of us would break.

I could feel his breath—warm and close—skimming across my cheek. I watched his chest rise and fall, slow and controlled, like he was holding back. But his eyes—they made mine catch. Locked. Waiting. Full of something that felt an awful lot like intent.

He was going to kiss me.

And I was going to let him.

And then the front door banged open.

"Honey, I'm home." Annie's voice rang out like an Amber alert in Sunday service.

Kevin jerked back, and I practically jumped off the couch.

Annie came around the corner. A bottle of wine in one hand, and a pink, fluffy foot spa in the other. "I thought we could do the mani/pedi thing..."

She stopped abruptly, a grin growing wider the longer we went without saying anything. "Well, this looks complicated," she said, eyes bouncing between us. "Why do you two look like two teenagers who just got busted for playing spin the bottle at church camp?"

18

Maggie

I was in the kitchen, flipping through my favorite cookbook, trying to figure out what to make for dinner. Joe was supposed to be leaving for work, but instead, he snuck up behind me, slid his hands around my waist, and kissed the back of my neck, the place he always went for when he wanted to distract me.

"If you don't leave right now," I said, smiling without turning around, "I'm marching you right back upstairs."

He laughed against my skin. "Tempting."

Still kissing the side of my neck, he mumbled, "It's an early day for me. Only one surgery. Want to go out instead of cooking? Annie and Mike could join us." He punctuated each sentence with a kiss, traveling the entire length of my neck.

I turned to look at him over my shoulder. "How about we eat in? Just you and me?"

His grin was mischievous. "Even better."

He slid onto the stool next to me, tugging mine a little closer. He leaned in and kissed my lips this time. His hands framed my face, and for a second, he just stared into my eyes.

"The day I met you was the luckiest day of my life. You know that, right?"

I smiled. With Joe, there was never a single second I questioned how he felt about me. He made it his mission to show me every day. It wasn't just the way he said "I love you," though he never missed a day. It was the way he looked at me—like I was his whole world.

I was loved fully, completely, and unconditionally.

And I knew it—always.

Being loved by Joe Bentley was the best feeling in the world. Joe taught me what real love looked like. Steady. Unshakable. Safe. He was the first person to ever really love me, and until I met him, I didn't know what it felt like to be someone's everything. But I did now.

It was one of those perfect North Carolina summer days. The sky was clear—the kind of blue that didn't seem real. It was already warm, but not sticky, with just enough of a breeze to keep the humidity at bay. I could hear the hum of the Curlee's lawnmower next door and the soft roar of the boats already taking laps on the lake. With the sounds and smells of lakeside living, I filled my lungs and let the comfort settle.

Summer in Hattrick Harbor.

There was no better place to be.

"I'll grab a bottle of wine on the way home," he said while swiping his keys off the counter on the way out the door. "I love you, Maggie."

I laughed and shouted after him, "I love you, too."

My eyes lit up. Lemon chicken and orzo—Joe's favorite.

Should I make dessert? Yes! Key lime pie—also Joe's favorite.

Three hours later, in the middle of making my pie crust, I got a call from the hospital.

"Mrs. Bentley, you need to get to the hospital right away. It's your husband."

I blew through every stop sign to get to the ER, begging, praying to God not to take him from me. But on the drive there, I felt my heart shatter. I knew it before I ran through the hallway and was met by his partner and mentor.

"I'm sorry, Maggie," Dr. Kurtz said. "There was nothing we could do."

He caught me before I hit the floor, and when I woke up, I was being rocked by Annie right in the middle of the hallway.

My husband, a world-renowned brain surgeon, had died from an aneurysm.

"Nails or toes first?" Annie plugged in the Dolly Parton Mani/ Pedi Spa machine.

"Ummm. Toes," I answered, dipping my feet into the bubbly water. "They're aching after a week of Joy barking out orders like a five-star general."

"She's pretty bossy for a pint-sized little sprite."

Annie lined up the bottles of polish, then finally asked, casually, "So...what was Kevin doing here tonight?"

I hesitated. "He kind of surprised me."

Annie raised an eyebrow. "Just stopped by?"

I nodded. "He wanted to explain who that woman was."

"You mean the Disney witch with the yacht-sized bank account?" Annie didn't bother to hide her skepticism.

"His ex-wife," I said quietly. "That's all I know. He didn't know she was in town."

Annie kept her focus on my toes. "It looked like maybe I

interrupted something when I walked in."

I exhaled and took a beat before responding. The memory of how close we'd been—his breath skimming my cheek, the almost kiss hanging between us—hit me hard. I wasn't sure if I wanted that moment back or to run far away from it. It had been years since I'd felt that kind of attraction, and it scared me to think how much I wanted more—more of him.

I glanced at her and added, "As always, your timing is impeccable."

"Of course it was." She smirked. "I have a sixth sense about walking in on emotional breakthroughs or hormone-fueled make-outs. Just ask my kids."

I rolled my eyes, but my laugh was half-hearted.

Annie leaned back and looked at me for a moment, and a low smile began to spread. "You *like* him."

I didn't answer right away, stirring the bubbles with my foot. "He's the first man in three years that has actually made me feel…something."

Something—that one word already felt dangerous. The word *nothing* was safe, *nothing* was easy, but *something* was messy. It meant wanting, it meant taking a risk. And wanting after losing Joe… well, that scared me more than anything ever could because I'd convinced myself that I would never feel anything so intense again.

Annie's lips tugged into a small smile. "Well, *something* is good, right?"

"No, it's not," I said softly. "It's terrifying."

"I know," Annie said, her voice strong and sure. "Watching you fight your way back after Joe died was one of the most heartbreaking things to witness. But also, one of the most beautiful.

You're inspiring, Maggie. You're strong. You're brave. And you're not the same woman you were three years ago."

I didn't say anything. Just let Annie's words land where they needed to. I wasn't the same woman I was three years ago—and I knew that. I'd lived through another hard chapter of my life, and it didn't break me. I wasn't stuck in grief. I just refused to believe that the universe was going to be that good to me again.

"I'm not doubting my strength," I said quietly. "Maybe just my luck."

Annie's expression softened. "Maggie, I want to say something to you, and I want you to hear me out."

I nodded, already feeling the heaviness of her words before she said them. "Okay."

She shifted slightly in her seat, folding her legs beneath her as she reached for my hands and held them gently between hers. "Mike was not the first man I ever loved," she said softly. "I've loved a few men in my life. Just because I love Mike now doesn't mean I didn't know love before him. It just means my definition of it has changed. Love evolves—just like happiness does. Every season of my life has taught me a different version of both."

Her voice was steady, every word laced with love. "I think that *you* believe that the only way you're going to be happy again is to find someone just like Joe. That happiness only has one definition. That love only looks a certain way."

I pressed my lips together and looked down, willing the tears to stay away. The idea of loving another man was something I hadn't let myself think about much. Being drawn to Kevin was already more than enough to handle.

Annie leaned in and squeezed my hands. "Don't get me

wrong—I loved Joe. He was part of our Fabulous Foursome. But Mike and I both pray that you find someone equally great. Not equally Joe. But great in his own way. And whoever he is, I hope he loves you fiercely…in *his* own way." Her voice became tender, tears glistening in her own eyes. "Because you deserve that."

I let out a shaky breath, blinking up at the ceiling, trying to keep the tears from spilling over. My best friend—condom distributor, sex toy enthusiast, and the one who gave all our boys the sex talk with a banana and a condom—could also be impossibly wise when it counted.

"You know I love you, right?"

Annie squeezed my hands and gave me her signature wink—the one she'd always pulled when she knew she'd struck a chord. "Right back at ya."

"But right now," I continued, picking up a bottle of Red Hot Chili Pepper polish and handing it to her, "I can't afford to get swept up in anything—feelings, distractions, or whatever this thing is with Kevin."

Because maybe it was easier to pour everything into the farm. The farm wasn't promised to me—not yet. I still had to win the vote of the city council and prove the land was worth saving. But people could disappear in a heartbeat—life had taught me that more than once. The land might not be guaranteed, but it was still a safer bet than trusting someone not to leave.

Annie didn't argue.

"I can't lose the farm, Annie," I said, sitting up straighter. "That land is more than just property. And it's more than just changing the footprint of this town—it's about changing the lives of kids who need it."

I paused, making sure my voice stayed even. "You know this as much as anyone. You were there when Joe and I took in the kids. You've seen the need. You've seen the difference a second chance can make. I can't imagine where Ethan, Mark, Evan, and Kal would be if Joe and I hadn't stepped in."

My voice caught, but I pushed through. "I want to do more, Annie. We can help a dozen kids at a time. Give them a home and a future. We can give them hope. And it's a legacy I can leave for Joe. He deserves that."

I took a deep breath and stared at my hands. Romance could wait. Hope couldn't.

"And if Kevin can't see how important that farm is—how much more it matters than building that casino, then..."

I trailed off. I didn't know how to finish that sentence. I didn't want to. Some things were just mine to carry.

"Maggie, does Kevin know your story?" Annie asked.

I shook my head. Very few did.

"You should tell him. It would explain a lot."

"I want him to decide that Hope Farm is the better option for this town and its people on his own, not because of what it means to me."

"But..." She hesitated. "Aren't they the same thing?"

"No," I said quietly, more to myself than to her. "No, they're not."

19

Kevin

Conrad: Be at the house tomorrow at ten.

Conrad: Don't be late.

Conrad: No exceptions.

Conrad: This is not a request.

On the way to my parents, all I could think about was sitting next to Maggie last night. The way my pulse had kicked up just being near her. The heat off her skin. The look in her eyes.

Those damn eyes.

They're trouble. Not because they're beautiful—because they were—but because I might be getting in over my head here. Trouble for me.

I had a job to do. Expectations from my father. From the company.

I'd spent months running the numbers, analyzing the Taylor Farm, mapping infrastructure, construction costs, and potential growth. Hattrick Harbor checked every damn box.

Strategically, it was ideal—the land was cheap. So cheap it was almost comical the price they were asking. Financially, it made sense.

A no-brainer.

But then there was Maggie. Her idea of Hope Farm. It had heart. It had Maggie Bentley written all over it. I tried to remember the last time my family had taken on a project with heart. Our company had passed on homeless shelters, animal rescues, and community centers because the projects hadn't been glamorous enough. They hadn't screamed prestige. They didn't come with ribbon cuttings or front-page headlines. And I'd gone right along with it. Never so much as blinked when we turned our backs on those projects. Never once stopping to ask what it would mean to say yes to something that could actually change people's lives.

Maggie was driven by compassion, while we were driven by ambition. She saw behind the idea—she saw the people. That made her different. And somehow, she made me see them too. She was the one woman who scrambled every thought in my head. Being around her felt easy. Like I could read her, even when she was quiet. Especially when she was quiet.

And last night? I *really* wanted to kiss her. It wasn't just one-sided either. I could see it, feel it. She had wanted it, too. And the fact that she didn't pull away—well, it made me want more. A hell of a lot more.

Maggie Bentley had cracked part of me open that had been

numb for a long time. She was a distraction…and I couldn't bring myself to walk away from it.

I pulled up to the iron gate and gave Rueben a nod. He'd been our head of security for over thirty years—same tight-lipped smile, same blue uniform. He waved me through like he had since high school. The house rose behind the gate like a monument—massive, impressive, with a fountain in front. But it was never really a home.

I rang the doorbell. We weren't the type of family who walked in unannounced—not even when our name was above the door. We waited to be greeted, then escorted to where someone was waiting. Everything in this place was formal—meetings, appointments, even arguments. Growing up, dinner felt more like a boardroom presentation, rather than a family meal. But that was my family's normal. I never knew any different.

Vera opened the door in her usual spotless uniform. She greeted me with a warm smile and a quick hug.

"It's good to see you, Vera." I bent in half to hug the small, frail woman.

"Hello, my sweet Kevin." Her voice was as weathered as she looked. "Everyone is waiting for you in the study."

Of course, they were.

I followed her through the marble entryway, passing all the things I'd never really paid attention to. I hadn't been home in a while, but everything looked the same. Every inch of the place gleamed. Polished brass fixtures. Oversized artwork, oversized chandelier, and the same stiff furniture no one ever sat on.

When I entered through the thick paneled doors of the study—the same ones my father had flown over from Italy—my mom was sitting in the leather chair by the stone fireplace, stoic face, ankles crossed, hands folded neatly in her lap. Ben and my dad were standing by the bar, already three fingers of bourbon poured, laughing about something. Ben slapped our dad on the back, holding on to his every word.

The moment my mom saw me, she stood, smoothing out her crisp skirt and white blouse like she always did. A nervous habit, maybe.

"Kevin." Her smile flickered, and her eyes softened.

She held out her arms, and I gathered her in mine. She was thinner than the last time I'd seen her. Everything on her looked meticulous—from her hair and the pearls around her neck, to the pressed skirt and Ferragamo shoes.

"You look good, Mom."

"Get over here, Kevin." My father cut in before my mom could say a word. "Let me pour you a drink."

"Just water," I said, already dreading whatever was about to happen.

"Nonsense." He picked up the bottle of bourbon and poured me a drink anyway.

I took it, but didn't sip. My father raised his glass and waited for Ben and me to join him.

"To Mitchell men," he toasted, his voice robust. Ben repeated the phrase, and I set my drink on the bar. Something was coming. My dad wore a grin that was too wide, too cocky, and he was way too sure of himself. Not that this was far from his usual attitude, but today it felt inflated. Unease settled in my gut.

"We're waiting for one more to join us," my father said.

My mother retreated to her leather chair, almost invisible. Ben didn't glance at her. And my dad never acknowledged her. Unseen. Unheard.

And just like that, it hit me—how long had it taken for her to shrink into the background? How many years of being talked over, dismissed, and overlooked until silence became her safest place? I looked over at her, gazing out the window, and it was like a knife twisting in my chest.

My mother looked…lifeless.

God, I was sad for her.

"Who are we waiting for?" I asked.

The study doors opened, and Vera appeared with Kristen right behind her.

"Mrs. Mitchell is here to see you," Vera announced.

I wanted my damn name back

"Here she is!" my dad bellowed. He put his drink down and acted like royalty had just entered the room. "Kristen!"

My dad stepped forward to greet her, arms wide, face lit up like a fucking Christmas tree. "Aren't you a sight for sore eyes?" He beamed.

Kristen leaned in and kissed my dad on one cheek, and then the other. "You sure do make a girl feel like she's home."

Ben stepped in, eyes sweeping over her. "Still beautiful as ever," he said, pulling her into a tight hug that bordered on sexual harassment.

Kristen cackled and slapped him on the arm. "You haven't changed a bit, Ben."

On the bitch scale from one to ten, she was off the charts. And by whatever scale measured family dysfunction, this was fucked up.

Then she came to stand by me.

"Kevin," she said, slipping her arm around my lower back, like we were part of a team.

I stepped away. Not subtly. I didn't care. There was a time I would have leaned into that touch—craved it even. Her cool, self-assuredness used to draw me in like a magnet. I couldn't get enough of it. Now? I couldn't get far enough away from it.

"When did you get in, Kristen?" my father asked, far too pleased for my liking.

She didn't answer him right away. Instead, her attention locked on me, her smile spreading like poison. "I made quite the entrance in town, wouldn't you say, Kevin?"

Ben let out a low chuckle and nudged his glass across the bar. "Late night then?"

Kristen let the insinuation hang in the air.

I didn't bother to hold my disgust. "It was *not*," I snapped, my voice edged with warning.

Ben was provoking me, and Kristen was enjoying every second. I ignored the heat crawling up my neck and shifted my glare to my father. "What is she doing here?"

He straightened his sleeves. "This is why I've called you all here," my father said smoothly. "With only a couple of weeks left before the city council vote, I've asked Kristen to help solidify the purchase."

Anger pierced through me. Of course he did. Of course, he brought her in—like this was a strategic chess match. Because that was what we were to him. Pieces. Positions. Leverage.

And somewhere in the middle of all of it was me—his son—

still playing by his rules. This wasn't strategy—this was cruelty disguised as business. For a man who'd built an empire, my father never seemed to understand the cost of the people he sacrificed along the way. There was a buzzing inside my head, giving off warning signals to abort.

"Dad, this is my project," I seethed. "It's *my* call who we bring in."

My dad took a swig of his drink, like we were talking about the weather. "While I'm still around, *I* make the calls."

Every inch of me was tense. My fists balled, shoulders locked. He'd bulldozed right over me. Any chance I had at helping Maggie—or even trying to find a middle ground where both sides won—was slipping away. How the hell was that going to happen when he'd invited the one person guaranteed to blow the whole thing up?

This was typical Conrad Mitchell.

"Don't get all bent out of shape, Kevin," he said. "While you're still the lead on this, Kristen is here to assist you. And she has some ideas she wants to share with us today. Ideas I think you'll find helpful."

He swirled the bourbon around in his glass like it was happy hour. "Kristen," he said, taking a seat in the leather wingback chair near my mother. "Why don't you fill us in on what you've found out and the strategy to help guarantee the vote swings our way."

Kristen stepped forward like she'd been waiting for this since she walked in the door. "Thank you, Conrad," she began, placing her designer bag on the sofa, then handing each of us a binder. "I've been researching our competitor with the Taylor Farm property. New Hope is a non-profit started by Maggie Bentley and her late husband. While Ms. Bentley has been left financially stable, she can sustain her lifestyle for a long time." She glanced at each of us, her voice rehearsed.

"However, from what I can gather, she cannot afford to maintain the foundation without its donation base. She has raised $2.5 million to date. Impressive—for a guidance counselor. But she has placed the same bid on the farm as we have. She has just enough left over to make the improvements and get her cute little New Hope Farm up and running."

I couldn't stand to hear Maggie's name and her life's work come out of Kristen's mouth, especially when she said it like that—clinical, dismissive, as if Maggie was nobody. Every muscle in me wanted to reach out and shut her up. And worse, my father had handed her ammunition to fire away. But I remained quiet, ignoring every impulse to fire back.

"And how is that good news?" Ben interjected.

Kristen continued. "Because all we need to do is offer more for the land. If we double the asking price—which would be very generous and affordable since the value of the land was underestimated—how can the city council say no to a fund surplus?"

A wave of nausea slammed into me, burning up my throat. Of all the scenarios I'd pictured, this was the one I couldn't stomach—Kristen going after Maggie's dream. If she destroyed Hope Farm's chance, it would crush Maggie. And I couldn't let that happen.

Kristen moved toward the bar and rested her elbow on the edge. "The idea is simple," she began. "We arrange a few key meetings with council members—perfectly legit. Show them profit projections, charm them over dinner, maybe a good steak and an expensive bottle of wine, or draft beer—whatever these simpletons drink. Make it clear that everyone wins with this casino."

She took her time glancing at each one of us.

Never acknowledging my mother.

"Then, the night of the vote, when we make our final appeal, we double our offer. It will look like a generous investment in Hattrick Harbor's future. Ms. Bentley will be blindsided. And even if she catches wind of it, she doesn't have the time or backing to match it. A sure-fire solution to guarantee the vote."

"Bravo, Kristen!" My dad beamed. "Brilliant."

I was fuming. My jaw ached from clenching, and the heat that crept up my neck was still there, suffocating me. After everything she'd done to blow up our marriage, my father went ahead and brought her back into the company. Invited her to be a part of this deal.

And when had we stopped giving a damn about people? About doing what's right when presented with options that would benefit both us *and* Hattrick Harbor? I used to believe that Mitchell Developers built legacies. Communities. Now, we were tearing them down and calling it brilliant. Maybe it had been like this all along, and I was just now starting to see things for what they really were.

I stared at Kristen, then at my father. "You want to double the asking price? Just to steamroll over a nonprofit and a guidance counselor who's trying to do something decent for kids who have nowhere to turn and no one to help them?"

I let out a disgusted laugh, but nothing about this was funny. "Why throw away a million dollars when we could take that money and invest it in a different property without all the community blowback?"

I locked eyes with my dad. "We get what we want. Ms. Bentley gets her farm. Everyone wins."

My teeth clenched. My patience thinned. And it took everything in me not to slam my fist on the table. "Tell me how *that* isn't good business?"

He didn't flinch. Just stared back at me, unshaken, his expression cold. "Sometimes, Kevin, it's not about business. It's about the thrill of the chase."

20

Kevin

Kevin: Maggie, I need to talk to you.
It's important.

I didn't wait to hear from Maggie—I went straight to her house after leaving my father. Last night, I'd left Maggie's feeling both disappointed and hopeful. Disappointed that her lips had been just inches from mine and I'd never gotten the chance to taste them, to feel them pressed up against me. Hopeful because she hadn't pulled away. If Annie hadn't walked in, I would've had my answer.

Now, I was back on her doorstep with regret and worry lodged in my chest. Regret that I may never know what it felt like to kiss her and worry about how Maggie would handle the news of Kristen's plan to undermine her.

Maggie hadn't answered my texts or calls, but I knew this was something she needed to know—sooner rather than later, and she needed to hear it from me.

My father had always pushed the boundaries on business deals, and he'd taught me to do the same. But nothing had ever felt like this before. Maybe I'd never looked closely enough or cared enough to understand what those boundaries truly meant. Now, I couldn't unsee it. As the lead on this project, I knew that telling Maggie about Kristen's plan would go against every rule my father had drilled into me.

But not telling her? That would be cruel. And that's not the kind of man I wanted to be.

When Maggie opened the door, I nearly forgot the reason I was there. Her hair was a complete mess—like she'd just rolled out of bed and hadn't bothered to tame a single strand—but somehow, she was gorgeous.

She was wearing what had to be her pajamas—an oversized sweatshirt just long enough to make me question whether there were shorts underneath or if this would be the ultimate test of my willpower.

I'd seen her in workout clothes and a power suit and everything in between—hair pulled back to sleek perfection and a messy bun. But this? Fresh-faced, sleep-heavy eyes, that early-morning rasp in her voice—it set me on fire in a completely different way.

She blinked up at me as if she wasn't expecting anyone, which, of course, she wasn't. My heart did that thing it never did—or hadn't until I met Maggie—it jumped. Then, it dropped just as fast as it had shot up because the news I was about to deliver might ruin whatever we had building between us.

She crossed her arms and leaned against the doorframe. "Do you ever call ahead?"

I lifted my phone. "Do you ever answer your texts? Or your phone?"

"Annie stayed over," she said, waving me in. "I lost my phone somewhere during the *Magic Mike* Marathon."

"I should've said I was Channing Tatum. Might've had better luck."

"Try that next time."

I laughed and followed her into the kitchen. Barefoot, wild hair, sweatshirt hanging off one shoulder, she grabbed a mug and held it up.

"Coffee?"

"Yes, thank you," I said, taking a stool around the granite island.

While Maggie pulled a second mug from the cupboard, I swiveled toward the living room. The coffee table had been shoved aside, couch cushions tossed on the floor, and a pile of blankets draped over what looked like some kind of makeshift kid fort.

"What happened in there?"

Maggie didn't even look up. "That," she said, pouring the coffee, "is what happens when Annie mixes wine, confidence, and *Magic Mike* choreography."

I raised an eyebrow. "Any injuries?"

"Maybe a pulled hamstring. She declared herself retired by midnight."

I grinned, taking the mug she handed me. "So, fort-building and a *Magic Mike* marathon with your best friend…"

"And a mani-pedi," she said proudly, holding out her hands and lifting her wiggling toes. "We also ranked the Hemsworth brothers and critiqued their dancing abilities."

"Who won?"

"Too close to call," she said, wrapping both hands around her coffee mug and taking a slow sip. "So, what brings you here on a Sunday morning?"

I was tempted to tell her that I'd been thinking about picking up where we left off on the couch, but there was a more pressing matter at hand. I hesitated, trying to buy time because she had no idea what was coming. "I had a meeting with my father this morning."

Maggie gave a slow nod, but I saw confusion starting to crease her brow.

"My brother was there," I continued, pausing just long enough to feel the weight settle in on what came next. "And Kristen."

Maggie blinked. "Okay," she said warily, clearly waiting for the other shoe to drop.

I took a deep breath and stared at the counter before meeting her eyes again. Then, I started on the conversation I'd been dreading for the last several hours. "Remember when I told you I didn't know why she was back in town?"

"Yes…" Her voice was cautious now.

Maggie shifted her weight, eyes narrowing the longer I stalled. Because that's exactly what I was doing—stalling, knowing what I was about to tell her would land like a sucker punch.

"Kevin, what's going on?" Her voice was gentle and steady,

but edged with concern.

No more waiting. I went for it, ripping off the band-aid. "Kristen was the attorney Mitchell Developers used on all its biggest deals. She's sharp, calculated—cold when she needs to be, which is most of the time. Her track record is flawless." I pushed forward. "My dad called her to help close the casino deal. Behind my back."

Maggie was quiet. Too quiet. Her face went still. No blinking. No movement. Just silence that settled like a boulder between us.

"What else?" Her face remained motionless, but she knew she hadn't heard the worst of it yet.

"Kristen's plan," I continued, about to give the final blow, "is to show up at the council meeting and offer double the asking price on the Taylor Farm."

Maggie's eyes widened. "Why would she do that?"

"She thinks if we do it publicly, it'll blindside everyone, especially you. Tip the scales in our favor. Make the council choose us because we're offering more. And she knows you won't have the time—or the money—to counter."

Maggie didn't respond. She stood there, perfectly still, looking at me. With each passing second, she stayed silent, and the air felt heavier and heavier.

I pushed the stool away from the counter and stood up. My hands felt useless, like they should be doing something—reaching for her, stopping her from hurting the way she was. But I didn't move. Not yet.

Then she turned her back on me. Shit. My heart lurched as I watched her retreat a few steps. Her shoulders slumped, and her posture went soft. This wasn't just a gut punch—it was a stab to her heart. Exactly the way Kristen aimed for it to land. I crossed the room, not wanting to spook her, but needing to be closer.

I wanted to write a check for a million dollars right then and there. Offer her anything to erase that look in her eyes. But I knew she'd never take it. I knew that for a fact. She was too strong, too proud. She'd want to figure it out on her own.

When I placed my hands gently on her shoulders, she didn't pull away. Relief hit hard. I eased her to turn and face me, and when she did, her eyes were glassy, and something inside me splintered. This woman had found her way into my heart, and I knew that because I wanted to obliterate anyone who made her look this broken.

"Why are you telling me this?" she finally asked, her voice barely above a whisper. It wavered, and all I wanted to do was take her pain away.

"Because I couldn't *not* tell you."

And I wanted to prove that I was nothing like the rest of my family.

Just as I lifted my hand to wipe away the tear that began to fall, she stepped back. Not dramatic. Not angry. Just enough that she was out of reach.

She gripped the counter and anchored herself, the magnitude of what she'd just heard—what she was about to say—left her needing something to latch onto. Then her sadness turned to something stronger. I saw the shift in her eyes.

"Joe and I helped four kids who had timed out of foster care," she said. "Emancipated is the technical term used, but that word sounds too hopeful, too positive."

She fixed her eyes on me, and I was riveted. Maggie was opening a door, giving me a piece of her story. Telling me more about her family in the picture I saw last night. I was afraid to make a move or a sound, afraid that if I did, she'd shut down. So, I stayed perfectly still, hanging on to every word, desperate to hear what she was willing to share.

"Those kids don't get a choice. One day, they're in a foster home, and the next, they're out. Done. Considered adults and expected to handle life—get a job, pay rent, manage bills. Most of them barely have a grip on high school. Some have to drop out just to survive."

I kept listening. Her words hit hard, opening a curtain to a world I didn't understand. Each word was like a key, unlocking pieces of her I was desperate to uncover.

"They were already on their own long before the state said they were. No warning, no guidance, just—'good luck out there.'" She let out a breath, tired and frustrated. "And without someone to help? Without someone showing them how to sign up for what little benefits they were offered, apply for school, fill out financial aid forms—most of them give up before they even start."

Her voice didn't crack, it sharpened, like she was warming up for a fight. "Ethan was living out of his car. Evan and Kal were couch-surfing from friend to friend. And Mark was living on the street." Her eyes never left mine. "None of them had family. None of them had a caring adult in their lives."

Her words hit dead center. And I just stood there completely undone by how little I knew about the world she was trying to fix—and how deeply I was starting to admire and care about the woman trying to fix it.

"These kids had nowhere to go. So, Joe and I gave them a place to stay, rules to follow, and supported them through college and trade school. Andrew and Jack loved having older brothers."

She drew in a breath, but she never stopped looking at me. "Hope Farm was our answer to that broken system. The answer to helping kids like the four we were able to take in. It's a passion project. It's a second chance."

It became so quiet in the kitchen that the hum of the refrigerator and the faint tick of the clock echoed in the still air. It was in that quiet that the idea behind her mission—a glimpse into her life—sank in.

"It's not just that I think a casino will ruin the very soul of this town. Yes, that's part of it, but Taylor Farm is the *only* property the foundation can afford. If we lose it, it could take another five years of fundraising to find anything close—and that's if anything like this ever comes on the market again, which is unlikely. It's undervalued, but it's perfect. But you know that, and so does Kristen. Everything I need is right there. That land is made for this project. *Not* a casino."

The more Maggie spoke about her family, about a foster system I had no clue about, the stronger she became—and the clearer her purpose was to me. Everything about her—every reason she wanted the farm, every word she just said—went against everything I'd been taught to value. My whole life was spreadsheets, profit margins, and closing deals. But Maggie was talking about real people. Real stories. Real life.

I ran a hand over my jaw. "You see what the rest of the world overlooks. That's what makes you different, Maggie. That's what makes you…extraordinary."

The tension in her face remained, and her determination was now more evident.

And standing in her kitchen, watching her stare me down like she was daring me to still pick the casino, I knew something had altered inside me. And it was going to put me on a collision course with my father—whether I was ready for it or not.

The divide was there now, a fault line separating the man I'd been from the man I wanted to become.

The line between business and Maggie Bentley was about to disappear. "There's something else you need to know."

21
Maggie

Mother Puckers 4-Life

Maggie: Don't mess with Hockey Moms. You guys are the best!

Joy: I've got poster board and glitter glue.

Katie: I have a Sharpie that smells like tequila. And bringing zip ties. No protest is complete without someone being tied to something.

Annie: Forget the zip ties. I'm bringing my furry handcuffs. I say we chain ourselves to the gate.

Maggie: Why are you always bringing furry handcuffs?

Annie: I never leave home without them!

Katie: Those and condoms.

Jules: I'm wearing camo and arriving on my Harley.
Joy: I made us matching T-shirts. And I'm bringing lemonade and cookies.
Jules: Never protest without Joy!

Before Kevin left yesterday, he warned me that his dad had secretly arranged for a local news crew to meet him at the farm today. It wasn't a site visit that we were both allowed—it was a full-blown media stunt. Conrad Mitchell wanted to parade around the property and pitch his casino vision straight to the people of Hattrick. Gloss it up. Spin it his way. Thanks to Kevin, we weren't caught off guard. The girls and I were ready—signs made, camo outfits complete, and a cooler of lemonade chilling for Joy's lemonade and baked goods stand.

If Conrad wanted press, well—he was about to get it.

Just not the kind he planned.

Joy hopped out of the SUV first, arms loaded with glitter-covered signs and a helmet tucked under her arm. "Who's ready to raise a little hell and have some snacks?" she called, slamming the door with her hip.

Annie stepped out after her, squinting toward the entrance of the farm. "I'm all for rebellion, but I'd rather not get arrested in a rhinestone visor and riot gear."

Joy practically skipped across the gravel, pulling behind her a cooler full of lemonade pitchers. "It's *sooooo* romantic," she sighed. "A man torn between family loyalty and the woman he's falling for. This is *Hallmark* gold!"

"*Hallmark* with back-stabbing drama," Katie said under her breath, unfolding a lawn chair with one hand and holding a travel mug in the other. "But, yeah, I'm invested."

"There's nothing romantic going on here," I insisted.

"I've seen the way he looks at you," Annie said. "It's not exactly subtle."

My face flushed, and I turned toward the road, pretending I didn't hear them—didn't see them side-eyeing me. But they weren't wrong. Kevin looked at me yesterday like I was the only person in the room. And if I were being honest, that look unraveled me at times. But I couldn't afford to have that feeling sideline me. Not when I was this close. I was going to tuck those feelings away and put that focus on Hope Farm.

This farm—it wasn't a "maybe" or a "what-if." It was everything. Joe's dream. My mission. A chance to close a part of my life that needed an ending. And right now, Mitchell Developers and Maleficent were standing in the way.

"Next thing you know, Joy's gonna organize a flash mob in front of the Channel 5 news van," Katie said.

"Oh, my God, can we?" Joy squealed, pressing her palms to her cheeks. "How great would that be? I already have a Spotify playlist, and I know all the TikTok dances!"

Jules adjusted her bandana and slung a picket sign over her shoulder that read *Higher Stakes, Higher Morals—No Casino*. "Let's just make sure we don't do anything that lands us in the slammer. I have Sunday school to teach," she muttered dryly. "Parents might complain if their child's religion teacher is locked up."

They all looked at me. I gave a small nod. "Kevin said it's all flash. They're doubling the offer, sure, but they're banking on public opinion flipping once they roll out the 'big-city' charm."

Annie snorted. "Let 'em try. I've got a bullhorn and I'm not afraid to use it or shove it places it might not belong."

"Or fit," Jules added.

I shook my head and was instantly filled with gratitude. Everyone needed a group like this in their life. Nothing said friendship like furry handcuffs, combat boots, and cookies. "You guys are the best!"

"And effective," Jules pointed out. "We chain ourselves to this gate, we control the narrative." She walked around the gate, tugging on the rusty metal pipes. "Solid. This'll work."

"I feel like you've done this before," I said.

"Let's just say, I have a lawyer on retainer for things like this," she replied.

"I still don't know if we can trust Kevin," Annie said, her eyes scanning the road. "He's gorgeous, sure, but that's how most bad decisions start."

Katie fanned herself dramatically. "Gorgeous? The man walks around in jeans like God personally tailored them to his ass. You give that man a bottle of baby oil and he could headline down at Spanky's."

"Katie!" I said, laughing and shaking my head.

"What? I'm just saying. There's civic duty and then there's... community appreciation." She rolled her eyes. "I'm just going to sit over there in my lawn chair. Wake me if Kevin arrives shirtless."

The group laughed, breaking the tension of the moment. Our homemade signs leaned against the fence, a row of angry glittered slogans shimmering in the morning sun. Our matching T-shirts, courtesy of Joy's late-night Cricut obsession, read *Don't Puck With Our Town.*

"Okay," I said, planting my feet. "Their plan is about more than spectacle. We're here to show the town—and the news cameras—what Hope Farm could be. Give them something real to believe in."

At noon, the crunch of tires sent a ripple of anticipation through our protest posse. Ready or not…here they come.

Joy shaded her eyes and rested her picket sign in front of her. "Black SUV at two o'clock."

Katie added, "Incoming."

Here we go.

I stood front and center with my four best friends behind me, arms crossed over their chests, like a small, but mighty, battalion of hockey moms turned revolutionaries. Each one of us in our camo-themed battle gear, wearing our shirts proudly, puffing our chests. Joy had her helmet on.

"Game faces, everyone," I said.

We looked legit. Especially with Jules decked out in combat boots, straddling her Harley.

Annie started cracking her knuckles. Jules began to punch her fist into her open palm with slow, deliberate menace. Katie slid her aviators into place, and even Joy gave her best imitation of a drill sergeant—if drill sergeants wore chocolate-scented, shimmered lip gloss and baked lemon cookies.

The black SUV kicked up dust as it came to a stop just feet from where we were standing. Four doors opened in unison. Out stepped Conrad, all smug and corporate arrogance, his face already fixed with a media-ready smile. Behind him, Ben, in an overpriced sport coat, chomped gum like a frat boy. Kristen followed in a sleek black skirt and a white sleeveless tank. Her shiny ponytail didn't move an inch in the breeze.

And then Kevin.

Black tailored pants, sleeves rolled up to his elbows, his stubble rugged, and Ray-Bans hiding those eyes I had no business thinking about at a time like this. He was a walking liability. I was trying to save a farm here, and he was trying to distract me with forearms and a jawline.

Joy elbowed me in the ribs. "I'll take two."

He caught my eye—and of course—smiled. Subtle. Private. Like we were in on something together.

I held my ground.

"Welcome to Hope Farm," I called out, digging my black boots a little deeper into the dirt.

"We have lemonade and cookies," Joy chirped sweetly. "But none for *you*." She flashed a dazzling smile and held up a tray of cookies like a pint-size version of Vanna White.

Kristen blinked, her expression cool and unimpressed. "Adorable," she muttered loud enough for me to hear. I didn't so much as flinch.

But Jules did. She straightened out of her Harley like my leather-clad personal bodyguard and revved the engine. "Prison doesn't scare me."

Katie placed her hands on her hips, scanning the scene. "I'm not afraid of doing a little time, either."

Ben took off his sunglasses and held them between his greasy fingers. His grin stretched too wide, revealing overly whitened teeth that made acid rise in my throat. Smarmy didn't even begin to cover it.

"Maggie," he drawled, oozing privilege and swagger he clearly thought was charming. "I told you we'd meet again."

Barf!

I tilted my head. "Looks like it's pig guts for dinner."

Kevin let out a sharp laugh, then caught himself, cleared his throat, and looked away.

"Ladies," Conrad drawled, eyes sweeping across the signs and lemonade stand. "This is quite the welcome. The press will love it."

"That's the idea," I said. "Thought we'd liven up your publicity stunt with a little local flavor."

Kristen narrowed her eyes. "You're seriously staging this in camo and homemade signs?"

"And cookies!" Joy added.

Kevin coughed. Definitely laughed.

Kristen's heels scraped along the gravel as she stepped forward, cutting the distance between us in half. Deep down, I was hoping those heels would snap clean in half and send her plummeting to the ground. She came within a foot of me, her eyes sharp, her voice low now—meant just for me.

"Do you really think your bake-sale army and homemade signs are going to stop what's coming? The casino will bring jobs and money to your dying little town. What are *you* offering?

A petting zoo and mason jars of canned vegetables?"

No way was I backing down from this bitch. This was a fight I wasn't going to lose.

I stepped closer, right into her Chanel-scented personal space. "I wouldn't expect you to understand. It takes a heart and a soul—two things you're clearly missing."

The gloves were off. She didn't just dislike me—she hated everything I stood for. And for the first time in my life, I could say the feeling was mutual. She could throw her money around and try to insult us, but I was here to fight for Hope Farm, and I didn't care how ugly it got.

Conrad had had enough. His fake amusement turned to thinly veiled contempt. "We're here to meet the press and present a professional case to the public. This hockey mom, small town sideshow won't stop progress."

"No," I said, calmly. "But it might remind them what you're destroying if that happens."

Kevin's gaze met mine again. He didn't say a word, but I saw it there—pride, worry, and something close to awe. I didn't know where we stood. But I knew this much—he warned us of his father's plan even though it risked putting him in the middle of a firestorm. I was able to get out in front of a media circus that might have helped *their* cause—instead, he helped *me* stay even.

He walked around his entourage and placed a gentle hand on my elbow. The heat of it was a direct contrast to the poisonous venom still lingering from my run-in with the ice queen.

"Ms. Bentley, may I have a word with you?"

I nodded, playing along, but the second we were out of earshot, I muttered, "I think I hate your ex-wife. And I've never hated *anyone* before."

We moved further away from the group, through the gate, and toward the barn. Once out of sight of his family and the wicked wench, he took off his sunglasses and hooked them on his shirt. His expression was unguarded, a mix of admiration and concern.

"It took me a while before I finally stopped taking Kristen's shit," he said, a grin tugging at his mouth. "You did it on day one. I'm impressed. You might be my new hero."

"She looked like she wanted to bite me."

"Her teeth are sharp. But Maggie," he took a breath, "you didn't look scared. What you did—that takes guts that most people don't have."

"Thank you," I said. "It's easy to fight for something you believe in."

"Well," he marveled, "you're really good at it."

His words hit hard, as did the way he looked at me when he said them. For so long, I'd been pushing through, holding it together, figuring things out on my own. And to have Kevin recognize this? He didn't pity me or treat me like I would break in half. He noticed. And for reasons I couldn't put into words, that mattered to me.

"I've been digging into the properties you flagged for us. I'm already familiar with three of them, but that fourth one—it's interesting. I'm heading out there tomorrow to take a look. If it checks out, I'll use it to try and change my father's focus—work him from the inside and try and get him off the Taylor Farm property."

"Why not just walk away from the project?"

Kevin's jaw tensed. "Because if I walk, I'm just some pissed-off son who went soft. He'll push the casino through just to spite me. It's how he works. But if I stay, I have a shot at steering him off course."

Before I could respond, a familiar chant erupted from the front of the farm as the news van rolled up.

"Hell no, we won't go! Hell no, we won't go!"

I peeked around the corner of the barn just enough to see the ruckus. Jules was standing on her Harley, holding a bright pink bullhorn to her lips with her fist in the air. Annie cupped her mouth and chanted along.

"Hattrick Harbor is not for sale," Jules yelled.

"We've got a list of demands and a flare gun," Katie added flatly from her lawn chair. "I'm staying near the snacks."

Kevin raised an eyebrow. "Your friends are something else, Maggie."

With a rush of affection and a laugh bubbling inside me, I said, "They sure are."

He grinned, the kind that went straight to my heart. "They're a bit unpredictable. And I love it."

Just then, Joy came into view and waved her arms like she was landing a plane. "Press! Press! Over here, if you want the truth *and* cookies!"

Kevin let out a quiet laugh and glanced back at me. "You've got backup. That's rare."

Then, I spotted movement near the SUV.

Kristen.

She stood rigid, fists at her side, eyes locked on us like a laser-guided missile. Her nostrils flared. If we were in Spain, she'd come charging down the street, and I'd be dressed in red with a bullseye on my back.

Her glare said everything.

"And the ice queen watches," I said quietly.

Kevin didn't even glance her way. His eyes stayed trained on me. Steady and intent. "Let her."

Something in the way he said it—not cocky, but defiant. Certain. And for the first time, I wasn't entirely sure what mattered to him more—winning the land deal and impressing his father or standing here with me.

"Maggie, I want to help you. Can you trust me?" he asked, his voice quieter now. Ernest, even.

I dropped my head, buying myself some time. I struggled with that word. Trust didn't come easily for me. I took a moment, found my footing, then met his eyes.

"Kevin, I know you don't know me very well, but trust—for me—isn't handed out. It's hard-earned."

"I figured as much," he said, with a slow nod. "I guess I'll have to earn it."

He held my gaze, not backing down. "Proving that doesn't scare me," he added.

Something about the way he said it made my heart skip. Without thinking, I asked, "What scares you then?"

His smile was vulnerable and honest. It landed somewhere deep. "You, Maggie."

22

Kevin

The office felt like every other Monday for the last twenty years. Assistants milled around, catching up on weekend gossip. Colleagues dragged themselves in from two days of kids' soccer games and carpools. My dad, already in his office with the shades drawn, was probably orchestrating something borderline unethical. Ben hadn't even bothered to show up yet.

And Kristen—of course—was camped out in the extra office. The one right next to mine. Convenient for her. Frustrating as hell for me.

I used to love Monday mornings. The fast pace. The pressure. The clean slate. A packed schedule and a deal to chase, and I was in my element. I thrived on it.

But lately, something felt off. Like I was showing up for a job I didn't recognize anymore. Everything felt hollow. The adrenaline I used to live for? Gone.

Even now, sitting at my desk, nothing felt right. I wasn't sure when things had started to change, but somewhere along the way, the whole place stopped feeling like mine.

And maybe it wasn't. My dad was still the puppet master, pulling strings behind closed doors. Ben rode on my coattails and collected credit, and Kristen shared my office wall. The whole damn thing felt wrong.

The truth was, I'd started to dread walking through the doors. The job I'd spent my whole life working toward—the life I thought I wanted—was beginning to look like something I didn't want at all. Half the time, I was pretending to give a damn. And today? My mind was somewhere else.

Maggie.

I'd made her a promise. One I desperately wanted to keep, but had no idea how to go about it.

I pictured her yesterday—boots planted, chin high, an army of her hockey moms at her side. She didn't as much as blink when Kristen got in her face. She was fearless. Unshakable. And yeah, terrifyingly beautiful.

I couldn't get her out of my head.

What the hell was happening to me? She'd gotten under my skin so fast it didn't feel logical. I wasn't that guy. But with Maggie…she made me want things I hadn't thought about in a long time. A different kind of life. A different kind of future.

One that mattered and made a difference.

But Maggie wasn't looking for anything beyond her farm. She had made it perfectly clear that was her priority. While my feelings were starting to get the best of me, I knew better than to think I had a shot.

But the way she looked at me yesterday, wanting to believe she could trust me, made me want to be better. To try harder.

It had me thinking whether the life I thought I was building was mine at all—or just the one my father had laid out for me.

Standing next to Maggie, behind the barn, all I'd wanted to do was grab her hand and drag her out of there—away from the cameras, away from my family, away from all the noise. Somewhere quiet. Somewhere private. Where I didn't have to share her with anyone else. Close enough to feel her breath. Close enough to taste her soft lips. I started to imagine what it would be like if she were mine.

That scared the hell out of me.

And that's why I said those words when she asked what scared me most.

You, Maggie.

I wasn't lying.

She was scaring the shit out of me. Not necessarily her, but what I was starting to feel when I was around her. What it might mean. What it might cost me if I leaned in—or worse, if I didn't.

I opened my laptop and clicked on the tabs to the properties she'd sent weeks ago—potential alternate casino sites, proposal drafts, and zoning impact statistics. Maggie had done her homework, that's for sure.

One click led to another. Before I knew it, one article turned into five, and five turned into a dozen. What started out as a review of Maggie's alternate property searches had inadvertently turned into a deep dive of Joe and Maggie Bentley. Article after article popped up—Joe and Maggie smiling, giving back, and making their corner of the world a better place. Joe, the head neurosurgeon at Cedar Medical, had started a community garden. Maggie was named Educator of the Year. Twice. Together, they spoke at a state hearing about foster care reform.

Every headline painted the same picture. Joe and Maggie Bentley were almost too good to be true. The kind of couple people admired. The kind of couple others strived to be. Overachievers with life and with love.

And that's when the next link popped up—*Remembering Joe Bentley—Celebration of Life*.

I hesitated.

Then, I clicked.

Someone had recorded Joe's Celebration of Life, and it had over a million views.

The screen filled with a wide shot of a packed gymnasium. Standing room only. A slideshow rolled with sad music about life, dreams, and love playing in the background—Joe in his college hockey jersey, their wedding day, their honeymoon, Joe holding Andrew and Jack the day they were born. Each photo had been taken with someone he loved—family, friends, neighbors, patients. Every one of them showed a good-looking, magnetic man with a smile a mile wide. Every picture told a story.

In any other context, the pictures told the life of a loving man, who was loved equally in return. If pictures could talk, they would have said, *I have it all*.

I knew I should exit the link. I should've stopped there.

But I didn't. I kept watching.

Maggie and six young men took the stage after the video ended. As soon as I saw her, my heart dropped into my stomach, and my breath caught in my throat.

Everything about her knocked me out.

No one in the crowd wore black. It was a sea of bright colors—Hawaiian prints, loud colorful shirts, and hockey jerseys everywhere. Someone in the third row wore a giant parrot hat, and no one batted an eye.

But my attention was drawn straight to Maggie. She was stunning—even on the worst day of her life. A floral print dress, hair swept on top of her head, and a smile that didn't quite reach her eyes, but she tried, nonetheless. It was impossible to concentrate on anything else.

They were a small army—all good-looking, all protective of Maggie. Three on one side of her, three on the other, holding each other together. They stood united—arms linked, backs straight, and shoulders square.

They didn't break formation and stood as one—one heart, one family, one force.

Two young men in their early twenties stepped to the mic first. They had to be Andrew and Jack. One looked just like Joe, the other was all Maggie. Both had his smile. Both had her eyes. They took turns speaking.

Our dad wasn't just a great father—he was a great man. He was our family's compass. He taught us what it meant to be good men, not by telling us, but by showing us. Every single day.

He was the real deal. He taught us how to be strong by teaching us how to be kind. That doing the right thing mattered. That taking care of people wasn't optional—it's who you were. He taught us to show up even when things got hard. To listen more than we talked. To lead with our heart, not our ego.

He taught us how to be a good friend. To always have someone's back. To be the guy your friends could always count on—no matter what.

And he taught us how to be a good husband. The way he looked at our Mom, every single time he saw her, like she was the center of his world. He loved her with his whole heart, and he never made it a secret.

Not a day went by that we didn't know we were loved. It defined the way he lived. If you were lucky enough to have Joe Bentley in your life, you know exactly what we mean. He loved hard—his family, his friends, his neighbors.

We were lucky…

Andrew and Jack stepped back into the family formation, and the other four young men came forward. The oldest of the group spoke first.

My name is Ethan. I never knew what it was like to have a father. They were foreign to me—something other kids had, and something every young boy wanted. I was no different. When I turned eighteen, I lamented the fact that having a father never happened for me.

But all that changed on the day I came to live with Maggie and Joe. Andrew and Jack were twelve years old at the time. Overnight, I had a family. A mother, two pesky younger brothers, and a dad.

Finally, I had a father.

I wasn't sure of what to make of Joe Bentley, but I found out quickly.

I was loved unconditionally, like I'd always been his own. I was supported completely. And I was shown what it meant to be a man. Someone who walked the walk and talked the talk. He taught me the real definition of integrity because he lived it every day.

Joe was only in my life for a short time, but in that brief window, he'd taught me everything I needed to know. Most importantly, I learned that family wasn't about biology. It was about someone having my back even when I didn't think I deserved it. It was about learning how to live a good life and never forgetting about the people you loved most. Listening to them, taking care of them, and loving them.

My brothers and I were the luckiest men in the world to have had Joe Bentley as our dad. I promise to be the man, the father, and the husband he showed me and my brothers to be because we learned from the best. It came so naturally to him.

Thank you, Dad, for being the best man I've ever met. The best father a boy could have. It wasn't long enough, but it was enough.

I'll take it from here.

One by one, the other three young men stepped up to the mic and spoke about Joe Bentley. About their dad.

He and Maggie saved my life…

My darkest day was the turning point in my life…

He always burned the bacon…

He woke up smiling…

He hated the Bruins. And was a Tampa Bay Lightning fan even when they sucked…

Word after word. Minute after minute. I laughed. I was moved. And by the end of it, I felt the loss of a great man I never had the chance to meet.

After all six boys spoke, Maggie stepped forward. She took her place behind the podium, both hands holding on to the sides like she needed to steady herself. For a long moment, she just stared down at the paper in front of her. Then, finally, she looked up, and the weight of her loss was clear.

All I saw was utter heartbreak.

I slammed the laptop shut the moment she started to speak. I couldn't bear to watch or listen as Maggie talked about the man she loved—and lost. It was too much. It felt like I had intruded on something very private, like I was eavesdropping on a conversation I wasn't supposed to hear.

I pressed the heels of my hands to my forehead and leaned back in my chair, trying to breathe through the tightness in my chest. I'd watched the twins—Andrew and Jack—stand tall and grateful. They spoke about their dad as if he'd hung the moon. Then came the other four boys, each with his own story, each saying that meeting Joe Bentley had changed his life. The man they called their father without any DNA connecting them.

If a man could walk on water, it might've been Joe Bentley.

Questions began running through my mind as I processed what I'd just watched. Would anyone talk about me like any of those young men talked about Joe? Had I ever been loved or admired that much? And then a thought so terrible crossed my mind, I hated even to acknowledge it. Would I have talked like that about my own father? The answer was shameful.

The weight of it clung to me as I sat in my corner office, in my designer suit and my nameplate on the door, wondering what the hell I'd done with my life. I'd built massive ballparks, closed multi-million-dollar deals, and made enough money to keep three generations of Mitchells rich.

Months ago, I would have bragged that I'd had everything I wanted. Now I wasn't sure I had anything that actually mattered. Joe Bentley had changed lives and left the world better off just because he was in it. And me? I was sitting here wondering if I'd ever be the kind of man a woman like Maggie could love.

There was a knock on my door, and it opened without waiting for a response. Kristen entered my office as if she belonged here.

Veronica Beard power suit—bone white, precisely tailored. Not a hair out of place, perfectly blown out. The sharp strike of her spiked heels against the hardwood was enough to set me on edge before she opened her mouth. She moved like a predator—measured, methodical, ready to take her shot.

None of it worked on me like it used to. There was a time I would have welcomed her into this office, locked the door behind her, and bent myself in knots to win her approval. But I wasn't that man anymore. Not yet the man I wanted to be, either. Everything about the last ten minutes made that perfectly clear.

And still, she moved into the room, closing the door gently behind her before leaning against it, ankles crossed.

"I miss this office," she said, eyeing the space like it was some nostalgic memory worth revisiting. "You always kept it so...perfect."

I didn't look up from my desk. "There are three other empty offices on this floor. Go reminisce in one of them."

She laughed softly, the fake kind that used to charm a court-room full of people. "You used to like it when I stopped by."

"I used to like a lot of things," I said, flatly.

That did it. She walked toward my desk, deliberately running her fingertips along the bookshelf. She propped herself on the edge of my desk, planted her arms behind her, and arched her back. "I've been thinking a lot about us since I've been back."

"There is no *us*, Kristen. Hasn't been in quite some time."

"This office. This city." She ran her hands over my desk. "This desk…"

"There is zero chance"—I motioned between the two of us—"that this is happening."

She let out a humorless laugh. "Playing hard to get…I like it. It's hot…to tell you the truth."

I pushed away from my desk and stood, leveling my gaze at her. "It's not hard to get. It's *done*. You left. And I've finally stopped wondering why or even caring."

This woman used to be everything I'd wanted. Now, I couldn't imagine wanting her at all, and I don't feel an ounce of remorse, sadness, or regret.

This. Was. Over.

A beat passed, and then she shifted gears. "What's her story?"

My stomach tightened.

"Maggie. The cute widow." She sat up and examined her nails. "The little wanna be farmer, with the brutish friends."

Every muscle in me went rigid. It took everything I had not to blow my temper. "Don't bring her into this."

"Why not?" Her tone was light, but there was an edge to it. "Touch a nerve?"

I stepped forward, heat flared in my chest, and fists curled before I forced them to relax at my sides. "Because she's not a part of whatever this is. You don't get to talk about her."

Kristen's smile faded. "Interesting," she said. "She means more to you than you're letting on. Conrad might not like that."

I didn't respond. My face remained expressionless.

She turned to walk out and paused at the door. "Be careful, Kevin," she said. "She seems sweet until she gets in your head."

I stared back at her. "No, Kristen. That was *your* move."

She huffed, cold. "Please. I was never sweet."

Then, with a wicked whisper and a dark gleam in her eye, she added, "And you know me. I always love a good fight."

She disappeared down the hall, and I let out a slow breath, dragging my hands through my hair. I shouldn't have let Kristen see that Maggie mattered to me—not with the deal hanging by a thread and my father watching me like a hawk. If Kristen sensed weakness, she'd weaponize it. And I had just handed her a reason with a damn bow on it.

But I couldn't stomach letting Kristen drag Maggie into her games. Hell, I couldn't stand to hear Maggie's name come out of her mouth. I might've made everything ten times harder—for me, for Maggie. And yet, the worst part? Hiding how much I was beginning to care for Maggie was becoming increasingly difficult.

23

Maggie

Mother Puckers 4-Life

Annie: I'm putting together a welcome basket for Kristen. Who wants to contribute?

Jules: Count me in for one large broom.

Jules: And a bottle of holy water.

Katie: I'll add a black hat.

Katie: And a DVD of The Other Woman.

Joy: I'll make her a T-shirt that says, "This is my resting witch face."

Annie: I'm getting her a gift certificate for an exorcism.

Joy: Should I add cookies...with Ex-Lax?

Jules: Let's add a framed picture of Kevin staring at Maggie.

Maggie: You are all terrible. Please drop off before 5.

The grocery bags were digging into my fingers as I reached the front porch. I hadn't even made it up the last step when I spotted it—another glossy flyer tucked between the door and the frame like a neon slap in the face.

Thinking About Selling Yet? Let's Talk!
—Sherri Templeton, Realtor

I let out a sigh and snatched it down, crumbling it before I'd even unlocked the door. Not again. That made three flyers this month. She was like a vulture circling roadkill—relentless, opportunistic, and weirdly cheerful about it.

I turned the knob and kicked the door open, bags still cutting off circulation in my hands, when a chirpy voice behind me nearly made me drop everything.

"Oh! Maggie! Perfect timing—I was just leaving you a note!"

I turned around slowly. And there she was, like a walking Lilly Pulitzer Ad—Sherri Templeton, dressed in head-to-toe neon pink with oversized sunglasses, holding a clipboard and flashing me the kind of smile you gave someone before offering them 'the deal of a lifetime.'

"Hi, Sherri," I said flatly, juggling the bags in my arms.

"I was just in the neighborhood and thought, *Why not pop by and see Maggie?*" She smiled and threw her arms out wide. "This place is so special, and I have several clients who'd die to have this view. A gentleman approached me and specifically mentioned your house."

Miss-Open-House-Barbie looked out at the lake, licking her lips like she could already taste the commission. I'd need to be desperate to call this woman.

Her first flyer had arrived at my door one week after Joe died, and they'd been coming on a consistent basis ever since.

I met her perky smile with a flat stare. "You've mentioned that before," I said, pushing the door open wider. "Several times." Then added quietly, "for several years."

She tilted her head in faux sympathy and stuck out her lower lip. "I know, and I'm sorry—it's just, well, this is a big house for one person. You must be rattling around in there all by yourself. The echoes must be deafening."

There it was. The dig, coated in powdered sugar.

This woman had balls.

The sad truth was that she was right on some level. This house was big. The yard was big. The upkeep was a lot. Perfect for six boys, a husband, and weekly hockey pasta dinners. But all that had changed. The boys had their own lives, and my husband…well, Sherri liked to remind me that *He's no longer with us, God rest his soul.*

If I really thought about it, the house was getting too big when it was just me and Joe. But I refused to give Sherri the satisfaction that she'd struck a nerve. "I manage just fine."

Her smile faltered for a half second. "Just take a minute. Imagine the freedom. Less maintenance, no yard work, a new chapter. Don't you think it's time?"

I looked her square in the eye. "This house isn't just about square footage and resale value, Sherri."

She blinked and tried to recover with a strained smile. "Well, if you ever change your mind…you know where to find me.”

Sherri held out her card as if it were a peace offering. I didn't take it. "Have a good day, Sherri."

And with that, I stepped inside and shut the door.

Hard.

Joe showed up at my door five minutes early, dressed in a pair of jeans, a button-down, and a smile that always triggered my own. It was impossible not to smile with him around. I swear I could be worried about a paper I had to write or having enough money to pay for my food plan, but when he smiled, every worry melted away.

I was sitting cross-legged on my floor, makeup bag open, deciding if the night called for eyeliner.

"Almost ready," I called, reaching for my mascara.

That's when he noticed the binder. I'd had it out earlier today and forgot to stuff it back under my bed. It was an oversized, overstuffed thing with hundreds of magazine pictures taped to every cream-colored page.

"What's this?" he asked, already crossing the room to sit on my bed, making himself at home.

"Joe don't—" I nearly tripped over my bag trying to stop him. Heat rushed to my cheeks. Of all the things to leave out in the open.

He turned it over in his hands, brows arched. "Looks serious."

"It's not," I said, trying to snatch it out of his hands. "It's silly. Just a stupid binder."

His grin softened. "Doesn't look stupid to me. Can I see?"

I hesitated, hugging it to my chest. I'd never shown it to anyone. It was something I had begun when I was a little girl. Something that helped me escape and gave me a reason to dream.

But Joe sat on my bed, eyes pleading, patient. That was the thing about him. With me, Joe never pushed. He just…stayed.

With a sigh, I sat down beside him and reluctantly opened to the first page. "Fine. But you're going to think I'm ridiculous."

"I doubt that."

Page by page, I showed him clippings I'd saved of the house I had dreamed about living in one day. A blue cottage with a wrap-around porch, window boxes overflowing with flowers. A kitchen with an island so big that the entire family could eat breakfast around it. A fireplace in a living room with windows facing the direction of the sunset.

"I want to live on a lake," I admitted. "A place where I could watch the sunset every night."

He glanced at me, his thumb tracing every page.

"And I want a house where everyone wants to hang out. Family, friends, kids, lots of noise. Laughter. I want a house where people never want to leave."

The more I talked, the less embarrassed I felt. The dream spilled out of me. A big family. A large backyard. A porch light that never turned off.

Joe listened raptly to every word. Not teasing, not dismissive. He just sat and listened, asking questions every now and then.

We had lost track of time. By the time we flipped to the last page, we had missed our dinner reservations. But Joe didn't care.

He reached over and, with his thumb, lifted my chin so I'd meet his eyes. "Maggie, I promise to build that house for you one day."

That was the night I fell in love with Joe Bentley. Not because he promised to build my dream house, but because he sat with me on the floor in my room for hours, looking through the pages of my childhood binder, and thought it was the most important thing in the world.

Because I loved and cherished it, Joe did too.

The lights were dimmed. Tranquil music played softly from overhead speakers. A lavender-scented mist floated in the air, meant to relax and center us.

It wasn't working.

Wednesday night yoga class.

"Breathe in calm and gratitude. Exhale stress and negative thoughts," Destiny murmured from the front of the studio.

"You'll never guess who Maggie came home to," Annie whispered, already halfway into child's pose. "Go ahead, guess."

"Patrick Dempsey," Katie said flatly. "Please tell me Patrick Dempsey."

"I wish," I said, placing my mat between them. "Nope, Sherri."

"Ugh, Zillowzilla," Jules said. "Did she bring cookies and a drone this time?"

Joy hissed. "Shhh."

Katie sneered at Joy. "You're just mad Sherri's perkier than you."

"I heard that," Joy snapped, but it came out more like a forced exhale.

"I'm just saying, she's really pushy," Annie whispered.

"Gratitude," Destiny called out, louder this time. "Let go of tension. Be here now. Ground yourself in the present."

"I swear Sherri's been watching too many *Selling Sunset* reruns," Katie said dryly. "She even has a Swarovski crystal clipboard."

"It sparkles," Jules added, attempting a tripod in her faux leather leggings and a tank top that said, *Jesus Loves Hockey Moms*.

Destiny raised her head. "Ladies in the back corner, please remember this is a shared space. Let's respect the zen of others."

Joy sent us all a death glare in the middle of her downward dog, somehow maintaining perfect form.

"I'm serious," Annie whispered. "She popped out from Maggie's azaleas like a damn squirrel."

"Find your center," Destiny said, in a voice that barely masked her growing irritation.

Katie leaned over from two mats away. "I'd like to find Sherri's center and shove a For Sale sign right up her—"

"Ladies!" Destiny barked, officially pissed.

"*Someone* needs to find her zen," Katie muttered.

We all pressed our lips shut like scolded schoolgirls.

Miraculously, we made it through the rest of class without getting shushed again. Jules slipped into warrior pose, looking like Catwoman at a candlelight retreat. Annie moved like she was born on a yoga mat. Joy flowed through every motion gracefully. And Katie fell asleep during pigeon pose.

The class ended with a soft chime, and we rolled up our mats.

As we moved toward the cubbies, a familiar face approached us—Donna Russo. City Council Member. Former Hockey Mom. Occasional margarita buddy.

Her eyes darted around the room. "They're moving the vote up," she whispered. "Next week. Thought you should know."

And just like that, all my zen disappeared.

24

Kevin

"My office, 9 a.m.," my dad barked as he stuck his head through my doorway. No "*Good morning, Son,*" no small talk, just an order, a command. Just Conrad Mitchell being Conrad Mitchell.

Typical.

However, nothing could ruin my mood today.

Maggie and I had plans—and yeah, I'd been looking forward to it for days.

Technically, this cornhole tournament was all part of Maggie's schedule that she'd given me weeks ago. Part of her *Operation No Slots—Just Slapshots Tour*. The name of her tour kept changing, but her mission hadn't. She wanted the farm—needed it.

And if I were honest, she'd already made her point loud and clear. I wasn't showing up for research anymore. I was showing up for her. Spending time with Maggie was becoming my favorite part of the week.

Scratch that. It *was* my favorite part of the week. No contest.

But I hadn't forgotten what had brought me here. How could I? It was my family's firm gunning for that land, and I was the one who had started the initial ball rolling, choosing Hattrick Harbor for the casino in the first place. And it would be up to me to figure out how to save the town I initially wanted to destroy.

I'd been racking my brain trying to find a way out of this. A way for Maggie to get the land she needed for Hope Farm and an alternate spot for the casino and resort that Mitchell Developers wanted to build. Everyone would win. I was close to having something mapped out, something that could actually work. But I needed more time.

Kristen wasn't making it easy. Still, I wasn't giving up. Not on Maggie. Not on her town. I was seeing her tomorrow night and getting closer to figuring out a resolution to this clusterfuck.

When I walked into the boardroom for the nine o'clock meeting, I had one goal—don't let Kristen push my buttons or my father spoil my day.

Kristen was already there, of course, perched in the seat right next to mine in her usual work attire. Everything about her was engineered for effect—blood red suit, heels to match, and diamond studs the size of marbles. Kristen wanted to intimidate anyone who met her, and she wasn't afraid to craft her persona to do so—right down to her pointy manicured fingers that looked less like nails and more like claws.

"Miss me?" She flashed a grin with lipstick too red for the boardroom that said she was up to something.

"Like a root canal." I never looked her way.

Conrad walked in on cue, clapping his hands, looking like a

game show host. "Great news, everyone," he announced. "We're gaining traction. That interview with Channel 5 gave us some excellent press—even with Ms. Bentley and her little band of cheerleaders trying to drag our name through the mud."

Kristen scoffed. "Who's taking business advice from a gang of small-town hockey moms, a cookie baker, and a biker chick who didn't scare anyone with her Jesus T-shirt."

"That's enough," I said, cutting her off without looking at her. "Can we leave the petty name-calling out of this? It lacks professionalism."

Conrad cleared his throat and kept rolling. "More good news. I got a call late last night. The city council has moved up the vote. It's happening next week."

I stiffened. The words hit like a full-out body check, knocking the breath clean out of me. All my newfound hope started to slip, unraveling thread by thread.

I couldn't prove anything. But if I were in Vegas, the safe bet would be that my dad had something to do with the sudden date change. I bit down hard, heat coiling at the base of my skull.

That moved the finish line out of reach. It took Maggie's chances of raising any additional funds from slim to impossible. And it cut the time in half I'd needed to stop this train from rolling right through her farm.

Conrad took a seat at the head of the table, folding his hands in front of him. Far too confident. Far too controlled. "Let's get right down to business," he said. "As you know, there are six voting members on Hattrick Harbor's City Council. If the vote ends in a tie, then Council President, Fred Cummings, gets the deciding vote."

He leaned back in his chair and flipped through the notes he had in front of him. "That said, I don't think it will come to that." He glanced across the table at Kristen, and his smile widened. "Kristen has been doing her homework and has come up with a plan."

He gestured smoothly in her direction. "Kristen, the floor is yours."

Kristen rose from her chair and walked to the large screen on the wall. "I've compiled research on our city council halfwits. Here's what we're working with."

I bit down on my tongue, holding back the urge to call her out. If she had the opportunity for a cutting remark about Hattrick and the people who lived there, she took it. People I'd come to like. A town I'd grown comfortable in. My father didn't just allow her unprofessionalism—he admired it. They both spoke the same language—disdain, hypocrisy, greed. And me? I was starting to wonder if I'd ever belonged here at all.

Photos began to appear one by one. She pointed the controller toward the screen. "Donna Russo. Hockey mom. Longtime fangirl of Maggie Bentley. Hard no. Waste of our time."

I smirked.

"Colleen Colasanti," she continued. "Husband owns the barber shop in town. Small business. Would benefit from casino traffic. Worth a meeting."

Kristen clicked on the next photo. "Bill Lombard. New to town four years ago. Well-liked and ran a good campaign. Hard to tell which way he'll vote. Worth the meeting."

"Dalton Coyle," she continued. "Owns the biggest car dealership in town. Financially motivated. Leaning yes."

"Tess Holcomb," she said with a dramatic sigh. "Goalie's mom. Bentley loyalist. That's a no."

She clicked on the last picture. "Tony Heckman. Wild card. Teaches civics. Quiet man. We don't know where he stands. Worth the face time."

Kristen launched into her detailed plan of attack. "As it looks right now, Russo and Holcomb seem to have already made up their minds. Meeting with them might be a waste of valuable time. Instead, we need to focus our efforts on the remaining members."

She didn't wait for our response. She just kept talking like she ran the show. "Colasanti, Lombard, Coyle, and Heckman are all worth talking to. If we play it right, talk about all the benefits we'll bring to Hattrick, then we're one step closer to securing the vote for our casino."

"*Our* casino?" I questioned.

Kristen said, "Yes, Kevin. Like it or not, I'm part of the team now."

Of course, she was. She'd muscled her way back into my life. I clenched my jaw, doing everything in my power not to let it show. Because the more she spoke, the clearer it became. She was here to win. And if she got the chance to step on Maggie's throat… well, that'd be a bonus. No wonder my father adored her. She could take jabs at me all night—I'd lived through that marriage. But I knew if I weren't careful, I'd lose the one chance I had to help Maggie. My blood boiled on the inside, and on the outside, I sat stone-still, every inch a picture of composure.

Kristen slid a stack of printed itineraries and detailed city council bios across the table. "I've taken the liberty of setting up meetings with all of them. Ben, you'll meet with Colasanti and

Lombard. Kevin and I will meet with Coyle and Heckman. We'll all meet with Cummings."

"I'm fine to meet with Coyle and Heckman on my own," I said, sharper than intended. "I don't need a co-pilot."

"Nonsense," my father interjected before Kristen could respond, slamming his palm on the table. "You and Kristen have always worked well together. You'll continue to work together as long as she's here."

I kept still and bit back a dozen arguments. My father might've thought we made a good team once, but now...this felt like purgatory.

"I'll tag along with Ben," he continued. "Then we'll all tackle Cummings together tonight over dinner."

Ben shifted uncomfortably in his seat. "Ummm. Dad, I can't make it tonight. I have plans."

Yeah, this should go over well.

"Not anymore, you don't," he said, never glancing up. "Tell whatever bimbo you have plans with that you're busy."

My eyes flew up at his comment, and I checked the reactions of the other two. Nothing. Why was I the only one who cringed at the language my father used? Suddenly, it felt like I was hovering overhead, watching the whole scene play out. I glanced over at Ben, and he just looked disappointed that he wasn't going to get laid tonight. Kristen wore a twisted grin—she didn't bat a fake eyelash. I was beginning to feel like I was in an alternate universe. The longer I sat here, the more I wanted to jump out of my skin.

I'd been practicing the art of keeping my mouth shut, and it was getting harder to do every time I stepped foot in the office. Every time I was around my father. And every blistering second

I was in a room with Kristen.

But I'd learned something. The more I spoke out—the more I pushed when they pulled—the more trouble I caused Maggie. If I could swallow my pride, clamp my mouth shut, and picture myself anywhere but here, I might be able to help her. The fewer waves I made, the better my chances. I'd suffer through the meetings. I'd sit across from Kristen and pretend we were on the same team because I needed eyes on everything. I needed to see where the council members stood and strategize on my own.

"And just a reminder," my dad said, taking off his reading glasses and staring at the three of us, "we have the Museum Gala Saturday night. I expect all of you to be there. Kevin, you can bring Kristen since she knows what to expect and has been there before with you."

"I already have a date," I said, gathering my notes, "but Ben can bring Kristen."

The silence was satisfying. It almost made up for the rest of the spectacle. Kristen's fake smile faded, Ben looked like he'd just been handed courtside seats for Game Seven, and I felt pretty damn good.

The meetings with Coyle and Heckman went as expected. Lunch at Slapshot's Café was over before it began—at least with Dalton Coyle. He practically shouted "yes" before his ass hit the chair. He owned the biggest car dealership in three counties and had already dreamed up a luxury rental fleet for high rollers.

"People don't just want to gamble," he said, waving his fork in the air, "they want to roll up in a Cadillac Escalade with tinted windows and a mini bar in the back seat."

He chewed with his mouth open. "I appreciate what you folks are trying to do for our town. I'm not saying yes, of course, but I can promise you, I'll be giving it thoughtful consideration."

Coyle would vote for the casino. He was in it for the money, plain and simple. He didn't care what it would do to Hattrick Harbor. Never mentioned a worry about the town at all. It was all about what the casino could do for him. The money *he* could make. The early retirement *he* could plan. And how *he* could turn his dealership into a fleet-hub for high-end rentals—maybe even find a way to slap his name on the shuttle service that ran from the casino to his lot.

Perfect city councilman to be elected *by* the people *for* the people. We could have mailed him a sandwich and gotten the same result.

Tony Heckman, on the other hand, was an entirely different species. Quiet, awkward, glasses perpetually slipping down his nose. High school civics teacher, single, and probably hadn't had a date in years—and Kristen saw her opening. She turned on the charm. Laughed too loud, leaned in too close, and wiped an imaginary crumb off the corner of his mouth.

"Oh, my gosh, has anyone ever told you how handsome you are?" she purred, letting her fingers casually brush his sleeve. "I bet your students adore you."

Heckman blinked behind his smudged glasses. "Uh—I, well—some of them, I suppose."

At one point, she even placed her hand on his leg underneath the table and said with a syrupy grin, "I just love a man who understands the importance of community impact."

I thought the poor guy was going to combust. His face turned fire-engine red, and his eyes bulged like he'd been poked with a cattle prod. I just sat there watching the sideshow unfold, wondering how the hell I got myself into business with these people and how far they were willing to go for the sake of winning.

He didn't come right out and say it, but he was leaning yes. Probably because Kristen had short-circuited his frontal lobe. Heckman was going home to take a cold shower, and Kristen was ready to take a victory lap.

Later that evening, we all met Fred Cummings for dinner at Ed's Chop House—his choice—a no-frills, hometown steakhouse with wood-paneled walls and laminate menus. Kristen looked like she'd stepped into the Bass Pro Shop by mistake, nose wrinkled and eyes scanning the room like she expected someone to offer her a beer and an axe. My dad looked equally out of place, adjusting the collar of his pristine white dress shirt. Ben was still sulking, clearly irritated that this meeting cut into whatever plans he had with the waitress he'd picked up last weekend.

I, on the other hand, felt perfectly at home.

The hostess—who knew Fred by name—greeted us with a friendly "Hi, y'all" and waved us toward a corner booth like we were regulars.

Conrad didn't waste any time and dove in fast. "Fred, thanks for meeting with us. We know your time is valuable, and we're excited about what our casino and resort could mean for

Hattrick Harbor."

Fred sipped his whiskey, studying the four of us. "Mm-hmmm. Been hearing a lot about it." He glanced at me. "But I've also known Maggie Bentley a long time. Our boys played hockey together. Good people, the Bentleys."

Kristen leaned forward, trying out her sultry vixen voice. "Absolutely, but personal connections aside, we believe this project could offer economic growth—jobs, tourism, infrastructure improvements. The entire town stands to profit."

Her charm wasn't working like it did with Heckman. None of this moved Fred. He ignored her comment completely. Instead, he set down his glass and looked thoughtfully toward the window.

"Sure was a terrible thing when Joe died. Maggie's living in that big house on the lake all by herself. Shame, really. But I'll give it to her—she hasn't stopped trying to make good on the farm she and Joe dreamed up years ago."

Fred wasn't wrong. She'd been carrying that dream on her back with nothing but grit and grace. That was Maggie. Fighting for what mattered—even when the odds were stacked against her. Even with monsters as enemies. And damn, if I didn't admire her for it.

Ben didn't say a word, just nodded as he downed his bourbon and attacked his ribeye.

"But," Fred added, voice firm and louder now, "I've got concerns about the casino. We're a small town. We like knowing our neighbors. And I'm not sure bringing in tourists with deep pockets and deeper vices is what Hattrick Harbor needs."

Kristen jumped in. "With all due respect, Fred, the positive economic impact—"

He held up a hand, shutting her down. "I've read your packet, ma'am. Appreciate the pretty pages."

Then, his eyes found mine. "But if it comes down to a tie, I'll be voting with my conscience. And right now?" He shrugged. "That farm feels a hell of a lot more like Hattrick than a roulette wheel ever will."

By the time dessert got to the table, I was the only one breathing easy. My dad looked like he'd bitten into a lemon. Kristen had gone radio silent. Ben was still pouting.

Fred ordered Myrna's Famous Apple Pie and left.

I ordered a celebratory beer and waited.

Ben reported from his meetings earlier. Colasanti and Lombard were both wild cards, but if Ben had to guess, they'd stay loyal to Maggie. Between Colasanti and Lombard, Maggie only needed one of them to tip the scale and force a tie.

She was the one with traction now. Things were leaning in her favor. I began to picture Maggie on the farm—the smile on her face when she'd won the vote. Hope was a funny thing—it wasn't something I thought about much, but right now, it felt possible.

Conrad folded his napkin and said, "We still have the surprise in our back pocket. When we double the asking price for the property, those votes will swing."

He turned to Kristen. "Let's continue to do our due diligence. I want you to dig into Colasanti and Lombard. Find out what it will take to get them on our side."

Panic started to leak through the cracks in Conrad Mitchell's polished facade—and my dad didn't get rattled. That alone spoke volumes about this town. About its loyalty. Hattrick Harbor trusted its own, and no amount of money would change that.

Let him try. Let Kristen dig. Let them throw their millions at a town that already knew where it stood.

My money was on Hattrick Harbor doing the right thing.

25

Maggie

Maggie: Still on for Cornhole tonight?

Kevin: I'm all in.

Maggie: There's one minor problem.

Kevin: I'm afraid to ask.

Maggie: We have team uniforms. Wearing it is not optional.

Kevin: Did Joy make them?

Maggie: You know it.

Kevin: Do we have a team name?

Maggie: Of course, we do.

Kevin: And????

Maggie: The *Hole Busters.*

Kevin: Tell me you're kidding.

Maggie: I can't make this up.

"You're going to owe me big for this." Kevin chuckled as he walked up beside me, tugging at the stiff collar of his red and white checkered shirt as if it might strangle him at any second. "No photos. A digital footprint can't exist with me in this shirt."

"Relax," I said, grinning as I adjusted my own matching eyesore. "Humiliation builds character. Anyway, you have bigger problems than being photographed in that."

Kevin shot me a look. "Like…"

"Helen's here. She's been asking for you."

His laugh turned to worry. "She already tried to corner me. Grabbed my bicep and asked if I was still single and limber."

I laughed. "She does love a man in uniform."

"She loves a man with a pulse," he muttered. "This shirt might actually be too much for her."

"Don't worry. That group never travels without a cardiologist or a defibrillator."

We made our way past the cornhole boards, and the Lakeside Grill glowed under a canopy of string lights, nestled right up against the edge of Lake Hattrick. The scent of pine trees drifted in on the breeze, blended with the grill's signature fried pickles and the famous Lakeside BBQ Chicken Sandwich. It was a perfect fall evening—cool, clear—and the whole town was buzzing with excitement.

The annual Lakeside Cornhole Tournament was a town tradition. Once a year, the whole town came out for a night of overly competitive beanbag tossing and epic smack talk. If you weren't playing, you were watching. My friends and I entered every year, and we'd never come close to winning—ever—but this year felt different.

We had a secret weapon. Not talent. Not a battle plan.

Matching uniforms. Ridiculously hideous ones.

Annie's husband, Mike, stood next to Kevin with a beer in his hand. "I'm going into Witness Protection on Monday. My coworkers already saw me walk in with this thing on. I'll never live it down."

Just then, Joy skipped over, beaming with pride like she'd just been named queen of small-town fashion week.

"Look at us!" she said, spinning in place. "This right here is what team unity looks like. This…" she waved her arm at our collective fashion disaster, "…this is how champions dress."

Jules, naturally, had thrown a black leather vest over hers, which did absolutely nothing to tone it down. "I feel like an outlaw at a picnic," she said, tying her matching bandana around her head that Joy had made "especially for her."

Annie raised her beer. "Only way to survive this matching polyester tragedy is with alcohol. Drink up!"

"It's like a 1980's diner meets a bowling alley," Katie said, sipping from her wine tumbler.

Joy perked up. "Next year—matching shoes!"

Kevin leaned over, his voice low and playful in my ear. "I draw a line at matching shoes."

A ripple of heat slid across the back of my neck and down my spine, catching me completely off guard. I should've been used to it by now—the way his voice did that to me—but every time, it struck like a bolt of lightning—quick and unexpected.

I smiled, but kept my gaze fixed on the group, afraid that if I looked at him, I might forget what mattered. Kevin was here as part of my tour to win him over and have him fall in love with my hometown. But I also had ulterior motives. We didn't really need another player on our team, but I'd asked him anyway. Being with him felt better than being without him.

And I wasn't so sure I needed to convince him that the casino was a bad idea anymore. After the protest and his confession about wanting to help, I let myself believe him. Because I knew he was trying. Really trying. Every step he'd taken lately—giving me the heads-up on the publicity stunt, the notes from his meetings with the city council members—pointed toward someone who wasn't toeing the company line.

But there was a lot at stake for me.

I couldn't complicate matters and let broad shoulders, a wicked grin, and a man who's defying family to cloud my judgment. The farm had to come first, and I had to finish what I started. And yet tonight, the lines were blurred. Even seeing Kevin in a pathetic polyester uniform didn't lessen my attraction to him. If anything, it made it worse. He slipped it on and owned it, like he was ready to go to battle with all of us. He was a good sport, laughed, and kept reminding me that I'd "owe him."

He'd better play cornhole half as good as he looked, because God help anyone who came between this group and a plastic trophy.

The Lakeside patio had become a war zone. We'd won our first three matches and made it to the finals—first time ever. I'd wanted to say it was because of our skill, but really, our trash talk had been better. Even Kevin was doing his fair share of taunting. It was all infuriatingly effective and annoyingly attractive. Unfortunately, for me, all of that was not ideal for staying emotionally detached.

Even the defending champs, *The Cornstars*, folded under the relentless barrage of Katie and Annie's Grade-A trash talk. Katie's delivery was as dry as sandpaper—like being insulted by your therapist—while Annie leaned in like a full WWF wrestler, pointing fingers and calling names. If there were a tightrope, she'd launch herself from the top. Joy's whistle didn't hurt either—blowing it as if it were the final seconds of a World Cup match. And Mike, with his long dreadlocks and bulging biceps, looked like he benched small furniture for fun. Our group wasn't exactly intimidating in the traditional sense, but we were menacing in various other ways.

As if by some strange cosmic alien attack, our final opponent was *Helen's Hellions*. Every team they played against got disqualified.

Joy blew her whistle. "Bring it in, *Hole Busters*." She waved us into a tight circle. We huddled together, arms looped, bodies bent forward.

"Someone is taking her job very seriously," Kevin whispered.

Damn goosebumps.

"Listen up," she said, eyes darting around the circle, making sure to have contact with each of us. "I have it on good authority that Helen and her misfits are playing dirty. She faked a hip cramp mid-throw and got the other team disqualified for unsportsmanlike conduct after someone tried to help her up. Don't fall for it."

"Isn't Helen, like, ninety-three?" Kevin asked.

"Ninety-three and a half," Joy snapped. "She faked a dizzy

spell in the first game and still managed to throw a perfect game. Don't make eye contact. Don't offer help. If she so much as limps, you turn away."

Then she added, "If she falls down, you walk over her." She looked like a miniature version of a Navy SEAL. "You got it?"

We all nodded, afraid not to.

"I'm not losing to a group of orthopedic tricksters," Annie said, looking more determined and battle-ready than ever.

"That's the spirit!" Joy shouted. "This is our moment. This is our time. Be alert—be ruthless. And whatever you do, do not help Helen back to her feet."

We put our hands in, and Joy yelled, "One. Two. Three."

"Hole Busters!" we all shouted.

When we broke apart, Kevin squeezed my elbow. "Am I wrong or were we just told to commit light assault on a grandma?"

"No mercy, Kevin." I bumped his shoulder, trying not to notice how solid he was or how close he was. "This tournament brings out the worst in us."

Game on.

We rotated through the lineup like clockwork. Every time we took the advantage, Helen's Hellions kept throwing on target.

The game was tied.

Helen tried every trick in the book. The fake hip-out-of-socket routine got her plenty of sympathy from the crowd, but none of us fell for it. Not after Joy's threatening pep talk.

"Eyes on me," Joy shouted from the sideline, whistle clenched between her teeth. "No empathy. She's trying to break you."

There were four players left to throw. Kevin and I for the *Hole Busters*, and Helen and Lois for the *Hellions*.

Each team rotated players carefully.

Lois was up first.

From her lawn chair, Annie was doing a solid job, throwing off Helen's second-in-command, and just as Lois was about to launch, she yelled, "Do we need to get you some bifocals for this round, sweetheart?"

Lois's bag veered off three feet and landed in the grass. She responded by giving Annie the middle finger salute.

Three players left to throw.

Helen—all four-foot-eight of her—hobbled over to Mike sitting on the sideline, clutching her cane like it had just snapped in half. "Young man, could you lend a hand? My cane seems to have malfunctioned," she said sweetly, batting her beady eyes in a cloud of perfume that smelled suspiciously like mothballs.

Mike didn't miss a beat. "Glad to help." He smiled widely, baring his teeth. "Right after we whup your ass, ma'am."

That fired Helen up like a bottle rocket. Her spine straightened, and she grew two inches, her cane miraculously sturdy again. Now, she turned her sights on Kevin, who took his spot opposite me.

Even though Kevin and I were on the same team, we stood twenty-seven feet apart, which put him next to Helen—well within the danger zone.

"Oh, honey," she purred, getting entirely too close, "you sure do know how to handle your bags." Her voice dropped to a husky rasp. "I wonder what else you're good at."

"Helen," I called out, unable to help myself. "Aren't you dating Jerry?"

She waved a hand. "He's deaf and half-blind. I'm practically single."

Kevin didn't flinch. He was zoned in. All we needed was a solid toss to stay alive.

He focused. Lined up his feet. Took one smooth step and let the beanbag fly.

Plunk!

He landed inches from the hole!

The *Hellions* needed to sink theirs just to stay even. If they did, it would force me to land on the board. I'd been doing that all night. But if they missed? Then I could throw mine straight into the bushes and walk away a champ.

Helen was their final thrower.

She'd been on fire all night, despite her psychological warfare.

"This one's for you, sugar buns." She winked at Kevin. "Let's get dinner after. I'm buying, but *you're* dessert."

Helen stepped up, tossing her bag high in the air. A perfect arch. The crowd held its breath. It didn't just land on the board—it collided with Kevin's bag and knocked it completely off.

Thunk!

The crowd gasped. Kevin's bag was in the grass.

We *lost* points.

Helen jumped so high, I thought she was going to break a hip for real this time. But she was surprisingly spry and rebounded just fine.

The *Hellions* were at twenty points.

It all came down to me.

The only path to victory was to sink it.

"Just breathe," Joy whispered behind me. "You've been hot all night. This'll be a piece of cake."

Across the patio, Kevin cupped his hands around his mouth.

"You got this, Maggie."

I took a deep breath. Closed my eyes and counted to ten.

Opened and focused.

Then launched.

The beanbag flew in a high, steady arc.

Whoosh!

Right. In. The. Hole.

Pandemonium erupted.

Joy cried. Annie screamed. Katie jumped on the scorer's table.

Mike took off his checkered shirt and waved it like a victory flag. The women of Hattrick had been waiting all night for that and swooned.

Kevin crossed the patio in three strides and scooped me up in his arms before I could even blink. He laughed—loud and unrestrained—and spun me in a circle, his breath warm against my ear.

"Maggie, you did it!"

I couldn't stop laughing. My arms wrapped around his neck instinctively, as I held on, breathless. For a moment, there was only the rush of the night air, the cheers from our team, and Kevin's arms locked tightly around me.

When he finally set me down, we didn't step apart right away, and his hands lingered on my hips. My hands stayed on the front of his chest, standing close enough to feel the heat of his stare.

Neither one of us moved, unwilling to break the thread between us.

For one suspended breath, everything faded.

The noise, the people, Helen's cries of "rigged cornhole

boards"—we didn't hear any of it. There was only the look in his eyes, the warm pressure of his hands, and the way my body leaned toward his without thinking.

A slow heat curled to life. His eyes stayed trained on mine like we were the only two people left standing under the glow of the lights and the navy sky. I swallowed hard, suddenly flustered. The soft affection in his eyes made my stomach flip.

"Nice shot," he said barely above a whisper, and for one dangerous second, the vote was the last thing on my mind. And right there, standing in the midst of Helen's temper tantrum and Joy's obnoxious jubilation, I felt my resolve starting to slip.

I smiled. My voice was completely useless.

I took a small step back, hoping it would calm the storm inside me, but it did nothing for the flutter in my chest that wasn't going anywhere, anytime soon.

I felt warm all over, dizzy in the best way. Not because of our big win or watching Joy hoist the six-inch plastic trophy above her head.

It was him.

Kevin.

Being in his arms didn't feel wrong or complicated—it felt easy. That was the only word that came to mind. Like an old sweater you put on when you want to feel cozy. And it felt nice—the kind of nice that made me wonder how something as simple as a hug could feel so good.

Then, the air shifted.

A rush of cold wind hit me, and out of the corner of my eye, I spotted someone standing completely still while the crowd celebrated.

Kristen.

Standing at the edge of the patio, watching us.

Correction—she was watching *me*.

Her glare sliced through the crowd, her expression unreadable, but icy enough to raise goosebumps on my arms.

I blinked, and just like that, she vanished. I scanned the patio again, but she was gone. The chill lingered. So did the unease. Her presence had unsettled the perfect night.

Kevin turned slightly, following my gaze. "What is it?" he asked, brushing my arm with his.

"Nothing," I said quickly. "Thought I saw someone I knew." He nodded, but my pulse didn't slow down.

Kristen was up to something.

And seeing me with Kevin just accelerated whatever it was.

26

Kevin

Kevin: Time to pay up.

Maggie: What's my penance?

Kevin: An event my family is sponsoring.

Maggie: Will I need heels, a hard hat, or
bail money?

Kevin: Heels. Pick you up at six.

I arrived at Maggie's, straightening my tie as I came to the door.
I don't wear tuxes often, but tonight called for it. Still, nothing
could've prepared me for the moment the door opened.

There she was.

I stood frozen, voice completely useless, like a high school
senior picking up his prom date—realizing she was way out of
his league.

Maggie wore a deep green strapless dress that made her eyes greener and her smile brighter, if that were even possible. Her hair was swept up in some soft, effortless twist that showed off the long line of her neck and the delicate curve of her shoulders.

And then there were her heels. Strappy and tall enough to make a man think dangerous thoughts. Tall enough to send my mind racing. Breathtaking didn't even begin to cover it—lucky didn't describe how I felt.

Then my mind wandered.

If she were mine, we wouldn't make it out the front door. I'd scoop her into my arms, carry her right back up those stairs, and lose myself in her—slowly, completely, over and over again. We wouldn't leave the house all night.

"Kevin?" Maggie asked, catching the strange look on my face.

I shook my head to clear every sex-starved thought barreling through my brain.

"You…" I started, still having trouble piecing together one complete sentence. "You… look beautiful."

"Oh." She smiled shyly, tucking a loose strand of her brown hair behind her ear. Her cheeks began to flush as she smoothed out the invisible lines on the front of her dress. "Thank you."

Shit, who was I kidding? We'd never make it back upstairs. I'd have her screaming my name right here on the floor in this entryway. Fuck the fundraiser. Fuck this monkey suit I no longer felt comfortable in.

And that dress, I pictured what it would look like in a pile on the floor.

Get a grip, Kevin.

We hadn't made it five steps into the gallery before heads started turning. Conversations paused. Champagne flutes froze mid-sip. It was like someone had flipped on a spotlight, and suddenly, every set of eyes in the room swung toward us.

Part of the attention wasn't just about Maggie. It was about *us*. Because I didn't bring dates to this event. Not since Kristen.

But the real showstopper was the woman beside me—the way she smiled, the way she moved—graceful, classy, and completely unaware that every female there was sizing her up and every man was sneaking second glances.

Maggie.

She walked with quiet confidence. We didn't hold hands, she didn't link her arm through mine, but we were side by side, and it was obvious she was here with me. That in itself was enough to stop traffic.

Mitchell Developers had sponsored the annual Charlotte Metropolitan Art Gala for as long as I could remember. Nothing screamed affluence like a ten-thousand-dollar painting. Conrad Mitchell knew it—he'd bought plenty over the years. More for show than any real love for the arts.

The Art Gala was just as stuffy as I remembered. It smelled faintly of varnish and something overly floral. Voices bounced off the stark gallery walls. A jazz trio was tucked into the back corner, and tiny food was passed around on silver platters by men and women in bow ties.

The people attending were the same, too. Board members

with pocket squares and inherited money. Art snobs. Old-money types with practiced smiles.

I already missed the cornhole tournament.

Maggie leaned in and whispered, "I'm guessing we're not drinking draft beer tonight."

I smirked. "Only if it's served in a gold-rimmed glass."

My hand found the silky fabric of her dress, and a jolt of awareness hit me, knowing just how near she was. I flattened my hand firmly on her lower back, feeling the heat from her skin, and boldly pulled her closer. My heart jumped for joy when she let me. I gently guided her to the center of the room, and heads kept turning as we passed.

We found my mother alone at a high-top table, staring into her empty wine glass. Her dress was simple and understated. Classic pearls were draped around her neck. Her expression was distant—like she was physically present, but emotionally absent.

I bent over and placed a soft kiss on her warm and wrinkled cheek. "Mom, I'd like you to meet Maggie Bentley. Maggie, this is my mother, Maureen Mitchell."

She offered her hand to Maggie, graceful as always. "It's lovely to meet you, Maggie."

Instead of taking her hand, Maggie reached in and hugged her. It threw my mother for a moment, then she softened, and a warm grin appeared on her lips. My heart tugged at the sight.

Across the room, my father's voice boomed. He was holding court at the bar with a ring of board members, laughing too loudly, gesturing too broadly.

"Can I get you ladies anything to drink?" I asked, glancing between them.

"A Chardonnay," my mother answered quietly.

"I'll have the same," Maggie added with a smile.

I nodded and turned toward the bar. Time to face the man holding court. I'd rather be anywhere else, but avoiding him would only be worse.

Better to walk straight into the storm than pretend it wasn't coming.

I approached my dad and the group of board members gathered around him, practically falling all over themselves, all too eager to laugh at his every word, like he had a key to their fortunes. He probably did.

"Kevin!" he shouted the second he spotted me. He clapped a heavy hand on my shoulder and tipped his drink toward me. "Hell of an entrance."

I offered a tight smile, shaking hands around the circle. "Evening, gentlemen."

"Kevin," Old Money said, his voice dripping with self-importance, "are you looking for more investors for that casino deal? Because I'd like in before the rest of these guys start crawling all over each other."

Art Snob, wearing his designer scarf, leaned in. "I'd like in on the ground floor as well. The sooner we get the ball rolling, the better. That land is a gold mine."

"Same here," Country Club added, his vintage Rolex on display for everyone to see. "This sounds like a once-in-a-lifetime opportunity."

I forced a nod, but my jaw clenched. They were all the same. Every man who stood around this bar. Every man my father called a "friend." They all had something to gain, something to sell, something to prove. Everyone wanted to be first in line for the next big thing. They were playing the *Whose Dick Was Bigger?* game.

No one cared about Hattrick and what it stood to lose in the process. And the people of Hattrick? Sure as hell, no one cared about them. How their lives would change. How the community would change. That was never a concern. Just dollar signs and how fast they could turn them.

This place—this room—wasn't about art or charity. It was about power and positioning. Every handshake had motive behind it. Every so-called "friend" wanted something in return.

I wanted to watch them squirm, so I said, "Well, right now, we're not taking on any more investors. And the city council votes next week. We're not even sure which way the vote will swing."

My dad jumped on that because if there was money willing to be thrown his way, he wasn't turning it down. "The vote is just semantics. I'm confident the council will be voting with us."

His confidence had taken a 180-degree turn since dinner with Fred. I paused a beat to wonder why the sudden change in attitude.

"Kevin's the brains on this one," my dad said, turning toward the group with a wide grin.

"Guy's got an eye for opportunity. Bringing Ms. Bentley here—genius move!"

Bile churned in my stomach. I knew exactly what he was doing. Reducing Maggie to a bargaining chip to win at any cost. She was just another casualty lined up in his war of control. There was no motive behind bringing Maggie here, but of course, he'd like to think I was conniving—had some kind of master manipulated plan— because that's exactly what he would do.

"Keep your friends close and your enemies closer," my dad continued. "Kevin here will do whatever it takes to seal the deal."

I forced myself not to react—but inside I bristled. He had no idea what I was willing to do—and who I was willing to do it for.

Art Snob chuckled like it was the cleverest thing he'd ever heard. "Smart. I like your style."

I shot my dad a look that said, *shut it*, but he ignored me, basking in the attention of his corporate robots.

"Yeah," I said tightly, my voice flat. "She's something else."

The second my dad started talking about Maggie, I regretted bringing her here. Maggie wasn't part of some game, and I'd be damned if I let anyone in this room think otherwise. I hadn't brought her here for strategy—I brought her here because I wanted to be with her. Because I couldn't stand *not* being with her. Maybe that was selfish. Maybe that wasn't fair. But having her here made this whole night feel tolerable.

We only had a couple of days left until the vote. Then, we wouldn't have a reason to spend as much time together. And that reason—the simple selfish one—outweighed all the logical arguments.

As they kept talking—boasting about profit margins, casino revenue projections, and whose name would appear on the next Mitchell project—my attention drifted. I glanced across the gallery and spotted my mother.

For the first time in months, maybe longer, she was smiling. Not the polite, painted-on kind she used for charity events. And not the timid one she used at home. This one was real. Soft and easy. And she was *laughing*. I couldn't remember the last time I'd seen that. And the reason behind it all was standing right beside her.

All it took was Maggie.

But I shouldn't be surprised. Maggie had that effect on people. Being around her was magical. If that dress and those heels didn't do it for me, then her standing there, making my mom laugh—well,…that struck something else inside me.

But then that bubble burst because right then Ben and Kristen joined Maggie. Kristen stepped right in front of my mother as if she didn't exist, blocking her out completely. Maggie frowned, gently guiding my mom back into the circle and standing at her side like a shield.

My hand curled into a fist.

I didn't even realize I'd cut off Country Club mid-sentence until I heard my own voice. "Excuse me."

I made it to Maggie in record speed.

Ben leaned an elbow on the high-top with a smile that was all teeth and mock sincerity. "Maggie Bentley," he said, like her name was dessert he wanted to bite into. "You clean up nice. What's a small-town girl like you doing in a place like this?"

"Trying not to step in whatever you tracked in," Maggie said sweetly, tilting her head.

My mom snickered.

I broke in immediately. "She's with me tonight," I said, sliding into the space between them and placing my palm on her lower back. My tone—my hand placement—left zero room for interpretation.

Kristen's lips tipped into a slow, venomous smile. "Well… isn't this unexpected?"

Maggie didn't blink. "About as unexpected as you showing up without your broom."

My mom choked on her drink. Then, cleared her throat.

Kristen's eyes narrowed at Maggie. "I guess Kevin always did have a thing for…projects."

My blood boiled. "That's enough, Kristen," I snapped.

"Oh, I'm definitely a project. But one well worth it, which is more than I can say for a bad investment."

I did a double-take.

Holy hell. That was *hot*. Watching Maggie stand there, unflinching, throwing verbal punches at my ex without batting an eye—yeah, fucking hot. I'd seen Kristen rip people apart, but Maggie just didn't hold her own—she left Kristen speechless.

Something about her defending herself—defending me—hit me harder than I expected. It was bold. Fierce. It was fucking sexy. My blood was already running hot with Ben and Kristen standing in front of me, but now all I thought about was pulling Maggie to me and kissing the hell out of her in front of everyone.

Ben chuckled and leaned into Maggie. "What do you say we ditch this place and find somewhere a little more fun, let these two hash things out."

I dug my nails into my palm, welcoming the bite of pain. "One more word, Ben, and I don't care where we are, my fist will knock that smug look off your face."

Maggie must've sensed my barely contained rage because she slipped her hand into mine, giving a soft squeeze. It took everything I had to stand there and not take a swing, but the warmth of her touch cut through the anger, grounding me.

"I'm done here," I said, my voice sharp enough to silence the table. My eyes found Maggie's. "You ready?"

She didn't hesitate. "More than ready."

I turned to my mother. "Can I take you home, Mom?"

Her distant smile had returned. "No, sweetheart. I need to stick around with your father."

I hated the way her eyes skittered nervously toward my dad, who hadn't moved from the bar—still near his loyal suck-ups—ignoring my mother, leaving her alone. She deserved better.

"Alright," I said, leaning down to kiss her cheek. "Call if you need anything."

With Maggie's hand still firmly in mine, we cut across the room, past the murmurs and side-eyes that followed. I didn't look back. Not once. I was done giving anyone in that room another second of my time.

Outside, the night air felt like freedom. I finally breathed.

I stared down at Maggie and the way our fingers stayed tangled together, as if neither of us wanted to let go. I'd dated women who played games, women who cared about image, the money, the power. Hell, Kristen was the queen of that kingdom. But Maggie wasn't any of those things—and it was exactly why she terrified me. I knew she was different. And I knew my heart had figured that out, too.

Leaving this place, my family behind, I realized something.

There was no denying it anymore. I wanted her. And not just wanted, needed. The kind of need that settled inside my bones and made me question every damn thing I thought I knew about myself.

27

Maggie

The car ride was quiet. Not the uncomfortable kind of quiet, but the kind when both people were lost in their own thoughts. For me, I replayed the entire evening in my head. Kevin could wear a tux better than most—trim shoulders, tapered waist, and a couple days of stubble looked really good on him.

But it was also the way he stood behind me—solid and steady—and the feel of his palm on my back when I squared up against Kristen. He didn't jump in to save me—not right away. He stood at my side, letting me fight my own battle. And when he did step in, it was the perfect moment. It struck me how rare that was, to have someone who knew when to stand with you and when to let you stand on your own.

Joe had always been my shield. I loved that about him. But since he'd been gone, I'd learned to fight my own battles, find my own voice. And tonight? It felt really good.

And Kevin's mother? She was lovely, but her eyes were so sad. It only took a few stories about my hockey moms—the cornhole tournament and team shirts—and she perked right up. But then Kristen and Ben showed up and she was right back in her shell. They treated her like she was invisible, and that didn't sit well with me. Some people have no idea what it was like to *not* have a mother.

Kevin's world…it was nothing like I'd ever known. All the money flaunting, the power playing, the way everyone measured their worth with who they could impress—it all felt cold and loud and far too shiny. I didn't belong there, not for a second.

And yet, sitting next to Kevin, I couldn't bring myself to run away from it all. Maybe it wasn't his world I needed to understand. Maybe it was the man whose hand I was still holding.

When we pulled into my driveway, Kevin turned in his seat, fully facing me. His voice broke through the silence, guarded and uncertain.

"Do you think I'm anything like my father?"

Not what I expected.

I turned toward him. His face was pained, shadowed by the dim lights. I shook my head. "No," I said softly. "You're nothing like him."

He let out a long breath and sighed. "Many think that I am."

"What do *you* think?" I asked gently.

He thought for a moment, then said, "I used to want to be just like him." He shook his head. "But lately I can't stand the thought of turning into him."

I studied his eyes—they looked defeated, even pained. "Just because we've lived a certain way our entire lives—doesn't mean we're stuck there. People change when they need to. Sometimes the life we've been living doesn't fit the one we want anymore. It's never too late to reinvent yourself. I should know."

A small smile tugged at his mouth. "You make it look pretty damn easy, Maggie."

A genuine laugh slipped from my lips. "You have no idea."

He stared back out the window and didn't say anything for a long time. He didn't pull his hand away and let me hold it while he contemplated what I'd said. Finally, he exhaled, and his shoulders dropped. Worry was etched in every line of his face. "After tonight, they'll all be watching me—Ben, Kristen…my dad. My loyalty's being questioned as we speak."

His eyes flooded with guilt, maybe even regret—and my chest bottomed out. I wasn't sure how to answer that. "I'm sorry."

His eyes found mine. "You have nothing to be sorry for. This is on me, Maggie. I wanted to be with you tonight, and I didn't stop to think of the repercussions it would have for you. I owe you an apology."

I blinked, thrown off.

"I never should have subjected you to my world." He shut his eyes like the words hurt to say out loud. "You didn't deserve that."

The sincerity in his tone tugged at me. I could see how much it bothered him. How much he hated dragging me into that corporate world of bullshit, but I'd agreed to go because a part of me—a bigger part than I was willing to admit—wanted to be with him tonight too, no matter what the cost.

"I knew what I was getting myself into," I said, wanting to ease his guilt. "Besides, anytime I get a chance to spar with Kristen and your brother, I'm all in."

A small smile broke through his stormy expression, and seeing it unlocked something inside me—something I'd been holding onto a little too tightly. This man was lethal. The smile, his sincerity, the way he took my hand and led me out of the gallery away from Ursula and her sidekick. I had wanted to turn around and stick my tongue out, but I thought I was a little too old for that.

"Would you like to come inside?" I asked before I could second-guess it. "You look like you could use a drink."

Kevin followed me inside, and his presence filled the empty, lonely space of my kitchen.

I grabbed two beers from the refrigerator, popped both the tops, and then handed him one.

When he took it from my hand, our fingers brushed, and the zing started from my chest and split in two. One path led to my head, the other to my heart.

I forced myself to take a breath and feigned composure. I leaned against the counter for support, no longer trusting my legs, completely pissed off at every hamstring curl and leg press I'd done because they'd failed me in every sense of the word. I planned on having a few harsh words with my trainer on Monday.

"Thanks," he murmured, still holding my gaze.

For a second, neither one of us moved. The air between us sizzled, humming with an energy I desperately wanted to cling to. I took a drink from the bottle, pretending I wasn't hyperaware of the mere feet between us.

He broke the silence first. "Maggie…about tonight…" His

voice trailed off. He was hesitant, unsure how to finish that sentence.

I shook my head. "You don't have to say any more about it."

"Yeah, I do." He set his bottle next to him. "Because the truth is…" he paused, his eyes holding mine in a way that made the room close in around us. "Call me selfish, but I don't regret taking you. Not for a second."

I didn't know whether to eliminate the space between us or try to keep protecting my heart. My mind raced. My pulse quickened. And the air locked up in my lungs. "This could get complicated."

His voice stayed even with an open and honest expression. "It already is."

Kevin didn't move at first—just watched me as if he was memorizing the exact shade of my eyes. Then, slowly, he reached out, his fingertips brushing a loose strand of hair from my cheek, his touch trailing softly down my jawline.

I didn't move. I couldn't. Not when every part of me already knew that this was it. I'd spent weeks trying to convince myself that this was wrong—bad timing, bad idea, bad everything. But standing there, with his soft touch against my skin, I finally stopped fighting it. My heart had already made the choice.

Without saying a word, he reached for my beer, and his fingers curled around mine briefly before he took the bottle and set it on the counter next to his.

I felt like all the air had been sucked out of the room the second he touched me, and I looked down at my dress to make sure it hadn't disintegrated.

His hand skimmed my bare shoulder, his thumb brushed the curve of it, and I reveled in the touch of him. His fingers traced down my arm, featherlight, like he was mapping out every inch of it. Goosebumps rose in their wake, and his eyes followed every one of them.

Then he bent, his lips near my ear. "Do you know how hard it is to be around you and not want to reach out and touch you?"

I opened my mouth, but nothing came out. My whole body was failing me. First my legs, now my words. All I could do was breathe him in—clean and warm—something I knew I'd already crave again. I wondered what his lips would feel like pressed against mine, what he'd taste like, and that thought alone made my pulse race.

Kevin laughed softly. "So. Damn. Hard."

Yep. That did it. I was done pretending that I wasn't drawn to him. I wanted him—more than I ever expected to want anyone again. My hands found the lapels of his jacket and pulled him closer. I could feel his breath on my lips, hear it even. My heart wasn't just beating fast—it was a full-on sprint. His fingers drifted back up my arm, grazing the side of my neck, and his lips tilted into the faintest, knowing smile.

"Did you wear your hair up so this neck of yours could torture me? Because it worked."

He didn't wait for an answer before his lips found the tender spot below my ear. My head tipped back on instinct, and a whimper escaped before I could stop it.

He pulled back just enough to search my face. "Is this okay?"

"Do you always ask a woman's permission before you kiss her?" My resurrected voice sounded breathless.

"You're not like any other woman I've ever known, Maggie."

I tipped my head to the other side because, honestly, what

kind of monster would I be if I let one side of my neck have all the fun? Kevin's hands slid to my back, pulling me flush against him. His mouth brushed mine—then claimed it.

A low growl rumbled in his throat when our lips met, shuddering right through me. His kiss was soft at first, then deeper—like he wanted to taste every single part of me. I melted into him, my fingers gripping his waist, like it was the only thing keeping me upright.

Every inch of me ignited, and my pulse surged as his mouth moved with mine. Perfectly in sync, stealing my breath, leaving me dizzy, and desperate for more.

His hand skimmed up my back, tracing the line along the zipper of my dress. I shivered so hard I reached behind me and gripped the counter.

"Kevin…" My voice was a whisper I barely recognized.

He smiled against my skin. "I love hearing you say my name."

I wanted to respond, but words were in short supply tonight. His hand curved around my waist, anchoring me, as if he didn't trust me not to run—or himself to let go. He gripped the back of my head, his fingers threading through my hair. Then his mouth found mine again, possessive, hungry, and a sound broke from his chest that made me tremble all over.

Whatever control I'd been clinging to snapped. Every ounce of resistance melted away as I matched his hunger with my own. The world narrowed to only desire and the need for him. This kiss wasn't just a kiss—it was raw, consuming, and impossible to pull away from.

But then he did.

Kevin broke away suddenly, and for a second, I just stood

there, stunned. My pulse was still racing, my lips still tingling, and I couldn't quite make sense of what just happened—why he'd stopped when everything in me wanted more. His chest heaved as if he needed air as badly as I did. My hands fell to my sides, his taste still on my lips, and my body ached for him to erase the space he'd put between us.

"You have no idea how hard that was to stop," he said, his voice rough.

"Then why did you?" The loss of his mouth on mine left me empty and breathless all at once.

"Because if I didn't…" His jaw flexed. "I wouldn't have stopped at all."

"And that would be a bad thing?"

His eyes darkened, his control visible as if he was holding himself together by a thread. "Bad? No. Dangerous? Absolutely."

Kevin took one step, his thumb brushing over my bottom lip so light my goosebumps had goosebumps.

"Maggie, you're all I think about. Standing here, looking at you in this dress with those heels…" He exhaled sharply. "I've wanted to kiss you since the day I met you."

I'd never wanted anything so fiercely. I wanted his lips back on mine, his hands behind me, and our bodies pressed together. I craved all of it. And the way his eyes held mine, like I was the only thing in the world at that moment…I loved the way that felt, too.

"You think I have any control when you look at me like that?" His voice frayed. "Because I don't. Not even close."

"So why are you fighting it?" I asked, almost daring him.

His fingers brushed a slow line down my throat, his voice a low promise. "Because when this happens…I don't want it to be just one night. I want more than that, Maggie."

The words hung between us—too hopeful, too terrifying.

"I want more," he said again, steady this time, "but I know I need to prove myself first. I haven't done that yet. But I will."

He cradled my face and kissed me again—gentle, careful, so tender it made my chest ache—and I silently cursed his moral compass.

"I care about you, Maggie. More than you know. So I'm going to walk away a gentleman—which may be the hardest thing I've ever done in my life."

He kissed me one more time and stepped back. "I'll show myself out."

And if that wasn't enough to turn my insides out, he stopped at the door. "And Maggie?"

I caught my breath. "Yes?"

"When this happens…" He gestured between us, his mouth quirking just slightly. "You'd better leave the whole night open. I promise that it will be worth the wait."

Then, he was gone—leaving me standing in the kitchen, breathless, confused, and already pulling up my calendar to see when I had a large block of free time.

The kitchen was silent after the door clicked shut, but my heart wouldn't stop pounding. *I want more.* His words echoed. He wasn't stating an opinion—he was declaring a fact. And more with Kevin Mitchell wasn't going to be simple.

I touched my lips—still swollen and warm from his kiss. *Could I trust this man? Could I love again?* I'd never thought either was possible. The very idea made my chest tighten, not with dread this time, but with the faint, thrilling ache of possibility.

Trust wasn't just a word—it was an action. And I'd trusted very few in my lifetime. I'd loved once—deeply—and I wasn't sure I'd feel like that ever again. But Kevin…Kevin was forcing me to rethink everything.

What would love look like with Kevin Mitchell? His world was nothing like mine—that much had been painfully clear tonight. But the strange thing was, it didn't seem like it suited him that well either. I'd seen Kevin in my world—one he'd slipped right into and looked comfortable doing it. But his? The power-playing, cutthroat, business one—it wasn't a place I'd ever belong.

And yet asking him to walk away from a life he'd built, just because it wasn't one I could live in—that didn't feel right either.

28

Kevin

Kevin: You free tonight?

When it came to Maggie Bentley, I had no control. None. I couldn't look at her without the need to touch her. And I couldn't touch her without needing all of her. She wasn't just beautiful—her heart was twice the size of anyone's I knew. She was fearless. And being in her world made me want to stay. I liked who I was when I was with her, and more than that, I liked the idea of who I could become the longer I stayed.

I'd promised I'd give Maggie space, but ever since I walked out of her house, I couldn't stop thinking about that kiss. I wasn't used to wanting something so badly and not just taking it. Closing that door behind me, leaving her in the kitchen asking me to stay had been the single hardest thing I'd ever done. Not because I wouldn't have given my left arm to stay and devour every part of her, but because I had something to prove. It wasn't one kiss or one night I wanted.

I wanted everything. Her smile. Her trust. Her body. The woman had affected me like no other woman had. The way she looked at me when she thought I wasn't paying attention. I was *always* paying attention. But wanting it wasn't enough.

If I was ever going to be the man she deserved, something had to change. I wasn't there yet—but I would be. And all of that would begin or end with the city council vote.

I had a plan—one already in motion. It would take the better part of my morning and a few well-timed phone calls. If it all came together, Maggie Bentley just might believe in me. And if I were lucky…I might have a real shot at something more. Something extraordinary.

My morning had been productive.

All three phone calls had worked out exactly how I'd hoped. Quiet moves, nothing flashy, just outsmarting the opponent. Just enough to shake the ground under the Mitchell family machine. It was subtle. It was strategic, and I was relying heavily on the goodness of Hattrick Harbor and its people.

With renewed hope, I arrived at Maggie's door, anxious to see her.

I'd waited all damn day for this.

I didn't want to play it cool. I didn't want small talk. I just wanted to see her again—to be near her. My mind had played on a loop all day—her lips, her hands, the way she'd melted against me. And if she thought she could take up every corner of my mind since I'd left her house and get away with it—well, she was about to find out otherwise.

Yeah, I'd have to dig deep, summon every ounce of control to keep it in check. But I would. Because being with her was a hell of a lot better than *not* being with her.

So, when I arrived at her door, there was only one thing on my mind—

I knocked.

And waited.

Then, knocked again.

Finally, the door swung open—abrupt, fast.

I stood there, anticipation skyrocketing out of my chest as every thought wrapped around her.

But the moment I saw her face, everything inside me braked.

She wasn't smiling. She wasn't teasing. She looked pale, and her eyes—always so full of life—were clouded with something else. Fear. Panic.

"I need your help," she said with urgency.

The answer was instinctive. "Anything."

She left me standing on her porch and disappeared inside. Seconds later, she returned, pulling two large suitcases behind her.

"Put these in your truck." No explanation.

I didn't ask, I just grabbed the suitcases and put them in the bed of my truck, adrenaline already kicking in. Something was wrong, and whatever it was, she trusted me enough to help her.

When I slid into the driver's seat, she was already punching an address into the GPS. "I need you to take me here," she said quickly without looking up. "When we get there, I will need your help. I can answer your questions later."

I nodded, gripping the wheel. "Alright."

As we pulled away from her house, Maggie got to work on her phone, texting, making calls, and hanging up, frustrated when no one answered.

The drive was short, just on the other side of the lake.

Before we pulled into the driveway, Maggie turned to me, her voice controlled but clipped. "Please stop the car."

I hit the brakes. She looked down the driveway, then back at me.

"I'm not sure what we're walking into, but I have an idea. Try not to say anything, just follow my lead."

I didn't need answers. The tone in her voice and the look on her face said all I needed to know at the moment. It was the most serious I'd ever seen her. Whatever she needed from me, I was in.

I eased the truck down the gravel path and came to a small white house surrounded by trees—paint peeling, gutters sagging, porch leaning. In the front yard, a young man was picking up clothing being tossed from a second-story window.

Maggie unbuckled and jumped out. "Grab the suitcases," she said over her shoulder, "and start picking up those clothes."

I did exactly what she asked.

"You're not my problem anymore!" a woman yelled from the window.

I recognized the young man right away. Cody was the team's hockey captain and a student of Maggie's. He was kneeling on the front lawn, surrounded by T-shirts and socks. His body shook while clothing rained down around him.

"Where do you expect me to go?" he cried, his voice breaking.

Maggie didn't hesitate. She walked straight to him, knelt down, and gathered him in her arms, where he completely unraveled.

"Good," the woman sneered. "They can help you get this shit off my lawn."

I froze. Who the hell talked to a kid like that?

Maggie's eyes darted to the woman on the second floor and gave her a look I didn't know she was capable of—so cold, so sharp. If looks could kill, that evil woman would've dropped dead.

I handed Maggie a suitcase and got busy with the other, picking up underwear, jeans, and tennis shoes scattered across the lawn. The woman kept yelling vile, horrible things. Not just at Cody—some were aimed directly at Maggie.

Maggie caught my eye and shook her head. *Don't. Not worth it.*

"You're nothing but an orphan now," the woman screamed. "Don't ever come back, you hear?"

"You're pathetic," she spat, then cackled. "You have two minutes before I call the police."

Maggie had asked me to stay calm, but after another minute of that woman spewing filth, I couldn't take it any longer. I wasn't entirely sure what was happening here, but there was no fucking way I was going to stand around and let this woman say another word and make that young boy feel any worse than he already did. And *no one* was going to talk to Maggie like that. Not when I was around. I felt like a rubber band pulled too tightly, and I snapped.

"ENOUGH!" My voice cut like thunder, even surprising me. "If you say one more word, you're going to wish you hadn't." I pointed at her. "Go ahead and call the police. I'll be more than happy to give you a reason to."

The old hag just huffed and slammed the window shut.

The lawn went still. Both Maggie and Cody froze mid-suitcase stuffing, their wide eyes on me. They looked at me in shock, their mouths slightly ajar.

I cleared my throat, realizing I might've gone too far. "I'm sorry," I said. "I couldn't just stand here and let her talk to either of you like that."

Maggie quirked an eyebrow, and over the top of Cody's head, she gave a slight smile and mouthed the words *Thank you*.

We finished collecting everything in the front yard while Cody grew increasingly despondent by the minute, eyes glued to the ground. The same young man who skated fearlessly on the ice—the team's star player, who had hugged Maggie at the dance with a bright smile and talked about his college applications—now stood before us, six feet of solid muscle reduced to something small and fragile, clinging to Maggie like she was his lifeline.

Once we loaded the suitcases into the bed of my truck, I opened the back door for him and placed a hand on his shoulder as he stepped onto the running board and slumped into the back seat without a word.

Right before I put the truck in reverse, Maggie placed a hand on my wrist. Her soft eyes had turned to steel.

"Give me a minute?"

Before I could answer, she was already sliding out the door. Her feet hit the ground, she crossed the front yard in several quick strides, and climbed the porch's rickety steps. Then, with the side of her fist, she pounded on the front door. Hard.

I didn't wait. I was out of the truck in seconds and came up behind her. No way in hell was I going to let her confront this woman alone.

The door swung open, and the woman's eyes bore into Maggie, who didn't flinch once. In fact, she leaned in.

"You may not care what happens to Cody, but plenty of people do. That kid, in that car, has ten times more people who love him than you do. And just know this…" she leaned in further, past the threshold. "You didn't break him. You just showed him the kind of person he will *never* become."

Every time the woman went to open her mouth, Maggie stepped a little closer until she was inches from her face. When she tried to slam the door, I reached past Maggie and stopped it cold with my hand.

"She wasn't finished yet." I forced the words through gritted teeth.

Maggie jabbed a finger into the woman's chest. "If you ever try to contact Cody after today," she bit out, "I will have you arrested for harassment. Do you understand?"

The woman shoved against the door again, but I held it open and met Maggie's eyes. "Are you finished saying what you need to?"

Maggie didn't break eye contact with her. "One last thing."

She came nose to nose with the woman. "The health department will be here tomorrow. I see a minimum of three code violations right now—who knows what else they'll find."

Maggie stepped back, leering at the woman, giving no sign of fear or apology. The door finally slammed shut with no resistance from me.

I stood there for a second—stunned. Maggie Bentley just didn't protect the people she cared about. She fought like hell for them. Faced monsters for them. And kicked ass doing it. If I wasn't falling for her before, I sure as hell was now.

Before we got back in the truck, Maggie grabbed my elbow and faced me. Her eyes had turned soft again, pleading with me. "Kevin, do you mind if we change plans tonight?"

"Not at all, what do you have in mind?"

She glanced back at the truck, then spoke softly. "Can we take Cody to dinner? He turned eighteen today, and there's no way I can let him remember his birthday like this."

I swallowed the lump in my throat. "I think that's a great idea."

"Thank you."

I nodded and guided her toward the truck, helping her into the passenger seat. I circled around the front and climbed in beside her.

Maggie faced the young, broken boy in the back seat. "Cody, would you like to get dinner with us?"

He didn't respond—just stared out the window. After a long pause, he gave a small nod, then lay down across the back seat.

Maggie picked up my phone, programmed an address into Google Maps, and handed it back. Her eyes met mine, and I nodded. I didn't need the details—I knew she had a plan, and I'd follow her lead wherever it went.

Maggie's eyes, the same ones that lit up a room, were dim now. The joy that always radiated from them was missing, and it about broke me. I hated seeing her like this. I wanted nothing more than to shoulder her pain and carry it myself. Instinctively, I reached for her hand and gently squeezed. She didn't pull away.

I backed out of the driveway and started following the GPS. One left turn, then a right, and soon we were out of view of

Cody's house and the awful woman who undoubtedly changed his life forever.

About a mile down the road, Cody shot up in the back seat.

"Please pull over!" he shouted, already unbuckling and throwing the back door open.

I swerved onto the shoulder and barely made it over before Cody had two feet on the ground, running before I shifted into park.

"Kevin, get me a towel." Maggie ripped off her heels and took off after him.

I found a towel in the bed of my truck and a water bottle next to it.

Cody was doubled over in the weeds, heaving. Maggie was already beside him, rubbing circles on his back until he was done.

I made my way over and dropped beside them. Unscrewing the bottle, I handed it to him.

"Here you go, buddy."

"Thank you," he said with shaky hands. He took a drink, swishing it around in his mouth, and spat it out in front of him.

He stayed kneeling, hands pressed to the ground. "I'm sorry you had to see that," he said, deflated.

Maggie knelt in the dirt in front of him and gently placed her hands on Cody's trembling shoulders.

"Look at me, Cody," she said softly but firmly, lifting his chin with two fingers to face her.

Cody's eyes shifted for a second before they dropped again. His shoulders sagged, too heavy to lift, just like his heart. Every bit of fight this young boy had in him was gone.

What was left was a child—not yet a man—abandoned on his

eighteenth birthday, kneeling in the dirt, because the people who were supposed to care about him the most didn't give a damn.

It gutted me.

Here I was, next to a boy I barely knew, watching the most horrible moment in his life play out in front of me. And beside him, Maggie. Barefoot, tender, and unwavering. Comforting him, doing the right thing, saying the right words.

"You are not alone. You will *always* have me," she said.

He sobbed. "But Ms. B, where am I gonna go? I have no home. No family."

"You have me, and I will help you figure this out," she promised.

Cody hung his head, and Maggie quickly enveloped him in her arms, rocking his body as he continued to weep. I didn't know much about this boy, but I'd just watched his entire world fall apart. And I witnessed Maggie promise to help him pick up the pieces.

I placed my hand behind Cody's neck and bent down beside him. I didn't say a word, but with my steady hand, I squeezed to let him know I was there, too.

The three of us stayed like that for a long time. When he was ready and his eyes had dried, we climbed back into the truck. I knew Maggie was strong, but tonight I'd seen the size of her heart—and it damn near leveled me.

29

Kevin

We arrived at Antonio's thirty-one minutes later. Maggie had been texting the entire ride.

Antonio's was old-school Italian. The faded sign out front of the brick building almost looked like it might be a place you'd drive by and never think to stop. But inside, pictures of the Italian countryside hung on the walls, checkered tablecloths were on every table, an abundance of red wine was stocked, and the Italian flag was proudly displayed over the bar. No one knew about this place—you had to be *told* about it.

A short, round man with a thick mustache and a pressed white shirt stood at the hostess stand ready for us.

"Antonio!" Maggie said with a grin.

"Maggie!" He threw his arms out wide.

She walked right into them, like it was something they'd done a hundred times.

"Antonio," she said, when they pulled apart. "I'd like you to meet Kevin—and this is Cody." She glanced back at us as Cody and I came forward.

Antonio's eyes immediately softened when he saw Cody. "Happy Birthday, young man," he said, clapping a hand over his heart.

Cody managed a faint smile. "Thank you."

"I have your room ready—right this way," he said, gesturing for us to follow him.

Antonio led us down a long hallway—the smell of garlic and fresh bread trailing behind us—until he stopped in front of a set of double wooden doors. Maggie glanced at me with purpose in her eyes before she pushed them open.

"SURPRISE!"

The lights turned on, people jumped out, the music started playing, and everyone began singing. Cody froze in the doorway—unable to move, unable to blink, unable to comprehend exactly what was happening.

The room was decorated with birthday streamers, large bouquets of balloons in every corner, and a banner that read, "Happy Birthday Cody." Along the wall, a long table was piled high with wrapped presents. I saw Annie and Mike, Joy, Katie, Jules, and their husbands. Liam was there, and Parker was bouncing in his arms, clapping. Helen was also there, surrounded by her cornhole team, and many people I didn't even recognize.

Cody stood still, waiting for the singing to stop, staring, like his mind couldn't process that this was all *for him*.

Two of Cody's teammates, wearing their hockey jerseys, came up first, slapping him on the back and pulling him into a hug.

One by one, the rest of his team took their turn. Helen and her Hellions were next, their voices warm and welcoming.

Helen grabbed his cheeks. "Happy Birthday, kid."

Cody's lip trembled—he tried to hide it, but I saw it. This wasn't just a birthday party. It was a reminder that people cared about him.

While everyone was taking their turn wishing Cody a happy birthday, Maggie looked on.

How the hell did she pull this off? The room, the people, the balloons, the gifts—it was more than impressive. It was impossible. And yet, here it was.

Maggie Bentley moved mountains.

I'd spent years around people who had power—real power. People who could broker million-dollar deals over a good scotch. Developers who could change city skylines. Politicians who could swing a vote with one handshake and a favor. But none of them could hold a candle to the quiet force of this woman.

Watching her tonight...I just knew. I knew that this could very well be the most important relationship of my life.

And that's when it hit me all over again. This woman did more for other people in one day than most did in a week. Hell, she did more in one day than most people I knew did in a year.

She didn't do it for attention. She didn't do it for recognition. And she didn't do it to gain anything in return. She did it because that's who she was.

Maggie moved through the room—checking on Cody, hugging her best friends and their husbands, picking up Parker, and laughing with Liam. I was mesmerized. Everyone in that room was there because Maggie asked them to be. They all showed up for Cody—for no other reason than love.

I couldn't stand there and not compare what was playing out in front of me to the world I lived in. In Maggie's world, there were no agendas, no politics—just heart. In mine, everything was a transaction. Every smile had a reason behind it. Every favor came with strings attached. No one did anything without wanting something in return.

But here? There were no power plays. Just genuine people doing something kind for a kid who desperately needed to know people cared.

The two worlds couldn't be further apart.

And the more time I spent in hers, the more I wanted out of mine.

Maggie had a plan tonight—probably a few phone calls, maybe a few texts—and somehow *this* happened. Not because anyone owed her. Not because anyone wanted to climb the social ladder. They wanted to be here for her and for Cody.

And me? I couldn't peel my eyes away from her.

I was so caught up in watching her that all the buzz in the background faded, until it was only her voice that I heard, only her face that I saw. Hell, a damn bomb could've gone off in that room, and I would've stood in the same spot, unfazed.

This woman utterly disarmed me.

She had all of me—right there, without even knowing it.

"She's something else, isn't she?"

I had no idea how long Annie had been standing next to me, but I was caught red-handed, eyes locked on her best friend.

"She's a goddamn unicorn," I responded without thinking twice, admitting to her best friend that I was in way over my head.

"She sure is," she said with a sincere smile.

I hesitated, then asked the question that had been sitting in my chest for days.

"How do I compete with a ghost, Annie? With the memory of a man she loved that much?"

She looked at me, no judgment in her eyes. "You don't have to."

"I never met Joe, but I'll admit—I've done my research. The guy was practically a saint," I said, trying to keep it light. But even I recognized the jealousy in my own voice about a man who'd been taken too soon from the people who loved him most.

Annie didn't jump in right away. She let the silence settle.

"Joe was a great man, there's no doubt about it," she said. "But the girl who married Joe is not the same one you're staring at now."

She nodded toward Maggie. "He'd be proud as hell, but he wouldn't even recognize *this* Maggie."

I frowned. "What do you mean?"

"Joe worshiped the ground Maggie walked on. Treated her like fine china. And that's who she was back then—warm, careful, guarded. But she's grown into this fierce woman who has learned to stand on her own. Who learned how to carry pain without letting it drown her. She's got the same heart, but now, she's…different. Stronger. She doesn't need anyone saving her anymore—she needs someone fighting *with* her."

She continued. "Joe loved her so well. He made it his life's mission to protect her from anything that could ever hurt her again. And he did that until he couldn't anymore."

"She loved him for that," she added. "We all did."

Then, with a quiet breath, "But while he was everything she needed back then, in some ways it made her soft. Safe. The Maggie we know today? She's not looking for someone to shelter her. She's building something—and she needs someone to build it *with* her."

"Is that why she's so careful with people?" I asked quietly.

"That's not my story to tell," she said.

Annie and I locked eyes briefly, then she gave me a look—maybe a warning.

"And Kevin…"

"Yes?"

"You'll never get a chance if your father takes that land from her, and you stand by and let him do it."

That hit me hard.

"And one last thing," she added, her voice firm. "Trust is everything to Maggie. Prove you're worthy of that. You'll get one chance. If you blow it,"—she exhaled sharply—"you'll never get another."

She squeezed my forearm and walked back toward her husband, leaving me to wrestle with her words.

I dropped my head, knowing the task in front of me.

Because I knew exactly what I was up against. My father. Kristen. Two people who only fought harder and dirtier when threatened. They preferred a throwdown. When they smelled blood, they pounced.

But neither one of them knew what I was capable of when *I* had something to fight for.

30

Maggie

I just needed to breathe.

I pushed through the double doors and onto the patio. The air was cooler now. It was quiet out here. Woodsmoke filled the air like someone had a campfire nearby. Crickets chirped, and an owl hooted in the distance. I could smell the pine trees and feel the breeze coming from the lake, and for the first time all night, I could hear myself think.

It was a stark contrast to everything going on inside, where the volume level hovered somewhere between a Luke Bryan concert and a demolition derby. Leave it to the hockey moms to treat a quiet Italian restaurant like Friday night at the rink. If Joy started ringing her cowbell, I wouldn't be surprised.

I smiled despite myself, placed my hands on the wooden railing, and exhaled slowly.

One minute, I was furious, and the next, I was so heartbroken—so much it felt like my chest was going to crack in half. No matter how many times I helped a kid like Cody, no matter how many times I witnessed a teenager face the worst day of their life, it never got easier. It was always personal. The fury never subsided, and the heartbreak stayed the same.

Every. Single. Time.

I saw the exact moment Cody realized he had nothing—no one. Eighteen years old, months from graduation, no money, no job, and not an adult in the world responsible for him.

The one person who should have loved him the most had left him years ago, and the people who had sworn to protect him had failed, too.

I watched that knowledge hit him, watched the light fade from his eyes. The day his childhood ended. The day everything changed. And that was something that had stayed with me.

The fury should have numbed the emptiness inside me, but it never did.

"I had a feeling you'd be out here." A voice that had become so familiar in such a short amount of time cut through the darkness.

I turned toward Kevin, and all I could think about was the way he stood beside me today—without question, without hesitation. He was heartbroken, too—I saw it in his eyes.

I wasn't sure Cody ever had someone stick up for him like Kevin did today. Sure, his teammates had his back on the ice, but this was different. It was real life. When Kevin had yelled at Cody's foster mom, Janet, and threatened to call the police if she'd said one more word, I could've run over and hugged him—kissed him.

Then, when he stood behind me while I gave Janet a piece of

my mind, he didn't step in or interrupt. He just stood there letting me fight for Cody. Letting me say what I needed to.

Weeks ago, Cody's teammates approached me with their concerns. He'd been doing his laundry at the rink because his foster family wouldn't let him use the washer at home. The team even took up a collection for socks and underwear because he didn't have more than a few pairs. Janet had stopped feeding him—he'd been surviving on school lunches and dinners with the Dentons after practice.

No kid should ever have to live like that.

I'd never understand the foster care system, which was broken in more ways than I could count.

I knew Kevin had questions—dozens of them—but he kept them to himself. He was giving me space and wasn't pressing me for details, but I probably owed him some.

Part of the reason I needed to step outside was because of watching Cody tonight face the worst day of his life. But there was another reason, and he was standing a few feet in front of me.

Kevin Mitchell.

The man who stood on the other side of the land I desperately needed. Land that could help kids like Cody and give them a place to belong. A place to call home.

He wasn't just standing in front of me—he was standing between everything I wanted and everything I couldn't lose.

I was still sorting it all—Cody, the land, Kevin—when I felt him move a little closer.

He didn't say anything at first. Just stood beside me at the railing, close enough that I heard the quiet steadiness of his breath. Close enough that a slow calm seeped in.

"He's going to be okay, you know?"

I turned to him. "How do you know?"

"Because he has you," Kevin said.

My heart fluttered.

He wasn't looking at me when he said it. He kept his eyes on the darkness, hands resting beside mine on the railing. Like he knew that looking straight at me would undo me. He didn't crowd me, didn't push.

"Thank you for helping tonight," I said quietly.

He glanced over. "I was just your backup. You were the storm."

That made me smile. "You were a little more than backup."

He moved and, without thinking twice, pulled me into his arms. For half a second, I forgot how to breathe—and then I went easily, sinking into him like my body had been waiting all night to do just that.

My cheek rested against his chest, right over his heart, and I closed my eyes. The steady beat beneath my ear was slow and gentle, making me temporarily forget that everything tonight had broken my heart in a hundred different ways.

Kevin's arms were strong, wrapped around me like he had no intention of letting go. And mine stayed tucked against his chest, folded between us. His chin rested on top of my head, and after a quiet minute, when he leaned back to look at me, I felt like maybe things would be okay.

Because he saw me. Every part of me. The part that fought, the part that cried, the part that was trying to hold it together. And he never looked away once.

His arms anchored me. They didn't make me feel weak or incapable—they just reminded me that I didn't have to be strong all the time.

But as the calm settled in, the question that had haunted me since he kissed me in the kitchen crept back in: *Could I fall for a man who came from a world I was fighting against?*

Before either of us spoke, Annie cleared her throat.

"I'm sorry to interrupt, but it's time for cake and presents. I didn't think you'd want to miss it." Annie winked before she went back through the door.

The next hour passed in a blur—cake, ice cream, presents, and more love than Cody knew what to do with. He'd never had a birthday party before, so this was all new to him. Liam and Parker gave him a Panthers jersey, Helen crocheted a blanket, and Annie and Mike gave him a pair of AirPods. He opened each gift like he couldn't quite believe they were all for him.

The Dentons were giving Cody the extra bedroom at their house. He'd be staying with his best friend and teammate as long as he needed to.

A weight had been lifted off my chest—for now.

One by one, I thanked my friends and hugged them as they said goodbye. Joy paused at the door and gave me a not-so-subtle nudge.

"Why does he always look like he's ready to star in a cologne ad?" she muttered. "It's rude, honestly."

"Joy," I warned, already smiling.

"I'm just saying, if he's planning to stick around, tell him to tone it down. Some of us are married and trying to behave."

"Goodnight, Joy."

I laughed, watching her waltz out the door. When the dust finally settled, and the last of the presents had been piled into the Dentons' car along with the two suitcases, it was just me and Kevin.

The restaurant was quiet, and the lights were dim. The waitstaff were busy popping balloons.

Kevin's hand slid into his pocket, his eyes never leaving mine. "You can tell me you're fine all you want, Maggie, but I don't believe you."

I blinked.

"I've watched you all night," he added. "Your smile is the same. But your eyes? They tell me a different story." He paused, letting his words settle. "I'm not going to press if there's something you can't tell me or if you're not comfortable telling me. I'll respect that. But I need you to know whenever you're ready, I'm here. For whatever you need."

I didn't have words for him. But I offered something else.

"Do you want to take a ride?" I asked.

His brow lifted slightly. "Sure."

We walked quietly to Kevin's truck. He opened the door for me, stepping back so I could climb in.

"Where to?" he asked.

Our eyes met.

"Take me to the farm."

31

Kevin

The old Taylor Farm.

Acres and acres of untamed land stretched out in front of us, once thriving now forgotten and neglected.

Maggie and I sat on the bed of my truck, shoulder to shoulder, taking in the land that, at first glance, seemed like a lost cause—a broken-down tractor, a barn that tilted a little too far to the left, half-dead trees with broken limbs, and a *No Trespassing* sign we clearly ignored.

This land…it was the very thing that had brought us together, and the very thing that stood between us.

It had been one hell of a day. All I wanted was to pull her onto my lap, tuck her head under my chin, and hold her until the weight she carried didn't feel so heavy anymore. But Maggie had asked me here for a reason, and I figured she had something she wanted to say.

So, I waited.

Hell, I'd wait all night if I had to because I was content just being near her.

Silence with her was comforting. The air was still, and the smell of dirt, grass, and the lake filled my lungs. I took another breath, this time deeper, like I couldn't get enough of it. No exhaust fumes, no city grit—just clean, honest air that made me want to stay a while. I inhaled it, cleansing my city lungs—out with the mess and in with the kind of peace that felt more like her.

"Thank you for bringing me here," Maggie said, her voice low, almost fragile. Her shoulders sagged like everything that had happened had finally caught up to her—but there was something else, too. I saw it in her eyes—something that looked an awful lot like contentment.

"Whatever it is you're going through, don't think for a second you have to go through it alone," I said.

Silence settled in again before she spoke.

"Tell me what you see here," she questioned me, her eyes fixed on the darkness ahead.

I tore my eyes away from her and looked out at the property. Most people would see an empty field covered in waist-high weeds. A barn with broken stalls and a sliding door hanging crooked off its track, and an old farmhouse that looked so abandoned it made people wonder how anyone could've lived there in the first place.

That's what *most people* would see.

But I wasn't "most people." Not when I was sitting next to a woman who made me see things differently. A woman who changed the way I breathed just because she existed.

"I see a place that makes you breathe easier," I said, and the reality of that settled deep in me.

She turned her head toward me. Her mouth, the one I couldn't seem to stop thinking about, curved into a hint of a smile.

"You want to know what *I* see?"

I nodded. "Tell me."

"I see a garden right there in that field—one that could grow sweet potatoes, tomatoes, and cucumbers, maybe pumpkins in the fall—possibly a row of fruit trees in the back. I see the barn fixed up with stalls full of boarded horses. And that farmhouse…" Maggie pointed toward the house with broken shutters. "I see a house full of kids like Cody who would have a place to call their own."

Her eyes stayed on the property like she could already see it alive and full of color. The massive undertaking never once dissuaded her. She wasn't thinking about the enormous amount of work she'd be responsible for—she was thinking about the farm's possibility.

But if my father got his way, it would all be destroyed. Bulldozed. Blown up. Dismantled, right down to the very last fence post, and replaced with concrete, flashing lights, and slot machines.

That's what brought *him* peace.

Maggie's dream would no longer be a possibility. And that's when I realized this wasn't just about saving part of her town, and it was more than saving a piece of land—it was personal.

She kept her gaze fixed on the dark outline of the barn, her hands gripping the tailgate of my truck. A slow tear leaked from the corner of her eye, catching the faint glow of the moon, and before I had a chance to reach for it, she wiped it away.

I leaned in slightly, keeping my voice low. "Maggie…why is this so personal for you?"

Not pushing. Not demanding. Just asking because I needed

to understand. Because I cared. This woman had become all I could think about in such a short amount of time. She filled every corner of my mind—at the office, in the gym, even at home—lingering in my subconscious, no matter where I was. The more I was around her, the more I found myself reaching for a life with her in it.

She didn't answer right away. Her eyes stayed on the barn, lost in thought. When she finally spoke, her voice was quiet and steady. "Because I was Cody."

The words hung there, heavy in the still night air.

I knew that Maggie and Joe had basically adopted four boys who had aged out of foster care. Raised them with the twins as if they were their own. Shit, I'd heard their stories on YouTube. But I'd never once considered that Maggie had lived it. I thought she and Joe had found a cause and threw their support behind it. Now, I knew better. There *was* a story behind it. *Her* story. My heart didn't just break for her—something deeper cracked.

I didn't say anything—just waited. I watched her carefully weigh her next words, wondering whether or not she could trust me with whatever she was going to share.

"I went into foster care when I was ten. On my eighteenth birthday, my foster parents locked me out of the house. I came home from school, and my key no longer worked. Two trash bags of everything I owned were left on the front porch with a note that said, 'Good luck.' That was it. I had no money. No plan. I was months away from graduation, and suddenly…I had nothing."

Her words hit me like a body blow I never saw coming. I'd watched Cody go through it hours ago, and now I was hearing that she'd lived the same damn thing. My body thrummed with rage.

Fury ripped through me so fast I had to unclench my fist before I broke something. I wanted names. I wanted addresses. I wanted to find the people who thought throwing an eighteen-year-old Maggie out on the street with a couple of garbage bags was acceptable—and make them regret it. Make them wish they'd never taken another breath.

At the same time, I was momentarily blindsided by this urge to protect her and hold her so damn tight that nothing bad could ever hurt her again. Fury and love—two emotions I wasn't used to feeling at the same time—slammed into me like an avalanche. And right then, I knew I'd do whatever it took to make sure she'd never feel that kind of abandonment again.

I stayed quiet, letting her have the space to breathe. Then, without even thinking about it, I reached over and hooked my pinky around hers. It wasn't much, but enough to let her know I was there, that I was listening, and whatever came next was safe with me.

She glanced down at our hands, then back toward the darkness. I felt the smallest squeeze against my finger, and that was all I needed to know that she was ready to keep going.

I steadied myself.

"I had nowhere to go. No one to call. Except for my guidance counselor, Mrs. Davis."

Her voice softened. "She didn't even hesitate. Came to get me that night, helped me load the garbage bags in her car, and took me back to her house. She gave me her extra bedroom, and for the next four years, her house was a place I called home."

Maggie's mouth lifted at the memory, just barely. "Between my good grades and Mrs. Davis, I got a full scholarship to State

College. If it hadn't been for her, I don't know what would've happened to me."

I watched her for a minute, then entwined our fingers. If I couldn't have her in my lap, I needed to be touching more than just her pinky, so I held her whole hand and held on tight. "And that's where you met Joe?"

Her eyes met mine. "Yeah, that's where I met Joe."

Her smile was soft and wistful—the thought alone was enough to warm her.

"Do you want to talk about him?" I swallowed the jealousy. I was asking the woman I was pretty sure I was falling for about the man who had loved her first—and loved her well.

She was quiet. Her gaze still fixed on the outline of the old farmhouse. "Joe changed my life in so many ways. He gave me everything I never had growing up—a family, a home, security. For the first time, I knew what it felt like to belong somewhere. To someone."

If it was possible to be jealous and grateful for a man who was no longer alive, I was. My emotions were taking a beating tonight, and my heart was getting a workout. Not only was she abandoned as a child—twice—but she also lost the one man who gave her everything she never had.

Maggie turned around to face me, the silver moonlight making her goddamn breathtaking.

I'd never met Joe, but I knew enough to know he'd been a good man—exactly the kind she deserved. A part of me wished I'd been the one to give her all that, but more than anything, I was grateful she'd had him when she needed him most. And sitting here with her, I couldn't shake the thought that I wanted to be that for her now. The man she could count on.

She looked back toward the field, her voice softer. "That's why this farm matters, Kevin. Kids like Cody…kids like me… they don't get second chances unless someone gives it to them. This place could be that second chance. A home. A fresh start. A place where they know they matter…*Hope Farm.*"

Her hand tightened slightly around mine. "I had Mrs. Davis. I had Joe. But not everyone does. And if I lose this farm, I lose the chance to be that for someone else."

Damn it. This woman was a firestorm to my heart. Every time I thought I'd reached the depth of how much I could feel for Maggie Bentley, she cracked herself open a little more—and I fell harder. She was strength and softness. Beauty and heart. And I was completely undone by it all.

Right then, I made myself a promise. Whatever it took— whatever lines I had to cross or bridges I had to burn—I'd make damn sure she won that council vote.

Her head turned slightly, and our eyes met in the soft wash of the moon. No words. Just a small, almost ghost of a smile before she rested her head on my shoulder.

It wasn't much. But it was everything. And it was enough to tell me I'd fight like hell for her.

This just became personal to me.

When she lifted her head, our eyes locked. I lifted my hand and let my knuckles brush gently along her cheek, feeling her breath shudder beneath my touch.

"Maggie," I said quietly, "it's my turn to show you something now."

32

Maggie

Once Kevin started driving and we left the farm, he reached over and took my hand. He didn't say anything—just lifted it to his mouth and pressed a kiss to the inside of my wrist, right where the skin was soft and sensitive. A slow warmth curled through my chest and into my throat so fast I couldn't swallow past it.

I knew I was about to cross a line I had drawn in the sand. One I hadn't planned on crossing until the deal had been settled on the farm. But when he looked at me, every clear thought I had started to slip. Boundaries I'd put in place with good reason suddenly didn't feel so necessary. That was the dangerous part. Not his hand in mine or the way he looked at me—but how easy it was to need more of him.

I didn't know where we were going, but I didn't ask. I didn't care. The way his thumb brushed over my knuckles, the way the night wrapped around us—I let myself follow him. Maybe blindly. But there was something about being with Kevin, sitting at the farm tonight, that made the unknown a little less scary.

And the kiss we shared…it hadn't left me. It lived somewhere between my pulse and my thoughts, replaying every time he got close. It was the kind of kiss that the memory didn't fade and my body was fully aware of it. And even now, with his fingers laced through mine, I could still feel it. The softness. The heat. The way he left me wondering and wanting more.

As we wound our way through the backcountry roads until the trees thinned, we came upon a sleek iron gate. Kevin punched in a code, and it swung open without a sound. The driveway curved through a dense patch of woods before opening up to a house that looked like it belonged on the cover of a high-end architecture magazine. All clean lines and sharp edges. The landscape was just as meticulous—low, sculpted shrubs lined the house, beds mulched with precision, and not a weed in sight.

"We're here," Kevin said quietly.

He kissed the top of my hand, then came around to open the passenger door.

"This is where I live." He guided me toward the front door with a steady hand on my lower back. The large steel door opened, and he let me step inside first.

He'd followed me to the farm without any question, so I figured I owed him the same respect. I didn't know why he'd brought me here, but I trusted that he'd had a reason.

"Just so you know, I've got an Airtag on my key ring, in case you plan on kidnapping me or locking me in your basement," I said.

Kevin's grin tugged at the corner of his mouth while he studied me. "One, I don't have a basement. And two…" He tossed his keys on the table in his entryway. "Never tell a kidnapper you have an Airtag."

"Good point," I conceded.

I wandered through the living room, letting my fingertips trail along the leather sofa. The inside of Kevin's house mirrored the outside of it—sleek, modern, masculine. Sexy, even. Industrial lighting, wide-planked, wood floors, and palettes of gray on every surface—the walls, the furniture, the framed artwork. Everything was high-end, but not flashy.

It was spotless—impressive, yet expected. I absorbed every detail and committed it to memory. It was all so…Kevin. Controlled. Strong. Intentional. I believed I could learn a lot about someone from their home, and this place—while beautiful—told me just how carefully he kept his life in order. It didn't feel like a Mitchell lived here.

He watched me closely, as if trying to gauge my reaction.

"Tell me what you see," he asked, still trailing behind me with his hands in his pockets, content to let me wander.

"It all makes sense," I said.

"What's that?"

"Your house."

He tilted his head, waiting.

"It feels like you," I added softly. "Separate from work. From your family. I get the feeling that *this* is where *you* breathe easier."

He didn't say anything. He watched me, his brow lifted like maybe he wasn't expecting me to read him that easily. Or maybe he was—and that's why he asked.

A low sigh escaped his lips as he settled back against the wall, arms folded, his eyes tracking my every move.

"Yeah," he said, his voice low and even.

He tried to smile, but he was also unnerved that I saw him so clearly. I didn't need to walk through his house to understand what kind of man Kevin Mitchell was. I saw it in the way he treated Cody, the way he listened to me at the farm, and the anger in his eyes when I told him part of my story. I was inexplicably drawn to him, and the more of him I saw, the harder it was to pretend I hadn't fallen at all.

"How long have you lived here?" I tilted my head, my voice soft but curious.

Kevin eased off the wall, watching me like he was weighing how much to give away.

"When Kristen and I divorced," he said, "I needed to start over. I built this house. Purposefully, away from my family. Away from…everything."

His eyes never left mine.

"You're the first woman I've ever brought here."

That pulled me upright. "Why's that?"

"Why do you think, Maggie?"

I wasn't prepared for that confession. But the way he looked at me—like he was letting me see a part of him no one else had—made everything shift. My pulse quickened. Not because I was nervous, but because of something I longed for.

"Don't do that. Don't answer my question with your own question. Why haven't you brought another woman here before, Kevin?"

His expression sobered, replaced by something deeper—heat, honesty, hesitation. "I've never felt like sharing this space with anyone."

"And why me?"

I wanted to know what he was thinking—what he was feeling. It had been a really shitty day, but one of the unexpected bright spots was how Kevin made me feel. I'd tried to hold back, keep him at arm's length, never fully giving in. But I didn't want to do that anymore. Not tonight.

He took a step closer, and every rioting emotion inside me went still. Being near him had begun to have that effect. No longer was I nervous or scared. When he came near me now, I didn't think about fear—I thought about *what if…*

"Are you the only one who gets to ask questions tonight?" His voice was warm under the gravel, wrapping around me instead of cutting through.

Another step. The air thickened between us.

My eyes stayed trained on him, waiting for an answer.

"Because I've never known anyone like you," he said, quieter now. "Tonight, you trusted me with something personal. This is me trusting you."

He glanced around the room. "This is where I come to think. I shut out the noise. I step away from being my father's son. This place is mine…and I wanted you to see it. I wanted to see you in it."

Well, that did it.

I didn't care that his last name was Mitchell. I knew he was on my side, knew who he was when his family wasn't watching. I saw it tonight. I trusted Kevin, and that was enough for me.

He was inches away now. The heat from his body fired through me in a way that left no doubt. Being around Kevin made me feel alive again—like the part of me that was shut down had come back to life.

My hand moved first. I reached up, fingers brushing the button of his shirt, rubbing it between my thumb and forefinger—bold and unafraid.

His hands slid to my waist, warm and strong, then he drew me in until our bodies were chest to chest and hip to hip. He lowered his head, his cheek grazing mine in a slow, almost reverent way. I closed my eyes, letting the scratch of his stubble tease me as his hands settled low on my back.

I inhaled. Cedar and pine and something darker—strong, masculine—rushed through me, leaving no place untouched. He was intoxicating.

My hand tugged gently at the fabric of his shirt, guiding his mouth toward me. His lips brushed my throat—so faintly I opened my eyes to make sure it was real. When his mouth moved lower, slower this time, my breath shuddered, and a tremor ran through me.

"Kevin," I whispered, his name tumbling out, soft and desperate. "Please, don't pull away this time."

His teeth nipped my shoulder, and desire ripped through me like a switch had been thrown.

He eased the thin strap of my dress aside, his mouth finding the bare skin. Every kiss was slower than the last, lingering like he couldn't stop himself. Each touch left my body humming, aching for more, and by the time he finally slid the strap back into place and stood to his full six feet, his eyes were molten, hungrier than I'd ever seen them.

My pulse pounded in my ears. I couldn't wait another second. My hands slid up, tangling in his hair, and I pulled him to me. The decision was mine—bold, inevitable.

The kiss was soft at first—testing, tasting. I matched his rhythm, moving with him, until need overpowered caution and we lost control completely. Our tongues collided, the heat spiked, and the kiss turned fast and hungry. We couldn't get close enough or survive without the other.

A low sound came from his throat—part growl, part groan— and whatever it was, it worked on me like a match to gasoline. My arms wrapped around his neck, pulling him tighter, until there was no air left between us. His hand gripped my ass, firmly, possessively, and I gasped against his mouth.

I wanted him. All of him.

His hands roamed, like he was learning, memorizing the shape of me. His mouth was urgent as if I were the only thing that would satisfy him. It wasn't just passion—it was deeper than that. A fire that had been smoldering between us was now blazing out of control with every heartbeat.

But…then…

Kevin abruptly broke the kiss, stepping back like he'd been burned. His chest rose and fell quickly as he laced his fingers and placed them on top of his head. He blew out a sharp exhale. I stood there stunned, lips tingling, heart stammering, caught somewhere between confusion and craving.

"What's the matter?" My body was still humming from the way his mouth devoured mine, and I felt the empty space immediately.

Kevin stepped back another foot, his hands still on top of his head like he was holding himself together by sheer will. His voice was hoarse, strained. "I don't have much strength left around you."

"Why do you keep pulling away from me?" My voice cracked from uncertainty. "You've kissed me like you meant it. Twice. And both times you stopped like you regretted it."

His jaw tightened, eyes locked on mine. "Regret it? God, no. But this…" he motioned between us, "this would be me taking advantage of you, and I won't do that."

I blinked, heart pounding. "Taking advantage of me?"

"Yes. You've been through a lot today, Maggie. This isn't what you need right now."

"And how do you know what I need?" I shot back, daring him to look away.

His hand dropped to his side, fingers twitching like he couldn't decide to reach for me or bolt—except this was his house, and he had nowhere to go. "When this happens," he said, his voice tight, "I don't want you to feel like it was a mistake."

My pulse plummeted. "Do you think it would be a mistake?"

Maybe I'd gotten it all wrong. Maybe I wanted something that wasn't supposed to be mine. I stood in front of Kevin and basically gave him the green light. But he was quiet, and I couldn't figure out if he was trying to protect me or let me down easy.

He stared at me. "I'm trying to do the right thing here, Maggie."

"And this is the wrong thing, why?"

He didn't answer. Just stood there watching me, his chest rising and falling in sharp, heavy waves while the space burned so hot that standing still was torture.

"Look, if you don't want this to happen because it's not what you want, that's different," I said. "But you don't get to stand there and tell me it's not what *I* want or that it's not good for me."

I'd never been that bold before, but I wasn't backing down. Not after tonight. My heart was already tangled up in his, and I needed to know where he stood—even if it shattered whatever fragile thing was between us.

If I'd misread everything, if I was wrong about him, then I'd walk away.

I waited. Nothing.

So I turned to go—

And that's when Kevin caught my waist—stopping me cold.

He didn't move. Didn't speak. Just held me there, his breath warm against my hair, and I waited again…

My back to him, my pulse climbing so high it hurt to swallow. He didn't say a word, just hovered over me, the heat of his body at my back.

A long exhale left him, hot against my neck. "You think I'm not interested?" he paused, his voice gravelly and low as it rippled straight through me. "Do you know how many times I've come home from being with you and how many cold showers I've had to take?"

Oh, I was listening now. Every inch of me.

He pulled me in even closer, his hand trailing up my arm to my shoulder before gently turning me to face him. His eyes searched mine, like he needed proof I was real.

"Do you have any idea how many times I've pictured you in my house?" he asked, barely above a whisper. "Bringing you here. Having you in my bed. I work in that office—I picture you on my desk. I cook dinner, and I think about all the things I would do to you on this counter. I've pictured you and me in every room of this damn house."

He slid his hand up to cup my cheek, thumb tracing the curve of my skin before settling on my jaw.

"Every time I walk through that door, I see you."

His touch drifted lower, his fingers grazed the column of my throat. I tipped my chin up, offering him more of me.

And that's when I moved.

I reached behind me and unzipped my dress, then slipped one strap off my shoulder—slowly. His hand stilled at my neck, and his lips parted with a sharp exhale. His gaze followed the fabric as it slid over my shoulder. Then the other strap. The silk skimmed down my arms until the dress pooled at my feet.

I stepped into him, our bodies flush.

"Are you going to make me put that back on?" I asked, breathless.

His entire body clenched.

And then he moved.

33

Kevin

Maggie Bentley stood in my kitchen in black lace, mile-high heels, and her dress around her ankles. She was all but telling me to take her.

There was no way she had to ask twice.

I closed whatever distance was left between us, not giving my brain a second to overthink it. I'd wanted Maggie Bentley in my bed the second I'd met her. The only difference between now and then was that now, I wanted her heart, too.

"You're breathtaking," I sighed, taking her face with both hands. I'd been holding back for her. Out of respect. Telling myself she'd been through enough today, that the last thing she needed was me pushing her into something too soon. But every second I stood there, the restraint felt like a noose around my neck.

Then, she looked at me—like she could take me apart piece by piece—and I knew I was done holding back. Whatever restraint I'd been clinging to snapped, and I stopped thinking altogether.

I claimed her mouth with mine as urgency took hold. When she groaned, I responded with my own, making me so damn desperate that I was close to losing my ever-loving shit. My hands slid into her hair, tangling the silky strands around my fingers as I tilted her head enough to deepen the kiss. She tasted so damn good that I needed more.

Her fingers fisted in my shirt until every inch of her was plastered against me, her curves molding perfectly to mine. I angled her back, swallowing every muffled sound she made until I couldn't separate her need from my own, only that I was drowning in the taste and feel of her with no intention of coming up for air.

My pulse went from zero to a hundred, and I felt her breathing quicken under my touch. Every brush of her body against mine, every sound that came from her mouth, made it harder to keep control.

The intensity between us vibrated, and the electricity that drew us together was addictive. One thing was perfectly clear—having Maggie one time would never be enough, and that scared the hell out of me. But I was going to take whatever small piece she was willing to give me because never having her scared me more.

Nothing else mattered. Take my job. Take my house. Fuck the family name. I could lose it all and wouldn't care—so long as she was still standing there, looking at me like that.

Maggie Bentley was worth it all.

My hands slid lower, lifting her off the ground. She let out a breathy sound—half surprise, half desire—as her legs wrapped behind my back, and her arms locked around my neck.

"Goddammit, Maggie…" My voice was already wrecked, more of a growl than any comprehensible word.

Her chest pressed to mine, the soft curve of her breasts burning through the thin fabric of my shirt. I carried her a few steps to the counter and set her down, pulling her to the edge as she wrapped her legs around my waist, locking me in. My palms gripped her, unable to stand the thought of letting go.

She shifted, and the friction made my control strain to the breaking point. A slight frown ghosted across her lips when she realized how much I'd wanted her.

"You're playing with fire," I warned, though my hands were already sliding over her hips and had no intention of stopping.

I chased her mouth for another taste before giving in and letting my forehead fall to hers. My chest heaved uneven, her warmth against my lips made it impossible to think about anything else.

"I have one question for you."

"If you're asking me to put my dress back on, the answer is no."

I ignored that—mostly because that never entered my mind. "Hard and fast or soft and slow the first time?" I quirked an eyebrow.

"First time?" she asked, her lips curving.

"I told you last time I kissed you. You'd better block off the entire evening because if you think this is happening only once tonight…" I let out a huff. "You'd better think again."

She laughed softly, a breath's distance between us. "Then we'd better get to it. I have a meeting in the morning."

My mouth reclaimed hers, deeper this time. As my thumbs grazed her hardened nipples through the thin lace, she trembled, and I drank in every reaction, taking a mental note of what made her shudder under my touch.

I'd thought about this—hell, I'd played it out in my head more times than I'd admit—and now I finally had her. I could've rushed it, taken everything in one greedy, uncontrollable sweep, but not tonight. Not with her.

I eased Maggie back onto the counter, her hair spilling over the edge, and took my time running my hands down the curves of her body. Every inch was mine to explore, and I planned on taking my damn good time.

"Fucking flawless," I murmured, "and totally *mine*."

I let my palms glide over the black lace, down the smooth planes of her stomach, lower still. Her back arched in response, and the sound of my name left her lips like she'd been made to say it.

"Maggie," I warned with a low growl, "just so you know…I don't have neighbors. And when you say my name, I fucking want to hear it."

Her lips curled into a wicked little smile. I hooked my thumbs on that lacy roadblock and tugged, watching the rhythm of her body change under the touch of my hands. I already knew I'd be keeping score tonight, finding every way possible to wring my name from her soft lips.

Challenge accepted.

I'd lost track of how many times she'd said my name. Instead, the only thing I kept track of was how many rooms we'd hit, making damn sure she saw every bit of my house. I wanted to walk into any room when she wasn't there and see her, feel her, remember how she looked—hair tumbling down her back, lips swollen, and her green eyes locked on mine like she'd never wanted anything more, begging me not to stop.

Once she'd fallen asleep, I made sure she never left my arms. I'd stayed awake another hour just watching her—the way our bodies were entwined, feeling her heart beat next to mine. I knew I'd never been more content. Then, I closed my eyes and had the best sleep of my life.

Hours later, when I woke and the morning light began to seep through my bedroom window, I let myself really admire her. Her skin—cashmere soft. Her body—smooth and lean. The sheet had slipped low, giving me just the briefest glimpse, making my pulse climb. But I had learned, Maggie wearing clothes or not, my body reacted the same way. And lying there with her naked body next to mine made it damn near impossible to remember why I'd thought keeping my hands to myself was a good idea.

Last night, our bodies moved perfectly in sync as if we'd done this a hundred times, yet every touch was new. The way she'd looked beneath me, the way she'd said my name, it all played on repeat. How was I supposed to do anything productive today when a flood of memories overtook every corner of my mind?

My body begged for an encore performance.

But I had important work to do today. Last week, there had been closed-door meetings between my dad and Kristen. Meetings I hadn't known about. When confronted, my dad had replied that they were discussing "the legalities of the zoning commission." At the time, it didn't seem out of the ordinary, but it still didn't sit right with me. Nothing they did sat right with me.

Before the first city council meeting, my father had rarely been in the office. But lately, he'd been staying later than even I did. It didn't take a genius to figure out that he and Kristen were up to something. It looked like desperation. Lines had already been drawn with the city council members. Sides had been chosen. Maggie had the edge. It was all over except the gavel pounding.

This nightmare would all be over soon. Maggie was going to get her farm, and I was going to get my shot at something more with her. This time tomorrow, the farm would be Maggie's.

It took everything in me to slip out of bed instead of waking Maggie, stealing her lips all over again. She was tangled in the sheets, the early light spilling across her body, and for a moment, I almost stayed.

But reality was waiting.

I showered fast, dressed, and made my way to the kitchen. While the coffee pot dripped, I grabbed my phone for the first time all weekend—forty-three new emails since Friday and multiple missed calls from my father and Kristen.

A knot formed in my gut before I even started scrolling.

Halfway down the list one subject line jumped out. Harbor Banking: Immediate Action.

Not familiar. Not good.

I opened it—and froze. Fred Cummings. The name hit like a punch. *Loan Application…Privacy blocked…Second Mortgage.*

Sweat prickled at the back of my neck. My pulse started to climb, sharp and fast. The email wasn't addressed to me—it was sent to my father. I was blind copied. Why the hell was my father getting a private email about Fred Cummings' financial updates?

I stared at the screen, coffee forgotten. The walls felt like they were closing in. The morning light suddenly too bright.

The clear answer here was that there was no good reason.

Maggie couldn't know. Not yet. Not until I figured out what was going on. Telling her would drag her straight into Conrad and Kristen's crossfire, and I couldn't let that happen. This was my problem to fix.

I shut off the phone, the screen going black, my reflection staring back at me.

My day just got a hell of a lot more complicated. Less than twenty-four hours until the vote—and now a secret that could blow everything apart

Not after last night.

Not after Maggie was beginning to trust me.

Not after I started to believe I could be worthy of her.

I made my way back to my bedroom and leaned against the doorframe. And stared.

God damn Maggie looked good in my bed.

Her hair was splayed across my pillow, her lips parted enough to make every muscle in my body tighten. It took everything I had not to climb back in, wrap her body around mine, and erase the world outside this room. For one selfish second, I almost did.

But the world was already knocking, loudly.

She stirred, eyes fluttering open, a sleepy smile tugged at her mouth. The sight of her—the bare shoulder and tousled hair, my sheets wrapped around her—slammed into me. I wanted this. Her. All of it.

She shifted, propped herself up on her elbows, her bare shoulder visible in a way that made my pulse jackhammer.

"Morning," she mumbled, her voice still warm from sleep.

"Morning, beautiful." I crossed the room and leaned in for

one small kiss, then handed her a mug.

She rested against the headboard and took the cup with both hands. "Thank you."

"I'm sorry I have to leave," I said, the lie already bitter on my tongue. "Something came up at the office that I need to take care of. You can stay as long as you want. In fact, if you want to stay in that same spot until I get back, I'd be perfectly fine with that."

Her brows lifted. "Work meeting?"

I hesitated, because what I had to say next mattered. "I know we haven't talked lately about the city council vote, but…I need you to know, I am going to try like hell to help you."

She stilled, and her fingers gripped the mug a little harder.

"I know trust doesn't come easy for you, Maggie," I said softly. "But I'm asking you to go out on a limb here and trust me."

She didn't answer. Just watched me over the rim of her cup, quiet and unreadable.

I moved to the side of the bed and crouched down, so we were eye level. "I know what the land means to you. I just…need you to know that trust might look a little different than you think it would."

Her eyes searched mine like there was some kind of catch.

"I'm asking you to trust me," I said again, "even when you think you can't."

I leaned in and kissed her. Not the teasing kind from last night. This one was deep and meant to sink in and stay. Her lips softened into mine.

I tore myself away. "My driver's out front, ready to take you wherever you need to go," I said finally. "Have dinner with me tonight?"

She nodded. "Okay."

"Clancy's? Seven?"

"I'll meet you there."

I kissed her once more, memorizing the way she tasted, the way her lips molded to mine, praying that I could undo whatever my father had done. Then I forced myself to stand, gave her one last look, and headed for the door before I lost my nerve.

My hand was already on the doorknob when the weight of what I was up against hit me—the email, Fred Cummings, the vote, the secret sitting in my chest.

Whatever was going on at the office, I'd find out—one way or another.

Because Maggie deserved that land—she deserved to make her dream real.

All I could hope was that fighting for her didn't mean losing her. That would be damn near unbearable.

For the first time in my career, I arrived late at the office. And I didn't even care. I'd refused to get out of my bed any sooner than I had to. But the weight of what I needed to do weighed on my mind for the entire drive.

The elevator doors opened, and the usual Monday hum felt different. More intense. Secretive. Every assistant was in their seat. No one was talking, and eye contact was minimal. Two IT guys were crouched outside my office, cables spread across the floor, one of them muttering about network access and sync logs. They froze when they saw me.

"Morning, Mr. Mitchell," one said quickly.

"What's going on here?"

"Just doing some routine scans and checking for viruses for your father."

I gave a nod and kept walking, but my gut tightened. IT didn't do unscheduled maintenance, and they sure didn't do it on a Monday morning.

My assistant caught my eye as I approached. "Morning," she said carefully.

I leaned over her desk. "What's going on, Mary Kay?"

She hesitated, then glanced toward my father's glassed-in office. "Your father and Kristen were here before I got in. Kristen has been in and out of your office all morning. She had the IT guys in there." Her tone said the rest.

"Thanks," I said.

Mary Kay nodded subtly, then looked back at her keyboard, pretending to type.

I walked the rest of the way down the hall, pulse steady, mind spinning. The panic I'd felt earlier started to double.

Conrad's laugh carried through the door before I stepped in. Kristen's sharper one grated on every nerve. No doubt. Something was up.

"It's about time," my father said when I entered. "You're late."

Kristen turned, a smile sliding into place. "Kevin," she said. "Glad you could join us."

My dad spun in his chair. "You were hard to get a hold of last night."

Kristen didn't bother hiding her smirk. "You must have had other…important plans."

I smiled tightly. "I turned my phone off. Went to bed early. I figured I deserved it after the week we'd had."

My dad's gaze lingered a second too long before he nodded. "We've had some issues with network security. I'm going to need your phone. I have a replacement for you."

I swallowed hard. "Excuse me?"

"Security issues. Possible information leaks. We're issuing new phones to everyone on the board. Just heading off any possible problems." He held out his hand for my phone. "You understand."

"Since when does IT sweep executive phones?" I kept my tone steady and took a slow breath.

Conrad leaned back in his chair and clasped his hands behind his head. "It's all precautionary. You know how it is, right? Making sure we're all on the same page. We've all handed our phones to IT. We have a company-issued one for you until the scan's done."

"I understand." I nodded toward the door. "It's in my office. Let me grab it."

I turned and walked out before he could say anything more. My pulse picked up the moment the door shut behind me. At my desk, I opened my phone and deleted all of Maggie's texts and information.

A hard knock on my door came seconds later, and Kristen entered. "Your dad wanted me to let you know that he wanted you back in his office—immediately."

"No problem. I was grabbing my notes." As she crossed the room, I quickly powered off the phone. I picked up the file on the Taylor Farm and followed her back to my father's office.

When we walked in, my dad was hanging up the phone. "Good. You'll be with Kristen today. The architect is flying in at noon, and I want you two to button up all the loose ends before tomorrow. Tighten the visuals, finalize our final argument to the city council. I expect it to be perfect."

"Got it," I said, convincing.

"Excellent. I'll need you both here all night if that's what it takes. Don't plan on leaving that conference room."

I nodded, and every muscle in my body wanted to rebel. Spending all day with Kristen was the last thing I wanted to do, but walking out now would blow any chance of finding out what that email was all about—and why everyone in the office was on edge.

I handed over my phone along with any connection I had to Maggie.

Kristen shot me a knowing glance as she powered up her laptop. "Let's get to work, shall we?"

We'd been working straight through the day, meeting with the architect, and we were still nowhere near being done. Ben left hours ago for "an appointment." My money was on some happy hour or chasing a tall blonde in a skirt. Hell, anyone in a skirt.

I watched the clock tick. Minute after minute. Hour after hour. Maggie was waiting for me. Finally, I excused myself to use the restroom, but instead I went right to Mary Kay's desk before she left for the night.

"Mary Kay, can I please use your phone to send a text?" I asked, keeping my voice low.

She looked around to make sure no one was watching before sliding it toward me. "Be careful, please," she whispered, her eyes darting nervously around the empty office.

I typed the text quickly, aware that Mary Kay's phone was likely being monitored as well. Still, I hit send and gave it back.

"Thanks, Mary Kay," I said quietly.

"Kristen's coming," she murmured, snatching her purse and disappearing through the stairway.

Kristen appeared seconds later, her voice sharp. "Kevin, what's taking you so long?"

I took a deep breath and swallowed my pride. "On my way."

I brushed past her with a tight-lipped smile and went back to the conference room. I returned to my seat at the table, pretending to focus, but my mind was a million miles away—on the woman I left in my bed this morning and sent a single line text to, praying that one line was enough to hold her until I could make this right.

34

Maggie

I arrived at Clancy's near seven and decided to wait for Kevin at the bar.

I'd walked around all day with a smile on my face that had nothing to do with the fact that Molly's Bakery had a **BOGO** on her glazed lemon cookies and everything to do with Kevin Mitchell.

Fucking flawless and totally mine.

I was thinking of getting a T-shirt made with those exact words on it.

Maybe a hat to match.

There was no way I was letting Kevin walk away from me again. Not after he had kissed me like that. Not after he looked at me the way he did. If he wanted me, I wasn't letting him pull away.

And it had been incredible. Just as I'd imagined it would be. The sex was hot—playful even. But it was how he'd said my name that turned the night into something else—desperate, hungry, and urgent. The way he worshiped my body and the way I responded to his—it was nothing short of extraordinary.

I ordered a glass of Chardonnay and sipped slowly, trying very hard not to look like the woman sitting alone, grinning at nothing. But that was hopeless when I kept thinking about how Kevin had whispered my name and my body unraveled under his touch.

"I think I would call this fate," said a voice I'd heard repeatedly in nightmares. "What's a beautiful woman like you doing sitting all alone?"

I turned. Sure enough—there he was, looking slimy and predatory—same smug smile, perfectly styled hair, and the same look in his eye that turned my stomach.

Ben.

The man I was certain had a spot on the National Sex Offender Registry.

"For my personal safety, you should probably keep your distance. My rabies vaccine is overdue," I said.

He leaned in and invaded every bit of my personal space, his cologne overpowering. "You know, there are thousands of women who'd die for my attention."

"And here I am. Alive and well. Immune to your charms," I said, suddenly hoping I remembered to put my pepper spray back in my purse.

Ben laughed. "I think you just called me charming."

"And I think you're hallucinating."

Ben flagged down the bartender. "Blanton's."

When the bartender appeared in front of us, Ben never looked at the guy and kept his beady, rodent-like eyes on me. He wasn't polite. He was dismissive and demanding. Even the way he ordered his drink dripped with entitlement, and it reminded me so much of his father that I wondered how Kevin was related to either of them.

"Don't you have to go search the dark web or something?" I didn't know how I could make it any clearer that I didn't like him.

I looked at my watch and then checked the door. Kevin was late.

Ben took a pull of his drink and set the glass back on the bar with a small thud. "The big vote takes place in the morning." He spoke casually, swirling the amber liquid in his glass like we were making small talk between friends.

"Yep. Less than twenty-four hours before you leave my town and move on to your next project—destroying an orphanage, tearing down a retirement home, or bulldozing a soup kitchen. Which one is it?"

"Have I ever mentioned how I love your sharp tongue?"

"Have I ever mentioned how small your brain is? Unfortunately for you, it's probably proportional to other body parts."

His laugh grated on every nerve. Ben didn't care that I hated him. He stayed parked next to me, uninvited, and didn't seem to take no for an answer. The man wasn't just repulsive—he was dangerous.

"I wouldn't be so confident that you're getting rid of us." There was pure arrogance wrapped in every word. I was beyond annoyed, and the last person I wanted to talk to about Hope Farm, the city vote, or my town was Ben Mitchell.

"And I wouldn't be so confident that your slick city values can upend small town morals," I said.

"Except…" He took a swig of his drink and leaned an elbow onto the bar, inching closer to me. "Right this very minute, the details are being hammered out by my brother and our brilliant lawyer."

Kevin? With Kristen?

The words hit harder than I wanted them to. Kevin would be here. Even if he were late. "Well…it's going to take a lot more than high heels and Botox to sway Hattrick's City Council."

He laughed, sharp and oily, like he was enjoying a joke at my expense. "You haven't done your homework, Maggie. Kevin and Kristen are unbeatable. They've never lost a deal when they work together. It's all that pent-up sexual chemistry they have."

Ben was trying to push my buttons. I couldn't wait to watch Kevin wipe that arrogant look right off his face.

"They have this…arrangement," he added, dragging out his last word like it was juicy. He swirled the ice in his glass like he had no place to be and all the time in the world to sit and needle me.

"Is that so?" My voice stayed flat, but my patience was running thin. This conversation was starting to irritate me by the second.

Where the hell was Kevin?

Ben's smirk turned dark. "Mutual. Convenient. No strings." Then he leaned in and whispered, "Friends with benefits."

My spine stiffened, and my heart dropped before I had time to stop it. Heat crawled up the back of my neck. I told myself that Ben loved to stir trouble, but my stomach still knotted.

"They've been divorced for years, but you'd never know it

when you see them together. You saw firsthand at the Gala. All that anger between them. It's just foreplay. They can barely keep their hands off one another in private. In fact, he was supposed to come with me tonight, but…"

I casually looked at my watch. Kevin was late, and I hadn't gotten a call yet.

"They decided to"—he paused to make air quotes with his grimy fingers—"'*work late*' at the office."

Don't bite. Ben was trying to paint a different picture. This was all part of his plan to rile me up before the vote tomorrow. Kevin asked me to trust him, and I won't let Ben play games with my head.

Still, the words clung to me, and I couldn't help the twinge of unease that formed. The small knot just got tighter.

I felt my phone vibrate and pulled it out of my purse. A text came through from a number I didn't recognize.

Unknown Sender: Remember what I
asked you this morning.

Kevin? Whose number did he call me from? Why the secretive text and why stand me up?

He was thirty minutes late. Kevin wasn't coming.

Trust me, even when you think you can't.

His words flashed through my mind like a warning light. Did I really know Kevin enough to give him that kind of trust? When he knew what the word meant to me—and still asked for it.

Ben and his thick skull leaned in. "Aren't you tired of playing hard to get with me, Maggie?" His hot breath made my insides recoil. "You know what they say. There's a thin line between love and hate. Close enough that they're interchangeable. Think of how explosive we could be?"

"Explosive like diarrhea?"

Ben's grin didn't falter. In fact, I thought he was enjoying it. His voice turned low, and he said, "Careful, Maggie. You keep insulting me with that pretty mouth of yours, and I'll start thinking you have bigger plans for me."

He'd love nothing more than to get a reaction out of me. I wanted to throw my drink at him or, better yet, introduce his balls to my knee, but I wasn't giving him the satisfaction by causing a scene the night before the city council vote.

I refused to give him any power.

I let a slow smile spread across my lips and moved in close enough for him to hear every syllable I spoke. "The only plans I have for you are watching your face crumble when the vote goes my way."

I slid off the stool, swiping my purse from the bar as my feet found the floor. "Good night, Ben."

Ben's laugh followed me out the door. "Don't say I didn't warn you."

35

Kevin

Staying late at the office the night before we put a deal to bed was nothing new to me. I'd slept on the leather couch more times than I cared to count. It never bothered me. But this? This was busy work. I was being monitored. Controlled. Babysat. Every word fit the scenario.

I'd been in the conference room—trapped—since I came in this morning. Lunch and dinner had been delivered, and my father started escorting me to the restroom. Clearly, he didn't trust me. Or maybe he was just paranoid enough not to take any chances with his own son. Either way, he wasn't wrong.

They were making sure any communication I had with Maggie—or any they *thought* I might have—was completely cut off. I was on a short leash, and they weren't giving me any slack.

So, I decided to stay the course. Flip the table and play their game.

My father and the architect were on the other side of the room reviewing projections when I turned toward Kristen. If I wanted to learn anything, she was my best option. Only, I knew she wouldn't offer up information unless she had something to gain. And in this case, that was me.

I gave myself a pep talk and reminded myself what really mattered…Maggie. I choked back my pride and took a slow breath and then—

I casually leaned back in my chair and gave Kristen the easy grin she used to fall for. "You know this feels like déjà vu. Late nights, too much coffee, hammering out a deal near the finish line."

She smiled and set down her pen. "This feels right," she said. "You and me."

I held back the sour taste in my mouth. "It does."

She crossed her legs slowly and let the slit in her skirt fall to the side. "So, tell me, are you done having your little fling with the farmgirl?"

I grinned, but inside I was cringing. "Jealous?"

Kristen laughed. "Hardly. Just surprised. You always had better taste."

I bit down the urge to defend Maggie. The words rose in the back of my throat, but showing my hand now would cost more than my pride.

"I've waited years for you to be jealous, Kristen. Why now?"

She tilted her head, studying me. "You know me, Kevin. I always want what I can't have." Her tone turned possessive. "And she took something that was *mine*."

The edge in her voice made my blood run hot, but I kept my expression blank.

"It was…impulsive."

It was anything but impulsive. It was the most natural, inevitable thing I'd ever felt in my life.

Her smile thinned. "It didn't look impulsive at that ghastly cornhole tournament. It looked rather cozy to me."

"It was just a fling. Tell me you haven't had your share since our divorce."

"It looked like more than a fling when you stormed out of the Gala," she said, all jealous and territorial.

"The truth—" I leaned back in my chair. "It came in hot and flamed out fast."

Kristen's eyes gleamed, and her entire demeanor changed. She stood, circled the table, and perched on the edge of it, brushing up against my arm. "Maybe you just need to be reminded of what we had."

"Careful," I said. "You'll make me blush."

Someone hand me the goddamn Emmy.

She leaned in and came inches from my face, her voice dripping with pure seduction. "I can do a lot more than make you blush."

My dinner was working its way back up my throat. "Very tempting," I said, fighting to keep my voice even. "But nothing gets started until after the vote in the morning. And that's *if* we have something to celebrate."

"Oh, I'm positive we'll be celebrating." She ran her finger down my shirt. "I can wait a day. Are you sure *you* can?"

I gave a low laugh. "And how are you so sure? From where I'm sitting, Ms. Bentley has the edge on us."

"Trust me—I'm sure."

"Then, how about you share your little secret. I'm quite sure I've earned that kind of respect."

She studied me, eyes glittering. "That smile. God, I've missed that." Her nails grazed the side of my cheek. "We're grown adults, Kevin. Why are we waiting? Haven't you missed me?"

I ignored her question and kept my voice light. "What am I missing here? How are you so sure?"

Spill it, Kristen. I could practically see the temptation pool behind her eyes. She actually got off on crossing the line and calling it business.

"Let's just say, when your father wants something, he doesn't play fair. And I get paid very well to help him get what he wants. How about you give me what I want?"

My insides twisted. *I was in fucking hell.* "Not until you tell me why you're so confident the council sways toward us."

Her smile turned wicked. "Okay…you want to play? Once you give me what I want…" Her fingers trailed down my shirt again. "I'll tell you. I can wait until tomorrow when we're celebrating. And if I know you, you'll be chomping at the bit to get me back to my room as soon as President Cummings slams that stupid gavel of his. Some things," she said, smiling, "are worth the wait."

She winked and sauntered down the hallway.

I stayed in my seat, stomach rolling.

What the hell was I not seeing? And what did Fred Cummings have to do with it?

I pressed the heels of my palms to my eyes and exhaled, praying that somehow Maggie would forgive me for standing her up.

Just a few more hours. Get through the vote, and I could put all this behind me—tell Maggie how I really felt. I'd wanted to say to her last night that I'd fallen in love with her—that I breathed easier around her. The words almost slipped out multiple times, but not with this vote still hanging over our heads. Not while my father still had his claws in me.

If Maggie and I had a future—and I believed we did—it had to start with a clean slate. After the vote. After I found out what was behind the email, why it was sent to me, and why my father was going to such great lengths to contain me.

I leaned back in my chair, exhaustion clawing at me.

Just a few more hours.

By the time dawn broke, I hadn't left the conference room all night. My suit was rumpled, my tie hung loose, and I hadn't slept a minute.

In an hour, I would be walking into the council chamber, no closer to discovering the truth than I was last night. All I'd learned was that something was buried deep, and Kristen knew what it was. My act needed to continue until this damn thing was over.

I kept telling myself that the council would do the right thing. At the very least, Fred Cummings was on Maggie's side. That should bring me some relief, but it didn't. Fred was involved in this mess, and I wasn't sure how.

When I saw Maggie today, I'd have to pretend that she meant nothing to me. Pretend I didn't know the sound of her laugh, the way she felt in my arms, and how she looked underneath me.

Please, Maggie.

Just trust me.

Please know I would never hurt you.
Trust me, even when you think you can't.
I begged my heart to stay caged just a little longer.

36

Maggie

I woke up early the next day without a message from Kevin. Not a call. Not a text. Nothing. I lay there staring at the ceiling, wondering if trusting Kevin Mitchell was the biggest mistake I'd ever made. I picked up the phone and called him, but the same automated message I heard last night repeated itself. *The number you have dialed has been disconnected and is no longer in service. Please check the number and try again.*

I checked and tried again. Same response.

Trust me, even when you think you can't.

What did that mean? Trust was trust. He was asking me to hand it over without an explanation. It wasn't something you could twist and mold to fit the moment. It had one definition. No fine print. Kevin was telling me there was some in between—a grey area I was supposed to step into blindfolded.

Blind faith? I'd never been a fan. It had taken Joe years to earn mine. Longer for everyone else. But Kevin? I'd known him for a month. He was asking for a lot.

I wanted to believe him. I just didn't know if I *could*. Or if I *should*. There was a lot more riding on the line than just my heart.

But I didn't have time to pick apart any of it—the cryptic text, Kevin's no-show, Ben's insinuations. Today was important. I had a small army of hockey moms to talk out of matching riot gear and keep them out of jail.

Most importantly, I had to make *the* call. The one I'd been dreading, putting off. But if there was ever a time to take a risk, it was now.

I was used to being underestimated, but I was going to do whatever I had to do to help secure New Hope Farm. I'd even taken the week off from school, just to prepare, which probably said more about how much this really meant to me—I never missed a day of work. After the vote, I figured I'd have plenty of paperwork—and emotions—to last the rest of the week.

The Boys

Ethan: You got this, Mom!

Andrew: Dad would be so proud of you.

Jack: Can't wait to drive the backhoe!

Kal: What do the girls have planned?

Maggie: I was told "not to worry about it."

Evan: Frightening

Mark: Odds are Joy made T-shirts.

Ethan: And Annie passes out condoms.

Maggie: That could work to my benefit.

Andrew: Keep us posted.

Jack: We love you.

Maggie: I love you too.

The minute I walked into the Lakeside Grill for our "pre-vote" pep rally, Joy pounced.

"Ta-da!" She whipped a stack of folded T-shirts from her tote bag.

"Not again," Katie moaned.

"Yes, again," Joy said, shaking one open to reveal the glittered slogan "Hope Farm Needs YOU!" On the front of the shirt, it looked like a picture of a woman pointing Uncle Sam-style.

I blinked and did a double-take. "Joy, is that a picture of me on the front of that shirt?"

"Sure is," she said.

There was so much sparkle on it, my face could be seen a mile away—and possibly all over the local news tonight, depending on how much attention my friends wanted to draw. "This is how we show our support for Maggie and Hope Farm. Plus…" She reached back into her tote and pulled out a large Tupperware container. "I baked these last night. I plan on passing them out to all our supporters."

"Bribing with baked goods?" I asked.

"Who can vote against my cookies and your face?"

"Why does *this* have to be our thing? Why can't we show up like normal, civilized people?" Katie tried to argue, even though she was already putting on her shirt.

"Why do they look like the American flag?" Jules held hers up.

"We look like Betsy Ross gone rogue," Katie muttered.

"We'll be easy to spot for the news cameras, and we have a

theme, go with it." Joy beamed, shoving mine into my hands.

I laughed and pulled it over my head. "Joy, you really outdid yourself."

"Wait, there's more!" Annie shouted, placing the cardboard box on the table. She popped the lid to reveal cheap, shiny pom-poms in red, white, and blue. "We're handing these out to everyone who walks into the council chamber this morning."

"Subtle," Katie deadpanned.

"Subtle is for boring people," Annie said, already pressing pom-poms into the hands of two confused kayakers who'd just walked in for breakfast.

"Pom-poms, plus patriotism, equals victory!" Joy threw her hands in the air.

"Exactly! No one will be able to ignore us." Annie started making her way around the restaurant, recruiting the staff and customers to our cause—wearing a T-shirt with my face on it, my finger pointing at everyone she talked to.

"Alright, ladies," I said, gathering my speech in one hand, my poms in the other. "Who's ready to shake things up?"

"We are!" they all shouted and shook the hell out of the crinkled plastic on a stick with my face dancing on the front of their shirts.

I laughed, but it came out a little shaky. Annie looked ready to lead a parade. Joy started marching—knees high—and Katie reluctantly followed, because she was in it no matter what she had to wear. Jules led the way on her Harley. And I was grateful for all of them.

I picked up my phone to check my messages. Just more good luck messages from the boys.

Nothing from Kevin.

I felt like a prizefighter entering the arena. Annie and Joy led us down the middle of the council chamber like they were my trainers, their confidence pulling me along despite the butterflies in my stomach. Every head turned in our direction when Annie hit the *on* button on the boom box, and "Eye of the Tiger" blasted from the speaker.

Katie groaned. "Let me guess—the *Rocky* soundtrack is our thing too?"

"Apparently," I said, trying to keep a straight face.

We continued our parade down the center aisle, looking like we were ready to take the title from Apollo Creed. Annie and Joy worked the crowd, high-fiving every Hattrick citizen in arm's reach, passing out pom-poms to everyone on the right side of the aisle—the Hope Farm side. The left side? Casino Country—they didn't find us as charming as most of the town did.

When a man from the left side tried to snag one of Joy's chocolate chip cookies, her chin shot straight up in the air. She turned her back and slapped his hand away.

"These are for Hope Farm supporters ONLY." She enunciated the last word. Loudly.

We reached the front row on the right side and took our seats, Annie on one side of me and Joy on the other. I let my eyes scan Casino Country until I found him.

Kevin.

Right between his father and Kristen. I had to look twice.

Heart-stopping gorgeous, sure—but his eyes looked tired, exhausted even, and his shirt was slightly wrinkled. His posture was stiff, his eyes glued to the papers in his lap until Kristen leaned in to say something. And then…he smiled. Not the glare he reserved specifically for her, but an actual, easy one.

A warning shot went straight to my heart. I tried to get his attention, willing him to look at me. To give me any kind of sign that he was still on my side—even though he was sitting between the enemy, smiling.

But he didn't so much as glance my way. He never acknowledged me. Not even a shift in his seat. He knew I was here—he had to. Heck, the whole town knew we'd arrived. But Kevin stayed firmly in his little trio, as if it were exactly where he belonged.

The knot in my stomach wrenched tighter.

Trust me, even when you think you can't.

Those words were a broken record in my head. Is that what he meant? Pretend like last night never happened? Smile and nod while Kristen sat glued to his side? I couldn't tell if he were playing some long game or if I'd just fallen for the oldest trick in the book. Either way, my heart sank.

Fred Cummings looked paler than usual as he pounded the gavel and called the meeting to order. The room was packed shoulder to shoulder—standing room only—every seat was taken, and the air was thick with anticipation, as if it could snap and erupt at any second.

Fred pulled a folded towel from his pocket and swiped it across his forehead. I didn't remember him being much of a sweater, but it looked like he'd just run the length of Main Street to get here. His hand lingered on the towel, patting once…then twice…

before setting it down next to him.

"City of Hattrick," he began, his voice scratchy. "We are here today to…" He trailed off, cleared his throat, and picked up his glass of water.

I checked to make sure the town doctor was in the building. Fred didn't look good.

He drained half the glass before continuing. "We are here to vote on the two proposals for the old Taylor Farm." Another sip. Another pause.

The air in the room grew heavy, like a storm cloud ready to break.

"We will hear from Mitchell Developers first. And then the New Hope Foundation and Maggie Bentley."

An eruption of applause and a pom-pom explosion occurred from my right.

Whack! Whack! Whack!

Fred slammed the gavel to silence my friends and winced at the noise, then dabbed his forehead again. "Ms. Bentley," he said, looking at me like he might throw up, "please…" His voice faded.

I shrugged, waiting for him to recover.

Then, I looked toward Kevin. Instead of meeting his eyes, I met Kristen's. She looked at me like she'd already won. Haughty. Triumphant. Then, without breaking eye contact, she placed her hand on the top of Kevin's thigh. Not casual. Not by accident. She put it there with purpose. With intent. Making sure I saw it.

And Kevin just sat there. Staring straight ahead.

Trust me, even when you think you can't.

Heat surged up my neck, and my palms went slick. I took three deep breaths. In through the nose, out through the mouth.

Nope. That didn't help one bit. Why wouldn't he look at me? And why was he letting Kristen touch him?

Fred's voice came again, weaker this time. "We will hear from Mitchell Developers now."

He nodded to the left side of the room.

All heads swiveled toward the front row. Kristen looked at Kevin—and he smiled—actually smiled—before he nodded at her. What was going on? I got nothing, and the she-devil in Prada got the smile? The smile that came so easily with me. The one I was already starting to miss.

Her fingers squeezed his thigh like a *thank you*. Then she stood up, smoothed her skirt, and sauntered to the podium. She stacked her notes neatly, adjusted the microphone, and let the silence stretch long enough to feel like a power move.

I reached my arm around Joy and clamped a hand over her mouth before the "boos" could start.

"Members of the council, citizens of Hattrick Harbor," Kristen began, her voice smooth as silk. "Mitchell Developers believes in opportunity, in growth, and creating destinations that will put your town on the map. The old Taylor Farm is more than a wasteland—it's a chance to bring new life to this community."

She let her gaze sweep the council members. "Mitchell Developers envision a first-class entertainment complex—a casino that will not only create jobs, but also attract tourism, generate significant tax revenue, and bring new businesses to Hattrick. Imagine restaurants, live entertainment, boutique clothing shops… all within walking distance of downtown. Even more, think of every business owner doubling, even tripling their yearly income."

Kristen's fingers rested on her notes, but she didn't look down.

"And because the Mitchell family would like to demonstrate how serious we are about investing in Hattrick's future, we are pledging to donate one million dollars up front so the town can benefit immediately."

A stunned silence hit first, followed by a collective gasp that seemed to suck the air right out of the room.

I sat still. So did my friends. We didn't so much as budge. Joy filed her nails. Annie tilted her head like she was mildly listening. Jules looked bored, and Katie pretended to fall asleep.

Kristen's eyes swept our row, hunting for shock.

She found none. Her gloating eyes landed on mine, purposefully. I smiled, and her eyes caught fire.

Fred's gavel got to work again. "Did I hear you correctly? Mitchell Developers is prepared to donate one million dollars *over* the negotiated price?"

Kristen's mouth curved into a menacing smile. "That is correct. We love this town as much as Ms. Bentley does, and we want to make that known." She turned, eyes locking on mine as she flashed a self-satisfied grin, then returned to her seat.

I really hated that bitch.

Annie's hand found mine, squeezing once. Joy grabbed my other hand and gave it two quick pumps.

Across the room, a low hum of whispers swirled, people still buzzing over Kristen's surprise "gift" to Hattrick.

Fred cleared his throat. Swallowed hard. Took a deep breath like he was about to dive underwater. He still couldn't meet my eyes.

"We…will now hear from Ms. Bentley."

It was my turn.

Every head turned toward me. I stood from my chair and

walked to the front of the room. Never once looking at Kevin.

This was it. The moment I'd been waiting for. I believed in Hattrick Harbor. All I could do was trust the people sitting in this room—the people who knew and loved this town as much as I did. Deep down, they knew right from wrong. I had to believe in that.

I stepped up to the podium, my hands holding both sides for a second before I spoke. "Members of the council…my friends of Hattrick Harbor," I began, my voice steady and sure. "Taylor Farm is part of this town's history. Generations of Taylors have lived in that house, gone to school with our kids, worked that land, and fed us from its garden. I want to preserve every part of it—not for me, but for kids who have no one."

I took a breath, letting my eyes rest on each council member before I went on. "The old farmhouse will become a six-bedroom home for young adults who time out of foster care. A place where they can live until they finish college or trade school. A place they can truly call home. While they live there, they'll work the farm—plant the garden, care for it, tend the barn, and board the horses. They'll learn skills, responsibility, and the value of caring for something that belongs to them."

I felt my throat tighten, but I kept going. "Many kids who've aged out of foster care have no family to call on. Nowhere to go. At Hope Farm, they'll have more than a roof over their heads— they'll have a second chance. Hope for a future. Hope for new beginnings. And best of all, a family they can call their own."

I started to step back from the podium, then stopped. "Oh… and one more thing." I looked over my shoulder and found Kristen, then looked back at the council. "I also match the million dollars."

The reaction was immediate. My friends erupted into a frenzy of pom-pom waving and cheers. Katie jumped on her chair and gave a loud "Whoop!" Across the aisle, Kristen and Conrad's mouths dropped to the floor, frozen in disbelief.

Kevin stayed perfectly still.

I leaned back toward the microphone. "Now that money is no longer the deciding factor, I ask that you vote with your heart and not your wallet."

The room exploded. Voices shouted over one another, chairs scraped, cookies went flying, people stood—clapping, arguing, waving arms in the air. Fred's gavel pounded, but it was useless— Hattrick Harbor had gone full pandemonium.

During the uproar, my eyes found Kevin's. He didn't move, didn't blink, just watched me through the storm like he was trying to say something in a language only the two of us understood. My pulse kicked harder, but I didn't look away.

Fred's gavel slammed over and over again.

This meeting was far from over.

37

Kevin

Chaos rang out around me, but I didn't hear a thing. All I saw was Maggie and those emerald green eyes that pierced every part of my soul. One look and I always knew exactly what she was thinking—good or bad. And right now, there was no mistaking it. She thought I'd sold her out. The confusion was there, but it was buried under betrayal. It was like she didn't even recognize me.

Every part of me wanted to run to her. Kiss the hell out of her in front of the whole damn town. I needed Maggie to know that *everything* I was doing or about to do was all for her. For Hope Farm. Not for me, or my father's company, and it sure as hell wasn't for Kristen.

But the longer this mess went on, the harder it would be to unwind.

My fingers flexed with the urge to reach for her. I locked eyes with Maggie, desperate for her to read what I couldn't say out loud. *Trust me, Maggie.* If I broke now, reached for her too soon, the whole thing would blow.

The hurt on her face stole my breath.

Whack! Whack! Whack!

"I will not stand for this behavior!" Fred Cummings' voice echoed in the microphone.

It took every bit of ten minutes for the crowd to stop shouting, to get Katie down from her chair, and to clean up a shit ton of chocolate chip cookies that flew across the aisle.

"Can you believe the behavior of those *so-called* grown women?" Kristen sneered, pulling chunks of cookie crumbs out of her hair. "First, they parade in here like some kind of drunk PTA do-gooders wearing mom-craft-night shirts, then they have the audacity to actually throw food like we're in a female version of Animal House."

She huffed. "They should be embarrassed."

I forced down every comeback that was stacking up inside me. "Let's just sit and get ready for the vote."

"You're absolutely right. *We* should take the high road." Kristen smiled and then placed her hand on my cheek. I forced my expression to stay neutral, but every muscle in my body revolted. I turned, praying Maggie wasn't watching.

She was.

Our gaze caught for a moment, and I saw it—pain, before she masked it. It hit harder than any punch I'd ever taken. I wanted to scream and tell her it wasn't what it looked like. But all I could do was turn away and hope she'd hang on a little longer.

The room settled back to a quiet hush, and Fred brought us all back to the matter at hand. He banged the gavel one final time, hard enough to rattle his microphone. He dabbed his forehead for the tenth time tonight.

"We will now proceed with the vote," he said, sounding a lot surer of himself than he looked. "Council members, I will call your names in alphabetical order. When called, please state your vote clearly so the clerk can record it. There will be no discussion during the roll call."

His gaze swept the room and parked it when he reached Maggie and the hockey moms. "I'd like to remind the gallery to remain silent until all votes have been cast and the results announced."

Kristen leaned toward me, close enough for anyone who was watching to misinterpret her actions. "Let's see if Hattrick's hockey moms can make it two minutes without looking classless."

Her voice rubbed every nerve raw. I wanted to get up and walk across the room—show everyone where my allegiance was. But if I left now, abandoned this plan of mine, then Maggie may never get what she wanted.

Something was off. I could feel it in my gut. I was missing a piece of the puzzle—some deception my father and Kristen had concocted—and until I found it, I couldn't risk a wrong move.

If anyone had asked me two days ago if I was worried about the vote, I would've confidently said no. I knew this town. I knew its people. There was no way they were going to support the casino and turn their backs on one of their own. But that was before Conrad Mitchell and his greed machine came to town. Now, I wasn't so sure.

Money could twist people. Make them do things they'd swear they never would. Greed could tilt the world on its axis. I'd seen it. Hell, I'd lived it my entire life. Money had power.

Today, I was crossing my fingers and relying heavily on the

goodness of Hattrick Harbor. More specifically, on one person.

Fred straightened the papers in front of him and wiped his brow again.

"We will start the voting tonight with Colleen Colasanti." Colleen was a wild card from the beginning. No one knew which way she'd vote. She leaned toward her mic, glanced at Maggie, and said, "Hope Farm."

One down.

Fred called the next council member. "Dalton Coyle." No mystery there. The guy had already hired an architect to make room for his fleet of Escalades. "Casino," he answered at once. No surprise.

"Tony Heckman."

I could practically see his pulse jump when he looked at Kristen like a lovesick puppy waiting for a treat. The civics teacher fiddled with his glasses and wiped the drool from his chin. "Casino." Predictable, considering he'd basically gotten a hand job from Kristen under the table last week. He grinned at her like a fool. She didn't bother to return it, just turned away. He didn't know it, but she was done with him.

"Tess Holcomb."

This was a no-brainer. Tess was one of Maggie's good friends, and she made sure everyone in the room saw her look Maggie dead in the eye when she said, "Hope Farm."

I caught the way Maggie's fingers clenched around Joy's hand. Two down.

Fred continued with the roll call. "Bill Lombard."

Lombard leaned into his mic and spoke clearly. "Casino."

Bill was another wild card, and I was hoping he'd flip. But

the fact that his son owned a tire store in town probably had something to do with the way he voted.

That left Donna Russo, another good friend of Maggie's, one of the people I'd counted on from the beginning. The pressure in my chest began to ease when she leaned in. "Hope Farm."

Three votes for the Casino.

Three votes for Hope Farm.

The council tied.

Per city council bylaws—the president of the council would be the deciding vote.

In any other situation, I would've thrown my fist in the air. Fred Cummings had told us himself that if the council tied, he'd be voting for Maggie. He was adamant about it. Loyal to Hattrick. Loyal to Maggie.

Then, yesterday happened.

Yesterday, I was standing on the edge, looking to start something new. Something real. And today, I was in the fight of my life for Maggie's dream, not knowing if she'd be waiting at the finish line.

I could feel my pulse speeding up for a different reason.

Fred wiped his forehead again, the towel damp now, and leaned toward his mic. "In the case of a tie," he began, "the City Council President will cast the deciding vote."

I watched him—sweaty and pale—looking like he might pass out at any second. But then Fred looked at my dad and Kristen, and the room turned cold. My dad muttered loud enough for only Kristen and me to hear him, "A man's gotta do what a man's gotta do."

Kristen's mouth curved into the same confident smirk. I

sat between them, turning my head from one to the other, then looked at Fred.

My dad and Kristen looked far too sure of themselves to be concerned about the conversation we had with Fred not too long ago, when he'd said that Maggie's idea of Hope Farm felt a hell of a lot more like Hattrick Harbor than any slot machine ever could.

Kristen reached over and squeezed my hand, and bile rose in my throat.

Fred's gaze drifted to Maggie. She sat rigid in her chair, lips pressed tightly together. Annie and Joy each gripped one of her hands. Katie and Jules both had a steadying hand on her shoulders. She didn't look away from Fred.

Fear spread across her face—real fear. I wanted to tell her to have faith in her town. To have faith in people doing the right thing. But even as I thought it, I didn't believe it anymore.

Fred leaned into his microphone. "I vote. . ." His voice caught. He coughed.

Looked at my father.

At Kristen.

Then at Maggie.

He closed his eyes.

"Casino."

The word landed like a wrecking ball. All the oxygen drained from the room.

Maggie's face went slack, and her hand flew to her mouth. I felt something inside me splinter. And then something else formed. Fury. Disgust.

And that's when it happened.

It was fast—like a pressure valve blowing open—and all hell

broke loose. The hockey moms went crazy. So crazy that their husbands rushed in to restrain them. Even Joy was swearing while thrusting her fist into the air, as her husband lifted her off the ground, holding her back from charging the council. Mike tossed Annie over his shoulder, carrying her out the back door, screaming bloody murder.

Maggie sat motionless.

I realized the fight wasn't over just yet. I swallowed down every bit of anger and frustration that welled up and willed myself to keep control.

The word still hung in the air as my father jumped out of his chair. "Yes!" he barked. Ben was already reaching for his hand and shaking it like he had anything to do with the outcome. My father acted like he'd just won the deal of the century.

Kristen jumped out of her chair before I could react and circled her arms behind my neck. "Time to celebrate!" She breathed triumphantly into my ear.

Over her shoulder, I caught Maggie—just long enough to see a tear run down her cheek.

If my heart could shatter any more than it had, it just did. God, I wanted to go to her. Wrap her in my arms. Wipe the tears from her face, but the fight wasn't over.

Conrad slapped my back. "I knew you'd get it done," he said, grinning like he never doubted the outcome.

Kristen grabbed my hand, but I pulled it away almost instantly.

I turned to look for Maggie. She was gone. Jules and Katie had whisked her away.

Her face—pure devastation, burned in my mind. I'd planned for every scenario, every move, and every possible swing of the vote. Except for this one. The way Fred wouldn't meet my eyes. The way he looked at Maggie. The slight nod my father gave him before the roll call started. Kristen's overconfidence.

Deceit—it all reeked of it.

Think, Kevin. Think.

I had one card left to play.

Kristen.

My father would never admit to wrongdoing, and my brother doesn't have a moral bone in his body. Kristen was the way back to Maggie.

I grabbed Kristen's hand and led her out the back door to the narrow strip of pavement along the side of the building. I ran a hand through my hair, took one deep breath, and then pivoted toward her, with a smile I had to reach deep down to find.

This just might kill me.

"We won," I said, walking toward her. My hands found her waist, and I walked her backward until she hit the rough brick wall. I let one palm trail over her shoulder, down the length of her arm—slow enough to make her think it meant something.

"Now this…this is more like it," she purred.

She tilted her chin up to kiss me, but I moved just enough for her lips to miss me.

"Still playing hard to get," she teased. "I love this game." She let her head rest on the building like she was settling in.

I let the lie roll off my tongue. "Kristen, it's always been you."

Her eyes lit with satisfaction. "We've always been so good together. I'm just glad you finally came to your senses."

"I couldn't resist any longer," I said, my face inches from hers—closer than I'd been in years, closer than I'd ever wanted to be again.

"Does this mean we're heading back to my hotel?" Kristen said with a slow, triumphant smile.

"A deal's a deal," I said with a laugh that made my skin crawl.

Inside, every instinct told me to push her away. But if I wanted answers, this was the only way to get them—my last chance.

"And tell me again how your little hockey mom was just a fling?"

"She meant nothing." The words felt like acid rolling off my tongue. This was what she needed to hear. She needed to know that she'd won—that Maggie was a blip in the radar to getting back what she wanted, what she thought was hers. This was me stroking her ego.

When Kristen peered over my shoulder, her lips curled, and she started to laugh. Not a laugh that was genuine—this one was mean.

I pulled back to see what she found so funny.

Maggie.

Standing there, having heard every word. And Kristen knew it. Reveled in it.

The color drained from her face. Her lips were parted slightly, shock flashed in her eyes like she'd been slapped. Her eyes—the ones I loved so damn much—were filled with sadness. A sadness I'd sworn would never be my doing. If the vote hadn't wrecked her, this just finished the job.

"How does it feel to lose twice tonight?" Kristen said to Maggie, finding enjoyment in someone else's pain. "Haven't you figured it out yet? Kevin Mitchell will do *anything* for a deal."

Kristen didn't care about anyone but herself. She never had.

Maggie, on the other hand, cared about everyone. That was the difference between the two women standing in front of me. One woman fed on power, the other gave away pieces of her heart to anyone who needed it.

I wanted to tell Kristen to shut the hell up. To tell her she didn't know a damn thing about me. But if I wanted to get to Maggie, I had to go through this vulture of a woman.

"Maggie, please leave," I begged, feeling every bit of my heart breaking watching Maggie crumble in front of me. But she would never give Kristen the satisfaction of seeing it. Pushing her away felt like ripping my lungs out. I mentally urged her to give me a little more time.

Maggie didn't say a word. She didn't need to respond. I knew what she was thinking. *I trusted you.*

"Maggie, unless you want to stay and watch, you should probably leave." Kristen actually got off making other people feel small and defeated. There weren't enough words to describe how much I hated her.

Another tear slid down Maggie's cheek. This time, she didn't bother to wipe it away. She turned her back on me and left, and my heart fucking shattered.

Everything in my body ached to run after her, to tell her this wasn't what it looked like. But if there was one chance to get to the bottom of what happened tonight—give Maggie the farm—it was here, right now. I just prayed I didn't lose Maggie in the process.

I dragged in a deep breath and forced my attention back to Kristen.

"Now, where were we?"

38
Maggie

Mother Puckers 4-Life

Annie: Maggie?

Joy: We're all worried.

Annie: We're coming over.

Joy: I have tissues and tequila. Sadly, Kristen was wearing all my cookies.

Jules: Katie and I need Kevin's address, please.

Katie: Just gotta swing by home for my taser.

Joy: He's officially off my Hall Pass List.

Annie: Maggie??

Maggie: I'm okay. I just need time by myself, I think. Heading south for a bit.

Annie: We can come. Girls' trip!

Katie: Motown Night at LaTavola is calling our name.

Jules: Didn't they ask you not to come back for a while?

Katie: I'll wear sunglasses. They won't recognize me.

Maggie: I love you guys. I'll call when I get there.

Annie: Maggie?

Maggie: Yeah?

Annie: We love you.

Jules: Same.

Joy: Ditto.

Katie: Me too.

Maggie: I know.

Even the clock in Dr. Passek's office was taunting me.

Sometimes I hated clocks.

Lately, most of the time, I hated clocks.

After Joe died, I'd begged God to turn back time—one hour, one day. Long enough for me to change something. I would've dragged him to the doctor, demanded a CAT Scan, done anything to have prevented what happened. If I'd known what was coming, maybe I could've saved him.

I kept doing the math in my head. One week ago today, Joe was grilling chicken in his swim trunks. One month ago today, we were celebrating his birthday. This time last year, we were at that concert that he swore would "change our lives." Time never seemed to be my friend. I was always wishing it backward.

So why should it start now—sitting in my therapist's office, listening to the annoying sound of a clock ticking, wishing it could rewind a million ticks when Joe Bentley was still alive. If I gave it the middle finger, Dr. Passek would surely have me evaluated for being officially off my rocker.

"You seem tired today, Maggie," she said gently.

You think?

Maybe it was my body language, maybe it was the way I'd kept giving the clock the evil eye. But Dr. Passek knew me. I'd been coming to see her for a year, and she could tell when something was off. Today, I was quiet.

Three hundred and seventy-eight days ago, my husband went to work, and I never saw him alive again.

"I guess you could say that," I muttered, my voice a little more sarcastic than I meant it to be.

She studied me for a moment. "Care to share with me what has you agitated?"

"I feel…" I searched for the word, my fingers twisted in my lap. "Claustrophobic."

"Okay," she said, her voice calm, inviting. "Why?"

The words flew from my mouth. "Because lately, everywhere I go, he's there. The grocery store. The ice rink. Even walking past the diner downtown—Joe's laugh, his smile, is just…everywhere. Our house is the worst. Every corner has him in it. Every memory is still so alive I can barely breathe."

"That sounds exhausting," Dr. Passek said.

"It is. I love Hattrick Harbor. And I love the summers in Hattrick Harbor. But that's when I have too much time on my hands. Sometimes it feels like I can't go anywhere without tripping over memories of our life together." My voice cracked. "And I don't know how I'm supposed to move forward when I can't go to the hardware store without remembering the time he'd bought the wrong screws, then playfully told me he could 'never have enough screws.'"

We both started laughing. I wiped the tears away. The sound then faded to silence.

More clock ticking.

Dr. Passek sat at the edge of her chair, resting her elbows on her knees. "Maggie, you're stuck. You've built your whole world out of memories with Joe, and you love him—of course, you do. But your whole life right now is revisiting a world wallpapered with old photographs. Everywhere you turn, you're surrounded. What you don't have is a space that belongs only to you. A place where you can escape that doesn't take you down memory lane."

I frowned. "And where exactly am I supposed to find that?"

"I don't know," she said. "Maybe it's somewhere new, maybe it's something you create. But it needs to be a place that feels like yours, Maggie. A place you can go when memories get too heavy. A place where you can start making new ones."

I let that sink in.

A place that was mine. The idea sounded impossible. And sad. A place without Joe? And yet, something inside me stirred.

I left Dr. Passek's office, chewing on her words. A place that's mine. Somewhere I can breathe.

By the time I reached my driveway, the clock was ticking again—loud and relentless. Every second dragging me back. I passed the porch light that Joe had installed, the basketball hoop he put up for the boys, and the flowerbeds we planted together. Footprints. Everywhere I turned was another reminder that time kept marching forward, and I was still wishing for a past that wasn't coming back.

I went to sleep that night thinking about what brought me peace.

I woke up early the next morning and started tossing clothes on my bed—jeans, flip-flops, my favorite T-shirts, a few sundresses, my yoga mat, and my running shoes. I threw the bag in my back seat. I didn't stop to overthink it.

The car was already pointing south.

The farther I drove, the lighter I felt. Mile markers slipped by, exit signs blurred past, and the knot in my chest loosened. I didn't know where I was going, but I put on my favorite playlist and knew I had to keep driving.

Hours blended together with gas station coffee, empty stretches of road, and the sun climbing higher as my thoughts got quieter. I kept driving south. Passed signs for Charleston, Hilton Head, and Savannah, but never stopped. I stayed on 95 South. Hit Jacksonville and decided to keep going. My car found its way to 75 South, and I still kept going. I was on autopilot. I didn't stop until…

Ten hours later, I crested the S.S. Jolley Bridge, and my breath caught as Marco Island sprawled out in front of me. Water glimmered on either side, and palm trees waved like they'd been waiting for me. At the bottom of the bridge, a sign read, "Welcome to Marco Island."

I was pretty sure Dr. Passek didn't really mean take a ten-hour road trip on your own to find this place, but desperate times called for desperate measures.

I pulled to the side of the road and got out of the car right away. For the first time in a year, I felt something shift inside me. Not joy, not yet. But it felt an awful lot like hope.

The cloudless sky was a deep blue, stretching for endless miles, and the warm sun sank into my skin like it was trying to thaw me from the inside out. The sound of the Gulf rushed in, the waves lapped at the shore as a boat sped by, its passengers laughing and waving. I smiled and waved back, surprised by how good it felt. The air smelled of salt and sweetness—a blend of flowers and sunscreen.

And then, a tear ran down my cheek. But for once, it wasn't one of sadness; it was layered with something else, like the first crack of sunlight breaking through after a long dark storm.

Dr. Passek told me to find a place where I could start making memories of my own—a place to breathe when things got too heavy. With my eyes closed, head tilted toward the sun, and the sound of the Gulf wrapping around me, I whispered to myself—I think I found it.

I don't even remember turning on the ignition and pulling onto Hattrick's Main Street after leaving Kevin and Kristen on the side of the building. My hands were on the wheel, my eyes were on the road, but my head was somewhere else entirely.

Trust me, even when you think you can't.

Kevin's words were hollow—they mocked me, like a cruel joke.

How could I have been so stupid? I let my heart get caught up in something it wasn't strong enough for. I'd guarded it for most of my life. And then Kevin Mitchell walked in.

I let myself believe he was different—that maybe love wasn't done with me yet. I convinced myself he was nothing like his family, but the evidence was right there in front of me—his lips inches from hers, his hands around her waist, backed up against the brick wall.

She meant nothing.

The words stung. Was I really that lonely that I'd imagined every good thing between us? None of it made sense.

My hands were wrapped around the steering wheel, my knuckles white, embarrassment simmering under my devastation. I wasn't just angry at him. I was furious at myself. I should've known better. My instincts were always spot on. But with Kevin… I'd never heard one warning bell. In fact, every part of me said to run toward him. I'd let my heart trump my head.

And here I was, not only heartbroken but humiliated by the one person I was beginning to trust. I'd told myself early on that I shouldn't risk it, that I wasn't ready—but Kevin made me believe.

And now? I felt like a punchline.

It was cruel how vindictive the universe had lined it all up. As if Kevin breaking me wide open wasn't enough—the very thing that had given me purpose again had slipped right through my fingers.

Losing the vote had felt like a stab to my heart. I'd mapped out every possible outcome. The worst-case scenario was that the council would end up in a tie. But even then, deep down, I knew Fred Cummings would *never* vote for the casino. He'd looked me in the eye and promised me that much.

Turns out, I was batting a thousand.

I passed Carlton Drive. Passed Lake Hattrick. Called the boys to tell them I would be okay. Then reminded the school that I'd be out for the week. I pressed on the gas and headed toward the highway. I wasn't going home.

The tears blurred my vision, but I didn't slow down or turn around. I drove south. I'd made this drive so many times over the past two years. I silenced my phone and turned on the familiar playlist, but even that couldn't drown out the questions rattling around in my mind.

Hours passed. The day stretched on, and road signs flicked past, one after the other.

Somewhere along the way, the anger and sadness dulled into exhaustion. My tears dried, and I stopped questioning. I just drove.

The hum of the tires on the empty highway filled the silence. The world outside grew quiet—almost hypnotic—and passed in nothing but a haze, other than the occasional flash of a headlight and a billboard advertising the nearest exit to the Winn-Dixie.

None of it really registered, though. I felt numb. Every muscle in my body was tired, and my heart was just plain worn out.

I kept my hands on the wheel, and before I knew it, the sun was beginning to sink low in the sky.

And then, just as the sky began to turn gold and purple, the road ahead curved to the Jolley Bridge.

Marco Island.

The place that gave me strength.

Everything here called me home—the Gulf, the breeze, the palm trees catching the last light of day. Marco Island was starting to wind down, and I was there to watch it exhale.

I pulled into the small lot at the end of the bridge like I always did when I arrived on the island, killed the engine, and got out. I climbed onto the hood of my car, tucked my knees to my chest, and let the world slow down for the first time all day.

The sun melted over the edge of the water, and something inside me finally loosened. The questions, the humiliation, the failure—they didn't vanish, but on Marco Island, they didn't own me.

A seagull cried overhead. A fishing boat's motor rumbled in the distance. And the smell of coffee wafted through the air from the local coffee shop.

Pushing all my thoughts aside, I took a deep breath and started to believe that maybe not today, or even tomorrow, but someday, everything would be okay.

39

Kevin

Kevin: Please answer your phone.
Kevin: Maggie???
Kevin: I can explain everything.

My calls went straight to voicemail. Every damn time.

"Maggie, it's me," I said into the void, my voice rough, panicked. "Please—just let me explain. It's not what you think. I'm on my way over."

I ended the call. Tried again. Same thing. Another voicemail.

"Maggie, don't shut me out. Please—I can fix this. Just give me a chance to explain."

I fired off another text. Another call. Straight to voicemail.

By the time I hit the ignition, my chest was tight, and my head was pounding. I couldn't stop seeing her face before she'd turned and walked away—the pain in her eyes, the tears running down her cheeks.

The tears had been my fault. Every single one of them. I had sworn I'd never be the reason she'd shed a single tear, but there was no one else to blame, and now I couldn't get that image out of my head.

I threw the car into drive and didn't look back. I drove through stop signs, blew through every stoplight, and ignored horns blaring at me. All I could think about was getting to Maggie, hoping she'd hear me out.

I arrived in no time and turned down her long, paved driveway. I barely threw the car in park before I saw it.

A giant sign in the yard—a perky blonde in a yellow blazer, arms crossed over her chest, and an obnoxious smile plastered across the board. The red bold letters screamed one word: SOLD.

For a second, I just sat there, staring.

I shoved the car door open with my shoulder, bolted up her steps, and jabbed at her doorbell.

No answer.

I started pounding my fist against the wood, harder and harder, until my knuckles stung.

Nothing.

"Maggie, please—please answer the door," I begged, my voice sounded broken.

More jabbing. More pounding.

Same result.

Nothing.

Silence pressed back at me, cold and final.

I leaned my forehead against the door, my chest heaving. "Please, Maggie. I can explain. Just…be…home." The words came out like a whispered prayer.

When nothing happened, I turned around and sank onto the steps, my elbows braced on my knees and my head in my hands. I stayed there, waiting. Telling myself she'd be home any minute.

An hour passed. Then two. I'd lost track of how long I sat there.

Still nothing. The darkness crept in around me. No headlights down the driveway. Not even a text. And no return call.

Finally, I pulled out my phone with hands that wouldn't stop shaking. I scrolled through until I found Annie's name and hit call.

After three rings, she answered.

"What?" Her voice sounded like a blade.

"Annie, please don't hang up."

"Ha!" She gave a bitter laugh. "The only reason I answered was so I could rip you apart. And when I'm done, Mike wants a word. Tell me where you are. He'd like to talk in person."

"Ten minutes," I blurted. "Just give me ten minutes to explain."

"Fine," she snapped. "I've started my timer. In ten minutes, I'm sending Mike on a manhunt, and then I never want to hear your voice again."

It had been two days since Maggie had lost the city council vote. Forty-eight hours since she'd seen me with Kristen. Forty-eight long hours walking around like half my heart was missing. I couldn't eat. I wasn't sleeping. No matter where I went, I was looking for her. And no matter where I went, the ache followed.

Every call continued to go straight to voicemail. Every text went undelivered. I didn't need confirmation that I'd been blocked.

The silence was deafening.

The sky matched my mood today. Fall in North Carolina was usually blue and clear. But today, the blue sky was scarce, and ominous clouds were abundant. Every cloud pressed down, reminding me of what I'd lost. But I was going to try to change that. And I was starting here.

I never knew Joe Bentley, but I was sure I would've liked him. From everything I'd heard, I felt like I already did. That's how I ended up at the cemetery, sitting at the foot of Joe Bentley's gravestone, about to have my first conversation with a dead man.

Joseph John Bentley
Beloved Husband
Devoted Father
Cherished Son, Friend, Doctor
Jimmy Buffett Lover/Parrot Head
June 5, 1975 – July 10, 2022
Gone too soon

"Hey, Joe. My name is Kevin Mitchell, and I'm in love with your wife." I laughed softly and shook my head, knowing in any other situation, those exact words would get the shit kicked out of me.

I inhaled the freshly mowed grass and kept talking to his headstone. "In fact, I'm so in love with her that when I'm with her, I can barely see straight because everything else around me fades to black. Maggie enters a room, and I know she's there before I even turn around and see her with my own eyes. The air shifts, and I just feel it. She's a damn science experiment. It's like every crazy law of physics about energy and gravity gets rewritten the second she walks in."

I rubbed a hand over the back of my neck and took a swig of water from my bottle. "I know that a part of her heart will always belong to you, and I'm okay with that. I just want to have the rest of it for as long as she'll let me.

"I also wanted to come here today to say *thank you*. Because you've shown her what love looks like—what it's like to be unconditionally loved with your whole heart—you've shown me. I'm fifty years old, and I'm not sure I've known love or experienced it in a way that Maggie has.

"Knowing her makes me want to be a better man. I've learned that there is nothing more important than showing someone— proving to them—how much they're cared for. I'd walk to the end of the earth, give away everything I own, sacrifice it all to love her. And more than anything, I want to know what it feels like to be loved by Maggie."

My throat tightened, and I cleared it—realizing that saying it out loud hurt more than keeping it in.

"She's the most extraordinary woman I've ever met. She takes my breath away with every kind word, every crooked smile, and every laugh that slips out of her mouth. None of this is news to you. I know that.

"I'm not sure what I believe in as far as what happens to us after we die, but I want to believe that our loved ones can still see us—keep tabs on us. And if the love stays strong enough for the one left behind, you can't convince me that the one who's gone stops feeling it, too. I just don't believe that love dies when we do. That's why I think, somehow, you already know. Have you been watching her, Joe? She's fucking unbelievable. She's fierce—the way she stands up for everyone in her life and fights for them.

"I knew I couldn't go to her and beg forgiveness until I came to you. I want your blessing. I know that kind of sounds fucked up, and there's no way to actually get it, but coming here felt like the closest thing. Now, if the ground opens and swallows me whole, I'll take that as a no. But I'm choosing to believe that you're a man who'd want Maggie taken care of. You'd want her loved and cherished the way she was with you. So, I wanted to give you my word, Joe. If I can get her to forgive me—and I'm going to try like hell—I will love her with every breath in my body for every day as long as I'm alive. Just like you did."

I sat there for another fifteen minutes, staring at his name carved in stone. Half hoping for an answer. A sinkhole didn't appear, so I took that as something. Finally, I stood up, folded the small chair I'd brought, and brushed the damp grass off my jeans.

When I turned to leave, the heavy grey sky parted, a small patch in the clouds opened up, and the sun's rays peered through. I'd never been one to believe in signs or anything like that, but I believed in fate now. Meeting Maggie had given me no choice. And that small glimpse of sunshine on a day that's been nothing but clouds? No one could tell me that it wasn't Joe giving me the thumbs-up.

When I got back to my car, I typed in the address that Annie had given me and calculated the drive.

Seven hundred and seventy-two miles.

That was the distance between losing Maggie forever or getting a second chance.

40

Maggie

Two years ago, when Dr. Passek told me to find a place all my own—somewhere to go when things got too heavy—I found myself here on Marco Island. I was fairly certain she had in mind something like a lakeside bench with a pretty journal or possibly a weekly drive to the Statesville farmers' market. I doubt she had meant a spontaneous drive to Southwest Florida to buy a little cottage with green shutters in Hideaway Beach, one block from the water.

But then again, she never said not to.

My financial planner thought I was having a nervous breakdown, but I told her to try losing a husband and living in a town surrounded by ghosts and then see if she didn't end up scrolling Realtor.com as a coping mechanism.

After buying my cottage, I made my next major purchase…a wagon—the kind with inflatable tires, built to haul serious gear. Mine was always loaded with the essentials—a chair, an umbrella, a book, and a cooler. Every night, I wheeled it to the beach. Watching the sun sink into the Gulf became my favorite ritual— one I never let myself miss.

Today, the air smelled like coconut sunscreen, the kind that clings to every towel and sunburned teenager. Seagulls squawked and fought over someone's forgotten bag of chips in the sand, and the still water stretched for endless miles in front of me. When combined, they did what Marco always did— it made the world feel simple again.

I sat in my beach chair, my eyes focused in front of me, and couldn't help but hear the snippets of conversation drifting by. Evening dinner plans were being made—someone craved the grouper sandwich at the Island Gypsy, while the teenager lobbied hard for Cav's pizza. Two sisters discussed their brother's upcoming destination wedding at the JW Marriott. And a group of young women strolled by in a heated debate over which shows were binge-worthy on Netflix.

I smiled to myself. Everyone found a reason to be happy at the beach, and it brought out the best in all of us. It was therapy for some, relaxation for others. For me, it started as a place to heal, and as time went on, it became much more.

On Marco Island, my mind slowed down. Years ago, I survived grief on this beach. I became a little less heartbroken every time I came, letting the water carry away some of the pain for me. Maybe that's why I found myself driving south two days ago. I needed to figure out what to do now—to figure out my next step.

I'd lost the farm, and I'd lost Kevin—not that he was ever really mine to begin with.

I'll admit it. I'd run away. But sitting in my sun-bleached chair, watching the horizon change from gold to pink, I could feel real possibility—broken things could be mended. Hope still had a place in my heart.

I pulled a sweatshirt over my head and looked out at the water. And just as the heat began to fade and a soft breeze drifted in, I felt the prickle of awareness shoot through me. A tall, familiar figure appeared, walking along the shoreline. I didn't need to turn—I already knew who it was.

The closer he got, the more my body had a mind of its own—my pulse sprinted, and I moved to the edge of my chair like he was some super-charged magnet, and my body was doing what it naturally did.

There he was. Kevin Mitchell, standing barefoot in the sand, sleeves rolled, wind in his hair, like he walked straight out of a memory I'd spent days trying to forget. My stomach tightened. Of all the places—why here? Hundreds of miles from Hattrick Harbor.

He stopped a few feet in front of me, hands stuffed in his pockets, eyes searching mine.

I squeezed mine shut, convinced I was hallucinating. I'd heard of the sun making people see things that weren't really there, but last time I checked, Marco Island wasn't anywhere near the Sahara.

"Maggie."

Just my name. Rough. Unsteady. The sound alone hit me square in the chest.

That voice. The same one that could undo me with a single

word. The same voice that came from the man who'd had his hands on his ex-wife's waist and his lips near hers, telling her I meant nothing.

I didn't answer him. I had a million things I'd wanted to say when I saw them together, but I'd lost all steam. Two days weren't long enough to erase the images of him with Kristen or the words I'd overheard. I sat with my arms crossed over my chest like they were the last defense to protect my heart. Looking at him hurt. Wanting him hurt worse.

For a split second, my heart reacted before my head could stop it. But then I'd remember who he was and what he'd done. The man standing in front of me promised I could trust him—then proved exactly why I shouldn't.

He looked rough—maybe exhausted, like he hadn't slept in days. Not the confident man who walked into a room like he owned it. Not the man who kissed me like he needed me more than he needed oxygen.

No…the man standing in front of me looked nervous. He was tentative with every step, but the way his eyes captured mine—the way they pleaded—were the only thing that kept me from bolting.

"Haven't you done enough?" I said, standing up, my arms locked across my chest, hoping it looked more like steel than the sadness I felt inside. "I have nothing to say to you."

He shifted his weight, like he couldn't quite find his footing. Then, he shook his head. "I'm not leaving, Maggie."

That did it. Heat rose in my cheeks, and my head pounded in frustration. This was *my* beach, *my* peace, and he was disturbing both.

"Fine," I snapped. "Then I'll leave."

I spun, braver than I felt, ready to grab my things. But before I could take a step, Kevin's hand reached out and gently touched my elbow. The touch was careful—not a trap, but a plea. He turned me back to face him, his eyes burning with something between sorrow and determination as I freed my arm from his grasp.

"Not before you hear me out," he said, his voice raw but firm. "Please."

My skin tingled where his fingers had brushed, and my traitorous body sparked to life. Clearly, my body didn't get the same restraining order as my heart.

"Kevin, what could you possibly have to say to me?" It was my turn to look exhausted.

He didn't answer my question. Instead, he pulled an envelope out of his pocket. "Please read this." Then he held it out for me to take.

I hesitated, but curiosity got the best of me. I yanked it from his hand.

"What is it?"

"Just open it." His voice was still gentle.

I slid my finger under the flap and tore open the sealed envelope. Inside, neatly folded, was a notarized legal document. My eyes raced across the words. My brain tripped over each one. *I hereby rescind…changing my vote…New Hope Farm…Fred Cummings…resignation.*

The world tilted beneath me. I blinked back tears, certain I was misreading it.

"I don't understand…"

Kevin's voice broke my rambling thoughts.

"My father and Kristen were extorting Fred Cummings."

My head jerked up. "What?"

"He was never going to vote for the casino, but Kristen went digging. Fred liked to bet on horses. Apparently, he applied for a loan to cover his losses, but my father paid someone at the bank for the information. Someone anonymously sent me the email. My father threatened to expose it to his wife and family."

Extortion? The words hit harder than I wanted them to. "You're telling me that your father and Kristen blackmailed Fred?"

He nodded. His eyes stayed focused on mine. "Fred's not a bad guy. He made a mistake. One he was desperate to keep private."

"The farm is mine?" I whispered, daring to believe it.

"The farm is yours," Kevin repeated.

The words knocked the breath right out of me. For one impossible second, the world righted itself. A laugh broke free, tangled with a sob.

"The farm is mine," I said again, hoping that repeating it would make it feel real. The tears came fast and hard. It had been a long journey. It was what I'd been waiting for to end a beautiful chapter in my life. Relief crashed through me, joy so sharp it almost hurt.

This was a new beginning for me.

But even as the joy spread through me, the ache came back. A knot of hurt twisted inside, reminding me of everything I'd also lost. Kevin. Even standing in front of me, he still felt impossibly far away.

The farm was mine—he was not.

He betrayed my trust. Sold me out. Went back to that woman who gave every woman on the planet a bad name.

Kevin took one step toward me, but I instinctively pulled out of reach. He'd lied to me. Slept with me, made me believe there was a chance for something more with him. With us.

"You came all this way…why? To ease your conscience? Twist the knife?"

Then he reached into his pocket and pulled out a second envelope. "I need you to see this before I can give you the answers to the questions running through your mind."

I took it, though my fingers shook as I tore it open. Again, I skimmed the words of a second legal document. My eyes caught on a familiar name. *Sherri Templeton*.

My pulse hammered in my ears, and my heart squeezed. "What is this?"

His gaze never wavered. "It's the sale of your house."

"I know. I sold it," I shot back, heat rising in my face. "Why do *you* have the papers?"

"Because *I* bought your house, Maggie."

I blinked at him. The words didn't register. My anger turned to confusion. "You—what?"

He looked at the sand, then back into my eyes, moving forward. I put my hand up for him to stop. "Why did you buy my house?"

"I knew you'd never just take the money from me to match my father and Kristen's million dollars. But if I gave you a chance to do it your way…" He let the thought trail off.

I shook my head, trying to piece it all together. "*You* bought my house?"

"Yes," his voice softened. "But in a couple of weeks, the deed will be back in your name, where it belongs. You can pay me back if you want, but I was hoping you'd think of it as my investment in Hope Farm."

My mouth went bone dry. I wanted to argue, to tell him how

insane this all sounded, but all I could manage was, "How?"

"Hattrick's a small town," he said, his tone gentle now. "After I found out about Kristen's plan to inflate the price on the Taylor Farm property, I had overheard Sherri in the coffee shop talking about your house. She didn't know who I was, so I approached her and asked her to make you an offer. I figured if you knew there was an interested buyer, at least you'd have the option to get the money you needed quickly. Sherri helped me plant the seed, but you were the one brave enough to take the chance on your own."

My knees nearly buckled. I swallowed hard. My throat tight. "I don't understand *any* of this."

His eyes searched mine.

"I knew my father and Kristen were up to something, meeting in private all week. That should have been a red flag. Then, on the day before the vote, I received an anonymous email from Harbor Bank that was sent to my father about a second mortgage Fred Cummings applied for."

Tess Holcomb worked for Harbor Bank.

He raked a hand through his hair. "I needed to find out why that email was sent to my father, and I knew Kristen was the only way."

He had my heart spinning in circles inside my chest.

"She'd never give up information unless she had something to gain. And the only thing she hated more than losing in court was seeing me happy with someone else. With you." He shook his head, regret etched into his features. "It became a game to her. I let her believe that she could have me back. And I know how awful this sounds coming out of my mouth right now, but at the time,

I was running out of options, and I thought it was the only way. So, I told her what she wanted to hear. What she *needed* to hear."

Every one of his words landed like a blow. My instinct was to fold my arms tighter across my chest, to guard the ache pulsing through my veins, because it still felt like betrayal.

His gaze locked with mine, fierce and unflinching. "Do you know why I couldn't even look at you at the council meeting?" He didn't wait for my answer and kept talking, his eyes bearing every part of his soul. "Because one glance, Maggie…one single look at you, and everyone in that room would have known that I'm head-over-heels, can't-breathe-without-you, in love, and if Kristen had seen that, she would've dug her heels in deeper. So I kept my eyes away from you, even when it killed me."

Kevin Mitchell loved me?

His words sank into me until they reached someplace I didn't know was waiting.

"You told her I meant nothing. I heard you." The pain in my voice was obvious, although I was trying to hold strong. I didn't want to break.

Kevin's eyes hurt, the way a man's did when he was standing in the wake of his own wrecking.

"I know you did," he said quietly. "And I'll regret that the rest of my life." He took a step closer, then stopped himself. "What you heard—it wasn't real, Maggie. I said those things to get Kristen to talk. She'd never give me what I needed unless she believed I wanted her back. I hated every word that came out of my mouth, but I had to make her believe it."

His hand grabbed the back of his neck, and his voice wavered. "You weren't supposed to see or hear any of that. God, I wish you hadn't. I was lying to her, not to you. But the second I saw your face…I knew exactly what it sounded like. And I'll never be able to tell you how sorry I am for that."

I didn't trust my voice enough to answer. I wanted to stay angry, but something inside me began to thaw. The faintest crack in a wall I'd built years ago began to splinter.

I'd spent my whole life holding everyone to impossible standards. If they failed me, I shut them out. Turned them away. There was no room for error—no second chances. And maybe that was my mistake. I never gave *him* a reason to trust me, and he all but told me his plan without coming out and saying it.

Trust me, even when you think you can't.

His words came rushing back, the way he'd said them that morning. I hadn't understood it then. I thought he was asking for blind faith when what he was really asking for was a chance. He knew things might look wrong, even skewed, but was begging me to believe anyway.

But I hadn't. I'd done what I always did—what life had taught me to do. I anticipated disappointment, assumed people would fail me. For people to leave me. It was hard to get rid of the demons you grew up with, and I was so practiced at expecting the worst that I never stopped to wonder whether Kevin might've been fighting for me in ways I couldn't see or understand.

"Why not just tell me your plan from the start?" My voice was sharp, but underneath was the ache of someone who wanted to believe what he was saying.

Kevin's shoulders sagged, like I'd just asked the very question he'd been dreading. "I wanted to protect you from whatever game was being played. When I arrived at the office on Monday morning, a group of IT guys was tearing apart my computer. Then my dad claimed there'd been some kind of security breach and confiscated my phone. I knew none of that was about security, it was about control. They wanted to isolate me.

"From that moment, I knew I wouldn't be able to reach you. I knew I'd miss our dinner. Every call, every text, every email was being monitored. I'm so damn sorry, Maggie. I was trying to uncover the truth. My dad would never offer up any wrongdoing, but Kristen would—with the right incentive."

He looked physically sick. "If I could've done this differently, I would have. Maybe I should have, but I couldn't risk it, and I never wanted to put you in the middle of it."

He let out a long, shaky breath. "It was torture standing next to her, letting her believe she'd won, that you meant nothing. That's what killed me most because you mean everything to me, Maggie. And the only thing I wanted was to tell the whole damn world."

I didn't know what to say. My throat burned, and every word I'd rehearsed in anger felt small. Part of me wanted to believe him. The other part—the one still nursing the bruise he'd left—wasn't ready to let go that easily.

"Everything you'd worked for was at stake. You needed that vote, and you needed to match their price. I saw firsthand what had happened with Cody, and if that looked *anything* like what had happened to you, then there was no way in hell I could let them win. The farm didn't belong in the hands of Mitchell Development. It belonged with you."

"Did you sleep with her?" The words fell out before I could stop them. I had to know how far he was willing to go to get what he wanted. But one look from him and I had my answer.

"Absolutely not." His voice was more forceful than it had been since he'd arrived. He took a breath and slowly released it. "What you saw behind the building was as far as it went. My lips never even touched hers."

He paused. His eyes locked on mine. "There's only one woman I want."

His gaze was so potent, so unwavering, that it left me powerless.

"Maybe I should've handled it differently—but if losing you meant that Hope Farm would be yours, I'd make that trade again and again. Your happiness means more to me than my job. More than any blockbuster deal, more than every dollar my family has stacked in the bank. It means more than my father's warped idea of loyalty, more than the Mitchell family legacy. All of it. Even if it meant I couldn't have you."

I wanted to argue, but I wasn't sure what I'd be arguing. "What are you saying?"

"I quit," he said simply. "After I corrected my father's mess, talked to Fred, and begged Annie to tell me where you were, I told my father I wanted nothing to do with Mitchell Developers."

I stared at him, trying to process what he'd just said. "Kevin… that company's been your whole life." My voice cracked before I could stop it. "You worked your entire career for that."

He shook his head slowly.

"He's your family, Kevin," I said, trying—but failing—to make sense of it all.

"If anyone's taught me what family really means, it's you, Maggie. My father and I share the same genes, but he's no longer the man I respect—and that's not the life I want to live. I thought it once was, but you changed that for me. Family is where your heart feels at home, where it can rest at night. Blood and last names have nothing to do with it. It's about the people who make you believe you belong."

His words lodged deep inside me, and my heart began to soften. His dark eyes pinned me in place, the lump in my throat swelled until it was almost impossible to speak.

Trust me, even when you think you can't.

The words echoed through my mind—pulling me backward— to the night of Cody's party, to his house, to the morning before he left. He'd begged me to believe in him, and I hadn't. I told myself I was protecting my heart, but maybe I hadn't trusted *him* enough. Maybe *I'd* given up on him too soon.

Hearing him now—hearing that he'd given up everything so that I could have the farm—Joe's dream—broke down the last wall I'd been hiding behind. He'd stood up to his family. He'd chosen me.

And if I couldn't forgive him, he would've accepted it— because I had the farm, because *my* happiness meant more to him than his own.

Kevin had put *my* dream above all else.

An ache bloomed in my chest, as if my heart had been locked up for too long and was finally forcing itself open again. It wanted out desperately.

There was no denying it—Kevin Mitchell owned a part of it.

The thought scared me. Thrilled me. My chest felt too small to hold everything it was feeling.

I could turn and walk away, shut it all down—but that's not what I wanted.

"Can we go back to the part where you said something about

can't-breathe-without-me?" My voice came out softer now. My arms fell to my sides, leaving my heart wide open—and ready.

He closed the distance in a single heartbeat and cupped my face in his hands. He pressed his forehead to mine, and a soft, warming sensation took root.

"Do you want the short, condensed version," he asked, his voice low, "or the one where I try not to scare you away?"

"No shortcuts." The words came out like a plea.

His breath fanned over my lips. "My heart's been in a free fall since the day I met you. When I first saw you doing your sign language bit with Walt, I knew you'd change my life. I didn't know how—but I knew it was true. And after I kissed you that first night…" His lips hovered over mine, his jaw brushing my cheek. "I knew that loving you would be the greatest thing I'd ever get to do. If you give me the chance, I'll prove it."

I couldn't think. I couldn't breathe. There was no question that this man knew what he wanted—and it was me. And I believed him.

"You make me want to fight harder, stand taller, to be the kind of man who deserves someone like you. I want to stand beside you, get Hope Farm up and running. I don't have a job, so hire me to muck out the stalls, clear the field, build a front porch—I don't care. Just let me prove myself to you. Because I know where I belong and it's right next to you."

My heart had heard enough. My breath caught, and for the first time in days, the fight in me went still. Kevin Mitchell was standing in front of me—messy, unshaven, heart laid bare—and somehow against every ounce of self-preservation I had left, I felt myself lean toward him.

His hands found my back, pulling me close like it was all too good to be true. Heat rushed through me, but it wasn't just his touch—it was everything behind it. The apology. The faith. The stubborn, relentless way he'd refused to give up on us.

"Nothing means a damn thing to me unless you're with me," he said. "I don't expect you to tell me you love me, but one day I hope that you will. And I promise you this—I'll show up every single day, proving I'm worthy of it."

"Kevin…"

"Please let me finish," he said softly. "My heart belongs to you, Maggie. From the day I met you, it's been yours. And standing here, looking at you—I see the rest of my life in those incredible green eyes of yours."

I sucked in a staggering breath because I knew it was true, too. The day I set eyes on Kevin Mitchell, I knew my life would never be the same.

And just like that, the walls crumbled, the fear subsided, and I let go of it all.

The world stilled around us, like it always did when he looked at me. His hands gripped me like I'd slip away if he let go, but he didn't close the distance—he waited for me to do that.

"All I need is you," he said.

With those last words, he had me. My heart had known what it wanted long before my head could catch up.

"Good," I said, "because I need a stable hand. You're hired."

Then I wrapped my arms around his neck and pulled his mouth to mine. He kissed me softly at first, then hungrily, like relief had broken free and he couldn't get enough.

I let his mouth wash away every doubt and replace it with

possibility. I'd thought I was lucky enough to get one great love—that life could only hand me one happy ending. But here I was, on Marco Island, with a man who was ready to prove me wrong.

Kevin Mitchell was about to change my world.

I was turning the page—starting a new chapter.

And in that moment, I didn't just *feel* it.

I *knew* it.

Epilogue
Kevin
One Year Later

The porch swing creaked as I rocked it gently with my heel, coffee mug in hand. The sun was starting to climb over the garden Cody and I had started planting yesterday. The barn doors were open, and I could hear Chester and Birdie whinnying from their stalls. Two horses boarded. Not bad after moving in only a month ago.

This was my favorite time of the day—the silent hush of the cool, crisp morning with dawn breaking above the apple orchard. Being on the farm was a kind of peace I'd never experienced. It was a hell of a lot of work, but only a man with sweat running down his back and callouses on his hands could understand the satisfaction.

The screen door eased open, and my slow smile couldn't be contained. I didn't need to look. I knew who it was.

Maggie padded across the porch in her bare feet, hair messy from sleep, a blanket wrapped around her shoulders. She slid onto my lap without a word, curling into me like she belonged there—which she did.

Correction: *This* was my favorite time of day.

"Good morning, beautiful," I murmured, brushing a kiss against her brow. She lifted her face and pressed her lips to mine. Soft, familiar, and all mine. Every thought in my head slipped away when she kissed me.

When she pulled back, I studied her. No makeup, eyes so green they lit up the rest of her face, and wearing my T-shirt and sweatpants, which hung low on her hips. So beautiful. So sexy.

"How do you look like this every morning?"

She smirked, stealing my mug for a sip. "Like what?"

"Like I don't stand a chance thinking about anything else till I get you back in our bed," I said, meaning every damn word. How the hell would I be able to get any work done today with the image of her in *my* clothes?

Her laugh was quiet, and it rumbled against my chest. She leaned further into me as we both stared at the property that stretched all the way to the horizon.

My life could not look any more different from what it did a year ago. Everything had changed. Forty-hour workweeks in a suit and tie to sixty-hour workweeks in denim and steel-toes. Ralph Lauren to Levi's. Dining with clients at five-star restaurants to grilling lakeside with Maggie's hockey family. Coming home to an empty house to coming home to her.

From nothing to everything.

I woke up every day, feeling like I'd hit the Mega-Life Jackpot.

Helping Maggie bring this farm back to life had been the biggest reward of all. I'd never worked harder. My body had never been sorer. And my life had never been more fulfilling.

And to think I'd almost lost it all. Before I found Maggie on Marco Island, it took two long days after the city council vote to untangle the mess my father and Kristen created. Once Kristen believed she had a shot with me again, she spilled everything about their master plan to "win" Fred Cummings' vote—the leaked email and the threat to expose him to his wife. I'd left Kristen standing on the side of the brick building, gaping after me, realizing she'd just lost at her own game.

Conrad Mitchell loved two things more than money: his reputation and his freedom. I'd given my dad an ultimatum—walk away from Hattrick Harbor and never look back, and I wouldn't mention their little extortion to the police. I would've done it, too. He'd nearly stolen the farm from Maggie, almost ruined a small town, and tried to destroy a decent man in the process. Fred's part of the bargain was to come clean to his wife and resign from the city council after rescinding his vote. Fred had jumped at the offer, and my father had caved.

Once all that had been taken care of, I handed in my resignation to the Mitchell Development Company.

Before driving to Marco Island and begging for Maggie's forgiveness, I had gone to the bank and started the paperwork to put her name back on the deed to her house. Her boys wanted to keep it, and we planned to spend every Thanksgiving, Christmas, and Joe's birthday there.

Maggie's boys came home often, and on those weekends, the Sunday night pasta dinners went all night. True to their word, they'd been instrumental in getting the farm on its feet.

Sometimes when I looked at her, barefoot and laughing on the farm, I still couldn't believe she'd given me another chance. But I thank God every day that she did.

Would I do it again? In a heartbeat. I would probably do it differently, but for her, I'd risk everything. That old life was over now. The only one that mattered was this one—because life on the farm turned out to be more gratifying than I'd ever imagined.

And life with Maggie was exactly what I thought it would be. Perfect.

This was our new normal now. Maggie cut back to part-time at school to free up more time for the foundation. Together, we ran the farm. Saturdays and Sundays were our days to be the "parents" for the kids living at Hope Farm. Sunday nights meant family dinners. Everyone in the house cooked, and the hockey moms and their spouses crowded around the wooden picnic tables. My mom never missed a Sunday. She'd help in the kitchen and laughed every time someone called her Grandma Maureen. She loved it. I'd never seen her happier.

Watching it unfold week after week, I knew *I'd* never been happier either.

I tightened my arms around Maggie. The ring on her finger caught the early morning light, and my heart back-flipped just looking at her wearing it.

Maggie Bentley had said Yes.

"Thank you," I said quietly, nuzzling her ear.

She squirmed. "For what?"

"For this." I motioned around me. "The farm, this life, most of all, you."

Her eyes softened, and she kissed me again, slowly this time.

"Maggie…" I warned, a slow hum working its way from my throat.

"Yes?" she answered, her lips still trailing my jawline. This was the way it went for me. She kissed me, and I turned to putty. Every damn time. I couldn't wait to get this woman back to our house.

I glanced at my watch—T-minus twelve hours until I had her all to myself.

I smiled and played with the ring I had specifically made for her. Two carats, thin gold band. Simple. Stunning. Just like her.

"So…I was thinking. What do you say we not wait too long to make this official?"

Her smile was so wide it practically broke me in half. "I'm good with that," she whispered. "As long as all the boys can make it, the girls, and your mom, let's do it."

"Are you serious?" I hadn't expected her to say yes this easily, but hell, I didn't want to wait another second to call her my wife. Maggie Bentley would finally be mine.

"Where should we get married?"

"How about right here?" she said, looking out toward the garden.

I'd marry her anywhere. And sitting there with her on the swing, coffee cooling in my hand, and her heart beating against mine, I knew I was exactly where I was meant to be.

Maggie turned my life upside down. She'd given me so much over the last year that it would be impossible to count every blessing, but I knew a few.

A love I hadn't believed was possible.

A family I never knew I was missing.

A group of friends who made life richer.
A life that had never made me happier.
She was perfect.
Our life was perfect.

Before there was Kevin,
there was Joe. . .

Author's Note

I wrote this book to be a romance as much as an ode to female friendships—especially the ones I met sitting at a cold ice rink bundled up in puffer coats, sporting mittens and UGG boots. The friends I've met at the hockey rink are the most eclectic group of women in my life. On paper, our friendships don't make sense. But in real life, it just works. These women became my people, and the bond Maggie shares with her hockey mom crew was absolutely born from frigid pregame tailgates, book club shenanigans, group text threads, and the real-life dancing on tables, any tables. I'm sure some of my friends are going to read this book and think, *Oh God, that's me.*

They aren't wrong! Hockey moms have given me the best material to write with…no research necessary. I probably have another ten books in me.

As a high school English teacher, I loved the classics—Hemingway, Fitzgerald, Steinbeck, and Salinger—and my go-to was always historical fiction. Give me a book about WWII and the Resistance Movement, and I couldn't put it down. I find myself inspired and in awe every time. These were the books I gravitated toward.

Then COVID happened. A good friend of mine handed me a romance novel to read. I remember thinking, *Okay, not my thing, but I'll try it.* Turns out it was very much my thing! Who doesn't love love? I became obsessed with the emotional roller coaster—the ache, the laughter, the ugly cries, and the promise of a happily-ever-after. Romance reminded me that while the world may fall apart outside our doors, stories still have the power to put us back together. Since then, I've tackled all kinds of romances from all kinds of authors, and I've loved them all. And honestly, girls, don't be afraid to hand one to the man in your life—it's never too late to teach an old dog new tricks (just sayin').

Romance books teach us all how to love and be loved. But I could also argue that every book I've read—no matter the genre—has taught me something, challenged me to think differently, helped me dream bigger, and, in a way, shaped who I am today. My hope is that when you finish this book, you'll think about the friend who lost the love of their life, the need for foster care reform, forgiveness, second chances, and the idea that a little chaos is good for the soul.

I wrote my first paragraph the day of my oldest son's college graduation (Go Bucks!). I casually said, "Maybe I'll try writing a book," having absolutely no clue I had just signed myself up for the hardest freaking thing I've ever done. Writing became an anchor during one of the biggest transitions in my life—letting my boys go, finding myself again, adjusting to a quieter house that I wasn't ready for. I wrote through empty-nest days, cold winter nights, hot summer days on the patio with my animals by my side and my bird friends at the bird bath, and more "back to the drawing board" moments than I care to count. Two years and ten different manuscripts later, this story refused to let me go. Maggie and Kevin's story kept tugging at me, asking me to follow them until the finished version finally made its way into your hands.

Thank you for spending time with me in Hattrick Harbor

and Marco Island. It means more than you know that you chose to read my story. I hope you fell in love with Maggie and Kevin's love story, the farm that healed them, and the friendship of the hockey moms. And if this book found you during a season of change or a second chance of your own, I hope it brought a little comfort, a little joy, and a reminder that it's okay to start again.

Acknowledgments

My four hockey players—Pete, PJ, Anthony, and Dominick. This, like everything I do, is for you. Always.

Annemarie Biondi, thank you for treating this journey like your own and for loving Maggie and Kevin as much as I do. This never would have happened without you. Everyone needs an Annie in their life. I got mine!

Karen Kurtz and Mom, thank you for giving me the space this summer to get this book done, and for always timing your phone calls when I was free. Thank you for always asking questions and being so excited about my journey.

Pam McCarthy, thank you for your invaluable and steadfast support. There are no words to express my gratitude for meeting with me every week. Thank you for laughing and crying in all the right places. You still got it!

Beth Deluca, my social media manager. You nail it every time! Thank you for always having my best interests in mind and making everything look so…me. You're a ROCKSTAR!

Jen Elmore, my designer and illustrator, thank you for being so supportive and kind. Your cover design and every piece of artwork you've created for me have been brilliant. Thank you for also being my formatter and artistic consultant and for finding time in your hectic schedule to help me with all the loose ends. I'm so lucky to have met you for so many reasons.

Peggy Savage and Kelly Johnston, thank you so much for reading through two very different versions of this book and for being so willing and excited to do it.

To Vince, Dad, the extended Barnes family, cousins, Nana Suzy, and David Coyle, thank you for always asking about my book and its process. Because it was important to me, it was important to you.

Tess Ellenberger, thank you for allowing me to send you the first three chapters. A week later, you had read all forty-one of them. Thank you for always giving your input when I asked questions about the book, tagline, and blurb.

Angela Smith, Kristen Wackerly, Stacy Albright, Aunt Lee, Jennifer Schwenk, and Renee Brahler, your feedback and support on the original manuscript were invaluable. Thank you for always giving me love when I was ready to quit.

Virginia Tesi Carey, my editor and proofreader, thank you for being so excited to help me and for loving my story! (And for dealing with my lack of computer skills!) I am so appreciative of your expertise.

The OG Hockey Moms: Michele Holcomb, Mary Jo Clark, Jen Marez, Stacey Zahoranski, Sarah Halford, and Darcy France, you were the first hockey moms I met back when our kids were babies. I knew then that hockey moms would be my people!

OBX Hockey Gang: Kristin Mothersbaugh, Sarah Markham, Christina Steffl, Kelly Dearden, Juli Ambach, Thea Sears and families, thank you for making vacation with thirty people in one house (the kids outnumbering the adults) easy and so much fun. Ma, MEATLOAF!

Empty Nester Hockey Mom Book Club: Maureen Huscroft,

Julie McCarthy, Teri Kufel, Kim Colasanti, Molly Holtzer, Amy Firment, Ann Cook, and Judy Wilk, thank you for always asking me about my book and supporting me when I was ready to give up. Thank you for letting me talk for hours on the subject—that couldn't have been fun for you, but you listened anyway! Your support gave me courage.

Hockey Mom TikTokers: Kathy Dobrowsky, Sherri Dalton, Ann Lombard, Sandi Passek, Melissa Heckman, Tiffy Harvey, Casey Lindow, Santina Sprang, Theresa Wise, Carolyn Grossi, Kris Bangtson, and Amy Sprinzl, thank you for always doing what I ask, even when you didn't want to. And thank you for always being game for any video I wanted to create—you never said no (except when I asked if we could put on full hockey gear and pretend to check each other and race to the bar).

Hockey Moms Gone Wild: Shari Jaskiewicz, Lisa Backo, Donna Rossiter, Jeri Romanski, Bridget Coughlin, Tracy Kindall, and Jenny Lee-Atkinson, a huge thank you to the first group of Walsh Jesuit Warrior hockey moms who taught me not to worry so much about my kid. Our lasting friendship proves that hockey moms are irreplaceable.

Honorary Hockey Moms: Colleen Coyle, Mary Jo Fleishman, Jenny Minear, Melanie Curlee, Holly Wilt, Casey Juve, Diane Ross, Maria Hanson, Neetta Houska, Amy Marin, Angela Kohl, and Jill Weeks, thank you for being the best group of friends and neighbors a girl could ask for. You are some of my oldest and dearest friends, and your friendship is invaluable to me. Casey, thank you for being my friend, even if I'm old enough to be your mother—albeit a very cool, trendy one.

Sarah and Abby Minear, thank you for helping plot out my

book long before I started writing it. To Marco!

Carol Ann Eastman, thank you for always answering my texts when your life is so busy with your own parenting, writing, teaching, and yogaing! We've never even met in person, and your willingness to help me is so appreciated.

Beth Fink, thank you for offering your time when you have so little of it to give.

Judi Fennell, my first editor. Thank you for giving me a master-class on how not to write! I learned so much from your record-breaking 27-page letter and edits. My first manuscript was nowhere near ready, but you encouraged me not to give up, and you said starting over would be hard, but that I could do it. I believed you.

Miranda Liasson, thank you for offering your advice and reading my first three chapters. You made the entire novel better in our one-hour conversation.

Danielle Edgar and Renee Brahler, thank you for allowing me to ask questions about the foster care system and for reading through parts of my manuscript.

To any hockey mom from the Kent Cyclones and the Walsh Jesuit Warriors I had the pleasure of knowing, you've left an imprint on my heart. Each one of you is in every character of this book.

To all the Walsh Hockey Dads, I couldn't write a book about hockey moms and their friendship without realizing that you are the supporting characters to the lead actresses! Your friendship has also been one-of-a-kind to me and my family.

To all my friends in Akron, Ohio, who always asked, "How's the book coming?" It has always bothered me when people say they're going to do something and then fail to do it. I didn't want to be that person. Your constant checking in made me accountable for things I said out loud. I appreciated your interest in my journey (Dave, Tim, Steve, and Lois especially).

To all my soccer mom friends, I want to take a moment to thank you, as I love soccer moms too! Jackie Surowicz, Liz Mendel, Robin Banyasz, Denise Young, Angela Dollins, LaDonna Wagner, Erin Haslinger, Kim Kerekes, Marlena Rimac, Bridget Folds, Colleen Groves, Kim Hain, Michelle Poling, Caroline Cooke, Alisa Kolar, Joyce Nicholson, Polly Peters, Michele Sinnaeve, Jen Stone, and Beata Rogalski you're as cool and awesome as hockey moms!

To my furry friends, Kleo, Baby, and the two mourning doves I called Larry and Lois, thank you for hanging with me and visiting me every day this summer (check Instagram for pictures). You were the greatest companions!

Steven Denlinger and Laura Navarre, thank you for being tough and keeping me calm, even when I was anything but.

To Janet Aldridge, Wendy Dorfman, Amy Harkonen, and Kim Presta. We were all hockey girlfriends before we became hockey moms. Margarita Night originated with you guys! Thank you for your lifelong friendship.

To every former student of mine, I had one of the greatest jobs in the world—being your teacher. Keep reading!

Anita Calleri is a first-time author with a passion for a good book, cozy Hallmark movies, and the beautiful shores of Marco Island. She's a proud mom of three young men and is happily married to her college sweetheart, who can't understand why she buys so many books and has so many shoes. For Anita, Marco Island is paradise—days revolve around watching the sunset, reading her favorite authors on the beach, and her early morning six-mile walk. Her debut novel brings together everything she loves most: romance, second chances, everything Marco Island, and the friendships of Hockey Moms!